W9-AMX-146

CATHY MARIE HAKE

WHIRLWIND

BETHANYHOUSE
MINNEAPOLIS, MINNESOTA

Whirlwind
Copyright © 2008
Cathy Marie Hake

Cover design by Jennifer Parker
Cover model photography by Mike Habermann
Olympic Ship photo: Library of Congress, Prints & Photographs Division,
LC-DIG-ggbain-09363

Scripture quotations are from the King James Version.

All rights reserved. No part of this publication may be reproduced, stored in a
retrieval system, or transmitted in any form or by any means—electronic, mechanical, photocopying, recording, or otherwise—without the prior written permission
of the publisher. The only exception is brief quotations in printed reviews.

Published by Bethany House Publishers
11400 Hampshire Avenue South
Bloomington, Minnesota 55438

Bethany House Publishers is a division of
Baker Publishing Group, Grand Rapids, Michigan.

Printed in the United States of America

ISBN-13: 978-1-60751-517-3

Dedication

To my editor, Sarah Long, a million thanks, a vat of chocolate, and an industrial-sized bottle of aspirin are far less than you deserve for one day at your job . . . and then, you have to deal with me! What a delight you are to work with! In addition to your considerable professional ability, I know you also pray over my book. That means so much to me. You are an extraordinary editor and also an extraordinary woman of God. For all you have done for me and for all you do for countless others, surely there will be jewels in your crown in heaven.

Also, to Jennifer Parker, the incredibly talented woman who designs the covers of my books. From the very first one she designed for me, I've been enchanted. Each time the artwork captures the feel of the story, the location, and most of all, the essence of the heroine's personality—and that takes pure genius. It's said that a book is judged by its cover. Then I'm a very blessed author, indeed. Thank you, Jenny!

Books by
Cathy Marie Hake
FROM BETHANY HOUSE PUBLISHERS

Letter Perfect

Bittersweet

Fancy Pants

Forevermore

Whirlwind

CATHY MARIE HAKE is a nurse who specializes in teaching Lamaze, breastfeeding, and baby care. She loves reading, scrapbooking, and writing, and is the author or coauthor of more than twenty books. Cathy makes her home in Anaheim, California, with her husband, daughter, and son.

WHIRLWIND

One

I 've come to a decision."

Millicent Fairweather clasped her hands together at her waist and waited in silence for her boss to continue. The clock in the far corner of the dim study ticked loudly.

"My daughters are of an age to expand their horizons. A change is in order. Therefore, I've located a place for them."

"A place?" Millicent couldn't help echoing his word. A frisson of fear shivered up her spine. At eight and six years old, Audrey and Fiona were still little girls. Surely he couldn't mean—

"A young ladies' academy." He paced the length of the oak bookshelves. Chinese silk carpet muffled each step, and an opulent gem-encrusted globe glinted as a reminder of all the riches Mr. Eberhardt amassed on the travels that made him a stranger in his own home. He nodded to himself. "Education, deportment—my daughters shall have the finest of everything."

The air froze in her chest. "Mr. Eberhardt, your daughters are both of tender ages yet. Perhaps if you spend a little time with them . . ."

"No!" He wheeled around. "The decision is made. I've directed Mrs. Witherspoon to pack their things. A coach will be here by five."

Five? Millicent glanced at the clock—a quarter past noon. Struggling to control her emotions, she rasped, "We'll be ready."

He made a dismissive gesture. "I've arranged for someone to accompany them. Your services are no longer needed. I've written a letter of recommendation for you. Alastair will see to it that you receive two months' salary to tide you through until you find another position."

Millicent drew in a deep breath. A governess served at the whim of an employer. She had no recourse; but how could he do this to his daughters? "Fiona and Audrey will want to see you. Luncheon—"

"I have things to accomplish." He pulled a book from the shelf and studied the frontispiece.

"Perhaps tea?"

He snapped the book shut and shoved it back in place. "No. Do whatever you like with the girls until five. That is all."

Shaking, Millicent left the study.

Mrs. Witherspoon, ruddy cheeks streaked with tears, met her at the head of the stairs amidst a collection of trunks. "The girls shouldn't see me like this."

Millicent pulled the housekeeper into her own bedchamber. "This is going to be so dreadfully hard on them."

Mrs. Witherspoon buried her face in a sodden hanky. "We're the only family those children know. They don't remember their mama at all, and I can count on one hand how many days he's spent here each year for the past five."

Tempting as it was to gossip, Millicent quelled the urge. She picked up the picture she kept at her bedside. It had been taken the day before her parents died, and every time she looked at it, memories of an unforgettably fun day washed over her. Resolve straightened her spine. Mr. Eberhardt might separate them, but she could give Fiona and Audrey one very special last day.

"Mrs. Witherspoon, after lunch, I'll take the girls outside so you can be alone to pack. Please ask Cook to give us ten more minutes before bringing up luncheon." Once the housekeeper nodded, she put down the picture. "Also, please ask Alastair if Billy can go to town. I'd like Mr. Braston to come take photographs. I want him to bring whatever's necessary so he can leave the pictures here with us."

"Oh! That's a lovely idea."

Before opening the door to the nursery, Millicent took a fortifying breath. *Lord, it'll be so hard to let go of them. All these years, I've somehow thought of them as my own. Please guard and protect them and let them find love.*

She barely started to open the door when the maid hopped up, along with the two girls. "What happened?" the maid asked.

Millicent straightened her shoulders and smiled. The muscles in her face felt strangely stiff, but she refused to dwell on that. She didn't want to say anything about Mr. Eberhardt, either. He didn't want to see his daughters, so Millicent wouldn't let them know of his presence. Children deserved to be cherished, not rejected. "Thank you for keeping the girls company.

It's almost time for luncheon, so I'd best see to washing up with them."

Wearing a pout, Jenny dawdled out of the room. Since the day she'd arrived a few months ago, she'd shown a penchant for gossip. Millicent refused to fan the flames of her habit.

Once the door clicked shut, Millicent knew she needed to use every single moment to prepare "her" girls. Sinking onto a small chair, she announced, "I have something surprising to tell you girls."

Fiona galloped over. "You do?"

Audrey followed at a slightly more sedate pace. "Jenny said there was a rabbit in the vegetable garden. Is that what you're going to tell us?"

Millicent wound her arm about Audrey's waist and pulled her close. "No, but that was a good guess."

"Are we guessing?" Fiona perked up. "Is it a pony? I want a pony. A white one."

"No, poppet."

While Fiona sighed in dismay, Audrey guessed, "Are we going to town? For ice cream?"

"You're going even farther than that. You, my dearlings, are going on a trip. A nice friend of your father is going to take you, and you'll be leaving this evening!"

"Today?! Where?"

"You are such fine little girls, your father decided you should be allowed to go to a special school where they teach girls to be elegant young ladies."

Audrey frowned. "But you're teaching us that."

"I've started. You'll have teachers at the academy, but there's something more. At school, you'll have several other girls as your friends. You'll be with them every day."

"You'll have friends, too!" Fiona gave Millicent a tooth-less grin.

"I suppose," Millicent said, trying to make her voice sound light when her heart weighed a ton, "I will have an opportunity to make new friends, too. But . . ."

Audrey's little hand suddenly clutched Millicent's sleeve. "You're coming with us, aren't you? You have to. I want you to."

"Yes, we do!" Fiona chimed in.

Sounding as stricken as her little face looked, Audrey kept babbling, "We'll have lots of fun together. We always do. And you can teach our friends how to be fine ladies, can't she, Fiona?"

Fiona's head bobbed.

Drawing the girls snuggly against her, Millicent closed her eyes. *This is so hard, Lord. How am I to answer them when I don't know what to say?*

Audrey nestled against her, the lace of her collar crinkled and snagged. "Miss Fairweather, don't send me away. I'll be good. I will. I'll be better. I won't put my elbows on the table anymore. I won't—"

Millicent's eyes flew open. "You've not done anything wrong, sweetheart. This isn't a punishment; it's a special gift."

"A present?" Fiona brightened.

"Precisely!" Millicent rested her forehead against Audrey's. "I'm proud of you. You're a wonderful girl." Audrey's blue eyes swam with tears, and Millicent strove to keep from weeping. In an unsteady voice she promised, "You'll always be close in my heart and thoughts and prayers."

"You're crying." Audrey's lip quivered.

"They're happy tears." Fiona wrapped her short arms as far around them as she could and squeezed. "Just like when we drew the card for her."

Latching onto that lifeline, Millicent smiled. "Oh, how I adore that card! It's such a treasure to me. Just think how happy you'll make me when you write and tell me all about your school and new friends!"

Audrey burrowed her face into Millicent's neck. "Will you write back to me?"

"And me?"

"Of course I will!" The immediacy and certainty in her response caused Fiona to wiggle with joy.

Audrey pulled away just a little. "But I make ugly blots."

"Occasionally, I do, too. Once you practice more, you'll be making beautiful swirls and loops. Between now and then, I promise I'll be so happy to get your letters that I won't even notice if you have blots."

Finally, Audrey managed a smile.

"Before you go, I thought it would be fun to set aside all the ways we usually do things and have an extraordinary afternoon. Wouldn't you like that?"

"What will we do?" Fiona asked.

A fond memory popped into her mind. Millicent smiled. "To begin with, we're going to have a different luncheon—a special one. Come to the table, and we'll get ready." By the time Cook arrived, both girls sat at the table—but in a rare breach of etiquette, they'd turned their chairs around backward and straddled them. Millicent didn't try to brave that position, but she'd turned her chair sideways. The girls seemed satisfied with that. Eyes pleading with the cook to keep the atmosphere light, Millicent announced, "We're having a backward lunch. If you please, we'd all like dessert first."

The girls' eyes bulged.

Cook managed a wobbly, yet knowing, smile. "What a very interesting idea."

Millicent smiled at Audrey. "This way, we won't be too full to enjoy it!"

"Aren't we going to pray?" Fiona asked.

"Yes, of course we are." It warmed Millicent's heart how the girls loved to recite their prayers. "But since this is a backward lunch, we say our prayer at the end."

So the meal went, until they finished. Fiona clasped her chubby hands together. "Jesus, it is you we greet and thank you for the food we eat. Make us good and strong and kind, and help us have pure hearts and minds."

Audrey then prayed, "Jesus, help me be brave at my new school."

Millicent took her turn. "And grant the children a safe journey."

Fiona added, "And thank you for giving us new friends! Amen."

As they left the table, Millicent's mind whirled. No doubt, the school would use pieces from *The Book of Common Prayer*. She'd taught the girls the bedtime prayer her mother had taught her. She'd also made up the beginning of their mealtime prayer, and each of them always took a turn adding something more. *Father, I wanted them to talk to you not from rote, but from their hearts. Everything will change for the girls, and I haven't prepared them.*

A knock sounded, and the nursery door opened. To Millicent's amazement, the butler stood in the aperture. "Miss

Fairweather, Billy's returned. The photographer will arrive shortly."

"Thank you, Alastair."

He cleared his throat. "If I might be so bold, I'd like a picture of the girls, myself."

"Of course."

Twenty minutes later, the girls stood in the center of two lines of household staff. Everyone had hands at their sides, eyes focused on the camera. *Poof!* The flash exploded, and Millicent blinked. When she could see again, Mr. Eberhardt slinked past the open parlor door. She opened her mouth to call him back, but at the last second she stayed silent. A lady never raised her voice, hired help never summoned the master, but most of all, he'd ordered them not to tell the girls he was home. She consoled herself by thinking she'd spared the children the sting of his rejection.

"Miss Fairweather?"

She turned to the photographer. "I beg your pardon?"

"I suggested you sit on the chair, and I'll pose the lasses with you. I can make two copies so you can have one and they can take the other."

"Thank you, but I'd like three copies of this one so each of the girls may have her own." Millicent sat as he directed and gently tamed Fiona's curls, then straightened Audrey's bow.

"Girls, you must hold still." The photographer squinted, then scowled at Fiona as he tacked on, "And don't smile."

Fiona not smile? Unthinkable. Millicent adored her sunny disposition. "Fee, you must hold very still," she said, "but I'd love for you to smile."

Audrey looked at her, somber as could be. "Are you going to smile, Miss Fairweather?"

"Let's all smile. That's what we always do, and it'll make us happy to look at the picture and remember the wonderful time we had together."

While the photographer took over the upstairs bath to develop the pictures, Millicent took the girls out for a walk. A brook bordered one side of the garden. Impulsively, Millicent allowed the girls to wade. She committed the sight to memory—wanting to recall every giggle and delighted squeal. With no towel, she glanced about to make sure no one could see her, then used her eyelet-edged petticoat to dry their feet.

Watching Millicent tie up her sister's shoes, Audrey asked, "What shall we do next?"

"Why don't we gather a bouquet for Mrs. Witherspoon?"

Fiona clapped. "I'll make one for Alastair!"

"Silly, boys don't like flowers."

Millicent rose. "It would be nice to make a nosegay for each member of the staff." What would it matter if they stripped the garden bare? Mr. Eberhardt wouldn't stay long enough to enjoy the garden, let alone entertain or escort a lady out for a stroll.

By the time they'd tied ribbons about the small bouquets and delivered them to the staff, Mrs. Witherspoon was directing the livery boys as they carried down the girls' trunks.

Grief slashed through Millicent at the sight.

"Where's Flora?" Panic lent a shrill edge to Fiona's high voice. She adored the rag doll Millicent had made for her.

"In the trunk." Mrs. Witherspoon sounded overly cheerful.

"The trunk!" Fiona burst into tears.

"Don't worry, Fee." Millicent knelt down and took Fiona's hands in hers. "Flora's having fun riding down the stairs."

"Can I ride down the stairs, too?"

Throwing all caution to the wind, Millicent answered yes. A few minutes later, Millicent stood at the bottom of the stairs. "Slowly, now."

"No, go fast!" Fiona bounced inside the blanket-lined wooden crate on the landing. The boys lifted the box onto a large sheet of pasteboard, and Alastair held fast to the length of clothesline tied to the box.

"Wheeeeee!" Fiona shouted as the box sledded down the flight.

"It's my turn!" Audrey looked down from the banister.

"I want to go again!" Fiona scrabbled out of the box and raced back up the stairs.

"Millicent, you've succeeded in taking their minds off what's to come." Mrs. Witherspoon blotted at her eyes. "Bless you, I—"

"The pasteboard's all hooked up," one of the boys said, holding the bedraggled piece aloft for inspection.

"I'm sure it will last for at least Audrey's turn." Millicent couldn't bear to cheat Audrey out of a ride. Audrey was always the serious, sensible one who asked for nothing and felt everything deeply. But she'd wanted a ride.

Alastair inspected the pasteboard and shook his head. "This won't do. No, it most certainly won't." He looked down at the head housekeeper. "Mrs. Witherspoon, I do believe the trays need a good buffing."

Millicent couldn't believe her ears. Even at that distance, though, she could see the grin tugging at the oh-so-proper butler's mouth.

"Which one?" Mrs. Witherspoon called back.

Straightening himself and sounding absurdly dignified, Alastair said, "Every last one, Mrs. Witherspoon."

Over the next half hour, Fiona and Audrey rode square, round, oval, and rectangular trays down the stairs. Citing a concern that the box might dent the trays, Alastair took to tying the clothesline to a belt he buckled around the girls. All the servants abandoned any pretense of working and came to cheer for the fun.

Millicent noticed the butler down on his knees, whispering to the girls. From the day she'd taken her position in the household, Millicent had liked the stately old man. He possessed a sense of propriety and managed the entire manor with finesse. Watching him shed his stateliness and grin at the girls, Millicent blinked away tears.

"Miss Fairweather." He rose and suddenly took on the full mantle of his authority. "A word, please."

Lifting her skirts ever so slightly, Millicent mounted the stairs. "Yes?"

Audrey handed him a tray. Well, at least she tried to. The piece measured at least a yard long. "This one?"

"Indeed, Miss Audrey." Alastair lifted the piece, then poked his nose into the air in an officious manner. "Miss Fairweather, Miss Audrey and Miss Fiona have determined that you've not done your share of polishing the silver."

Disbelief shot through her, but the twinkle in the old man's eyes told Millicent she'd have to do some fancy talking. "The girls are right, Alastair. But governesses don't . . . polish silver."

"Yes, but those are ordinary governesses. You are an extraordinary governess."

"Thank you. How—"

"Quite simply," he interrupted before she could finish her sentence. "This is sufficiently long for you and the girls to . . . ahem . . . work on together."

Denial sprang to her lips, but Millicent looked into Audrey's hopeful eyes. Tugging on her sleeves, Millicent nodded. "Never let it be said I shirked my chores."

A few seconds later, Alastair tested the rope he'd secured about her waist. "Safe and secure, Miss Fairweather. I'm sure this will be a smashing success."

"That was hardly a reassuring choice of words," she muttered. To her relief, Alastair and the boys looked away as she sat on the tray. The only way to keep from having her skirts fly up was to gather her narrow hoops high and spraddle in the most unladylike way imaginable, but with the girls in her lap, all ought to be . . . passable. "Audrey . . ." Once the elder girl sat before her, Millicent beckoned, "Fee."

With the girls in place, Millicent glanced down at how her boots hung off the tray. "I'm afraid this simply won't do."

"Ah, but this will." Alastair popped a small, round chafing dish beneath her heels.

"Here you go!" One of the boys heaved against Millicent. As they started careening downward, Millicent suddenly realized they were going far too fast. *Alastair doesn't have hold of the rope!*

Thumpthumpthumpthump. How could anything drag and bump, yet move with such speed? *Dear God, don't let anything happen to the girls.* Terror sucked away any breath she'd use to scream, but in the few seconds of the dizzying descent, Millicent prayed a million words. Everything blurred, then they sent a shower of larkspur, roses, and fern in all directions and came to a skidding stop in the center of the marble foyer—directly beneath the massive oval table.

"Girls! Are you hurt?" Millicent's dry mouth made the words come out in nothing more than a croak.

Laughter bubbled out of Fiona, and Audrey shook with a fit of giggles. With her skirts beneath the girls' weight, Millicent couldn't move. She patted them, desperately trying to reassure herself they'd come through unscathed.

From the parlor door, an ominous voice rumbled, "What is going on here?"

Two

Fiona rolled onto her knees and peeked from beneath the table. "Who's that?"

Audrey squeaked, "Father?"

"Father!" Fiona scrambled out, and Audrey rolled away.

"Miss Fairweather." Alastair's hands curled over her shoulders. "Allow me to assist you."

Unable to speak, she nodded. As the butler pulled, the tray beneath her grated across the marble floor. He helped her to her feet. No, foot. One was stuck in the chafing dish.

A subtle twist didn't manage to dislodge the toe of her kid boot from the inner rim, and her heel wedged tighter still from the action. A swish of her skirts failed to cover that humiliating detail. Something tugged at her waist.

"Miss Fairweather." Mr. Eberhardt tilted his head toward the study. In a tone that rivaled a thunderclap, he added, "Now."

The combs and pins securing her prim chignon became traitors—abandoning her in her moment of need. Audrey tucked her hand into Millicent's. Millicent gave it a reassuring squeeze. "Curtsy to your father, girls. Then you may go with Mrs. Witherspoon."

As the girls dipped with very nice form, Millicent did her best to collect herself and correct whatever flaws she could. By the time she reached the study door, she wanted to regain as much order as possible. She didn't know precisely how she'd manage that feat, but anything would be an improvement.

Alastair murmured from behind her, "My apologies, Miss Fairweather. I cannot untie the knot."

Muffling a moan, she took an ungainly step toward the study, the metallic sound of the chafing dish echoing loudly. Acting as if the chafing dish wasn't there and pretending she didn't have a clothesline trailing after her like a tail, Millicent accepted the butler's proffered arm.

Mr. Eberhardt moved only enough to lean against the doorframe and watch her as she clung to Alastair for dear life. Every other step, she tried to subtly shake off the impossibly heavy chafing dish. It protested by holding fast and putting every drum in the queen's brigade to shame.

Fiona scooped up a spike of larkspur and galloped to her father. Oblivious to the deep furrows in his dark brows and the stern grooves bracketing his thin mouth, she thrust the flower at him. "This is for you!"

Mr. Eberhardt bent stiffly at the waist and accepted the broken stem. "Thank you."

Clearly hungry for his attention, Audrey scooped up every flower within reach and sidled closer. She bit her lower lip and looked at her father with longing in her big blue eyes.

"Go put the flowers in water," Mr. Eberhardt said in a remarkably gentle tone to Audrey. He added the larkspur to her armload and walked deep into the study.

In the moment the master's back was turned, the butler swooped down and yanked on the chafing dish. It came off—but took along Millicent's boot.

"Thank you," Millicent whispered. Anything was an improvement. She hastily repositioned a slipping hairpin and squared her shoulders.

His back still to them, Mr. Eberhardt ordered, "Leave us, Alastair. And shut the door."

Her skirts didn't dare even rustle as she crossed the floor and stood in the center of the room. To Millicent's astonishment, the photographs she'd commissioned lay across the desk.

"I'm waiting."

"My apologies, Mr. Eberhardt."

He wheeled around. "I didn't ask for an apology. I demanded an explanation. Just what were you doing?"

Making a ninny of myself. "I wanted to give the girls a special day to remember."

His brows hiked toward his hairline. "I'm sure you've succeeded."

She bit her tongue and folded her hands in front of herself.

Stalking toward the table, he lifted one of the pictures of her with the girls. "It would appear decorum isn't your strong suit."

Millicent remained silent.

"No reply, Miss Fairweather?"

"You made a statement. A man is entitled to his opinion—especially in his home and regarding his family." She watched in disbelief as he tucked the picture into his pocket.

"Is something wrong?"

"I'm sure you noticed how very young the girls still are when they offered you the flowers. Though I understand you make the final decisions, they would continue to benefit from a governess's care—"

"Indeed I do make the decisions and they are no business of yours."

Millicent stared at him in utter dismay. "You asked me what was wrong."

"My question," he enunciated, "wasn't an invitation for you to vent your opinion regarding my decision. You appeared distressed about something else."

"The picture." She swallowed. "I ordered three copies of that pose so the girls and I could each have a remembrance."

"Which leaves the third." His hand pressed over his coat pocket for a moment—an almost reverent gesture that was at complete odds with his cold, detached demeanor.

"Academies often separate children according to age."

"How would you know?"

Millicent met his intense gaze. He needed to know just how cruel it was to relegate his daughters to a boarding school. "Personal experience."

Something flashed in his eyes. "My daughters will be kept together."

"They're very sweet girls. Good and clever and—"

"I've read your monthly reports."

He had? He'd never responded to her letters.

"Fiona's lost several teeth since last month." He lifted another picture and stared at it.

"Yes." Millicent fought the urge to go scoop up the photographs. She'd paid dearly for them—a whole month's salary.

"Did you indulge in that fanciful American practice of having a fairy come collect her teeth?"

"Yes."

He hummed a noncommittal sound, then continued to study the photographs, shifting them into different places. Silence reigned. He'd not given her permission to leave. As long as her boss concentrated on the photographs, though, she fumbled with the impossibly huge knot in the rope around her waist. Her nerves stretched more taut with every passing minute. Why didn't he just fire her, rescind his recommendation, and be done with it?

Rustling sounded, and Mr. Eberhardt wheeled around.

Oh no. The girls knew about the doorway from the servants' hallway into the study.

"We put them in water, Father." Audrey carried the flowers with all the solemnity the queen would use to place a wreath on the grave of a fallen warrior.

Unable to ascertain whether anger or awkwardness caused his silence, Millicent filled in the uncomfortable silence. "Audrey, let's place those on the far end of the table. You did a lovely job with the arrangement."

"Indeed." Mr. Eberhardt pushed the photographs to the side.

Fiona tugged on her father's pant leg. "I helped!"

Audrey dared to whisper, "May I please see the photographs?"

Mr. Eberhardt pulled out the chair and sat down. To Millicent's utter astonishment, he popped his daughters into his lap. Fiona curled her fingers around his lapel. "Are we frontward again?"

"Frontward?"

Audrey nodded. "Luncheon was backward." Emboldened, she tacked on, "Fiona and I sat backward. Miss Fairweather turned her chair sideways."

As if that revelation weren't enough, Fiona tacked on, "We ate our cookies first."

So now he won't just rescind the letter of recommendation and send me packing, he'll keep the salary he promised.

"What else have you done?"

Millicent wasn't sure whether he'd asked her or the children. Regardless of who answered, he would learn they'd shed their shoes and waded in the garden pond—and she'd dried their tiny feet with her own petticoat. *Well, once he knows that, I'm going to have to walk to town, dragging my trunk behind me.*

"We cut flowers." Fiona basked in his attention, completely unaware of the strained undercurrents. "We cut all, all, all the flowers in the whole garden!"

"But we gave them away." Audrey gazed up at him, before looking pensively at the closest picture. "That's Mrs. Witherspoon. She cried when I gave her posies."

A governess ought not speak unless given leave, but Millicent figured she'd already destroyed any possibility of convincing Mr. Eberhardt that she'd been the quintessential governess these past four years. "They were happy tears, Audrey. Your gift pleased her. I'm sure when you give her that picture, she'll be happy."

Fiona tugged on her father's lapel. "May I please give someone a picture?"

In a matter of a few minutes, the girls decided to whom each picture should go. Their father kept looking at the clock.

Audrey let out a huge sigh. "We don't have enough photographs."

A knock sounded, and Alastair opened the door. "A Mrs. Brown is here, sir."

As if this situation wasn't already embarrassing enough! Millicent determined she'd gather the girls and exit through the servants' door.

"Yes. Show her in."

Mrs. Brown didn't wait to be summoned. She entered before Mr. Eberhardt finished his sentence. Dressed in a black bombazine traveling suit, she looked immanently respectable, but instead of dipping her head and murmuring a pleasant greeting, she gave Mr. Eberhardt a strained look. "The girls' trunks are already being loaded onto the carriage. We must be off at once."

The clock struck four; he'd said the girls would leave at five.

"Father, we don't have enough photographs," Audrey repeated. "Miss Fairweather won't get one."

Millicent knew full well Audrey wasn't just troubled by the missing photograph. She wanted to delay leaving the only home and security she'd known.

"Your father has a special present for you to give to her." Mrs. Brown grabbed a bracelet from beside the flower arrangement and boldly locked eyes with Mr. Eberhardt in a manner completely unbecoming a lady. "Isn't that right, Ernst?"

"Yes." He took the silver bangle and thrust it at Millicent. "Wear it always as a reminder of the girls' affection, Miss Fairweather."

Millicent hadn't seen the silver bangle before that moment, and she knew full well the jewelry wasn't intended for her. She couldn't accept it.

"Oh yes!" A beaming smile erased the lines in Audrey's worried little face.

"Is it from me, too, Father?"

He nodded curtly. "Yes, it's from both of you. Miss Fairweather won't ever take it off." He stared at her, his eyes every bit as hard as his voice. "Will you?"

"Put it on, put it on," Mrs. Brown urged Millicent.

At the same time, Mr. Eberhardt stood, lifting his daughters with him. "Miss Fairweather, please grab the pictures for the girls. You're right—they'll each want their own. You can write down your address, and I'll instruct the photographer to make another and send it to you."

Fiona wrapped her legs around her father. Audrey dangled awkwardly. Millicent jammed on the bracelet and reached for her. Audrey dove into her arms. "I don't want to go!"

Blinking back tears, Millicent bowed her head and kissed Audrey. Emotions choked her and kept her silent.

"Flora is in the carriage," Alastair declared.

"We gotta go." Fiona hugged her father.

"Alastair, carry Fiona. I'll take Audrey." Mr. Eberhardt transferred his younger daughter and tugged Audrey away from Millicent. Audrey didn't want to turn loose. "Come, now."

Millicent pressed a kiss on the crying child's cheek. "I love you. Be sure to write to me."

Fiona accepted a kiss, too. "I'll draw you pretty pictures."

Out in the foyer, Mrs. Brown put a restraining hand on Millicent. "It would be best for you to remain inside." She pried the photographs from Millicent's hand and left.

Standing at the window beside the front door, Millicent felt the cold of the marble floor creep up through her stockinged foot and match the chilly emptiness of her breaking heart. Mrs. Brown got into the carriage and immediately pulled the curtain shut, taking away her last glimpse of the girls.

Mr. Eberhardt didn't even bother to wait to wave them off. He strode back into the house and spared her an impatient glance. "Alastair will see to it you're taken to town. There's no reason for you to remain here."

Hands shaking in hurt and anger, Millicent pulled off the bracelet. "This—"

"Was a gift, and you told my daughters you'd wear it. Does your word mean so little to you, Miss Fairweather?"

"I didn't give my word, Mr. Eberhardt."

He turned his back and headed back to the study. "I have no time for nonsense. Cut off that ridiculous rope and be gone."

———

"Boat, Dadda! Boat!"

"Yes, son. This is our ship." Daniel Clark looked away from his little son's glistening brown eyes and braced the nanny's arm to coax her across the gangway.

She hesitated. Eyes wider than his son's, she stammered, "This boat doesn't look big enough to cross the Thames."

"Nonsense, Miss Jenkin. The *Opportunity*'s proven she's seaworthy. She's crossed the Atlantic several times." He made sure the nervous nanny gained stable footing before passing Arthur to her.

"Probably used up all her luck by now," she muttered.

A white-coated man greeted them, then escorted them down a mahogany-paneled corridor. Open doorways to a ladies' parlor, a ballroom, and an elegant dining room showed a plethora of lavish appointments. The sailor gestured toward a book-lined room. "Tradition is for the gentlemen to enjoy their own bon voyage in the library, sir." Though the *Opportunity* had once depended on the wind to push her across the ocean, she'd been converted to a screw engine vessel; nonetheless, the luxurious echoes of her past lent an aura of cozy welcome sadly lacking on many of the newer cruise line ships. Daniel was well pleased with the vessel.

"Here we are. Suite six." The glinting brass numeral secured to the door confirmed the sailor's announcement. He opened the door.

Daniel stepped into a compact parlor occupying the center of the suite. Doors winged in opposite directions from the parlor—one to his bedchamber, the other to the nursery. He nodded approvingly. "This will do nicely."

Warily eyeing their surroundings, Miss Jenkin shifted Arthur to her other ample hip. "How long before our belongings get here? I might need something."

A pock-faced man appeared. "Sir, I'm Tibbs, your room steward. Should you need anything—anything whatsoever—I'm at your disposal. Your luggage was right behind me. I'll be happy to help unpack it straightaway."

Putting down Arthur, Miss Jenkin breathed a sigh of relief. "There's my portmanteau. And my sewing bag. And Arthur's nappies. Especially those!" She started indicating different pieces that belonged in the nursery. "I'll see to those. Tibbs, you just tend to Mr. Clark's belongings. How long before we leave?"

Daniel glanced at his pocket watch, but before he answered, Mr. Tibbs stated, "The first mate's started processing steerage. We'll set sail with the tide in an hour and a half."

Miss Jenkin dropped her bag. "That soon?" She grabbed Arthur as he scrambled past.

"Time and tide wait for no man." Tibbs straightened the sleeves on his uniform. "Sir, would you prefer to have your son join you for meals in the dining salon or have him take meals here in your suite?"

"Here in the suite."

Miss Jenkin pulled Arthur upward and cradled him. "As soon as Mr. Tibbs unpacks your belongings, Mr. Clark, I'll have him bring tea and crumpets for Arthur and me. That way, I can put him down for a nice long nap. He's spinning about worse than a top."

"Very well." Daniel Clark appreciated order and schedules. Children and businesses thrived when kept in the confines of regimented expectations and predictable patterns. It had to do with efficiency, too. That was key. When the essentials were accomplished, that permitted spare time for leisure pursuits. In the past, he hadn't understood that part of the formula, but now that he did, he'd do better.

Daniel pressed a kiss on Arthur's brow. "You have a nice tea." Satisfied that the details had all been ironed out, he headed for the library. Two gentlemen sat to the side, arguing politics while ensconced in leather wingback chairs; another perused a newspaper. Four played cards at the table by the window. Taking a whiff of the cigar he'd removed from a tabletop humidor, a bald man hummed appreciatively. "Cuban tobacco. None finer." His companion carefully snipped the tip of his own cigar and nodded agreement.

"Bah! Tobacco. Port while in port, I say." A red-nosed man lifted his crystal glass in a solo cheer before downing the contents.

After lighting the one man's cigar, the steward turned to Daniel. "Shall I get a drink for you, sir? We have a vast selection of libations—port, whiskey, wines . . ."

"Coffee. Black." Daniel settled into another wingback chair and made himself comfortable.

A moment later, the steward appeared with a gold-rimmed cup and saucer bearing the ship's name. "Your coffee, sir. I took the liberty of bringing you a few finger sandwiches. Proper tea will be served after we set sail."

"Excellent."

The gentleman reading *The Times* set it aside. "Bivney. George Bivney. I'm on a buying trip. My specialty is gutta-percha."

"Daniel Clark. Sold my import business and I'm heading for Texas."

"Texas." Bivney's brows rose.

"I have family there." Daniel didn't go into particulars. The import business had required extensive travel. His wife, Henrietta, had cared for their son and filled the weeks of Daniel's absence by participating in a gardening club, visiting museums, and volunteering at a few charities. The minute he returned home, though, she always dropped everything just to be with him. Life was sweet indeed—until eight months ago. While he was away, Henrietta fell down the stairs. He'd received the telegram and rushed home at once—but not soon enough to be at her bedside as she and the child she carried slipped away. Though Arthur had Miss Jenkin, Daniel couldn't justify being gone so much of the time and leaving his son to the care of others. A child deserved a parent's time, attention, and affection.

So after a decade of building a thriving import-export empire, Daniel made a huge sacrifice. He sold it all. Remaining in England would pose temptations to reengage in grandiose deals, so he had removed himself and bought a thriving mercantile in a bustling Texan town. There, he'd guide his son to manhood while still earning a satisfactory living.

The *Opportunity* set sail. Understanding his son needed rest, Daniel stayed away from the suite for a few hours until the smaller waves characteristic of being close to shore changed to the large, gentle swells of the ocean.

Remembering Arthur's excitement over spying the "boat" earlier made Daniel smile. He decided to direct Nanny to pop his son into a coat so he could take little Arthur out for a toddle.

Arthur's wails echoed in the suite as Daniel entered. He waited for Nanny to settle his son . . . but he waited in vain. When a minute passed with no change, Daniel frowned. Was his son suffering seasickness? Impossible—not with him putting up such a fuss. Striding to the nursery, he called out, "Miss Jenkin, is something—"

"Dadda! Dadda!" Arthur stood in his cot and lifted his hands.

"There now." Daniel pulled a handkerchief from his pocket and mopped Arthur's face. "Nanny!"

Nanny Jenkin gave no response.

Daniel started to lift his son and discovered a very soggy nappy. His nose wrinkled. "Miss Jenkin!" Still no answer. "I hope she's not seasick."

It was then he caught sight of a folded sheet of paper on the bed.

$\mathcal{Three}$

The important thing is, we're together." Millicent flattened the center bunk against the bulkhead and secured it. The constant droning of the ship's engine filled the steerage compartment with a nagging sound and an odd vibration that even rocking ocean waves didn't hide.

Isabelle sank onto the lowest bunk and scanned their dank surroundings. "I don't think we could be any closer together. Millie, how will we ever endure a whole week of this?"

As the elder of the two, Isabelle always worried and Millicent admitted that her sister had ample cause for concern this time. Lucifer himself probably had had a hand in designing the *Opportunity*'s lowest deck. Narrow bunks stacked three high filled the "family" quarters. Thin mattresses smelled of stale straw, and a single thin-as-a-sneeze blanket would be all the warmth each passenger got. And those were the better aspects of the accommodations.

Here and there, a lucky passenger had grabbed one of the few life preservers and now used them as pillows. *Lord, please don't let anything befall this ship. Without enough life boats or preservers, we'd drown.*

Unaware of her sister's thoughts, Isabelle continued on in a whisper, "You ought to go get in line for the women's necessary so you can remove your bustle. Even though you're slender as a sapling, the extra inches the bustle adds are ones you don't have. There aren't even two feet of space between our bunk and that one."

Grasping at a chance to cheer up her sister, Millicent whispered, "What a grand idea! It's the horsehair roll, so we can take turns using it as a pillow."

"Millie!"

"Millie?" Frank, Isabelle's husband, squeezed in through the door and turned sharply toward them. "How did you shock Isabelle this time?" Deep worry grooves around his mouth returned as soon as his fleeting smile left.

"Isabelle and I are . . . solving problems. I'm sure if we put our heads together, we'll all find ways to make the journey tolerable. After all, it's one slim week, isn't that right, Frank?"

Isabelle's husband nodded. "Be glad Millicent came along, Isabelle. Had we gone ahead, I'd have refused to send for her. There's no way I'd allow your sister to travel like this alone and stuck in the single women's compartment."

"It would have been better if she took that position with the Grants. She could have saved up, and we would, too. Then she could have come second class."

"I can't believe you said that." Millicent popped up and swung around to face her sister. Her bustle caught on the post of the next bunk and slung her back to sprawl across Isabelle's lap.

Isabelle gasped.

Millicent burst out laughing and straightened up. "See? You would have missed that if I weren't here. With me along, you'll be entertained the whole voyage."

A squabble broke out nearby. Frank muttered, "We could do with less entertainment."

"You're the only family I have." Millicent decided sitting on the bunk with her sister was the only sensible option. She gave Isabelle a meaningful look. "We promised each other—"

"That we'd always stay together," Isabelle finished.

"And we will." Millie leaned forward to look at her brother-in-law. "So I'm warning you both here and now, you're going to hurt my feelings if you say anything more about wishing you'd left me behind. Why, I'll be downright cranky."

A wry smile eased some of the tension from Frank's expression. "I doubt you'll have a single cranky hour in your whole life."

Millie laughed. "So what did you find out?"

The worry lines returned. Frank cleared his throat. "The single men's compartment and the single women's compartment are on either side of the engine. We're at the back. There's a tiny deck at the stern for steerage."

"We'll let the men get windblown back there." Isabelle scanned the dank area. "I suppose Millie and I can sew in the dining room between meals."

"I'm sorry, lamb, but this is it. There isn't a dining room or any other space whatsoever."

Isabelle stared at the next triple bunk. "The way these are stacked—" her voice cracked—"I'm going to have nightmares about being trapped alive in a coffin."

"No you won't. Will she, Frank?"

Frank stroked Isabelle's cheek. "We'll pray about it."

Lacing her fingers with Isabelle's, Millicent nodded. "God will grant us fortitude. Besides, there's no way you could be dead and hear all this noise." In addition to the engine's pulse, babies cried, children whined, and adults talked.

Off to the left, a woman laid her baby on the bunk and started to change his nappy. Isabelle blushed. "There's no privacy."

Millicent patted her sister's hand. "I've thought that through. Frank was a genius, claiming the corner for us. Ours are the only bunks that flatten up against the wall. We can fold them out of the way, drape our blankets across the space, and we'll have a private dressing room!"

Thump. Isabelle used her heel to hit something beneath the bed. "Are you forgetting our baggage is under here?"

"I'll stack it to the side whenever you need me to, lamb."

Millicent gave her brother-in-law a look of gratitude. He understood her sister's penchant for fretting. He and Millie had an unspoken agreement: Between his patience and her creativity, they managed to help Isabelle control her worries. A week on this ship was going to take every shred of their collective strength.

Isabelle straightened her shoulders. "Once we reach America, I'll forget all about this."

Frank sat at Isabelle's side, his knees hitting the neighboring bunk. "I've been thinking of what we'll do in America."

"You've thought of little else since you decided we ought to go." Affection coated Isabelle's words.

Frank leaned forward. "Emporiums and catalogues sell ready-to-wear clothing. We need to cater to the more discriminating clientele. The wealthy won't blink at purchasing pricey items. It wouldn't take but a few customers, and word of mouth would take care of the rest. New York will be teeming. I was considering Baltimore or Boston. What do you think, Isabelle?"

Isabelle shivered. Millicent opened her shawl and shared its warmth. "Someplace sunny."

Teatime came and went without a single morsel of food or a drop of something to drink. Millicent ignored her rumbling stomach. Judging from the dismal accommodations, they'd be fortunate if dinner was edible. Millicent stood. "Why don't we go out on deck?"

Frank winced. "It's crowded out there."

"Some fresh air does sound good." Isabelle's gaze swept the compartment, and she murmured, "Is it safe to leave our things untended?"

"Sooner or later, we'll have to." Millicent shoved the bracelet beneath her cuff. "But it's wise to keep anything with us that's small and tempting."

Isabelle's hand went up to her throat. Beneath the high neck of her blouse lay Mama's locket. She never took it off. "I suppose my worry was for naught. We didn't have anything of much value to bring."

Millicent turned and eased into the aisle. Proud of herself for making it through without bumping her bustle or banging her head, she beamed. As soon as she saw the stingy four-by-ten-foot area where the steerage passengers could catch a breath of air, Millicent decided complaining wouldn't do any good. Instead, she squeezed ahead and tugged Isabelle along. "The salty air smells like the broth we made—remember?"

"Oh, I'd forgotten about that." Isabelle giggled. She couldn't turn, so she craned her neck and looked up at Frank. "One Christmas, since most of the other girls went home to be with their families, the cook let Millie and me spend time in the kitchen with her. We each thought she told us to add salt, so it got a double measure. In order to remedy the mistake, Cook kept having us add other things to the pot."

"It was the best soup I ever had." Millie turned her face into the little tunnel of fresh air that angled between two men. "Isabelle, do you—"

"Attention! I'll have your attention!" A crew member called down from the deck above. "We've a passenger who requires a nanny."

"Millie." Isabelle prodded her.

Pain washed over Millicent. She'd poured her love into Audrey and Fiona, only to have them ripped from her care. *Never again. I can't do that again.*

"I can mind a child!" A rawboned woman waved her arm in the air. A few more volunteered, as well.

"You—" The sailor pointed at the first woman. "Go to the starboard stairway."

"Millie, you should have spoken up. Don't you think so, Frank?"

While Frank nodded, Millicent shook her head. "No. I couldn't. We're going to stay together."

"That's not the real reason, is it?" Isabelle's eyes narrowed, then her lips parted. "Oh, Millie. It wouldn't be like with the Eberhardt girls. You'd just mind the child for a week. That's all. Besides, you'd earn a little money."

"I'd do it without pay, just to be up in first class," someone said from behind them.

Millicent squeezed Isabelle's hand. "I couldn't bear being up there, knowing I'd left you down here."

"Knowing you were up there would make staying down here more bearable. If there's another chance, promise me you'll take it."

Laughter bubbled out of Millicent. "That's preposterous. Someone needing a nanny is a fluke. Besides—"

"So help me, Millie, if you dare say something about staying together again, I'll do something rash. Don't you dare think I won't. I'd—"

"Pick me up and pitch me overboard?" Millicent grinned.

"Give way! Give w—" A woman towing a school-aged boy tried to shove through the crowd. They didn't make it to the side in time, and the boy got violently sick. The sight and smell triggered a revolting wave of nausea among several present.

Frank immediately shoved Isabelle back toward the family quarters and jerked Millicent along. Grim lines set his face. "If you can get out of this purgatory, do so."

"It's just a tickle in my throat is all." The woman who'd been selected as the nanny resisted her escort. A brace of coughs shivered out of her. "You have no reason to worry."

The uniformed man who'd originally chosen her scowled. His pockmarked face looked downright frightening. "You won't serve." He remained two steps up and nudged her back into steerage.

"My sister-in-law is healthy." Frank stepped behind Millie and rested his hands on her shoulders. "She's an experienced nanny. You couldn't find better."

Wariness furrowed the sailor's brow. "Come here."

Plagued with uncertainty, Millie made her way to the foot of the stairs. Up closer, she stopped noticing his blotched complexion and saw the worry in his eyes.

"Your cheeks are red," he said. "Are you feverish?"

"It's the wind." She lifted her chin. "I'm quite well."

"Fine." He beckoned her to follow.

The wind whipped at her, then suddenly stilled when she stepped into a protected alcove on the upper deck. The man kept striding along, and she did her best to keep up with him. His rolling gait accommodated the rocking of the ship; she had yet to develop her balance. *I didn't realize it downstairs because we were packed in so tightly; I could only shuffle.*

Hastily tucking in a few errant wisps of hair and poking in a hairpin, Millicent halted when the sailor did. He knocked sharply on a gleaming mahogany door bearing an ornate brass six. A deep voice from inside sounded, though she couldn't tell what he said before the sailor took a key from his vest pocket and opened the door.

Belatedly, Millicent smoothed her skirts and quirked a smile at the thought that the children wouldn't even notice her rumpled clothing.

The man whispered, "What's your name, miss?"

"Miss Millicent Fairweather."

"Miss Millicent Fairweather, sir. She's an experienced nanny."

"It's about time!" A tall sable-haired man strode out of an adjoining room. He held a crying toddler at arm's length. As soon as he saw Millicent, he came to an abrupt halt.

The child wriggled and wailed even louder.

"Allow me." Millicent swept the baby from him and took him back into the room they'd exited. "I assume you have nappies in here for . . . is it a boy or a girl?"

"A son. Arthur."

"Will there be anything else, Mr. Clark?"

"Yes. I expect I'll need to interview a few more prospects, as well. Bring the next candidate in a quarter hour."

Millicent's heart skipped a beat. *Do I want this job, or don't I?*

The woman moved with incredible ease, laying Arthur down, stripping him, pouring water into a washbowl, and bathing him. She cooed softly, completely unaffected by the stench of the soiled diaper. Almost the second she took possession of Arthur, he'd stopped squalling. A fold here, a twist there, a few pins, and she'd done more for his son than Daniel had managed in the past half hour. In action and in temperament, Miss Fairweather exemplified grace. Popping a fresh gown over his head, she said, "Peek-a-boo!"

Arthur giggled and grabbed a tendril of her nut brown hair. "Boo!"

She extricated herself and seated him on the floor. "You sit here for a moment."

Arthur clouded up again.

"Now, now." Miss Fairweather glanced about, a frown marring her youthful face and darkening the gray-green of her eyes. Obviously not seeing what she needed, she pulled a bracelet from her wrist and gave it to him. "See? Pretty!"

"Preeee!" Arthur snatched it with glee.

She turned back, tugged open a few drawers, then found sheets for the drenched baby bed. In a few moments, she'd changed the linen, washed her hands, and started tying a pillow slip into a series of knots.

Daniel watched her. "What, pray tell, is that?"

Pulling on two corners with a flourish, she declared, "A bunny rabbit! See, Arthur? This is your new friend. Come play with Bunny while your father and I have a chat."

When she took the seat Daniel offered, little Arthur promptly crawled into her lap. Gifting her with an angelic smile, he snuggled the knotted cloth and slumped against her bosom. She smoothed back his damp brown curls, started to rock, and softly hummed.

"It's plain to see Mr. Tibbs was correct. You have experience."

"I do."

"Have you letters of recommendation?"

"I have one in my baggage. I'll produce it if you'd like."

Brows lowered, he repeated, "One?"

"My first and only post lasted four years."

"Why did you leave?"

Pain streaked across her features. "My employer decided it was time for his daughters to attend an academy."

"You disagreed with his decision?"

"A father is responsible for making the decisions concerning his children."

She was discreet and loyal, handled Arthur with ease. From her speech and carriage, Miss Fairweather was a proper lady—probably one of the unfortunate types whose family money ran out and marriage prospects dwindled so she'd resorted to genteel servitude. She was everything he needed. He studied her. Fairweather wasn't just her name—it was an apt description. Sunny and breezy, she chased away the cloud of looming problems. All save one enormous predicament: A youthful and comely nanny sleeping in the adjoining room would fan unsavory speculation.

Why couldn't she be old and stout as Miss Jenkin had been? The mere thought of the former nanny had him bristling now. She'd been his wife's nanny, so when he and Henrietta had welcomed Arthur, it seemed comforting to summon Miss Jenkin to take charge of their nursery. All had gone well until Henrietta's death. Thereafter, Daniel noticed Miss Jenkin was frazzled at times, but he attributed it to her grief. The way she'd flitted off the ship and abandoned Arthur . . . Daniel ground his molars.

"I presume Arthur is teething?"

Daniel frowned at the way his son gnawed on Miss Fair-weather's bracelet. "Teeth keep cropping up. Is that why he's in such a temper?" He attempted to pry away the bracelet.

Arthur jerked back. "No! Mine!"

"Arthur." Daniel gave him a stern look.

"Good little boys don't tell their father no." Miss Fair-weather smoothly traded the cloth rabbit for her bracelet. "Bunny is yours, Arthur. As long as you listen to your father and obey him, you may keep the bunny."

"My buddy." Arthur ended the announcement by chomping down on one of the knots.

"Yes, that's a good boy." Miss Fairweather smiled at his son, then looked up at Daniel. "If he's teething, chewing feels good to him."

Guilt swamped Daniel. "I'm not sure he's had his tea. His nanny snuck off the ship before we set sail."

Her gasp hung in the room for a moment, then she recovered. "The steward—Mr. Tibbs was it?" When Daniel nodded, she continued, "I'm sure he could send for something."

"What do you recommend?"

"A finger of cheese, some diced chicken or shredded pork, and applesauce. He'd do well, though, to have hard biscuits to worry. It helps the teeth to break through." She bit her lip. "Sir, I have plans for when we reach America. It's only right that I tell you I'm only able to fill the position for the duration of the voyage."

Though Daniel needed someone for the long term, he figured it was highly questionable that he'd find anyone aboard who'd fit the bill. *I'd probably do better to hire an American girl for the position—that way she won't grow homesick and want to leave.* "I'll inspect your letter of recommendation and make a decision after conducting the other interviews."

Miss Fairweather left and Mr. Tibbs showed in the next candidate. She looked perfect—short, squatty, and ugly as sin. Mrs. Yannislov smiled and thanked him for the seat he offered. "This is my son, Arthur."

"Arthur!" She opened her arms, and his son ambled over.

"My buddy!" He thrust out the cloth rabbit for her inspection.

She nodded sagely. "Arthur and Buddy." Obviously pleased by her acceptance, Arthur crawled up into Mrs. Yannislov's lap.

"It seems my son has developed a fondness for that . . . rabbit."

Mrs. Yannislov nodded.

Pleased by how well things were going, Daniel launched into a quick speech. "I'm looking to engage a nanny for my son. The job will last only the duration of the voyage." He outlined a few duties and ignored a feeling that something wasn't quite right. "As it's a six-day voyage, I'll pay for seven, so in essence, you'll have a day off. You'll watch Arthur around the clock. When—" He halted. With almost every sentence he spoke, Mrs. Yannislov bobbed her head. A sinking feeling led him to ask, "Mrs. Yannislov, don't you speak English?"

"English!" She smiled again and tapped her breastbone. "Czech!"

Mr. Tibbs arrived with a tray for Arthur. Daniel took it. "Mr. Tibbs, I need a healthy, intelligent, homely old woman who speaks English and loves children. Please escort Mrs. Yannislov out and bring me someone whom I can hire."

"Yes, sir."

Daniel tied the serviette about his son's neck to form a bib, then sat him on the edge of the parlor table. Knowing his son had been abandoned, scared, wet, and hungry made Daniel furious. He scooped up a spoonful of shredded meat. "Daddy is going to be sure you're taken care of. Yes, he is."

Arthur reached over, grabbed the cheese in one hand and the spoon in the other.

"Hey. Daddy's in charge of the spoon." Juggling the tray, the spoon, and a wiggling toddler proved to be far harder than Daniel had imagined. In the end, he abandoned propriety for practicality. He held the plate and let Arthur poke, grab, and pinch bites, then shove them into his little mouth. Though applesauce wasn't a beverage, it did slide to the rim of the small bowl—so Arthur was slurping it when Mr. Tibbs arrived yet again.

"Miss Bernice Crookshank, Mr. Clark. I trust I've followed your instructions satisfactorily, sir."

"Indeed." With her salt-and-pepper hair scraped back into a severe bun, a huge beak of a nose, and thin lips, Miss Crookshank's age and appearance gave Daniel hope that he'd found a nanny. "Please do come in and have a seat, Miss Crookshank."

"Thank you."

Oh good. She speaks English.

Perching on the edge of a nearby chair, she set a bag on the floor and clasped her hands in her lap. "I'd far rather mop up your boy than sit here useless; but as Benjamin Franklin said, 'He that cannot obey, cannot command.' "

And she's intelligent.

"More, Dadda. More, peasssss."

"It's an odd time for him to be eating. Don't worry. I'll have him on a schedule quick as can be."

Schedule. That was an excellent sign. This woman understood order and pattern. "It's been an unsettling day." Daniel pried the dish from Arthur's hands and began using a corner of the serviette to swab his goopy face. "I'll be glad to have him on a routine."

50

"Permit me." Miss Crookshank rose, came over, and scrubbed Arthur's face with notable enthusiasm while he squawked and tried to wiggle away. " 'Do not consider painful what is good for you.' Euripides said that. See? You're orderly again. Just as you should be. How old is he?"

"A year and a half."

"And he's still in nappies?" Miss Crookshank *tsk*ed. "We'll correct that this week. Which way is the nursery?"

"Directly behind you."

Miss Crookshank scooped up Arthur, took him to his cot, and popped him into it. "Now you be a good boy and nap."

"No! No! No!" Arthur shouted his favorite word.

Without so much as a backward glance, Miss Crookshank shut the nursery door. A stingy smile yanked the corners of her mouth up for a fleeting second, then her lips went back to their pinched line. She resumed the same seat Daniel had originally offered her.

"Do you have letters of recommendation, Miss Crookshank?"

"But of course." She retrieved the bag she'd originally brought in and produced a stack of papers.

Daniel accepted them and scanned the first two. "I see you're noted for orderliness."

"Indeed." Nodding as if she were the queen acknowledging a peasant, she added, "Discipline is vital. According to Plato, 'The first and best victory is to conquer self.' "

Arthur's shouts changed to wails.

"My son—"

"Must learn to do as he's told. A firm hand instills obedience."

Shaking his head, Daniel paced to the nursery door.

Miss Crookshank reached it at the same moment. "You mustn't give in to his fits."

"Fright is entirely different than a fit." Daniel wrenched the doorknob and strode to the cot.

Reaching his chubby little arms between the slats, Arthur sobbed, "Dadda! Dadda!"

"Come, son." Arthur's tiny body shook with his sobs as Daniel carried him back out to the parlor. He patted and shushed, then glanced at Miss Crookshank's puckered face. "Arthur's nanny decided not to travel to America with us. She stuck him in that cot and skulked back to shore without telling me of her decision. I won't have him think he's being abandoned again."

Instead of reconsidering her tactics and realizing Arthur was terrified, Miss Crookshank shook her head. "Once you make an exception, a child believes he rules everything." Revulsion twisted her features. "What is that filthy thing you're giving him?"

"It's his bunny." Arthur clutched the cloth rabbit to his chest and tried to chew on one long ear between his choppy almost-done-crying breaths. "As you can see, Arthur finds solace in his bunny. I thank you for your time, Miss Crookshank, but I won't be engaging your services."

Face ruddy and lips pinched into a bloodless line, she forced her letters of recommendation back into her bag. After marching to the door, she turned around. "You're spoiling that boy. Seneca said, 'No evil propensity of the human heart is so powerful that it may not be subdued by discipline.' "

"The only way evil is subdued is by the grace of God. Good day, Miss Crookshank."

The door shut. Arthur slid an arm up around his neck, snuggled close, and sighed, "Dadda." Warmth radiated across Daniel's chest. It took less than a second before Daniel realized the warmth was also wet.

Four

Sitting on the lowest bunk, crammed beside Isabelle and Frank, Millicent peered at the watery contents of her tin bowl. No aroma wafted up from it—but she couldn't tell whether or not that was a point in its favor. "I'm not sure what they're feeding us."

"Frank, I'm glad you offered to pray." Isabelle sighed. "God would have known I was lying if I said I was thankful for this."

Millicent whispered in her sister's ear, "I'm thankful— after this kind of fare for the passage, it won't be hard to cinch myself in."

"But we paid more for this ship than we would for another because it included meals."

Wrinkling her nose, Millicent shuddered. "If you think it smells down here now, just imagine the reek if everyone had brought food with them."

Frank bowed his head. "Lord, grant us the strength to endure this voyage and direct us as we embark on a new life.

We pray for your protection and providence, and thank you for the warmth of this meal. Amen."

"The bowl is warm. It makes my hands feel good." Millicent continued to cup it in her palms.

Isabelle arched a brow. "You're dawdling so I'll test the first bite."

Millicent shook her head. "There weren't enough spoons. You eat first, then I'll use your spoon."

"Here." Frank's arm shot past his wife. "Take mine. You should have told me."

"Nonsense."

"We'll share my spoon." Isabelle took a bite, then passed the spoon to Millicent. "Eat up, Frank. Millie and I are used to sharing, aren't we?"

"Indeed." Millicent scooped up a small bite and plastered on a smile as she lifted the spoon to her mouth. "Mmm—I see a carrot."

"Vegetable soup." Frank's spoon clanked against his tin bowl. "Not bad. Not half as good as yours, lamb, but nothing ever is."

All around them, children huddled on the lowest and highest bunks to eat while their parents stood. Because the other bunks didn't fold up, the passengers moved the straw mattress off the center bunk and used the wooden board as a table.

"Fairweather!"

Since she was closest to the doorway, Millie handed her bowl to Isabelle. "Someone's calling for me. I'll go see—"

"No. I will." Frank set his empty bowl on the deck. Muttering an apology, he bumped over their knees as he climbed out to the aisle. A moment later he returned. "Millie, the room steward wants your letter of recommendation." She and Isabelle had to stand up so Frank could raise the lowest bunk to allow her access to her portmanteau. He took the letter and came back. "Isabelle, I want you to pray. Millicent, I'd like a word with you."

It wasn't as if they could find a quiet space and have some privacy. Frank hovered over Millicent and spoke in a low, forceful tone. "The family you went to see—you said nothing. Is there something I should know?"

"Mr. Clark's a widower traveling with his young son."

Frank's jaw hardened as he pulled away. Then he dipped his head again. "In one cabin?"

"A suite." She felt her cheeks grow warm. "There's a parlor with a bedchamber on either side of it."

He nodded. "If your bedchamber has a lock on it, you take the job. I want you out of here. With you gone, I'll do away with the center bunk and Isabelle can sleep on the bottom one without thinking she's trapped in a casket."

"I understand, but I'd want to pray about it."

"Isabelle's already praying. If God wants you to have this job, they'll send for you." Frank shifted—more from nervousness than from the boat's rocking, since his motions didn't correspond to the *Opportunity*'s movements. "It's not because of the money, Millie. The Lord knows we could use it, but that's not why. Isabelle frets over you. Knowing you'd be better off would relieve her of so many worries."

"Ma'am, if you're not going to eat that, I will." A lanky youth stared at the bowls Isabelle held.

"Of course the ladies are going to eat their soup." Frank took one of the bowls and pressed it into Millicent's hands. "It's warm and filling."

At best, the tin bowl felt tepid in her hands.

Isabelle patted the bunk, inviting Millie to join her. "It's not hot anymore, but I suppose it'll be filling. You know Frank." Isabelle gave her husband an adoring look. "He always finds the bright spot."

Millicent laughed. "If the devil walked by, Frank would find something nice about him."

"I heard that." Frank shook his finger at her.

"I'm sorry, Frank." Millie didn't bother to smother a smile. "You would have told him we're short on silverware and talked him out of his pitchfork."

The lanky youth laughed. Several others snickered.

No privacy. Isabelle's concern rushed through Millicent's mind. Manners and propriety dictated that everyone ignore the conversations of others. Such constraints were ridiculous in this situation.

"Fairweather!" a man bellowed from the doorway. Millicent turned toward him. Because Frank stood in the way, all she could see were the cuffs of a uniform and her letter of recommendation.

————

Arthur's diaper drooped low on his hips. Like a little savage in a breechclout, Arthur wore only that scrap of cloth. The gown he'd been wearing now sat in a soggy mess with Daniel's shirt in the washbasin. Dressed in a fresh shirt, Daniel didn't dare pick him up. At this rate, he'd have to ask Mr. Tibbs to do laundry right away. Otherwise, he and Arthur would both be as naked as heathens by tomorrow night. "Son, come here."

Arthur took the bunny's ear out of his mouth. "No!" The minute Daniel stood, Arthur spun around and streaked away, ducking beneath the table. Daniel lunged for him.

Miss Fairweather knew how to handle his son. Her former boss had given a glowing endorsement of the loving care she'd lavished on his daughters. Still, she was young and pretty and unmarried—all huge drawbacks in this situation. But Arthur's needs rated above any other consideration. Simply put, he'd found himself incapable of caring for his son, and a child's safety and survival counted far more important than the sordid and untrue suppositions people might form about Daniel and the hired help.

"Arthur, come out of there." Daniel dropped to his knees, shoved the tablecloth aside, and made a mad grab. Attached to the bunny as Arthur had become, the silly pillowslip animal would draw him right back out.

The door opened. Simultaneously the tablecloth swished back down, Daniel hit his head on the edge of the table, and his fingers captured a wisp of cloth.

"Excuse me, sir. You instructed me to bring Miss Fairweather straight in without knocking."

Resisting the urge to rub the back of his head, Daniel rose. The only thing salvaging his dignity was that he'd outsmarted Arthur. Any second now, Arthur would reappear and beg for Bunny. "Yes, I did, Tibbs. Thank you. Miss Fairweather, do come in. Tibbs, place her luggage in the nursery."

Tibbs did so and left. Miss Fairweather cleared her throat. "Do you need some assistance?"

"Arthur will be out in just a moment." Staring at the hem of the tablecloth, he held Bunny aloft for Miss Fairweather to see. Surely, she'd appreciate his clever solution to Arthur's misbehavior. Suddenly Arthur shot out and Miss Fairweather caught him. Arthur clutched Bunny.

Daniel refused to look at what he, himself, held.

"I'll pop that nappy on him." Miss Fairweather laid Arthur on his back on the floor while she spoke. Her black wool traveling skirts pooled about her as she knelt and reached for the nappy Daniel held. He watched in fascination as the woman unpinned his woeful arrangement, created a similar, far neater composition, and pinned it in place. Arthur wiggled the whole time, but it didn't seem to bother her in the least. "There you go!"

Arthur stood, curled his tiny toes into the carpet, and swiveled his shoulders from side to side. Gleefully, he cradled his rabbit against his chest. "My Buddy!"

Could a one-and-a-half-year-old child gloat? Daniel didn't know. Arthur seemed more delighted than boastful. *There's so much I don't know about my son.*

Miss Fairweather started to rise. Daniel assisted her. He turned loose of her hand as soon as she gained her feet. For the remainder of the trip, he'd stay away from the suite. Discretion required distance, and besides, Arthur needed the room to romp.

"Thank you."

Daniel nodded, then strode out of the cabin without another word.

After ascertaining the door had a lock, Millicent looked about. The top drawers of a hand-carved dresser held Arthur's necessities. A cursory search showed room for her small clothes in the lower drawers, the armoire held far more hangers than she required, and her bed boasted a luxurious satin-covered down duvet.

Millicent popped Arthur on the bed. She removed her traveling jacket and the mutton sleeves of her gray-and-white-striped blouse puffed out to give her more ease of movement. "I need to unpack my clothes. When I'm done, we'll play."

Arthur jabbered. As she shut the armoire, he crowed, "Jumpy, jumpy. Me jumpy!"

Swiping him from the mattress, Millie scolded, "We don't jump on beds. Ask Bunny—he likes to hop on the floor."

With Arthur hopping along, Millie inspected the parlor. A few books stood between a pair of golden fleur-de-lis bookends. Two chairs, a small settee, and the table formed a pleasant grouping that left sufficient space for Arthur to frolic. Another door branched off from the parlor, but Millicent didn't open it.

A tap sounded and Mr. Tibbs opened the door. "Supper, Miss Fairweather." He set the tray on the parlor table and lifted the silver domes to reveal two plates. "Veal, haricot verts, and potatoes au gratin for you, miss. The chef provided simpler fare for Master Arthur—diced meat and vegetables. Bread pudding and clotted cream for dessert. Is there anything else I can do for you?"

"This is delightful. Thank you, Mr. Tibbs."

After supper, Millie played pat-a-cake and peek-a-boo with the little boy. When Mr. Tibbs returned for the tray, Arthur begged, "More!"

"Is the boy still hungry?" Mr. Tibbs glanced at the plates.

"Oh gracious, no. He's asking to play more pat-a-cake. Supper was delicious." Millicent dared to add, "I feel guilty, wasting so much." Arthur curled his fingers around her smallest finger, but Millicent kept her attention on the steward. Something else was tugging at her heart. "Actually, Mr. Tibbs, my sister and brother-in-law are down below. Supper there was . . . scant."

He stared at the tray. "We don't give leftovers to anyone in steerage. Might cause unrest."

Disappointment washed over her. "I suppose it might." She glanced toward the nursery. "Could you please tell me about how I can wash the nappies? Arthur will go through every last one by morning after next."

The man's complexion went a sickly shade of green. "I'm to see to that."

"Unless . . ." Millicent's heart raced. "You provide me with the necessary water and soap, and somewhere to dry them. I'm more than willing to wash them if you can make a way for Isabelle and Frank Quinsby to have my leftovers. Or perhaps Isabelle could wash them . . ."

He moved a fork, then put it back where it had been. Next, he shifted the still half-full cup of milk. "I can't. The captain could fire me."

Millicent rose and propped Arthur on her hip. "I'm sorry, Mr. Tibbs. In no way did I mean to threaten your livelihood."

"I know, miss. Let me think on it."

"Thank you. That's more than I should ask."

Mr. Tibbs left, and Arthur started rubbing his eyes. Millicent prepared him for bed, then rued the lack of a rocking chair. She held him, swayed, and sang a song. He fought sleep.

WHIRLWIND

Soon, though, his head rested heavily on her shoulder and his body grew lax. "There, that's a very good boy." She laid him in his cot, tugged Buddy beside him, and tucked a soft blue-and-purple-striped flannel blanket about them.

Silence descended. After a day in the chaos of steerage, this solitude ought to be a blessed escape. But it wasn't. Millie was alone with her worries. Devising a few methods to entertain her charge the next day kept her occupied for a brief time. Next, Millie slipped into the nursery to fetch her Bible. She sat by the lamp and traced the top of her Bible to locate the thin silk ribbon that held her place. The seventh chapter of Matthew lay before her. *Or what man is there of you, whom if his son ask bread, will he give him a stone? Or if he ask a fish, will he give him a serpent? If ye, then, being evil, know how to give good gifts unto your children, how much more shall your Father which is in heaven give good things to them that ask him?*

Her heart lurched. *Please, Lord—could you please watch over Isabelle? Bread and fish—those would be far better than what she's had today. You gave me this job when I didn't even ask for it, Father. I have faith that you will shower her with blessings.*

Arthur's cot creaked, and he cooed a few sleepy sounds. Millicent paused a moment and examined her heart . . . Arthur was darling, but the warmth she felt toward him didn't begin to compare with the fierce love she held for Fiona and Audrey. *Isabelle was right. I was with my girls four long years. Love grew deep and strong in that length of time. This is different. One short week can't possibly be long enough for the affection I feel for this sweet little boy to develop into anything more.* Relieved by that insight, Millicent set aside her Bible. She tiptoed over and tugged the blanket up to Arthur's shoulders. A few of his baby curls coiled around her fingertips. Incredibly soft as they were, she didn't have to fight with herself much to draw her hand back.

It was still too early to turn in. Millicent took out a ball of crochet string and a hook. Frank's plan to cultivate an elite clientele made sense. Unfortunately, she didn't know what the latest fashions and patterns were. Diamonds? Flowers? Scallops? No more did she start a portion than she'd unravel it.

Time unraveled, too. Mr. Tibbs returned. "I've a cuppa tea for you, miss. Do you mind my taking the hamper out of the nursery?"

"I'll get it. I don't know whether Arthur is a light or a heavy sleeper." She emerged from the nursery with the wicker hamper, but the steward wasn't there. "Mr. Tibbs?"

"Here, miss." He emerged from the other bedchamber. "I just turned down Mr. Clark's bed. The Haxtons' nanny said her youngest charge usually wants a cup of milk at midnight. Shall I bring some for young Master Clark, just in case?"

"No, thank you. Arthur is a year and a half. At his age, if he awakens, he needs to go back to sleep."

"Very well." He opened the hamper, took out the heavy canvas bag inside, and inserted a replacement. "I'll have the lad's laundry back by midmorning tomorrow."

"Thank you, and good night."

Millicent retired for the night. Carefully locking the chamber door, she let her eyes grow accustomed to the dark. Each layer of clothing rustled, but when she unfastened her bustle, she accidentally also undid the latch on her hoops. The eighteen-inch diameter metal cage collapsed on the floor and atop the previous layers, one ring at a time, in a quiet series of chimes. Arthur slept through it all.

The door to the cabin shut. Steady, solid steps sounded in the parlor. They crossed toward the other room. Mr. Clark, no doubt. To her surprise, they then grew louder and louder. Closer.

Millicent's breath caught as the steps halted outside her door.

Five

E ven though Mr. Tibbs had twice sought him out and reported that he'd been in the suite and Miss Fairweather was doing right by the young master, Daniel still needed to assure himself that his son would have immediate attention if he awoke. Daniel tapped on the nursery door.

"W-what is it?"

Those three words sounded petrified. "I'm making sure my son hasn't been left alone again, Miss Fairweather."

"Arthur is sleeping peacefully, sir." Her voice started out a little shaky, but finished on a steadier note.

"Fine, then. Good night."

"Good night."

Had old Miss Jenkin been around, Daniel would have comfortably used the parlor for devotions; with Miss Fairweather, he'd relinquish all personal use of the parlor. Doing so would make it clear to the ship's staff that he observed all propriety. To punctuate his honorable intentions, he firmly shut his bedchamber door.

Daniel awoke the following morning to his son's giggles. He lay in bed and savored the moment. At home, the nursery was on the third floor—far enough away that Daniel hadn't ever started his day with his son's peals of laughter. That alone constituted an excellent reason for this move. Once they established their home in Gooding, Texas, Daniel would enjoy his son's presence at all times.

Quickly dressing, Daniel outlined the points of a conversation he'd have with the new nanny. Expectations, preferences, pay—the like. He'd ignore how he'd frightened the nanny last night. His son's needs were of foremost importance. Before he banished himself from the suite for the day, he'd outline what he required of her and steal a few minutes with Arthur. Everything planned out, Daniel opened his door. His thoughts scattered and the words he'd planned evaporated at the tender sight that met him.

Arthur sat on the nanny's lap. A bib covered most of him. Miss Fairweather's slender hands folded over Arthur's, forming a steeple, and she'd dipped her head to speak to him. "We'll pray to thank Jesus for our breakfast."

His dark brown curls blending with the nanny's black and brown blouse, Arthur piped up, "Foo good!"

"Yes, yes. We'll thank Him for our good food."

Daniel chuckled softly. "That was the prayer, Miss Fairweather. At least, that's the best Arthur manages at present. 'Thank you, Jesus, for my food and help me be so very good. Amen.'"

"'Men!" Arthur disentangled his hands from the nanny's, leaned forward, and grabbed a rasher of bacon.

"Good morning, sir. It's a darling prayer."

Poise like hers would stand them in good stead during the next week. Daniel couldn't help noticing how her hair and skirt were the exact same shade of golden brown. Nannies always wore black, didn't they? He couldn't say for certain. *Yes, I can say for certain. In this instance, I can dictate a uniform.*

"Miss Fairweather, we didn't speak about the particulars of your employment yesterday." He clasped his hands behind his back and watched as she buttered and cut Arthur's toast into little sticks that she lined up like a row of soldiers. Listing expectations seemed absurd; in the moments he'd seen her with his son, the woman had proven to be capable and creative.

Listing his preferences, however . . . This would be the ideal time to stipulate what she wore. This outfit made her look soft and gentle. Attractive, too—all qualities he didn't want. Daniel's chin lifted. "So there can be no question as to your role, henceforth you're to be clad in black and wear an apron. Am I correct in assuming you own such attire?"

She spooned a bite of poached egg into Arthur, neatly slipping a stick of toast into his fingers as he grabbed for the spoon. "I do."

"Wear it." With that settled, he pushed on. "My son is to be called by his full name—not Art or Artie." Henrietta had been quite firm in that, and out of respect for her, Daniel would see to it that her wishes were carried out.

Miss Fairweather smiled at her charge. "Arthur's a fine name for a strong boy."

On to pay, then. "The voyage is six days. Five now. That being the case, I'll pay you for a full week. Consider the extra day you're paid as your day off, at the rate of seven dollars."

Her eyes went wide. "That's most generous."

"My son is worth it. I believe that is all."

She set down the spoon and lifted the glass of milk, murmuring, "Both hands."

"All's well, then. The nursery and parlor are of a size to permit him room to play. Mr. Tibbs will keep informed as to my whereabouts. If my son needs me, send the steward."

"Yes, sir. Fresh air and a daily stroll do wonders for a child's health and spirit. With your permission, I'd like to bundle your son in his coat and take him out."

"Do." *And I'll maneuver so I can be along the way and spend more time with my son.*

By tea time, Daniel couldn't stay away any longer. Knowing Tibbs would be picking up the tray, Daniel stopped by the cabin to check on how Arthur fared.

"There you are," a soft, feminine voice soothed from the nursery.

"Buddy." Arthur's sigh carried with it utter contentment.

"You have a nice nap. Yes, let's cover up Buddy, too. Sleepy-bye." Miss Fairweather backed out of the nursery and pulled the door shut. Sometime between breakfast and now, she'd changed into a black skirt, plain white blouse, and a blindingly white apron.

"How is my son faring?"

"He's a delight." She pulled a face. "Most of the time, anyway. I took his ball away. It's so big and hard, I'm afraid he'll break something with it. I'll see if I can find enough yarn to knit up something softer for him to toss about."

"What about a pair of socks?" Her cheeks went red, and he immediately tacked on, "I've several pair, so I wouldn't miss them." He paced to his cabin, pulled out a pair of socks, and crushed them into a tight ball. Black. All of his socks were black . . . as were his ties. Such paltry symbols of mourning.

He and Henrietta had had a sound marriage. Pleasant, even—except for her mother's infernal meddling. Her mother's overbearing manner was what first captured Daniel's attention. While eating at a restaurant, he'd overheard Mrs. Renfroe at the next table. She spent the entire meal instructing Henrietta as if she were a small, wayward child, demanding she assert herself and insist upon playing the church organ. Though he didn't want to eavesdrop, it would have been impossible to ignore the litany of her daughter's faults Mrs. Renfroe listed. Among the worst, though, was that she'd reached the age of three and twenty without receiving a single offer of marriage. That pronouncement came just as the waiter served cake to them—a confection decorated with delicate pink icing roses.

No one deserved to be demeaned—and being humiliated while receiving one's birthday cake seemed so very wrong. As he rose from his table, Daniel intentionally stepped on the hem of Henrietta's gown. He'd not only apologized, but insisted upon making restitution for the damage by sweeping Henrietta to the local modiste for a new gown. While there, Daniel asked if Henrietta might recommend a church since he was traveling and unfamiliar with her town.

Three months later, Daniel and Henrietta exchanged their vows at that very church. Only once did she ever hint that her life before him had been difficult. She'd said Jesus was her Savior, but Daniel was her knight in shining armor. Daniel knew better. Too wrapped up in business to notice the little things, he'd missed the signs—or so Mother Renfroe later accused. Had she been the only one to say so, he might have chalked it up to her bitter tongue, but Nanny Jenkin also confirmed that Henrietta had been struggling with dizziness during that second pregnancy. Henrietta hadn't wanted to trouble him, so she'd not complained and tried to get by without his assistance as he put his business before his family. In the end, he'd not rescued Henrietta; his neglect had been the death of her.

———

The suite lay silent as Daniel let himself in. A single kerosene lamp swung from a ceiling hook over the parlor table. Some of the more modern vessels he'd sailed in had boasted electrical lighting, but the *Opportunity* counted far too many years afloat to feature such appointments. Many a mast still thrust upward from its ship's deck, bare sentinels to the years that sails had provided the power of navigation before technology made them obsolete.

Having brokered hundreds upon hundreds of business deals, Daniel understood the routine well. The suites on the upper level carried first-class passengers between the two shores, but what lay in the holds below depended on which direction the ship sailed. A vessel such as this would carry a multitude of products from the New World to England. For the return trip, the holds transformed to carry a different cargo entirely: immigrants.

All things considered, Daniel felt pity for the wretches enduring the purgatory below deck. Then again, their very presence had provided his son with a caregiver. Daniel cast a glance at the suite's second stateroom. At home, he'd been able to slip into the nursery. Indeed, he'd done so often. Originally, it was because he and Henrietta would marvel over the miracle of the child the Lord had given them. After Henrietta's death,

Daniel had been drawn there for solace and to relish every minute he could get with his boy.

Arthur had a habit of sleeping with his thumb in his mouth, his little knees tucked up beneath him, and his bottom in the air. More often than not, he'd escaped his blankets and needed to be covered. Was the new nanny conscientious about that important detail?

For the past two days, Daniel had enjoyed a scant fifteen minutes each morning with his son. Whiling away the remainder of his time on the deck and in the library prudently kept him and Miss Fairweather apart. Rigid adherence to propriety made sure others understood he wasn't taking advantage of the close quarters. *It's just for a few more days. All those weeks I traveled on business, I wasn't with Arthur; he didn't suffer from my absence . . . or did he?*

His son's lack of a mother nagged at Daniel, yet Daniel refused to let that loss propel him into marriage. A competent, caring nanny could nurture Arthur. Daniel had been so consumed with business matters that important things regarding his wife had slipped past his awareness. In the end, his inattention had killed her. After making such a horrific mistake, he couldn't imagine taking on the responsibility of a wife ever again.

Today's ocean calm had permitted Nanny to take Arthur for a stroll. Watching them through the window, Daniel had noted their route. Henceforth, he would occupy a deck chair along their path and instruct the nanny to bring his son to him at nine-thirty sharp each morning. The nanny could wander off and leave Arthur with him for an hour. Pleased with the plan, Daniel took the lamp into his chamber.

The supple leather of his Bible felt good in his hands as Daniel sat beside his bed. He opened to where the black strip of silk marked his place. Since the day he'd determined to make this trip, he'd decided to read a chapter each evening out of the book of beginnings—Genesis. The thirty-ninth chapter of Genesis told a chilling tale of how Potiphar's wife tried to seduce Joseph. Though Joseph resisted her, she made accusations. *Lord, is this just the next part of the history of your people, or is this a warning to me?* The image of Miss Fairweather flashed through his mind. Clearly, she took excellent care of Arthur— but Daniel knew almost nothing of her.

Troubled, Daniel knelt by his bed. "Almighty Father, I thank you for the safety of this day and that Arthur is thriving. You know my concerns, Father, regarding his present nanny. Grant me a spirit of discernment. Don't let me be blinded by her kindness to my son."

He'd no more than finished his prayer than an ear-splitting, grating sound filled the air. It died out, and Daniel remained still for a moment, trying to determine the cause. The ship wallowed through a trough and took a long while to level out. Daniel bolted to his feet. The ship wasn't moving forward.

Six

Millicent had just blown out her lamp when a horrid screech filled the air. She jumped out of bed, but it took a few minutes for her to realize the *Opportunity* felt different. The gliding sensation that accompanied the rocking had disappeared. Without the light, she fumbled and scrambled into her clothing. Completely oblivious to it all, Arthur continued to sleep.

Bang! The outer door to the suite opened.

Racing toward the nursery door, Millicent called out, "Mr. Clark?"

Silence . . . for a brief second. Then she heard shouting in the passageway.

Heart thundering, Millicent had to use the striker half a dozen times before lighting the lamp. *Please, Lord, keep us safe.* She found only one life preserver in the armoire.

Arthur protested sleepily as she lifted him into the impossibly big white vest. He rolled over, and his head slid through an arm hole. The straps each measured at least a mile long, and Millicent wrapped and knotted them. Belatedly, she jammed a cap as best she could on the top of the little boy's head. She stuffed a pillowcase with nappies, blankets, and a few more of his baby gowns, then scooped up Arthur in one arm and the supplies in the other. By the time she pinched the doorknob between her index and third finger, Millicent's prayer shrank down to two words she couldn't stop repeating. "Help, Lord. Help, Lord. Help, Lord . . ."

The parlor carpet squished beneath her foot. Her prayer shortened. "Lord, Lord, Lord."

A shadow loomed on the corridor wall, then a big male form filled the suite's door.

"Lord, Lord, Lord . . ."

"Miss Fairweather?"

"Mr. Clark! Here. Here's Arthur." Mr. Clark strode toward her and grabbed. "No, not the pillowcase— Here's your son."

"Miss Fairweather—"

His steady voice did nothing to calm her. The man simply didn't understand the gravity of the situation. "You've got him upside down!" She dropped the pillowcase and rearranged Arthur, then shoved her boss toward the door. "Hurry now. Hurry."

Mr. Clark refused to budge. "The ship isn't sinking, Miss Fairweather."

"You don't have to pretend with me, sir. I won't be hysterical. You're all Arthur has. Go!" The stubborn man didn't move an inch.

Arthur let out a muffled whimper. Millicent tamped down the urge to do the same thing.

"There's been a mechanical failure." Mr. Clark leaned forward and enunciated carefully, "Something broke in the engine room. They're inspecting it even as I speak."

"It has to be more than that. The floor is wet."

Tucking Arthur under his arm like an enormous baguette, Mr. Clark went past her, into the nursery. Arthur let out another, louder whimper. "Hush, there," Mr. Clark said in a reassuring tone. "Daddy has you." He emerged carrying the lamp. Looking down, he stated, "It appears as though the carafe spilled."

Disbelief and relief shot through her. Millicent laughed. "Merciful Lord, we're safe!"

"As ardently as you were calling upon His name, I'm sure the Almighty heard you." He set the lamp on the parlor table and studied the bundle he held. "What have you done to my son?"

Arthur's cap was swooped down, covering one eye. His head stuck out of the armhole, and he scrunched the other eye closed as he let out a wail.

"I'll have him out of that in a trice."

Mr. Clark's brow hiked upward. "I seriously doubt that."

Her boss didn't relinquish Arthur, so Millicent started to undo the knots. "If you could please lift—yes. And now this way . . ."

"Silk worms couldn't spin a cocoon this complicated." He finally shoved Arthur into her arms. "I have a pocket knife in my chamber."

"No!" Millicent didn't realize she'd grabbed Mr. Clark's sleeve until he gave her an odd look. Hastily releasing him, she said, "There's just this one life vest. You cannot cut it—what if we truly need it for your son later?"

"At the rate you're supposedly freeing him, he'll still be stuck in it when we dock in New York." He paced away and returned with the knife. "Hold him still."

Clutching the little boy to her bosom, Millicent inched backward, and Arthur let out another loud wail.

"Hush, son. Daddy is here."

To her amazement, the little boy drew in a few choppy breaths, but he stopped hollering. "Sit down, Miss Fairweather." Mr. Clark didn't really have to give the order. The moment the knife came close to her charge, her knees turned to jelly. Next to Arthur, the pocket knife looked like Goliath's sword. Teasing the tip of it into a knot proved impossible, so Mr. Clark repositioned the blade beneath the strap and sliced clean through.

His big hands stilled just before he cut through a second knot. "Must you do that?"

She loosened her hold ever so slightly.

"That's not what I meant. You're praying."

Heat suffused her cheeks. She hadn't realized she'd been speaking aloud.

"Where did you learn to tie knots like this?"

"While attempting to braid my hair as a child." She bit her lip. Embarrassment washed over her—for both her inane babbling and because Millicent realized her hair hung in a thick braid down her back. She was positively indecent.

Mr. Clark focused on the job and the last strap fell free. His big hands delved into the white life vest and curled around his son. Arthur wiggled and screeched with happiness.

"I fear your son is a bit too wound up to go straight back to sleep."

Mr. Clark gave her an assessing look. "So you don't hold with discipline and routine?"

"Indeed I do. Then again, when the extraordinary happens, one can scarcely expect ordinary behavior from a child so young." She took Arthur from his father, then stooped to pick up the pillowcase. As she straightened up, her braid swung over her shoulder. Millicent tried to console herself with the fact that she'd managed to pull on her clothes. The best thing to do was ignore her inappropriate presentation and hope Mr. Clark would, as well.

But then he reached over and flipped the braid behind her. Just as he finished the action, Mr. Clark's hand froze. Immediately shoving his hands into his pockets, he said in a brusque tone, "Sorry. Arthur pulls—pulled . . ."

She watched as embarrassment heated his face, revealing a chink in his usually reserved, composed nature. Wanting to rescue him, Millicent filled the silence. "It's a wonder all adults aren't bald from babies snatching handfuls of our hair. If babies weren't so sweet, I'd suspect they do it on purpose because they're jealous we have more hair than they. Only I can't say that about little Arthur. I mean, he's sweet. It's just that he's not jealous. He has no reason to be. Your son has a lovely head of hair." *I'm babbling like a fool. What is wrong with me?*

Pointing at what she held, Mr. Clark asked, "What's in that?"

Millicent looked down. Oh dear mercy. The hem of her shirtwaist hung askew, having been buttoned unevenly. If that wasn't bad enough, she hoped in the dim light her boss wouldn't notice that she'd put her skirt on inside out. Jerking the pillowcase upward to cover those flaws, she said, "Lifeboats can't possibly be supplied with nappies. Speaking of which, I'm sure Arthur needs a dry one."

Mr. Clark took the pillowcase. Brows shot toward his hairline. "How many nappies did you put in here?"

"All of them. It isn't all that many. Mr. Tibbs has most of them to launder. He goes through seven or eight nappies a day. I mean, Arthur does—not Mr. Tibbs." *Oh, why can't I just stop talking?*

"Tibbs!" A man in the corridor called out. "I demand to know what's happening!"

Taking advantage of the distraction, Millicent took possession of the bag. Mr. Clark's fingers released the pillow slip and curled around hers for a mere breath. "Stop shaking. You're safe."

After he vacated the suite, she stayed right where he'd left her. He'd calmed her considerably; she had nothing to fear . . . so why was she trembling?

Pulling up the collar of his coat, Daniel stepped out onto the deck. With the sky barely tinted the peculiar shade of predawn lavender and nary a star left in sight, the ocean formed a vast menacing shadow all about the small vessel. Waves that just yesterday seemed friendly swells now pitched and rolled the *Opportunity* in a show of might.

Huge coils of rope and bundles of thick white canvas abounded on the deck. Two older men stood by the captain. One gestured grandly while the other bellowed at him in such a thick accent that Daniel couldn't understand most of what he shouted. Then again, the words didn't much matter. Clearly, the captain had ordered sails to be hoisted.

A well-attired passenger strode into sight. Heading for the captain, he stomped directly over one sail, then on top of another. "I hold you responsible for this!"

One of the old men swung about. "Get yer boots offa my sails, else I'll—"

"Mr. Fogarty." The captain rapped out the name, and the sailor went silent. Not budging an inch, the captain then turned his attention on the passenger. "Mr. Haxton, until repairs are completed, we'll continue on the voyage under sail."

Huffing like a bull, Haxton didn't move. "Time is money."

"True." Daniel sauntered out just a few feet. "Good thing we won't be completely dead in the water. Captain, you're to be commended for striking sail so rapidly." He turned and served Haxton a jolly slap on the shoulder. "Haven't had my coffee yet, so you just might beat me in a game of cribbage."

Engaged in the game, Daniel missed his morning glimpse of Arthur. By midmorning, he sat in a deck chair and awaited his son's stroll. Right on schedule, Miss Fairweather came into sight. Head turned and slanted downward, she was paying close attention to Arthur's gleeful babble.

As she dropped Arthur off to play with Daniel, Mr. Haxton gave Miss Fairweather an assessing look. "With the ship delayed as it is, my wife and our maid and nanny are distraught. I should have thought of it sooner, having your nanny watch my child, too."

Daniel bristled at the man's rudeness. "Miss Fairweather has been hired to watch but one child. Staying busy with your children is undoubtedly the best cure for your wife and nanny's anxiety."

"You let the nanny rule your home?"

Daniel gave Haxton a cold look. "The Lord is the head of my home. As a man of honor, I set forth a contract that was fair and reasonable for both parties. I'll not go back on my word." Daniel didn't want Haxton ogling Miss Fairweather or making any further comments. He gave Arthur a big hug. "Back to Nanny now, son. Be a good boy and have a happy afternoon."

The day dragged on interminably. Daniel returned to the suite only to dress for supper, then for bed. By then, the parlor was silent. The "balls" Nanny had made by stuffing portions of his socks with beans each now boasted decorative zigzags of white and red yarn. Though Arthur's toy box contained much finer playthings, Daniel knew his son would gladly ignore everything else in favor of the nanny's creations. Straightening up, Daniel noticed the minuscule line of light glowing from beneath the nursery door. Pitching his voice so it would carry, he asked, "My son?"

"Sleeping, sir."

"Very well." At least he hadn't frightened Miss Fairweather this time.

Retiring to his bedchamber, Daniel planned out the sliver of time he'd be in New York. Such a cosmopolitan city would have several suitable nanny candidates. He took a list from his pocket and set it on the bedside table. Throughout the day, he'd jotted down pertinent requirements and concerns. Organization would narrow down his prospects and permit him to hire the right woman in short order. A Christian topped the list. She needed to be older and of impeccable character. In the morning, he would add the latest consideration that had occurred to him: A nanny ought to be a light sleeper. Pleased with his sensible plans, Daniel opened his Bible.

"Mr. Tibbs, it is imperative you return Arthur's laundry." Millicent stood across the table from the purser. "Arthur's got only two more clean nappies, and he doesn't own any more gowns."

Going a sickly shade of puce, Mr. Tibbs swallowed hard. "I'm sorry, miss. I tried. Maybe you could borrow from the Haxtons."

"I rather doubt they have any to spare. Even so, you'd still have to launder and return any we borrowed."

Removing the silver dome from the tray, the purser declared, "Breakfast is served, Miss Fairweather." He raced out of the cabin before she could say another word.

She and Arthur prayed and ate. As she had for the past two mornings, Millicent set aside the third coddled egg. Small as he was, Arthur didn't eat much. She often shared his plate so the food wouldn't go to waste. Her own food fit into a handkerchief, which she dropped into Frank's outstretched hands each day while on her morning walk with Arthur. Then they would saunter to the deck chair Mr. Clark preferred at the appointed time, as requested.

Determined to remedy the nappy situation, Millicent took the serviettes from the breakfast tray and went to the nursery. Once there, she folded them together and used them to diaper Arthur. Without a clean gown to put on the little boy, she took a tiny blanket and knotted it into a cape. "There! You are King Arthur. Let's go get your horsey."

Arthur rode about the parlor on his stick horse. "Gup! Gup!"

"Gup?" Mr. Clark lounged in the doorway to his bed-chamber, a puzzled look on his face. "I rather expected it might mean cup, but Arthur's not at the ta—" His voice halted abruptly.

"Arthur just learned 'giddy up' yesterday," Millicent quickly stated. "He's a very clever boy."

"Just what," Mr. Clark said in a disbelieving tone, "is he wearing?"

"His costume." Millicent strove to sound nonchalant. "He's King Arthur, of course."

Hunkering down, Mr. Clark beckoned his son. Arthur rushed to his father, clumsily stepped free, and thrust the little toy at his father. "Dadda, gup!"

"It's very nice of you to share, but you are King Arthur." Mr. Clark adjusted the blanket around his son's shoulders. "You ride. There you go now." Pleased with the attention he'd received, the toddler climbed back on the "horse." He didn't care that it was backward; he rode away, dragging the head on the floor behind him.

Mr. Clark straightened up and sauntered over to the table. Casual as could be, he put the two rashers of bacon on the remaining piece of toast, folded it over, and took a bite.

Disappointment speared through her. *Poor Isabelle and Frank. I won't have anything to give them other than the—*

Her employer picked up a knife, tapped around the egg-shell, and lifted the top. His brows knit. "Yolk's runny. How did you manage to get any of it into Arthur?"

"I cut his toast into little pieces and pour the yolk onto his plate. He dips the toast whilst I feed him the egg white." Afraid he'd reach for the serviette and find it missing,

Millicent blurted out, "Did you see his new tooth? It came in yesterday."

"So he's not gnawing on your bracelet any longer?"

"I didn't mind."

Mr. Clark nodded sagely. He disappeared into his bed-chamber and returned. "Son, come here."

"No!" Regardless of his word, Arthur trotted back toward his father.

"Daddy made you a boat. See?" Mr. Clark set down a trio of connected rectangular blocks. Each rode on cork wheels, but the middle portion's wheels weren't connected from the center. The offset axle made that block—and the carved wooden boat upon it—rise and dip crazily as he tugged on the string.

"Me do!" Arthur grabbed the string and pulled. The toy undulated toward him, and he squealed with glee. "Me boat!" Arthur dropped the string and tried to step onto the boat.

"No, no." Mr. Clark jerked the toy away from certain de-struction. "You're too big to ride this boat."

His forehead creasing exactly like his father's, Arthur lifted his foot again.

Millicent swept him backward. "Arthur, go get Buddy. Don't you think Buddy wants to see your new boat?" While he went to fetch the rabbit, she smiled at her boss. "The toy is charming. Children don't understand about size differences until they're a bit older."

"Then he's too young for this."

"Not necessarily." Millicent seized the opportunity. Perhaps she could coax him into spending a little more time with his son. "As long as he's supervised, Arthur will enjoy playing with it. Imagine how much fun he'll have, tugging it along as he strolls the deck! I'm sure he'll be very proud to show everyone his father's handiwork."

"There's only one problem with that, Miss Fairweather." Mr. Clark pressed the toy into her hands and headed for the door. As he turned the knob with one hand, he slowly withdrew his handkerchief from his pocket with the other. Studying the handkerchief, he asked in a blasé tone, "Do you know what that problem is?"

"Yes." She couldn't muffle her laughter. All this time, he'd pretended as if he hadn't noticed his son's makeshift nappy. "Everyone aboard might not have heard the story of 'The Emperor's New Clothes'."

"Indeed, Miss Fairweather." Arthur rounded the corner, without a stitch on him. His father nodded at him. "The king is wearing nothing at all."

———

"This one. Isn't it exquisite?" The Haxtons' nanny showed Millicent a copy of a recent *Godey's Lady's Book*. "I adore the brightly colored puffy sleeves, don't you?"

"They're beautiful." Millicent closed her drawing pad and rose. She'd been copying drawings and making notes about fashion. Being up-to-the-minute with the styles would help get Frank's business off to a good start. "Would you mind allowing me to sketch it sometime?"

"You can take it with you as long as you promise to give it back tomorrow."

The other two nannies and a pair of maids all rose and straightened their aprons. Whenever they had a few free moments, the servants gathered in an alcove near the stern. One sighed dreamily. "If I were you, Millicent, I'd be sewing a wedding gown. Mr. Clark is handsome and rich."

"Nonsense." Millicent slid the *Godey's* atop her sketchbook. "I have other plans for when I reach America. This is just a temporary job."

Waggling her brows, the maid said, "Plans can change. It's not like you're really one of us servants. Don't think we don't notice your fancy words and pretty ways."

"Leave off, Jilly." One of the others scowled at the maid. "You're in the right of it, sayin' Millie's a lady. Her bein' a lady means she wouldn't imagine settin' her cap for a man in mournin'."

"But he's got himself a poor, motherless son. Them's the kind what aim to marry up fast again."

Millicent shook her head. "Jilly, my dream is to start up that dressmaking shop with my sister and brother-in-law. I want an adventure, not an anchor. Who knows? Maybe someday you'll see one of the fashions I design or an article I write in one of the magazines."

"I never pay much attention to who writes the articles," the Haxtons' maid said. "I just read them. From now on, I'll make it a point to see if Millicent Fairweather is below the title."

"I want to make something of myself." Millicent held the magazine and sketchpad to her bosom and stared off into the distance. "I've had to live by a schedule all my life. For the first time, I'll be able to do as I want."

Jilly huffed. "If you marry a rich man, you won't ever have to do anything. You'd have servants to do it all for you. I know I'd rather wear those gorgeous gowns than have to sit and sew them for someone else."

"Of course you would," another maid teased. "The last time you mended your apron, the string pulled straight off the minute you tried tying it back on."

Glad for the lighthearted response, Millicent made a getaway. She didn't want anyone linking her romantically with Mr. Clark. Oh, he was handsome and well-off, but those were hardly recommendations. *Someday, if God brings me a fine Christian man who loves me as Frank loves Isabelle, then I'll wed—but not before then.*

Indeed, she'd given it considerable thought. Until now, she'd found contentment in whatever circumstances life brought—but that was far different than seeking and embracing what she desired for herself. Settling into a shop, decorating it just the way she and Isabelle fancied, building a business of their very own and creating their own trademark designs—it would be a challenge and a delight. Instead of following after the commands and demands of bosses, they would set their own goals and achieve their own dreams.

Heart aglow with plans, Millicent turned the corner and into the companionway. It took a moment for the sight before her to register. She burst out laughing.

Seven

Daniel's head shot up when he heard melodic laughter. He didn't bother to hide his smile. "I believe Arthur's getting tired."

"I wouldn't have suspected that in the least. It looks as if he's ready to dive straight onto his boat."

Facing backward and tucked under his father's arm, Arthur still gripped the string to his toy and pulled it behind them. His stubby legs stuck straight out from beneath his gown, his feet paddling the air. Every few steps he'd announce, "Boat! Boat, Dadda!"

Pleased with the solution he'd found to keep his son from sinking into the tantrum that had threatened only moments before, Daniel continued to walk down the passageway. Miss Fairweather approached from her direction, and they met at the suite door. She reached for Arthur, then hesitated.

Daniel wasn't sure how to pass his son to her. "I'd best set him down."

The minute Arthur's feet touched the deck, he whined, "No! Up! Up!"

Miss Fairweather knelt by Arthur. "Where is Buddy?"

A stricken expression twisted Arthur's face. "Buddy!"

Miss Fairweather lifted him into her arms. "Let's hurry and find him." Daniel opened the door and watched as she passed through the parlor and carried Arthur into the nursery. "Do you see him?"

"Buddy!"

Daniel plucked the pull toy from the deck and marveled at how the nanny managed to avert a spate of tears. Whenever Arthur grew tired, he became cranky. He'd been rubbing his eyes when Daniel scooped him up. For a few minutes Arthur had calmed, but his good will wouldn't last long.

"You hold Buddy." Miss Fairweather's kind voice drifted from the other room. "We'll pop you into a dry nappy, then you can help Buddy take a rest under your blankie."

Blankie? Miss Jenkin had never used baby talk with Arthur. Why would—

"Bankie." His son sighed the new word with weary relief.

From where he stood, Daniel watched as Miss Fairweather diapered, then cuddled his son. Slowly swaying to rock him, she murmured, "Sleepy-bye."

"Mmmm-ah."

Daniel started as the sound Arthur had made registered. He watched as Miss Fairweather brushed her lips against his son's cheek and heard the tiny, puckered sound of the kiss he returned. To his knowledge, Arthur had never kissed Miss Jenkin. In fact, the few times Daniel had been present when Miss Jenkin put his son to bed, she'd never kissed Arthur, either. He couldn't help but think that perhaps losing his nanny wasn't a disaster, but a blessing.

Gently, she laid him in the cot. "Yes, there you are. Cuddle Buddy, and Nanny will cover you both with the blankie."

"Buddy bankie seepy-bye."

Pride speared through Daniel. His son didn't have many words yet, and the best he'd done until now was to put two together.

Miss Fairweather reached between the slats and fussed over the blanket for a second, then nodded to herself.

Daniel turned toward the table, bumped something, and it plopped to the floor. Kneeling, he lifted the sketchpad Miss Fairweather had dropped off en route to the nursery. Precise drawings of women's fashions and detailed notations filled both of the visible pages. He rose and continued to study them. The nursery door clicked shut. "I know very little of what women consider stylish, but your drawings are quite appealing."

"I can't take credit for those. I copied them from a magazine." Miss Fairweather remained over by the nursery door.

A thought crossed his mind. "I've some catalogues from America. If you'd like, I'll loan them to you. They feature some ready-made wear as well as fabric and sewing fripperies."

"That's most kind of you."

A few moments later when Daniel gave her a Montgomery Ward and Company catalogue, she said, "One of Arthur's gowns is a bit short. Shall I pick out one of the tucks to lengthen it, or were you planning to save them?"

"Save them?" As soon as he echoed the question, her meaning sank in. The pleasure of the day evaporated. Arthur was his first child—and his only child. Instead of putting Henrietta ahead of all else, Daniel failed her and God. A man who couldn't keep his priorities straight didn't deserve to have a wife. The bitter realization of his failure and the fact that it also cost his son a mother and siblings tore at Daniel. "I'll not have more children, Miss Fairweather. Arthur is all I could hope for, and he's enough for me."

Daniel then left for the library. He knew he couldn't change the past, but he'd do everything in his power to make sure he'd lead a life where he'd be there for his son each day from now on.

For most of the day he pored over the Sears catalogue, taking notes as he went, to ascertain what items rural Texas mercantiles might carry. Sears touted "quality" and "The finest you can buy anywhere." If the claims were true, the prices seemed reasonable—even modest. How did local dry goods emporiums stay in business? His cousin promised the store was well stocked and served a thriving community. Even so, Daniel wanted to assume control at once and put his own stamp on things.

He dipped his pen again. The ship tossed unexpectedly, and the nib of the pen crashed into the inkwell. As the *Opportunity* righted, Daniel inspected the thin metal nib. Bent as it was, the thing rated as useless. Even after cleaning off the ink and trying to bend it back into shape, Daniel couldn't redeem it. *Little things. Daily needs. Ordinary objects. Unanticipated items that break or suddenly fail and must be replaced at once. That's where the bulk of my sales will be.*

He turned toward the household section of the catalogue. Though he'd imported and exported thousands of dishes, Daniel realized he had no idea how often sets were replaced. Cast-iron cookware would last an eternity, so common sense dictated he'd not need a large inventory. Lamp chimneys, wicks, oil—those were staples. Matches, too.

Unthinkingly, he put the pen to paper. An ugly black blot spread beneath the nib and spidered across the list he'd begun. A wry smile twisted his lips. Pens, too. One couldn't send off for a new one if the old pen was already broken. Another pen lay nestled in a shallow brass tray in the center of the library table. Daniel helped himself and took another sheet of paper.

"Sir, were you wanting any tea?"

The remnants of what once had undoubtedly been a tempting assortment of scones, cakes, biscuits, and cheeses littered the serving trays on the teak cart. Daniel started to send it away, then reconsidered. Arthur was teething, and Nanny said gnawing on things helped. "Put together whatever you have there. I'll take a plate back to share with my son."

Arthur would love his treat. That much was certain. Miss Fairweather might, too. Perhaps whilst she ate, he could ask her about how long a spool of thread lasted and whether steel, ivory, or wood were the best knitting needles.

———

Millicent had no more set up a tower of blocks and spools than Arthur delighted in knocking over the pile. She created yet another and leaned back. "Okay, Arthur. Get it!"

Gleeful squeals filled the air as he hit and kicked the tower. Blocks tumbled everywhere. It took a moment before Millicent realized they weren't alone. She turned. "Mr. Clark."

He rounded the settee and held out a plate laden with what looked like half of a bakery. "You said Arthur was teething."

"The biscuits are a good idea." She rose from the floor. "I'll put a few in . . ." Scanning the room, she spied a small pasteboard box. "This'll serve nicely."

A curt nod of acknowledgment accompanied the muffled thump as he set the tray on the table. Hitching his pant legs, Mr. Clark knelt beside his son. "Are you building something?"

Arthur shook his head. "Me boom!"

Her heart skipped a beat. Mr. Clark had thought of his son and was going to play with him! Lazily dropping the biscuits into the box one at a time, she watched father and son together. Her little charge now sat in his father's lap. "More, Dadda! More!"

"Here. You put that on top of my block. Daddy will help."

"Me do!" Blocks tumbled. "Uh-oh. Boom!"

"Next time, Daddy will help you."

Millicent glanced over and smiled. Every last block sprawled across the carpet in testimony to the fun father and son shared. She'd prayed for her boss to pay more attention to his little son. Gratitude filled her heart. Perhaps God had caused the ship's engine top to break so Mr. Clark would see the importance of getting to know his son. The creases in Mr. Clark's face eased, making him look significantly younger. *How old is he?*

Five biscuits filled the box. Two more remained on the tray . . . alongside a pair of tarts, three slices of pie, a chunk of cake, a half-dozen scones, and a wedge of shortbread.

Oh—and cheese. Several small cubes and domino-sized slices of creamy white and buttery yellow cheeses tumbled along the side of the tray. Isabelle and Frank would relish receiving even a few. Millicent clenched her fingers to keep from slipping some of the food into her apron pocket. That would be stealing.

Mr. Clark glanced up. "Miss Fairweather, if there's anything on the tray that appeals to you, take it."

Startled, she blurted out, "You don't mind?"

"Not at all. I'd rather fancy some of the cake. Didn't have any tea, myself."

"We don't have any plates or silver. I'll—"

He set Arthur off his lap and rose. "That's of no consequence. My son's taught me eating with one's fingers can be quite efficient." He picked up the chunk of cake. "Go ahead. Grab whatever you fancy."

"Thank you." Mind awhirl with plans, she took the biggest scone. "I'm not all that hungry now, but I'll save this."

Her boss stared at her.

Millicent flashed him an embarrassed smile. "You must think me a glutton."

"Not at all. Cookies in a box proved you to be resourceful. I'm waiting to see how you plan to keep the scone."

"I'll fetch a handkerchief." Carrying the scone into the nursery, Millicent formed a plan. She set the scone on the bureau, then took a fresh hanky from her drawer. Perhaps Mr. Clark wouldn't notice she'd brought the scone in with her. Now she'd go get another so Frank and Isabelle could each have one. Almost giddy with joy, Millicent went back to the parlor.

"Bite." Arthur tugged on his father's pant leg.

As Mr. Clark bent to share what little was left of the cake, Millicent wrapped some cheese along with the scone and placed it in her apron pocket.

Mr. Clark jerked away from his son. "I say! His teeth are sharp!"

"Yes. Are you—"

" 'Twas nothing. Here, son. Have a biscuit. Nanny and Daddy need to have a little chat."

"If he eats too many sweets, Arthur won't take his supper." The scone she held branded her as either a hypocrite or thief. With great reluctance, she set it down.

"I've never noticed my son eating much more than a few bites of anything." Mr. Clark gestured toward the abandoned scone. "Go ahead. Eat up. I was wondering . . ."

I'll nibble on it. Just a few tiny bites from one edge. The rest can still be for Isabelle. The faintest taste of vanilla and currants flooded Millicent's mouth.

Mr. Clark gave her an intense look. "How long does a spool of thread last?"

Millicent lowered the scone, hurriedly swallowed, and blinked in surprise. "Last?"

"Yes. A week? A month?"

"It depends—" She braced herself against the table as the ship dipped unexpectedly.

"Sit." He pulled out a chair for her.

Off balance not only because of the ship, but because Mr. Clark ordered her to be seated when she ought to be minding his son, Millicent demurred. "I'm fine. Truly." The words had no more than left her mouth when the ship bucked out of the trough it had dipped into and Millicent had to catch herself.

"It's foolish to stand on propriety when you can barely stand at all." Mr. Clark's gaze swept from her to the chair.

Millicent murmured her thanks and took the seat. In an attempt to get beyond the awkwardness she felt, she blurted out, "About the thread. A spool can last for a day or for years. It depends on the color and whether it's merely for mending or for making a new garment."

"Hmm." Mr. Clark tucked the remaining portion of his cake into his mouth. He followed it up with a few cubes of cheese. "I'd better take notes."

As he went to get a pen and ink, Millicent broke off a bit of her scone for Arthur. Happy to get more, he gave her a toothy grin and plunked onto the floor.

"You eat nicely for Nanny, don't you?" Mr. Clark ruffled his son's hair, then pulled a chair up to the table.

After hearing comments romantically pairing her up with her employer, the last thing Millicent wanted was for him to lounge about the suite while she was there. At least, she noted, he had left the door open to the companionway.

Mr. Clark gave her a cursory look. "How many spools would a skirt such as yours require?"

Such odd questions! "One would be gracious plenty. With an exceptionally ornate skirt, a second might become necessary." Arthur yanked on her skirt, so she slipped him the last biscuit.

"How many buttons are on a dress? And a lady's shirtwaist?"

The questions seemed vaguely improper. Millicent felt her cheeks growing warm. Curiosity provided a way to avoid answering. "Do you mind my asking why?"

"I bought a mercantile." He scanned the tray, reached out, and lifted a slice of pie. The tip of it drooped, but Mr. Clark swept it upward. What would have been fifteen or sixteen ladylike forkfuls for her amounted to four big bites for him. "Jet or mother-of-pearl buttons?"

Flummoxed, she realized she'd been staring at him. "Precisely what are the buttons for?"

"Shirtwaists and the like. How many do you women use, and what's the preference?"

His explanation made sense and took some of the awkwardness from his odd interrogation. The edge of the scone started to crumble between her fingers. Millicent shoved the scone into her apron pocket. *Oh heavens. I just stuck food into my apron with him watching me!* "The number of buttons varies tremendously. It depends entirely upon the style."

"Seven buttons. All of my shirts have seven buttons. I counted. Why can't women be just as standardized?"

Either Mr. Clark is the most diplomatic gentleman on the face of the earth, or he's the most oblivious. Please let him be the latter. Millicent disciplined herself to focus on the conversation. "Men are accustomed to a regimented life. The number and size of their buttons are predictable and functional. Therein lies the difference. Regardless of the pursuit in which a woman is engaged, she is expected to appear beautiful. Buttons therefore become an important part of the design and flair of her clothing. Several dainty ones can signal she is demure, while a few black jet quietly state she is a widow. There's nothing standard about being a woman, so women require a plethora of buttons from which to choose in order to express their style."

"That makes sense." He ate more cheese and turned the tray toward her, gesturing for her to help herself.

Well, as long as he didn't mind her taking the cheese. . . . Millicent took a few pieces and leaned over to give two to Arthur. "These are yummy. Your daddy likes cheese."

"Oooh."

As she straightened back up, Mr. Clark absently scratched his cheek with the end of the pen. "Did Arthur make that as a sound of approval, or was he thanking you?"

"I can't be sure."

What looked suspiciously like relief eased the furrows in Mr. Clark's brow. "So it's not just me; even with your experience, you don't completely understand him."

"No, I don't." A smile tugged at her mouth. "Though now that I think of it, he was fascinated with his coat buttons this morning. Perhaps you can have a conversation about them."

"No telling what he calls them. I've not been around children, and most of what my son says sounds like pure gibberish to me."

"Most tots only say a handful of words. I recall little Fiona's vocabulary seemed to blossom quite suddenly when she was about Arthur's age." The memory tore at her. Millicent dipped her head. "My apologies. It wasn't right for me to mention someone else's child."

"No apology necessary. It's a relief to know Arthur's progressing as he ought."

At the mention of his name, Arthur tugged on Millicent's skirt. He stood and pushed a misshapen lump of cheese flat-handed into his mouth. "Up." He lifted his messy hands.

Millicent lifted him onto her lap and briskly cleaned him. He promptly leaned forward and reached for the shortbread. Broken in half, it still filled his little hand. He held it up to Millicent's mouth.

"What a nice boy you are to share with Nanny!" She pretended to nibble the edge.

Pleased with her praise, Arthur twisted and aimed for his father's mouth.

"Daddy's busy." Mr. Clark picked up the pen. "We were discussing buttons and such."

Puzzled by his father's rebuff, Arthur turned back to her. She covered his hand with both of hers and took a tiny bite. *Why doesn't this man spare his son's feelings? Maybe he needs someone to show him how to act around a baby.* "That tasted wonderful! Thank you, Arthur. Here. You have a bite now."

While he happily aimed for his own mouth, Millicent rearranged Arthur on her lap. Her hand bumped her bulging apron pocket. *Oh goodness. How much have I tucked away?*

Unaware of her chagrin, Mr. Clark dipped the pen into the inkwell. "I thought it might be wise to keep a good assortment of sewing goods. I presume women purchase based on immediate need."

"Indeed."

Mr. Tibbs knocked on the doorjamb. "I have some of the lad's nappies."

Millicent started to rise, but the steward quickly said, "No need for you to get up, miss. I'll set them in the nursery. Mr. Clark, sir, the captain ordered the crew to inform the passengers that the repairs are almost completed. He anticipates we'll be under power at seven o'clock."

"Tonight, or in the morning?"

"This evening, sir. We'll pull into New York only two days late."

A curt nod acknowledged the information.

Millicent looked at her charge and held out her hand. "Arthur, your nappy's wet." Once she shut the nursery door, Millicent noticed only three nappies and one gown lay on the bed. Swiftly, she changed his nappy and gown, then went to address Mr. Tibbs, who hovered by the table. Mr. Clark was gone.

"Miss Fairweather?" he said tentatively. "With the delay, there's more wash to do than expected. Your recommendation—to have your sister launder the baby's clothes—I got approval as long as she does the Haxton child's, too."

"Excellent. My sister is below . . ."

He looked relieved. "I remembered. I'll watch the lad for a few minutes if you could fetch her. Oh, and here—no use in good food going to waste. Tuck these tarts into your apron for her."

Millicent smiled in thanks and ruefully wondered if he'd noticed her already bulging pockets.

———

"Come sit on Daddy's lap." The teak deck chair creaked softly as Daniel lifted his son. Arthur squirmed a moment, then rested his head against Daniel's neck and clutched Buddy to his chest.

"Here's a lap robe, sir." Miss Fairweather carefully tucked Arthur's blanket around him. Once done with that, she made sure Arthur's cap covered his ears.

"With the blanket and me holding him close, he'll be warm enough. You needn't fuss over that." Daniel reached to remove the cap.

"Please, sir—leave it on." Desperation edged Miss Fairweather's voice. "Surely you've noticed he's already sniffling a bit. By keeping his ears warm, we might ward off infection. Audrey—one of the Eberhardt girls I minded—sometimes got ear infections, and they were so frightfully painful. I want to spare little Arthur that."

Daniel cupped his son's head and thumbed the edge of the knit hat so it gave even better coverage.

"I'll bring my son back to you once the engines start up and he's calm."

Miss Fairweather took the hint and backed up. Hands clasped demurely at her waist, she murmured, "I'll be in the nursery." As she walked off, the setting sun's rays illuminated her brown hair, bringing out strands of gold and russet. The wind swooshing off the sails captured tendrils, pulling them free to dance in the cool breeze while her skirts and apron fluttered about her until she turned the corner and disappeared from sight.

Mr. Haxton escorted his wife around the corner. They approached and took a nearby pair of deck chairs. Mrs. Haxton slanted a look at Daniel, then stared pointedly at his son. "If your governess isn't working out, there must be dozens of other unfortunates in steerage who'd watch your boy."

"I want my son with me." Daniel didn't bother to explain. Had Mrs. Haxton truly held the merest scrap of concern for Arthur, she would have volunteered to allow her daughter's nanny to mind him. More often than not, Mrs. Haxton's conversation at the luncheon and supper table consisted of sly remarks and catty comments. As seating was assigned, Daniel chose to be civil enough to acknowledge her presence; but that was the sum total of his interaction with her. It hardly seemed right to request a change of tables and subject someone else to what he himself found objectionable. Citing his wife's abhorrence of tobacco, Mr. Haxton spent a good portion of each day and all evening on the deck with a cigar in his hand. Daniel suspected he used cigars as an excuse to escape her.

"When I disembark, you can be sure I'm going to report the laxity shown on this vessel." Mrs. Haxton wagged her head like a disappointed tutor. "Imagine, the crew going about in shirt-sleeves! It's indecent. Simply indecent."

Daniel ignored her. Explaining the men couldn't heave ropes, trim sails, and do any number of other chores while wearing the standard tailored jacket would be a waste of breath. Mrs. Haxton merely needed to complain. *Better to be single than wed to a woman like her. Far better.*

Arthur sneezed.

"God bless you." Before Daniel could pull out his handkerchief, Arthur burrowed his face into Buddy, effectively wiping his own nose. Oh well. The pillow slip was just as easy to launder as a handkerchief. Daniel dipped his head. "Remember what Daddy told you? There's going to be a big noise, and then the ship will move fast."

Completely unimpressed, Arthur stuck his thumb in his mouth.

Daniel refused to take chances with his son. The first time the engines had fired up as they'd prepared to set sail, Arthur had suffered a horrible fright, and Nanny Jenkin hadn't been there to soothe him. This time, it would be different. Daniel vowed he'd keep possession of his son until the sound of the engines became a welcome lullaby.

It didn't take long before Arthur's eyes grew heavy and his body went lax. Daniel relished simply holding him. The setting sun seemingly lit the water on fire—a display of scarlet, orange, and gold. The wind whipped the tips of some of the waves, and the resulting froth winked silver and gold. Under other circumstances, this time would hold nothing but contentment. As it was, Daniel waited with concern. When the engine started, how would his son respond? In the best of all possibilities, Arthur would sleep through it all.

About ten minutes later, already weary of the Haxtons' jaded opinions, Daniel wavered between impatience and pity for the ugliness in their hearts. To move would risk waking Arthur, so he tried to ignore their unpleasant conversation.

An almost imperceptible vibration began. The deck chair transferred the motion, letting him know the engine was starting. As it had in port, the engine slowly built up power.

Arthur slept through it all.

The Haxtons argued about whether the *Opportunity* ought to combine sail and engine power or to simply rely on the more modern propulsion.

"What do you say, Clark?"

Daniel didn't want to be drawn into their bickering. "I say my son's in need of his cot."

"He ought to have been in it already." Mrs. Haxton pulled the edges of her fur coat closer. "Keeping him out in the night air was foolish. He'll likely come down with a chill."

"My wife's right, you know. The nanny ought to—"

"I made the decision to have my son with me." Daniel rose carefully, trying not to jar his son. "Good night."

The minute he opened the door to the suite, Miss Fairweather hopped up from the table. She whispered, "How is he?"

"Slept through."

She murmured something that sounded like, "Praise God." The lamp in the nursery burned enough to give safe light, but low enough not to awaken Arthur.

When Daniel stopped at the cot, he lifted slightly and pressed a kiss on his son's curls.

Miss Fairweather carefully eased the blanket away, and he laid his son down. Arthur sleepily rolled over onto his tummy and wiggled until his knees tucked up beneath his chest. Daniel smiled as he laid the blanket over his son.

Miss Fairweather whispered, "Isn't it darling how babies like to sleep like that?"

"Do they?" Daniel whispered.

She nodded. "By next year, he'll sprawl like a boneless cat across the bed." She kissed her fingertip, then pressed the "kiss" on Arthur's cheek. As soon as she did, she looked away.

Even in the dim room, Daniel witnessed the faint blush in her cheeks. *She always kisses him before she puts him down. I thought it was for him—but it's not. Her affection for my son is unmistakable.* Miss Fairweather reached between the slats and scooted Buddy closer to Arthur.

Daniel gestured, "After you," and followed her out of the nursery. She wouldn't meet his gaze, and he suspected why. "Miss Fairweather, I'm thankful for your tenderness toward my son. After what happened, he needs to feel safe and treasured."

Her shoulders melted. "Arthur's a very lovable boy. You're exceedingly blessed."

"Indeed. Well, then. I believe I'll go look at the catalogues."

"Mr. Clark—you were asking questions regarding sewing items. If you'd like, I'd be willing to review the crochet and knitting goods in the catalogues for you."

"Would you? Excellent!" The words had barely left his mouth when a loud sound cut the air and the *Opportunity* lurched, flinging Miss Fairweather into his chest.

Eight

O h dear. I'm sorry." Millicent pushed away.
"Are you—"

Arthur's cry sent her rushing to his side. "Arthur!" He pushed himself up and sat in the center of his cot as he wailed.

Mr. Clark plucked his son out and awkwardly tossed the blanket over Arthur. The blanket descended to bury the boy, and his wails grew.

"There, now." Millie repositioned it and patted his back. "I bet you want Buddy, don't you? Buddy heard a loud noise. Do you think he's scared?"

Arthur jammed his thumb into his mouth and reached out with his other hand. Whimpers still spilled from his lips.

"We're fine. Yes, we are." Mr. Clark patted his son's back. "Let's go sit down. Maybe Nanny can find you a biscuit. Can you, Nanny?"

"Right away." Thanking God for having provided those biscuits earlier in the day, Millicent withdrew one from the box.

"Here you go." She held out the biscuit, and Arthur pulled his thumb from his mouth to accept it. "Here, sir. I'll take him."

"That's not necessary." Mr. Clark sat in a chair and didn't seem to mind that his son crumbled the biscuit all over both of them. He didn't say much, but the reassuring *thump, thump, thump* of his hand patting Arthur filled the silent suite.

It didn't take long for Arthur to calm. Millicent went into the nursery and brought out a fresh nappy. "Arthur feels safe with you. I thought—"

Something between panic and resolve mingled in Mr. Clark's eyes. "I'll try."

Millicent smothered a smile. "I'll change him. I simply didn't think he'd tolerate my taking him away from your presence at the moment."

Mr. Clark handed him over. Millicent changed Arthur, then set him on his feet. "All done!"

"Dah done." Arthur bobbed his head.

Her boss lifted his son. "Clearly, the engine repair didn't hold. I rather doubt they'll get it fixed tonight. Just to be on the safe side, I'll go make inquiries."

Millicent sat down and patted her lap. "Come here, Arthur. I'm going to tell you a story."

The little boy gave her a wary look.

"My story is about a man and his boat."

"Boat!" Arthur dove toward her.

"Yes. Once upon a time, there was a man named Noah . . ."

A short while later, Mr. Clark returned. He studied how Millicent cradled his son on her lap. "He fell asleep right after Noah put horses on the ark."

"At least he made sure of the important things." Mr. Clark stuffed his hands into his pockets. "The damage is significant. It looks as if we'll finish the voyage under old-fashioned sails. It'll take another week. I will, of course, pay you for the additional time."

Millicent bit her lip, then shook her head. "That's not right. I agreed to mind Arthur for the entire voyage for seven dollars."

"I appreciate your trying to be honorable, but I must be just as scrupulous. This has become more involved than we suspected."

Yes, it has . . .

"So I insist. I'll pay you for two weeks. You can safely put Arthur down—the engines won't start up again."

Millicent nodded and left the parlor. As she bent to put the toddler into his cot, Millicent's heart caught. *It's okay to like the child. I just don't need to love him.*

Her heart, however, whispered back . . . *liar.*

———

"Mr. Tibbs," Mr. Clark said as he helped himself to a piece of his son's toast, "Miss Fairweather is to have the day off."

"You aren't going to try to watch the lad all on your own, are you?" Mr. Tibbs looked horrified. "Not change him and all . . ."

"Which is precisely why I brought up the matter. Do you think you can find another woman in steerage who's equal to the task?"

Mr. Tibbs cleared his throat. "Yes, sir, I might."

Was he thinking of Isabelle? Millicent couldn't leave it to chance. "My sister is available."

"You have a sister?" Mr. Clark gave her an odd look.

Millicent busied herself with spreading raspberry jam on the remaining wedge of Arthur's toast. "Yes. Isabelle Quinsby."

"I can vouch for her, sir. She's been engaged to do the laundry for your little boy and the Haxton child."

Millicent flashed Mr. Tibbs a smile of gratitude.

Mr. Clark stared at the crust of bread he held. "Well, then, bring up Mrs. Quinsby." He waited until the steward left. "Somehow, I deduced incorrectly that as a single woman, you were traveling alone."

"My sister, her husband, and I are all together." She gave the food to Arthur and added a dollop of cream to his tiny bowl of oatmeal.

Mr. Clark thoughtfully chewed and swallowed that last bite of toast. "When you asked if the position as my son's nanny was strictly for the voyage, it wasn't because you're meeting a swain in America?"

"No, sir. Adventure lies ahead for me. I plan to own a dress shop and be a woman of independent means."

"Quite a tall order, that. Opening a business requires significant start-up capital."

"That's undoubtedly true. Frank, Isabelle, and I are committed to the venture."

"I've no doubt you'll work hard."

"Thank you, sir." She wiped a dab of jam from Arthur's chin. "America is the land of opportunity, and we anticipate even a humble beginning can flourish with time and effort."

Mr. Clark reached for a rasher of his son's bacon.

"Mine!" Arthur grabbed it and scowled at him.

Mr. Clark chortled. "You're a good eater, aren't you?"

Arthur nodded. He didn't put down the bacon and curled the stubby fingers of his other hand around his spoon. Half of the oatmeal plopped off before he got it to his mouth, but a gloating smile lifted Arthur's mouth.

The sound of a tap on the door accompanied its swinging open. "Mrs. Quinsby, sir."

Isabelle stepped into the suite.

Millicent fought the urge to dash over and embrace her. Instead, she held out her hand. Isabelle came over and clasped it. "Mr. Clark, this is my sister, Mrs. Isabelle Quinsby."

He dipped his head. "Mrs. Quinsby."

"Sir." Isabelle bobbed a curtsy.

Millicent caught the cup of juice before Arthur knocked it over. "This is Arthur."

Isabelle stooped a bit and smiled. "Gracious, aren't you a big boy!"

Arthur grinned and thrust the bacon at her.

"Why, thank you." Isabelle tore the bacon in half and gave a piece back to the boy. "We can share."

"Tibbs, my son has invited Mrs. Quinsby to breakfast. See to it she has a tray."

"Yes, sir. At once."

Mr. Clark started toward the door. "It seems my son has an interesting method of conducting an interview." He paused at the edge of the carpeting. "Miss Fairweather, feel free to pass the day as you will, but be sure to explain about my son's visit to me. I'll expect him at nine-thirty sharp as per usual."

Once the men left and shut the door, Millicent threw her arms around her sister. "It's so good to see you!"

"And you. It's so good to see for myself that you're okay."

"You've no worries over me. Arthur and I get along famously."

Isabelle scanned the parlor. "This is a grand arrangement."

"I feel guilty that you and Frank—"

"I won't listen to a word of that." Isabelle frowned. "Because you're up here, you've sent us good food each day. And with my doing the babies' laundry, I earn twenty-five cents, wash up, and even do a bit of my own laundry. Truly, Millie, your landing this position was a boon for us all."

Millicent urged her sister to sit down and start eating. "I worry about your being alone, doing the wash. Are you safe?"

Isabelle laughed. "Do you think any man is eager to be around dirty nappies?"

"Now that you put it that way . . ." Millicent's laughter stopped abruptly as Mr. Tibbs arrived with the other breakfast tray. "Mr. Tibbs, I'm thankful to you for your kindness and help."

"If the shoe was on the other foot, so to speak, you would've done the same for me."

"Thank you, Mr. Tibbs. It's all just a matter of the Golden Rule, don't you think?"

"Some folks don't abide by that. They got the gold, so they think they rule everything. Puttin' on airs. Not you, though."

Slathering jam onto her toast, Isabelle tattled, "Mr. Tibbs didn't accept my offer to launder his shirts, Millie."

Millicent gave him a you-naughty-boy look. "Mr. Tibbs, you'll be sure to allow us to do that as a token of our gratitude won't you?"

"Suppose I oughtta. This voyage is taking a lot longer than any of us planned."

"Then it's settled. I'll be doing some of my own laundry today. When you come fetch the breakfast trays, why don't you bring along your wash?"

"Millie, I'll—"

"Be watching Arthur." Millicent sprinkled brown sugar on her oatmeal. "Arthur, do you want Nanny to put some of this yummy on your cereal?"

"Yummy! Ummy ummy ummy!" He beat the table with his spoon.

"So what is this about nine-thirty?" Isabelle sipped her coffee.

Millicent cupped her sister's cheek. "We'll have about an hour alone, and you're going to have a bath and I'll help you wash your hair."

Hope flared in Isabelle's eyes, then dimmed. "How is that possible?"

"At nine-thirty sharp Mr. Clark will be sitting on the port side deck. I take Arthur for a stroll and leave him there so they can have a pleasant visit. It's a set routine. Mr. Clark returns him to the suite here about an hour later, just in time for Arthur to take his morning nap."

"Isn't that a bit unusual?"

Millicent nodded. "Yes, but Mr. Clark is a man unto himself. It's a refreshing difference."

"He's quite handsome." Isabelle shot her a sideways glance.

"You're right; Arthur is a very handsome boy."

———

"Mr. Quinsby." Daniel reached out and shook hands with Miss Fairweather's brother-in-law. The man had a direct gaze and firm grip. And even though he was traveling in steerage, he'd made the effort to wash up. Good. So far, things looked promising.

"Mr. Clark."

"Have a seat." Daniel sat down on one of the chairs near the bow. "With the vessel under sail, I've discovered this area doesn't get a huge draft. Another yard ahead, and the salt spray grows problematic; but this spot is surprisingly pleasant."

"Very pleasant." Mr. Quinsby took the proffered chair. His stiff carriage made it clear he felt out of place.

Daniel pretended not to notice. If things turned out well, he'd hire this man; if things didn't pan out, at least Miss Fairweather's brother-in-law would eat a decent meal and be assured she was being treated respectfully.

"I've taken the liberty of ordering lunch to be served here." The minute he spoke, Daniel spied the slightest twitch in Quinsby's jaw. Business dealings honed his awareness of those minor cues, and he immediately clarified, "A business luncheon for us, so to speak. I thought we might discuss your plans. Your sister-in-law mentioned a shop."

"Isabelle and Millie are very skilled seamstresses."

"I've seen a few of Miss Fairweather's sketches. She's also been embroidering something quite ornate."

Mr. Quinsby nodded. "They're both embellishing collars and cuffs so we can trim gowns as soon as we open the business."

"Wise use of time. Have you settled upon a location? Any family already in the States?"

"No, no family. We've discussed various cities. I've yet to make a final decision."

Frank Quinsby's direct gaze and diction would make him an asset to any business. He managed to be forthright, yet discreet at the same time.

While a waiter delivered twin plates that held generous slabs of roast beef, mashed potatoes covered in gravy, and green beans, Daniel casually mentioned, "I've bought an emporium in Texas. My cousin currently operates it; once I take over, he'll run the feedstore."

"Congratulations." Mr. Quinsby bowed his head for a minute. When he looked up again, he smiled. "It'll be nice for your son to be surrounded by family."

So Miss Fairweather's brother-in-law prayed. That boded well. Frank Quinsby struck Daniel as a man of innate nobility who was unafraid of work. Certainly, with him willing to ignore a possible business opportunity while he took time to pray, the man had his priorities well ordered, too.

"Actually, Arthur won't be surrounded at all. My cousin is a bachelor." Daniel started cutting his beef. "So you're a tailor?"

"Not exactly." Mr. Quinsby lifted a bite of roast to his mouth as if it were pure gold. "I was a caretaker and jack-of-all-trades on a modest holding. Did repairs and what have you. The owner recently sold the place, and the new master decided to replace me with an old family retainer."

"Thus, you're free to pursue other interests and possibilities. I presume you're looking toward building a more stable future for your family."

Mr. Quinsby nodded curtly.

They ate and conversed. Daniel eventually leaned back in his chair. "I'd like to make a proposition. . . ."

———

"Miss Fairweather? Mr. Clark wishes you to return to the suite at once."

Millicent looked up at the steward in surprise. "Is something wrong, Mr. Tibbs?"

"Dunno, miss. He sent me after you."

Quickly gathering up the catalogues and the sheets filled with her notes, Millicent strained to imagine why her boss summoned her. It had to be an important matter, or he wouldn't be interrupting her day off. She hurried along the companionway and into suite six.

"Frank?!" She blinked in surprise. What was he doing there? Clutching her husband's hand and sitting beside him on the settee, Isabelle looked . . . emotional. "Is something wrong?"

"Please be seated, Miss Fairweather." Mr. Clark gestured toward a chair.

Millicent lowered herself and held the catalogues tightly just so she'd have something to do with her hands.

Mr. Clark strode to one side of the parlor, then turned back and measured the same distance in reverse—his long-legged stride making short work of the action.

Isabelle lifted a hanky and dabbed at her eyes.

Unable to bear the suspense, Millie repeated herself. "Is something wrong?"

"How do you feel about going to Texas?" Isabelle blurted out.

"Texas?" Taken completely off balance, Millicent looked from Isabelle to Frank.

"Mr. Clark came up with a plan." Frank patted Isabelle's hand. "We'd like to discuss it."

Mr. Clark nodded at her. "In short, Miss Fairweather, I suggested a mutually beneficial arrangement. You and your relatives will immigrate to Gooding, Texas, along with me. Frank will assist me in the mercantile. As for Mrs. Quinsby, she could have a segment of the mercantile's floor in order to have a flourishing modiste's shop right there where patrons can select from the fabrics on hand."

"We wouldn't have to invest in fabric, so Frank says we could buy a treadle sewing machine!"

"You, Miss Fairweather, would continue on as my son's nanny. Is this arrangement agreeable?"

"I don't know a thing about Texas." The words leapt from her mouth.

"It's big. Very big." Isabelle beamed.

"Compared to England, the United States is huge."

"And there are cowboys." Isabelle chattered on—a rarity that underscored her excitement. "But we had dairy farms in England, so that's nothing different."

"I'll step out and give you a chance to speak freely." Mr. Clark's tone sounded clipped and businesslike.

Oh mercy. I've insulted him. Frank and Isabelle want to do this, and he was merely being polite to present it as a choice. He considered the deal all but closed.

Once he left, Millicent went to the nursery door and peeked in on the baby. After she shut the door, Isabelle took both of her hands and squeezed them. "I know what you're worried about. What if you fall in love with Arthur, and Mr. Clark marries?"

Before she could ratify or deny that supposition, Isabelle continued on. "Don't you see, Millie, that that's not a problem? We'll be right there in town anyway. You'd still see the little darling. Your heart won't be broken the way it was when Mr. Eberhardt stole his sweet girls and sent them away."

"With both of us earning salaries, and Isabelle opening the shop without an outlay other than the sewing machine, we'll be far better off than if we settled anywhere else."

The hope in Isabelle's eyes and the logic behind Frank's words made it clear how they felt. *They want this—badly. If I don't, they'll give it all up. But how selfish would that be of me? I don't have a single reason not to go along with this.*

"Isabelle and I prayed already, but I think that was hasty. We should have waited for you."

"You've prayed and feel this is God's will?"

"Yes." Frank motioned to them. "But we'll pray again, together."

Sliding her hands from her sister's hold, Millicent shook her head. "That's ridiculous. God isn't like the waves out there, tossed by the wind. He's unchanging. If you're assured this is His will, then I'll agree." She hastily tacked on, "As long as no one expects me to cook."

Peals of laughter bubbled out of Isabelle. "Millie, we know better."

"Good, because I don't want to murder anyone, and suicide is a sin." She laughed. "Murder is just as much a sin, but you know what I meant."

Frank shot to his feet. "I'll go tell him."

Isabelle hugged her. "It'll work out. Just you wait and see, Millie. God is faithful."

Millicent gave her a squeeze. "As long as we're together, it doesn't matter to me where we are."

They parted. "This is your day off. Go on and enjoy yourself."

"I can do whatever I'd like, and I want to be with you."

"How long does Arthur usually nap?"

Millicent glanced at the camelback clock on the wall shelf. "He ought to wake up any minute." She smiled. "He sings to himself when he wakes up. I can't understand a word of it, but it's always the same song."

"He's a darling little boy." Pushing in an errant hairpin, Isabelle tacked on, "One of these days, Frank and I will have children for him to play with."

"Isabelle! Are you . . ."

"No. Not yet." She glanced at her tummy with dismay. "I haven't changed an inch since the day I married Frank." A faint longing registered in her tone.

"Isabelle, I'm relieved you don't have a baby to worry about on the voyage."

"I suppose you have a point. It's especially hard on the women down in steerage who have babies and toddlers."

Sing-songy gibberish floated out of the nursery. Both sisters turned to respond.

"He's mine today." Isabelle served her a pointed look. "Go read or knit."

"I'll copy another dress from one of the magazines I have. There's a little alcove where the maids and nannies congregate. We all share magazines and books."

Isabelle entered the nursery and glanced over her shoulder. "So you have fashion books?"

"Yes. Empire cuts are no longer in favor. It's all skirts and blouses. I'm seeing some differences between French and English styles compared to the American ones. European skirts are gored in the back or have something called an umbrella train. In contrast, Americans still use bustles with some of the styles."

"Which, I notice, you're still wearing. Really, Millie, it's old-fashioned. It's no more practical to wear while you're minding a baby than it was for you to struggle with it when you were wedged into steerage. It's important for us to look stylish. I could probably just take out the bustle and rework the waist so the skirt takes on that umbrella train appearance."

Millicent laughed. "Whatever the rage is doesn't matter to me at all. I just don't want to be tripping over my hem whilst I chase after Arthur. He's a fast little imp."

"Me!" Arthur nodded agreement as Isabelle lifted him from the cot.

Millie laughed, stood back, and watched as her sister wiped Arthur's nose and reached for a fresh nappy. *She'd be a good mother, Lord. Frank would be a fine father, too. Please, Father, bless them with a child.*

———

Counting his blessings, Daniel prepared for bed. All things considered, the day had gone quite well. Though the voyage's length ought to have been a setback, he'd managed to engage help for his mercantile. Frank Quinsby's assistance would allow him to make up for the lost time as well as rearrange and restock the merchandise. It stood to reason that his store would benefit from featuring a dressmaker, too.

Best of all, Arthur would keep Miss Fairweather as his nanny. She'd mind Arthur all day, then Daniel would be responsible for his son during the night. Since she'd live with her sister and brother-in-law, there'd be no reason for anyone to look askance at the arrangement.

Daniel reached over, took the list of requirements he'd made for a nanny, and crumpled it. A light-sleeping nanny wouldn't be necessary. Besides, the considerations he'd enumerated were moot at this point. Miss Millicent Fairweather was a Christian, loving, and good with children. It didn't matter a whit that she was young and unmarried. Well, it might. Daniel punched his pillow. He didn't want someone sweeping her away.

I'll get her to promise me three years. Yes, three. And I'll offer an attractive bonus for that. By then, Arthur will be getting ready to attend school. Then, if she wants to marry . . . The thought bothered him. He didn't want some hayseed farmer or bowlegged cowboy dragging Miss Fairweather off. She was too cultured and delicate to live a life of drudgery.

Irritated with those thoughts, Daniel flopped over and sought a cool spot on his pillow.

———

"Mr. Clark. Mr. Clark!"

Daniel rolled over, then sat up when he realized he'd awakened to her voice.

The door to his chamber rattled as she rapped on it. "Mr. Clark! Please wake up."

"Coming." He slid into his pants and shrugged into the shirt he'd worn last night. The look on Miss Fairweather's face when he opened the door made his hair stand on end. "What is—"

"Arthur's sick."

Nine

"I can't be sure, but it reminds me of when the Eberhardt girls had the chicken pox. Audrey's rash looked just like this." Miss Fairweather ran a tepid washcloth over Arthur's chest. Just how long she'd been tending his son before summoning him, Daniel couldn't be certain. Miss Fairweather didn't seem the sort to cause an uproar over something minor. A glance at the clock said it was seven in the morning.

"There's no physician aboard the ship." Daniel paced only a few feet away and back. "The only other possibility—" He didn't speak the word.

Her head shot up. "No. It can't be. I'm sure. Remember how he's been sneezing and his nose got runny? Fiona had those selfsame symptoms the day before she came down with the chicken pox. Before we set sail, did Arthur play with someone who became ill?"

"Not that I know of. His nanny minded him whilst I made the final business arrangements." He pressed his hand to his son's forehead. "He's burning up!"

"Children are like that—their fevers run high."

"How can you be sure?" Daniel desperately wanted to believe her. "You said you'd only held that one position."

"Yes, but I allowed Fiona and Audrey to have other children visit. It's important for them to have little friends. When one of the boys took sick, I distinctly recall Mrs. Witherspoon, the housekeeper, saying such was the way children healed. She likened a fever to a refiner's fire burning away the dross."

Steady and gentle, the nanny's hands continued to cool his son's sizzling skin with the cloth she'd dip in the washbowl.

Almighty Father, please don't take my son. "If it's not the chicken pox . . ." Daniel gave her a strained look.

"I'll keep Arthur in the nursery. No one needs to see him. Have you had them?"

"Smallpox? No."

She shook her head. Small tendrils coiled at her hairline, making her look fragile. "Not that. Chicken pox."

"Oh. Yes. Of course. Haven't all children?"

"Dadda!" Arthur reached up with both arms.

"Come here." Cradling his son to his chest, Daniel felt the heat his tiny body radiated. "Poor boy."

"I'd best take him, sir." Miss Fairweather set aside the cloth. "Truly, I don't think it's" —her voice dropped to a mere rasp— "smallpox, but if anyone else does, we'll be quarantined and at their mercy. I'll keep him out of sight in the nursery."

She was right. "Go to Nanny." He pressed a kiss on his son's brow and relinquished him.

Miss Fairweather was halfway across the parlor when a tap sounded at the door. She rushed the remainder of the way and barely secured Arthur from view before the room steward entered.

"Good morning, sir. Breakfast for the lad and his nanny." Setting the tray on the table, Mr. Tibbs glanced about the suite.

They're always out here, ready for breakfast. Does he suspect anything's amiss? "Miss Fairweather just took my son back into the nursery."

"I see. Little Master Arthur's an early riser—I always deliver his breakfast first." Taking the dishes from the tray and setting the table, the steward moved with the smooth economy of a man accustomed to performing his job by rote. As he finished, the steward straightened. "With the voyage stretching longer, the menus need to be altered. The cook wants to assure you, however, that there's still plenty of food."

Instead of a pair of eggs at each place, there was one apiece. Toast, bacon, and oatmeal completed the trays. "The meal will suffice." A frown suddenly creased his face. "What about cream?"

"Milk's in the small pitcher."

"Tinned milk?"

"Aye, sir. Will there be anything else?"

Just in case the worst happens and we get locked in here . . . "Yes. Arthur's teething. A jar of biscuits for him."

"I noticed the damp washcloth." Mr. Tibbs emptied the washbasin into a bucket. "My sister used to have her wee ones gnaw on a wet one. Said it helped."

"By all means, then bring in several." A terrible thought rushed through Daniel's mind. "What about fresh water? With the voyage extended as it is . . ."

"Steerage uses sea water for bathing and such. Our drinking water supply is more than sufficient. I'll see to it that your son has plenty of biscuits. Will there be anything else, sir?"

The nursery door opened and shut. The very picture of composure, Miss Fairweather folded her hands at her waist. It took a moment for Daniel to realize what was different. She'd dressed in her black gown and white apron. He'd not noticed she'd been in her robe with her hair streaming down when she fetched him. Now, though, she gave the impression of the quintessential, unruffled governess. "I didn't mean to eavesdrop, Mr. Clark, but since your son is teething, willow bark can soothe the discomfort. If Mr. Tibbs brings it, I'll brew a little as needed."

Willow bark for fever. Excellent thinking.

"Poor lad. All you need do is summon me. I'll brew some any time he requires some; that's what I'm here for."

"Then a pot, Mr. Tibbs." Daniel nodded.

"Bitter as it can taste, could I trouble you to bring along some honey or a glass of apple cider?" Miss Fairweather smoothed back a tendril of hair that caressed her cheek. "The tea won't do a bit of good if I can't coax Arthur to drink it."

"Yes, miss. Right away."

Once he left, Daniel murmured, "I'm going to the library to see if I can locate a medical text. Is there anything else you need?"

She looked up at him, her eyes steady even though tension strained her features. The color had deepened—becoming far more gray than green, as if to mirror the storm inside her. "Nothing I can think of. I wish we could get word to Isabelle and Frank so they could pray."

"It would set off a panic. We're keeping this between us."

She nodded in agreement.

"Eat. I'll go fetch a book."

"Mr. Clark . . ." He turned to look at her. Compassion and worry mingled in her features. "I'll be praying."

"Do."

Five minutes later, his arms full of books, Daniel was back at the suite. "How is he?"

Miss Fairweather was coaxing Arthur to sip something. "Fussy and feverish. Did you find a book?"

"I did." He set the others off to the side and carried the medical reference to the table. Scanning the index, he found chicken pox and read the pages. "It says here cold-like symptoms, backache, and such occur prior to the onset of a fever and rash."

"That's what happened to Arthur." The little boy fretted, so she slipped off her silver bracelet. "Here, Poppet. Pretty."

"Preeee." He gnawed on it.

"According to this, the time of year is right." He cast a grim look at his son. "Supposedly chicken pox is a springtime malady, but so are smallpox, I recall."

"The girls both contracted the chicken pox right at Eastertide."

"Good. Good." Daniel caught himself. "Not that the girls were ill—that you know they had chicken pox at this time of year."

Miss Fairweather slid the damp cloth over Arthur's dark curls, then coaxed him to take another sip.

Though he'd rather shut the book, Daniel forced himself to look up smallpox. His mouth went dry. "The other . . . before the rash the patient seems to take a chill, have a runny nose, sneezing, and such. The fever and rash follow."

Miss Fairweather bit her lip. Suddenly, she looked at him. "With measles, the rash starts differently than other maladies. Where does it say the spots are for . . . it?"

"Face, arms, and legs primarily. Especially the palms and soles. With chicken pox, it's mostly on the trunk." He shoved aside the book and grabbed for his son.

"They're on his chest and back." Miss Fairweather's voice lilted with delight. "See? It's merely chicken pox. I'm sure of it."

Carefully checking every inch of his son's roasting little body, Daniel finally cradled Arthur to his chest. Closing his eyes, he breathed, "Thank you, Lord."

A few minutes later, Arthur wiggled and whined, "Anny."

"Yes, Nanny's right here." She quickly took him back and gave him a searching look. "After you left, it occurred to me that we'll not be able to keep this a secret."

"No, we won't." Daniel watched his son slump against the bib of his nanny's apron. "I'll have Tibbs get the captain. They must have a protocol for such things."

Miss Fairweather let out a small laugh. "Of course there is. We British have a proper way to do everything."

———

"How's the lad?" Mr. Tibbs brought in a tray of tarts and tea.

"Napping." Millicent gave him a weary smile. "You've been most kind, Mr. Tibbs."

A sad smile crossed his features. "Turnabouts, miss. Back during the '73 epidemic we all got the pox—the bad kind. Me mum and da both died, so a woman down the lane come and took me home with her. Wouldn't be fair for me to turn my back on a wee lad when someone nursed me, now would it?"

"I'm grateful for your help. I daresay, had you not been so reassuring that it's merely the chicken pox, the captain might well have nailed the door to the suite shut or tossed us all overboard."

"I can't take any credit. Mr. Clark made quite a convincing argument."

The door to Mr. Clark's chamber opened. "I overheard my name."

"Mr. Tibbs brought tea. He was crediting you with being the voice of reason when the captain paid Arthur a visit."

Mr. Clark sauntered across the parlor. "Your promise, Miss Fairweather, to remain quarantined with Arthur for the remainder of the voyage was the turning point." He gestured toward the delicate china tea service. "We'll need an additional cup, Tibbs. Henceforth, I'll be taking my meals here with my son."

"Yes, sir. Of course." Mr. Tibbs scuttled away.

It took every scrap of self-control for Millicent to wait until they were alone to speak. "Truly, sir, that's entirely unnecessary. You needn't trouble yourself."

"One might think you don't want me here."

"I don't!" As soon as she blurted out that reply, heat flashed through her. "I beg your pardon, sir, but you needn't hover. I'll take excellent care of him."

As if to make his point all too clear, Mr. Clark pulled out a chair. The stubborn man was going to sit there and let gravity win his argument. "Miss Fairweather." He gave her an excessively patient look, then indicated the chair.

She gasped. "You can't do this. I'm merely a nanny and—"

"We're immigrating, so British propriety no longer holds sway."

"We aren't in the States yet." Millicent slapped her hand over her mouth. Wishing he'd take the hint, she stared longingly at the door.

"If wishes were horses, Miss Fairweather, we all would ride."

"Feel free to ride—I mean, go free." *I didn't just tell him to feel free to go free. I'm a blithering mess. It's his fault, too. If he'd just go off and let me do my job, this would be so much less awkward.*

"Freedom allows me to choose what I wish. I wish to have tea here."

Mr. Tibbs entered and approached the table carrying another cup and saucer in one hand and a plate in the other. "I belatedly recalled that you have an affinity for shortbread, Miss Fairweather. This is fresh out of the oven."

"Excellent. Miss Fairweather was just about to take her seat."

Unable to devise a gracious retreat, Millicent accepted the chair and murmured her thanks as Mr. Clark slid it closer to the table.

"I take my tea plain." Mr. Clark took a seat.

Millicent waited for Mr. Tibbs to fulfill her employer's request, but the steward left the suite. Manners dictated she pour . . . then she'd find an excuse to slip away from the table. Even though the shortbread smelled heavenly.

Mr. Clark accepted his cup. "You were so busy with Arthur, you barely ate anything at breakfast or luncheon. You must be starving."

"I'm far from languishing for want of sustenance."

"Let's keep it that way." He passed her the plate of shortbread.

Temptation sat on that plate, beckoning. Just one tiny bite . . . *No. No, I'm not going to have anything.* Setting down the plate, she straightened her shoulders and opened her mouth.

"One might guess from your expression that you had all lemon and no tea." Mr. Clark helped himself to a tart.

"I need to—"

"Eat some of that shortbread and have yourself a nice cup of tea." He gave her an entertained look over the rim of his own cup. "Without lemon."

"Was that an order or a suggestion?"

"Both."

It wasn't until he answered that she realized she'd spoken aloud. Millicent moaned. "Now if you will please excuse me . . ."

"You're not excused." He had the nerve to chuckle as he reached over and took the largest wedge of shortbread. "Has it not occurred to you that I'll partake of meals with my son?"

"Yes, of course you shall."

He nodded. "Precisely. And do you consider me such an ogre that I'd expect you to go hungry rather than to share our table?"

Thoroughly disgruntled, Millicent stared at him.

His deep brown eyes sparkled. "What are you thinking?"

"You shouldn't ever ask me that." Dear mercy. The moment she said the words, Millicent wished she could take back her comment. Mr. Clark undoubtedly would take that as a challenge.

"You're the woman in whom I lay my trust. Nothing is more important to me than my son. Of course I should know how your mind works."

"You adored debate in school, didn't you?"

The right side of his mouth slid up slowly, giving him a rakish air. He set the shortbread on her plate. "You should take it as a compliment that I engage in such banter with you. I don't waste my breath on nitwits."

"Plenty of other people waste their breath on gossip. Prudence dictates I conduct myself in such a manner that safeguards my reputation and that of my employer."

He scoffed. "Under the circumstances, Miss Fairweather, allowances must be made. Out of respect for the other passengers, I plan to spend most of my time sequestered in the suite. You gave your word that you'd remain in quarantine with Arthur for the remainder of the voyage. As there is but one table, logic dictates we share it." He paused for effect, then stated, "Now let's address the dressmaking venture."

"Isabelle should really converse with you about that. After all, it will primarily be her business. I'll—" She started to pop up, then plopped down. "I can't go fetch her."

"I'll send Tibbs after you've enjoyed your tea."

She muttered to herself.

"I beg your pardon. I didn't understand you."

"You weren't supposed to." He gave her a searching look, and she fought the urge to wiggle in her chair. "Oh, all right. I said I want a minute alone with my sister to warn her about you. She thinks I have a stubborn streak, but I need to warn her about yours. Then she, in turn, will warn you that I possess the perfectly horrid ability to speak out of turn at inopportune times." She paused. "Now that you know the full truth, it's only honorable for me to allow you to back out of the deal. I'm sure you want someone biddable as your son's nanny."

"You're wrong, Miss Fairweather. I want you."

Ten

I *want you.* Oh, he'd said a mouthful. And the words echoed in Daniel's head all day.

It was true in more ways than bore scrutiny. He hadn't had much contact with Miss Fairweather until now, and she'd turned out to be quite a surprise—a pleasant one. Beneath that pretty exterior lay a sharp mind and a quick wit.

She was every inch a lady, though she sometimes slipped up in the tact department. It was downright entertaining to hear what she'd say next.

Even so, Miss Fairweather exhibited grace under pressure with his little boy. That admirable quality shone from her. Ignoring Arthur's crankiness, she patiently got a dose of honey-laced willow bark tea into him. She sponged him, rocked him, sang to him. Clever as could be, she popped tiny socks onto his hands so he couldn't scratch himself. As the day progressed into night, his fever didn't go any higher, but the rash continued to spread.

"Poor mite." Miss Fairweather laid Arthur down for bed. "He's more speckled than not."

Daniel touched his son's forehead. "But at least he's no longer burning up."

"From what I gather, his fever will come and go. You mustn't fret overly much about that. It's just part of the malady." She leaned over, murmured a sweet little prayer, then crooned, "Sleepy-bye." Her lips grazed Arthur's forehead.

Even with his hands enclosed in socks, Arthur reached up and cupped her face. "Mmm-ah!" His baby kiss glanced off her cheek.

"That was lovely. Now you go sleepy-bye with Buddy." She tucked the makeshift toy into Arthur's grasp.

Daniel didn't mind waiting to kiss his son. He relished the tender care Miss Fairweather lavished on Arthur. Arthur certainly sensed her comfort and compassion; a father couldn't want more for his son. A fortnight ago, he would have scoffed at the notion that a simple, ordinary pillow slip could be a child's most prized possession. Now he couldn't imagine Arthur going to bed without Buddy. Little loving touches—Arthur deserved all he could get.

And Miss Fairweather gave unstintingly.

When she slipped to the side, Daniel leaned over the cot. It seemed she'd created a bedtime ritual for his son, and if it helped Arthur slumber more peacefully, Daniel resolved he'd unashamedly tuck in his son with baby talk for as long as necessary. "Sleepy-bye, son." He pressed his lips to Arthur's forehead.

"Buddy mmm-ah." Arthur held up the bunny.

"He wants you to kiss his bunny," Miss Fairweather whispered.

Tending his son was one thing; kissing a pillow slip . . . *It's the same thing. It matters to Arthur. If it makes him feel better . . .* "Sleepy-bye, Buddy. Mmm-ah!"

They left the nursery, and as he shut the door, Daniel noticed Miss Fairweather dabbing at her eyes. She shrugged self-consciously. "That was the sweetest thing I've ever seen a man do. Your son is blessed to have a father who loves him so deeply and freely."

"That I do, Miss Fairweather. But he's also been most fortunate to gain you as his nanny. You've been a great comfort to him."

"We've only just begun the battle. He'll keep breaking out with more of the rash for another few days, and it'll be a week before everything is scabbed. It's not until all of the pox have scabbed that he'll be safe for other children. Do you think we'll reach land before then?"

I've been in a hurry to finish the voyage, but now I want it to lag awhile. It'll let Arthur recover, and it'll give me the chance to learn more about this woman. She'll be a huge influence on my son; I need to know her better. Daniel picked up the plate of shortbread. He'd ordered Tibbs to keep a supply of the nanny's favorite in the room in addition to tea biscuits for his son. Daniel extended the plate to her. "It depends."

"Upon what?"

"If you are the only Fairweather the Lord chooses to grant us."

———

Eight days later, as she opened the nursery door, Daniel informed the nanny, "We'll be in New York by noon."

"Do you think I'll be able to see the Statue of Liberty from the porthole?"

"I'm not sure which side of the ship it'll be on. If you don't see it, I'll be sure to arrange for you to view it. It's my son's fault you've been cooped up."

"It's no one's fault!" She lifted Arthur and sat him at the breakfast table.

"Goo food. 'Men." Arthur parted his hands and reached for his bacon.

Miss Fairweather took her seat. "He does love bacon, doesn't he?"

"I have yet to find a food my son won't eat." Daniel smiled.

As breakfast ended, a strange silence filled the air. Daniel identified it at once. "We must be in the harbor. They've taken down the sails."

"We're in New York?" Miss Fairweather's eyes shimmered with excitement.

"In a manner of speaking. We'll be processed, then released into New York." His own heart raced, but for an entirely different reason. Ever since Arthur broke out in his rash, Daniel knew the Americans could use that as a reason to deny them entry into the United States. He'd said not a word to Miss Fairweather, not wanting her to worry. Besides, her cheerfulness had made what might have been an utterly miserable time bearable. In fact, bearable didn't do credit to the sweet days she'd devoted to helping him and his son.

Daniel couldn't think of another soul who would have remained with someone else's child in that first hour when they'd questioned if his son might have smallpox. She'd shown rare courage and loyalty, and even after they'd ascertained it was merely chicken pox, Miss Fairweather had cared for Arthur with loving-kindness.

And what would her reward be? If the port authorities disagreed with their diagnosis and rejected Arthur, they'd undoubtedly send Miss Fairweather back to England, as well. He'd made up his mind: If the worst happened, he'd pay for the Quinsbys to return to England with them—first class. Because they wouldn't be eligible to reenter America for a full year, he'd rent a place and employ them all, and after the year lapsed, pay for first-class passage to America again. It would be costly, but it was just.

Unaware of his thoughts, Miss Fairweather disappeared into the nursery. Not long afterward, she called Arthur. She reappeared with her valise. Arthur toddled after her, clinging to the exquisite skirts of an off-white outfit that made her look ready to attend the queen's garden party. "I've just changed Arthur. He ought to be fine for a while."

Before Daniel could comment on her finery, a knock sounded. The captain opened the door. "Quarantine officers, Mr. Clark. They have to examine your boy."

A dark-suited man and a younger one carrying a clipboard entered. The elder peered through his spectacles around the room. "Where . . ."

"Arthur, let's show this nice man your polka dots." Miss Fairweather sidestepped to reveal Arthur's location. Smoothly, she knelt and lifted the hem of Arthur's gown.

"No." He wiggled.

She pulled the hem clear up to his little nose. "Peek-a-boo!"

"Boo!" Arthur giggled.

One of the doctor's brows rose a notch. "That's one way of gaining a tyke's cooperation. He's got a crop of lesions, doesn't he?"

"If you mean sores, he does. Especially on his tummy and back," Miss Fairweather admitted.

Horrified by her admission, Daniel hastened to add, "But almost none on his face, and not a one on his palms or soles." As the doctor checked for himself, Daniel added, "He's not running a fever, either."

Miss Fairweather flipped the edge of the gown over his son's nose, and Arthur tugged it back down. "Boo!"

"He's in high spirits and has a good appetite." Miss Fairweather turned loose of the gown.

The younger man jotted down a few notes on the clipboard as the doctor carefully inspected Arthur's arms. "I need to look in his mouth. Open up, boy."

Arthur scowled.

Daniel rested his hand on his son's head, fearing if Arthur didn't cooperate, all could be lost. "He's too young to understand."

"Hang him upside down." Miss Fairweather swept up Arthur and shoved him at Daniel.

He couldn't fathom why she wanted to upend his son, but she knew more about children than he did. Daniel trusted her. "Over you go."

"Ohh! Ohh! Wheeeee!"

"Turn him a little this way," the doctor ordered. He stooped over and craned his neck. "That's sufficient." He straightened and headed toward the door.

Heart in his throat, Daniel half croaked, "Well?"

"First glance had me wary. If Mama hadn't been so quick to show off his spots, I'd have sworn it was smallpox. Hard to tell at first, but it's chicken pox. The sores are in all different stages of healing. Smallpox erupt at the same time. That youngster has nothing more than chicken pox. Harmless as can be." He smiled.

"So you're clearing the *Opportunity*." Relief colored the captain's voice.

"Indeed." The inspector turned toward Miss Fairweather. "Ma'am, I'll have to recall those tricks for dealing with fractious toddlers. They're not standard method, but I can't argue with success."

The men left with the captain.

Miss Fairweather stammered, "I'm sorry, sir. I should have— Arthur's not— We—"

"He could have thought you the king of Burma and I wouldn't have corrected him. The important thing is, we're cleared to enter America now."

A smile lit her features. "Praise the Lord. I've been worried."

"You never said a word."

"I've said plenty while talking to God. I didn't want to worry you by bringing up a needless concern." She picked up her valise once again. "Isabelle, Frank, and I will meet you as arranged. Oh—and you might think to slip a biscuit into your pocket for Arthur. He's quite fond of them."

Mr. Tibbs appeared in the open doorway. "It's highly irregular, but we've received an order for everyone to go through Ellis Island—even the first-class passengers. I'm sorry for the inconvenience." The steward glanced about meaningfully. "I've arranged for Miss Fairweather's sister and brother-in-law to board the barge with you and the other first-class passengers, sir."

Daniel handed him an envelope containing a very generous tip. "You've rendered exemplary service, Tibbs."

"Thank you, sir."

Feeling relieved that Arthur was declared okay and Miss Fairweather would remain with them, Daniel lifted the biscuit tin and repeated exactly what she'd said just a moment before. "Miss Fairweather, you might think to slip a biscuit into your pocket for Arthur. He's quite fond of them."

Equipped with biscuits and nappies, Miss Fairweather held Arthur's hand. Wearing Buddy wrapped around his neck in capelike fashion, Arthur pulled his little boat down the companionway and onto the barge.

Mrs. Haxton let out a squawk upon spying Arthur. "You simply cannot think to expose us all to that!"

"The physician has cleared him." Daniel swept Arthur into his arms. "If you're worried, wait for the next barge."

"With steerage?!"

He shrugged. "Suit yourself."

Paper tags were pinned to their lapels. Once on shore, the prospective immigrants carried their small bags, but the heaviest were left to be reclaimed later with a receipt tag. "Women and children this way," a loud voice called out.

"My son . . ."

"I don't mind." Miss Fairweather claimed Arthur and headed the opposite direction.

Never had Daniel seen anything like it. Much like cattle, they were directed into lines. No allowance was made for first class any longer. Walking a mere two feet behind a complete stranger, Daniel entered a huge pine building and mounted the stairs. Men in starched shirts and jackets keenly observed those going up the stairs. One hustled down and reached for an older man's suitcase. "Here. Let me carry this for you."

"Mark my word," the man behind Daniel murmured. "They'll check him for heart and lung trouble. It wasn't help that youngster offered; it was a way of taking away the old man's excuse that the weight of his suitcase winded him. They're serious about only admitting the healthy ones."

At the top of the stairs, two physicians checked the men for a variety of problems. One marked the old man's coat with chalked letters *H* and *P*. In the pink of health, Daniel moved on through. The only portion of the process that bothered him was when a man pressed a buttonhook to his eyelid and flipped it upward. "Just a quick check for trachoma, sir. You're clear."

Eyes stinging from the crude examination, Daniel looked down at the buttonhook. "You won't do that to a baby, will you?"

"We have to do it to everyone. It's the law."

Daniel loathed the notion that they'd do anything so painful to his tiny son. Objecting would only serve to make the officers angry at him. They held the power to admit or reject him, so Daniel sat and prayed that whoever examined Arthur would be far more gentle.

And Miss Fairweather. No one ought to be treated roughly, and most certainly never a woman—but when someone was as compassionate as she, surely she deserved to be handled with special care.

The test for mental defect was laughably easy. While the man at the next table was copying geometric shapes, a man slid a book into Daniel's hand. "Read aloud."

"As you wish. *'Je voudrais réserver une place pour le train—'* "

"Whoops." The man snatched it back. "That's French. No mental problems for you. Go on ahead and wait for the next segment, sir."

When called to the next station, Daniel provided his papers. "I've purchased a mercantile in Gooding, Texas."

A few simple questions, and he expected to hear what he'd overheard many times by now—only it didn't come. Instead of the stamp of "Admitted" and a cheerful, "Welcome to America," he was directed, "You need to step to the far wall, sir."

"Why?"

"You're to be detained."

Eleven

"Where do you imagine they are?" Isabelle stood on tiptoe and craned her neck.

"More men are immigrating than women. It's probably taking them longer."

"You said that at least an hour ago. I don't believe it now any more than I did then. All of the children are with the women. If anything, I'd expect the men to be waiting for us!" Isabelle sat back down on the hard wooden bench.

All around them, women waited. They'd been grouped by country, but no one seemed to comprehend that Ireland and Scotland weren't England. The fact that they all spoke English was all that mattered. A segment of women nearby spoke in a Slavic tongue while German, French, Italian, and Greek also created pockets of noise. Over all of it, babies' cries and children's impatient whines added to the chaos.

Even though they'd been found healthy and mentally competent, one last condition had to be met. Deemed "likely to become a public charge" if they had no male relative to provide for them, women could not immigrate alone. They had to await their husbands, fathers, or brothers. Once the processed men claimed their women and children, they then left Ellis Island. A handful of single women waited for their fiancés to arrive. It wasn't enough to have a man send for them; that man had to appear at Ellis Island and marry them then and there.

Off to the side, one girl—built tall and solid like the Swedes—chewed her fingernails as she spoke to a matron.

Millicent busied herself keeping Arthur happy. A short while later, the woman next to her gasped. "I didn't think it was true, but it is!"

"What?" Isabelle leaned forward.

"See that blond woman? The matron took her over to that knot of men just fifteen minutes ago. Now she's going to the office with one of them. She's marrying a complete stranger, just to get into America!"

Millicent and her sister exchanged a disbelieving look.

"I would've picked a handsome one," an Irish lass said from beside Isabelle.

"She probably chose him because they speak the same language," someone else surmised. "It's a sad reason to marry."

The Irish lass mused, "Do you think God will honor the vow they'll make to love one another when they don't even know each other?"

Isabelle twisted her own wedding band. "God will honor the union—the question is whether they'll do their part."

Millicent took off her bracelet and recalled the first wedding gift mentioned in the Bible was when Jacob gave Rachel a bracelet. Arthur stuck his hand in and out of the silver bangle as Millicent said, "In Bible times, men and women married and love came later. Maybe it'll be that way for them."

Isabelle shook her head. "Frank and I love each other so very deeply. It breaks my heart to think that girl might never experience the joy of having a husband who cherishes her above all else."

A freckled young woman entered the room. "Attention! May I have your attention, please. I'll be calling names. If you are traveling with anyone whose name I call, you're to follow me. Roy Adams. George Ardell. Reggie Blackwell. Daniel Clark."

"Mr. Clark." Millicent turned to her sister. "Since I have Arthur, I suppose that means they expect me to go—but I can't leave you!"

"Just a minute. They might still call Frank's name."

"Steven Oates," the woman continued.

She was going alphabetically. Quinsby would come soon— if at all.

Isabelle reached over and held Millicent's hand.

"Frank Quinsby."

Air gusted from their lungs. Reassured that they'd be kept together, Millicent tugged the bracelet from Arthur and slipped it back onto her wrist. Walking in a trail like ducklings, the women and children associated with the listed men followed the speaker.

"You'll be staying in the dormitories."

A chorus of reaction swelled.

She stopped at the head of some stairs. "Your men are being temporarily detained. If any of you has another male relative who's been accepted or if you're here to meet with a family member who's come to claim you, you may go on ahead and enter the United States. Simply go down these stairs here." A smile tilted her mouth. "The foot of the stairs has been dubbed 'the kissing post' because of the understandable affection shared upon a reunion."

Once those women left, she looked at those remaining. Her smile melted. "You'll follow me down the center flight of stairs to detention. You must remain here until the status of your party is established."

"Detention!" and "Remain here!" sprang from the lips of many of the women. "My husband's healthy as a horse," one woman protested. "Why are you holding him back?"

"I don't have the particulars. These matters usually take just a few days to resolve."

"Likely as not, it's paper work," a woman said in French to the older woman with her. "If they're being detained, they passed the doctor's tests."

Isabelle was just as fluent in French as Millicent. She whispered, "But Frank had all the necessary papers. I'm sure of it."

"Something might have been misplaced. Don't worry. I'm sure the lady is right—that it's just something minor that won't take long to clear up."

The guide continued on. "The dining hall serves hot, nutritious meals thrice daily."

"How much does the food cost?" Isabelle's face creased with worry.

"There's no charge. While on Ellis Island, you'll not pay to eat."

Men and children played sports in the yard. Women congregated around the edge, many of them knitting or sewing. "It looks pretty nice, Isabelle. I'm sure it's nothing more than a minor inconvenience. At least we weren't separated."

"But we *are* separated. I don't know where Frank is!"

Shouting made them all turn around. Some of the men who'd been playing ball started fighting. Others dragged them apart.

"Probably Albanians." Wagging her head from side to side, the guide tacked on, "They fight at the drop of a hat." Their guide stopped at the bathhouse. "You're free to do as you will until supper." She cupped a little girl's cheek, and her voice softened. "We serve milk to all children and women in the dining hall, and there will be milk and crackers at night in the women's dormitory, as well."

Most of the women from steerage thronged to make use of the bathhouse. Hiking Arthur up on one hip, Millicent juggled her portmanteau in the other hand. "Let's go outside. Maybe the men will find us."

Daniel and Frank scanned the open field, searching for Millicent and Isabelle. When he spotted the sisters and his son, Daniel was thankful the women had decided to dress with more flair than the average traveler. Miss Fairweather's traveling suit was quite stunning, and Mrs. Quinsby stood out in a striking burnt orange garment.

Nothing had ever felt as good as the light, solid warmth of his son's little body as Daniel took him in his arms.

"Frank, what happened? Why are you and Mr. Clark being detained?" Wrapped in a tight embrace, Isabelle's words were muffled against Frank's suit coat.

"We don't know yet." Nodding at Frank, Daniel suggested, "Why don't the two of you see if you can find out?" Setting Arthur down for a moment, he took off his jacket and spread it on the grass for Miss Fairweather. "We'll wait here."

Once Miss Fairweather sat down, she pulled a sock ball out of her valise. "Mr. Clark, Arthur's balance is quite good. After being carried about all day, he might enjoy having you teach him how to kick."

Accepting the ball, Daniel smiled. "This sounds like fun." Indeed, Arthur's idea of kicking proved to be entertaining. He was just as likely to catch the ball on the backswing as the kick, so the ball wobbled all around them. Miss Fairweather picked up her crochet and kept her hands busy, yet she watched them. "Excellent, Arthur!"

Encouraged by her praise, Arthur stayed interested in the activity for quite a while. When his energy flagged, Daniel carried him back to his nanny. He sat down, stretched out his legs, and grinned. "I do believe that was a record for my son. He's usually bored with something after three or four minutes."

Miss Fairweather took a nappy from her valise and began changing Arthur. "Children long for their parents' attention. Your son is blessed that you make time for him."

Daniel absently toyed with his son's baby curls as Arthur continued to lie on the grass. "It's why I'm going to Texas. Business had me traveling a good portion of the time. When Henrietta was alive, Arthur had her; with her gone, I need to be with him."

Miss Fairweather didn't say anything for a moment. She looked at him, her gaze radiating unmistakable compassion. "My condolences on your loss." Her eyes grew misty. "A son cannot take the place of a missing spouse, but I hope that in the years to come, he'll bring you sweet memories of her. I do know that you'll be a wonderful father to him."

All the women he'd known were cool and proper. Miss Fairweather didn't pretend to have their reserve, and her lack of artifice made the honesty of her words count for full measure. "Thank you." He didn't want to spoil the moment by saying anything more.

Just off to his left, the Statue of Liberty rose in her majesty—a symbol of hope for a better life. Looking at her, then looking back at Miss Fairweather, hope flourished within him. He'd fill Arthur's life with love and safety. Just as he'd shown him how to kick a ball, he'd teach him all of the skills a boy wanted and a man needed. With Miss Fairweather's imagination and big heart, Arthur's life would be saturated with fun and tenderness. Working together, they'd ensure Arthur lacked nothing.

Arthur plopped into Daniel's lap and stuck out his arms. Stubby fingers opening and closing like winking stars, he said, "Buddy peassss."

"Here you are." She opened her bag, pulled out Buddy, and gave him to Arthur.

"Coo!"

"You're very welcome."

She pulled a rabbit out of her bag. The realization thoroughly entertained Daniel. He sat and watched as she picked up her crochet—just as she'd picked up the unraveled mess of his son's world and with careful attention and a deft hand brought back order. "My son's not the only one who ought to thank you. I should, too—for all you've done." *And all you'll do in the future.*

"It's been my pleasure." The crochet hook continued to move, but not with smooth, agile swoops and twirls. Biting her lip, she worked more furiously, then abruptly shoved everything back into her bag with a silent sigh. "You've no notion how relieved I am to stay with Arthur. At the outset, I promised myself that I'd enjoy him for the voyage and let go at the end. All too soon, I knew I'd set myself up for heartache. He's such a loveable child." Tears glossed Miss Fairweather's eyes.

Wariness set in. "Why are you distressed if you're glad to continue on as Arthur's nanny?"

"I am. Glad, that is. Truly. It's just that I miss my girls. They really weren't mine, I know. But after four years of doting over them, teaching them, and tucking them in at night, Audrey and Fiona . . ." Her voice grew too thick with tears for her to say anything more.

"Ahhh. I see." She fell in love with Arthur in a matter of days. How much more devoted must she be after years with those girls? If anything, that made her all the more essential for his son. He waited a moment. "How old are they?"

"Audrey's eight and Fee's just six." She blotted away her tears and steeled herself with a deep breath. "I know where they've gone to school. Yesterday I wrote to them and mailed the letters from here. Since I could give them a return address, they'll be able to write back." She let out a teary little laugh. "Audrey will write; Fee will send pictures. And I wrote during Arthur's naptime. I don't want you to think I'd ever—"

"When Arthur is awake, you couldn't possibly sit down long enough to pick up a pen, let alone write your name. As he learns to occupy himself, though, there's nothing wrong with you writing the girls while you mind my son. I'd be a sorry excuse for a man if I asked you to tend my son with diligence and affection, yet expected you to forsake those same tender emotions you've developed over the years for those girls. In fact, since Arthur is an only child, I would hope you'd make every effort to seek out playmates for him. His little world should be full of friends."

"Little friends," she echoed in agreement.

Something about the brave tilt to her shoulders as she set aside her handkerchief tugged at Daniel's heart. Miss Fairweather ached to hold "her" girls, yet she showed the courage to venture forth and risk her heart once again—all for the sake of his son.

Arthur crawled out of his lap and toddled over to her. Pressing Buddy's ear to his nanny's cheek, he exclaimed, "Mmm-ah! Aw bear."

"All better," she agreed. Setting aside her obvious heartache over the girls, Miss Fairweather kissed both Arthur and Buddy.

Then Frank and Isabelle returned. Frank cleared his throat. "I spoke to General Burns, the deputy here. It turns out Scotland Yard sent a transatlantic telegram. They think a murderer sailed away on the *Opportunity*."

Isabelle shuddered. "That means there might have been a murderer right next to us that whole voyage!"

Frank continued. "Any tall, dark-haired man on our ship who's between twenty and forty has to be cleared."

Outrage transformed Miss Fairweather's features. "Whatever happened to the American notion of innocent until proven guilty?"

"We're not processed yet." Daniel caressed Arthur's downy hair. "The agreement between Britain and America obligates them to hold us until the Crown releases us."

"How long is it going to take?"

Daniel wondered that himself. "No telling. These delays are trying my patience."

Isabelle leaned forward. "They mentioned that we need to be careful about our valuables." She touched her throat. "Mama's locket is safe. Millie, maybe you'd better take off

153

Grandma's cameo and hide your bracelet beneath your cuff. Frank, do you suppose we ought to take the money from our sewing baskets and have you keep it?"

"No." Frank shook his head. "Divided up, it's safer than if we keep it in one place." He patted his wife's hand. "The twopence is what counts the most."

A twopence? Daniel kept his expression neutral, but it took discipline. If a twopence was the largest denomination of money they had . . .

Frank smiled at him. "The traditional twopence Isabelle wore in her shoe for our wedding is special." He took it out of his inner jacket pocket. "It's the one her mother and grandmother carried, as well. Her grandfather etched this cross on it, and we're saving it for the next generation."

"And Millie," Isabelle tacked on. "She'll use it when she's a bride, too!"

Daniel looked at Millicent. It took no imagination to picture Millicent Fairweather as a bride. *Mine.*

The primal reaction shot through Daniel's mind so savagely, he froze. He'd buried his wife nine months ago and decided at that time never to marry again. He had a son, and that was good enough—or so he thought back then.

Mine. The word Arthur shouted possessively about his little toys suddenly became his father's.

Arthur already wiggled his way into Miss Fairweather's heart. What would it take for me to court her into opening her heart to me? I can't deny the attraction. It's been there from the start. He smiled. *But it's not about what I'd want in a wife. The issue is if I'm able to be what God would require of a husband.*

I'm not going to rush into this, he promised himself. *Whirlwind romances are for fools.*

Twelve

As night fell, Daniel and Frank went to the men's dormitory. Frank looked about. "Good thing Millie's with Isabelle. Being in a place like this is bound to bring back bad memories."

"I gathered they'd attended an academy. How old were they?"

"Isabelle was barely ten. Millie's four years younger."

"She was only six?" *She was nothing more than a baby!* "Who could send away their flesh and blood like that?"

"Their uncle. According to my wife, a distant relative wanted Millie. Millie begged for her to take them both and threw quite the tantrum when she refused. As a result, both girls went to the academy." Frank sighed. "Isabelle still holds herself to blame. Trying to console Millie, Isabelle promised her they'd always stay together. She never imagined her pledge would cause Millie to forsake the opportunity for a normal life."

"Adults ought never have placed the girls in such straits."

Frank shook his head. "It got worse. By the time Isabelle turned fifteen, their uncle had squandered the family funds. Isabelle found a school that would allow her to work in exchange for keeping Millie as a student. It was her way of honoring her promise."

"Your wife is to be commended."

His praise garnered a smile. "Isabelle's a remarkable woman. She's fretting over our being apart and Arthur's not being with you."

"God willing, we'll all be on a train together tomorrow." He grimaced. "Those little girls Miss Fairweather cared for—they're about the same ages she and Isabelle were."

"Exactly. It's stirred up nightmares for Millie and my wife, as well."

A man entered the dorm with another gentleman who held a sheet of paper. "Attention. I'm Tilson, superintendent of the watch. If I call your name, you're to line up."

Daniel could see the paper was a *wanted* poster. "If I don't miss my guess, that chap is a representative of the Crown. If he releases us, we could get out of here."

Daniel and Frank's names were called along with other young, dark-haired Englishmen. After walking down the line to look at them, the two men in charge held a quick conversation. Tilson then turned to the men. "You've all been cleared. First thing in the morning, you'll be permitted to leave."

Grinning like simpletons, the other men walked back to their bunks. Frank grabbed Daniel's arm. "Did you read that poster? See who was murdered?"

"Eber-something."

Grim as could be, Frank said, "Eberhardt. The man whose daughters Millicent minded."

"Are you sure?" Daniel didn't wait for a reply. "Do you know who the closest family is to the girls?"

"There is none. None whatsoever."

"Then a guardian. Did Millicent ever mention who the girls' guardian would be?"

"I don't know if one was ever appointed." Frank grasped Daniel's arm. "I'd rather not tell Millie anything about Mr. Eberhardt's death. She'll be distraught. Until I can ascertain what's to become of them . . ."

Daniel demanded, "How will you do so?"

"The butler. I can write the school, too. Millie mentioned the academy the girls were taken to. Surely between the two contacts . . ."

Superintendent of the Watch Tilson was walking by. Daniel strode toward him and Tilson stopped. "Did you need something?"

Pointing at the poster, Frank said, "We saw that. Eberhardt was a widower with two small daughters. There is no other family."

Tilson frowned. "What a tragedy for the girls."

"I know the telegraph here on the island must be closed for the night, but this is an emergency. I must send telegrams at once to ensure the children are looked after." Daniel gave the officer a level gaze. "I mean no slur on your integrity when I state that cost is not a consideration."

Later, as they walked back from an office after having sent telegrams, Daniel said, "At least now the academy and the butler know how to get in touch with us."

Frank stopped. "I'll ask you to give me your word that you won't say anything about this yet."

"Of course not. There's no use putting Miss Fairweather through needless anguish."

"Isabelle, either. You see, Mr. Eberhardt didn't come home for months or even a year or more at a time. On Millie's day off she'd often bring the girls with her, and we'd go on a picnic or out for a little fun. My wife's exceptionally fond of little Audrey and Fee. That's why I'm asking for a gentleman's promise to shelter both Millie and Isabelle from the truth until we can assure them of the girls' safety and well-being."

"You have my word, Frank. I'll do anything I can for them."

Back at their bunks, Daniel opened his Bible. Frank cleared his throat. "I had Isabelle keep our Bible with her. Do you mind reading aloud?"

"Not at all. I'm reading John. Chapter three . . ." He began reading of the time when Nicodemus went to Christ and was puzzled when Jesus said he must be born again. Upon finishing the chapter, Daniel looked up.

Frank lay across his cot, his head propped up on one hand. "Poor Nicodemus. The simplicity of Christ's message confused him."

"In the end, it was Nicodemus who gathered the costly spices for the Savior's burial."

"Yeah. It took time, but I guess he finally did accept the truth." Frank swung around and sat up. "That verse about the wind? Once, when my mother flummoxed my father, he quoted the beginning of that verse and likened women to wind."

Daniel opened the Bible again and read, " 'The wind bloweth where it listeth, and thou hearest the sound thereof, but canst not tell whence it cometh, and whither it goeth.' "

"Yes, that's it. Come to think of it, Isabelle's that way, too. She refreshes and cools me, and yet I can't ever be quite sure what she's thinking or why she does things."

"If Isabelle's like a wind, then Millicent is a whirlwind."

Crooking a brow, Frank said, "Oh?"

"She's the more lively of the two." Daniel set aside his Bible.

All around them, men found ways to fill their spare time. Playing cards, reading, laughing at coarse jokes; but a pocket of stillness formed between Frank and him. Frank gave him a long, steady look. "I'll ask you straight out: Are you starting to have feelings for Millie?"

I opened the door. I had to expect him to ask. Had he not, I wouldn't respect him. Until Millicent marries, he's her protector. Daniel's chin rose a notch. "It's my intent to pray about it. About her. I didn't expect to marry again, but I didn't consider that just as a man can be spiritually reborn, he can also experience a second love life. I'm not going to rush into anything. It's too early to declare any intentions other than to simply say that I'm seeking God's will."

A slow smile lifted Frank's mouth. "I'll pray about it, too. You're right, though. Millie's a whirlwind."

Daniel began to pray. *Lord, what I want most is to be in your will. I'll wait on you and let you lead me in this. Your blessing means everything to me, and if I'm not to marry again, I pray you'd take away the stirrings I feel for Millicent.*

Unaware Daniel was praying, Frank chuckled. "Yes, Millie's definitely a whirlwind."

Lord, I know only you can control the wind. Is that the answer? That I'm not to marry again?

"Miss Fairweather."

"Yes?" Millicent looked up from tying her shoe. All about her, women were getting ready to go to breakfast.

Mrs. Sloper, the matron in charge, was looking at her intently. "Could you come with me? You may bring the little one with you."

"Should my sister come, too?"

The matron didn't meet her eyes. "I'll fetch her soon."

Something seemed wrong, but Millicent didn't question the matron. She popped Arthur onto her hip and followed the woman through the building and to an office. Mr. Clark stood at the window, his face drawn and somber. Another gentleman stood behind his desk.

The matron's voice sounded strained. "Miss Fairweather, this is Colonel Webber, the director of Ellis Island. The young lady to his right is Miss Alma Matthews, the Methodist missionary to the island."

Millicent murmured polite greetings but inwardly knew something was wrong. She looked to Mr. Clark.

He took Arthur from her, gave him a quick hug, and passed him to the matron. The woman slipped out of the room with the little boy. Mr. Clark touched her arm. "Miss Fairweather, something dreadful has happened."

"Oh no. Frank didn't make it through processing?" She turned toward the colonel. "He's healthy and bright. Of all the men in the world, Frank is the most honest and hardworking."

Colonel Webber remained standing behind his desk. "That's not it. We thought to speak with you first so you could assist us. A fight broke out last night. Unfortunately, Mr. Quinsby walked in and became a victim."

Millicent looked from the colonel to Mr. Clark, then back. One looked grim; the other wore a bleak expression. The missionary was crying softly. Millicent rasped, "Was he hurt badly? Where is he?" Manners dictated she be silent and allow them to respond, but worries started to soar. "I'll get my sister. Isabelle ought to be with him."

Mr. Clark nudged her into a chair and stooped so his dark eyes were level with hers. Her fright escalated even more.

"Millicent."

He called me by my Christian name. That realization sent her into a panic. "Frank—"

"He's with the Lord, Millicent."

Feeling as if he'd pushed her into a snowbank—shocked, off balance, and ice cold—Millicent stared at him. "Fr— No. No, there's been a mistake."

"There's no mistake. I saw him." Mr. Clark warmed her icy hands. "I thought you ought to know first so you could collect yourself. Isabelle is going to need you to be strong for her."

"Isabelle. Oh, it can't be." Tears welled up as she looked at Mr. Clark's unblinking gaze. "My sister . . . she adores Frank."

"And he adored her. It's a tragedy." He pressed his handkerchief into her hand.

The colonel cupped Miss Matthews' arm. "We'll give you a few minutes." He said something more to Mr. Clark, but it sounded muffled and far away.

Again, Mr. Clark took her hands in his. "I cannot begin to express how much I regret your loss."

"It didn't really happen."

"It did. I saw him, Millicent. He's not with us anymore."
He tilted her face up to his. "We must help Isabelle through
this."

Shaking uncontrollably, she tried to calm herself. Mr. Clark
took off his coat and slid it around her shoulders. "It w-would
be best if I told her." She curled up within the warmth of his
coat. "Tell me what h-happened."

"Frank accidentally walked into a knife fight occurring
in the lavatory and was caught horrifically in the midst of
violent chaos. He passed on in a matter of minutes from the
injuries."

Millicent stared at him. Steady brown eyes gazed back.
"Please, Mr. Clark. Check again. It might be a mistake."

"It's no mistake. It's Frank."

"I have to see it for myself."

He jolted. "No!" Just as quickly, he lowered his voice. "The
wounds are . . . unsightly. Frank wouldn't want you to remember him that way."

"You said I have to be strong for my sister. We can't let
Isabelle see him. I-I'll do it for her. So I can tell her. She won't
believe anyone else. Only me."

The muscles in his jaw twitched. "You can believe me."

"I know I can, but Isabelle won't. She doesn't know you."

He knelt again. Slowly, he removed something from his
pocket and pressed it into her hand. "This will convince her.
Isabelle knows Frank wouldn't ever part with it."

Millicent didn't want to look, but she forced herself to.
Daniel had given her the twopence. There, gleaming in undeniable proof, was the cross that identified it. Her fingers closed
around it. In her heart, she knew that Isabelle would find
excuses to believe Frank was still alive and the coin had been

stolen from him. "Isabelle will need me to see." She swiped
the tears from her face and pled, "He's her husband. Let me
do this for my sister."

"This is against my better judgment."

Millicent bowed her head. *Lord, give me strength. I need
your help so badly now.* She opened her eyes and took a steadying breath. "God and I—we're all Isabelle has left. When our
parents died, they buried them without our seeing them. Years
later, we still imagined we saw Mother or Father here and there.
I have to see Frank so I can spare Isabelle those doubts."

Millicent had no memory of how she got to a small room.
A sheet lay draped over a form. Mr. Clark wrapped his arm
about her shoulders. "We can stay back here . . ."

Wetting her lips, Millicent shook her head and started
forward. When she saw the boots sticking out at the bottom,
everything inside her started to tremor. Those were Frank's
boots.

Mr. Clark's arm tightened about her.

Someone pulled the sheet back a tiny bit—just so she could
see from the top of the man's head to the beginning of his
moustache. The breath froze in her lungs. "It's . . . it's . . .
him."

Mr. Clark half dragged her from the room. "I wanted to
spare you that. Here. Sit down."

"No." She pulled free from him and pressed her hand
to her forehead. "I . . . he . . . Isabelle." She moaned, "Oh,
Isabelle."

Mr. Clark made a soothing sound and folded her into a
chair. "Sip this." He tipped a cup to her lips.

She swallowed, but the water had a hard time making it past the ball lodged in her throat. "What are we going to do?"

"There are only two choices: Either you and Isabelle go back to England, or you marry me so you can stay in the States. You've no one and nothing to go back to. I feel marriage is the best option."

Millicent stared at him. "I'm upset, Mr. Clark. I know I'm not hearing—"

"Yes, you are. I'm asking you to become my wife."

Thirteen

I don't love you." Millicent blurted out the words. "We respect each other, and we're both believers. Love . . . love can come later."

Wasn't that what she thought just yesterday when the Swedish girl married the stranger? That she'd hoped, like in the Bible marriages, love would follow the wedding?

"I cannot fathom sending you back to a life of poverty and hardship. As my wife, you and your sister will have your every need met," Daniel said.

"That's not a good reason to marry. Marriages of convenience are merely fictional devices in penny dreadfuls."

He pressed his fingers to her lips. "We'll not speak of that. Not now; not ever."

"If we do this, it will be for Isabelle and Arthur." Tears filled her eyes.

"I know what we're doing. Trust me."

Ten minutes later, they broke the terrible news to Isabelle. Millicent watched as every last vestige of color left her sister's face. "You're lying. You have to be."

Millicent wrapped her arms around her and whispered brokenly, "Isabelle, I saw him. It's Frank."

"You're wrong. I have to see him."

"It was him." Millicent pressed the twopence into her sister's palm.

Isabelle stared at the tiny coin. Her head fell back, and her blood-curdling cry tore through the room.

———

An hour later, the minister knelt beside Isabelle in the small chapel and said a prayer for Frank's eternal rest.

Mr. Clark then took Isabelle's hand into his and spoke in a soft, slow voice. "Isabelle, Frank loved you deeply, and he'd want you to be taken care of. Your sister and I are going to do that. There's only one way for me to shelter and provide for you. I mean no disrespect, but we have no choice. Millicent and I are to be married here. Now. It's the only way I can take you with me."

Instead of their being married in an office, Mrs. Sloper and Colonel Webber arranged for them to use the chapel. Miss Matthews had gotten the minister from the Methodist church across in Battery Park to come officiate at the wedding. She'd rounded up three flowers and tied them with a pale blue ribbon for Millicent to hold—a lily, a pink rose, and a red rose. The meaning of each flower registered in Millicent's mind . . . Death. Friendship. Love.

What am I doing? Love should be the only reason to marry. Lord, how can I do this? She stared at the flowers.

Mr. Clark extended his hand toward her. "Come, Millicent. It's time."

Her knees shook, but she rose. Pressing her forehead against her sister's, she whispered, "Isabelle?" She noted the black traveling suit her sister now wore. Her own off-white suit, in contrast, now took on a bridal air.

"Go" was her sister's simple response.

They repeated their vows, and Mr. Clark started to slip a ring on her finger. For a moment, she flinched. In a low tone, he said, "The ring was my mother's. I pray our marriage will be as strong and happy as hers." A second later, the insubstantial gold band encircling her finger proclaimed she was his bride.

The minister didn't invite her groom to kiss her. He skipped that and said a blessing.

Afterward, Millicent started shaking. *What have I done?*

As if he could read her very thoughts, Mr. Clark tilted her face up to his. "You did the right thing."

———

Mile after mile slipped past the train window. Daniel had tried to hire a Pullman car so they'd have privacy, but none was available. With so many people squeezed into a regular passenger car, the odors of food and unwashed bodies became overwhelming. Opening the windows helped, but ash and soot from the train's smokestack blew in. The thunderous sounds of the engine reverberated, too. *Two days of this.*

Millicent tried to console her sister as best she could, but she was mourning, too. Grief so raw needed release. Daniel considered disembarking and booking a hotel for a few days to give them time. Then again, what difference would that make? Shock usually blunted the loss for the first few days. After Henrietta passed on, he'd been numb for about a week.

It might be merciful to hasten on to Texas and get them settled before the full reality struck.

Deep, painful memories assailed him. *Henrietta loved me, was all a wife could possibly be, yet I failed her. I wasn't there for her to rely on. Just last night I told the Lord I'd wait upon Him. I'd wait for His leading and guidance—yet this morning I charged ahead and married. It seemed the only practical solution. I put logic ahead of spiritual wisdom. What have I done?*

Daniel sat in silence, glad Arthur was able to nap in the midst of the noise. The ladies were in no condition to converse, so he concentrated on the problem. What was he to do? He'd made a commitment to the Lord not to wed unless or until he was given leave to do so again; in the midst of the crisis, he'd acted rashly. Only now that the deed was done, to annul the marriage would be to make a mockery of sacred vows. He'd pledged before God and man to be her husband until death parted them. He'd proposed, placed his mother's ring on Millicent's finger, and told her she'd done the right thing. Annulment was . . . unthinkable.

So where did that leave them?

"I don't love you. . . . Marriages of convenience are from penny dreadfuls . . ." Her words echoed in his mind. She was right. This whole set of circumstances might well have been a plot for such a novel. They'd acknowledged that they were marrying for Arthur and Isabelle's sake. Watching Millicent carefully smooth a tiny wrinkle in the cape over Isabelle's shoulder and keep the barest murmur of reassurance going, Daniel knew she'd want to be by her sister's side for a long while to come. That would simplify matters in the short term. At least for the foreseeable future, they'd lead an in-name-only marriage. As time passed, Daniel would seek God's guidance. The Lord

would either grant him the self-control necessary to endure the deprivations his hasty actions would inevitably cost, or in great mercy the Lord would free him to have Millicent become his wife fully and completely.

Lord, forgive me for this mess.

———

The train pulled into Gooding, Texas, late the next evening. Millicent reached over and tried to take Arthur from his father's arms, but Daniel wouldn't turn him loose. Caught in the middle of that silent tug-of-war, the little boy didn't even stir. Millicent whispered, "I'll get Isabelle and him off the train. You have a lot to tend to."

"Not so much that I can't see to my family." Daniel hitched Arthur over his shoulder, rose, and lightly touched Isabelle's shoulder. "This is our stop."

Millicent pressed one of the valises into her sister's arms. "Isabelle, please carry that. I'll handle the rest."

The valises beneath their seat required a few good yanks to come free. When Millicent straightened, Daniel hooked his big hand through the handles. He helped them disembark and led them over to a bench beneath a gas lamp. "Stay here. I'll be back as soon as I can."

"We'll be fine." She dropped the bag and reached for Arthur. "I'll take him now, sir."

By the glow of the light, she could see Mr. Clark's frown. Was it because he'd just noticed that tears streaked down Isabelle's face?

"Call me Daniel, Millicent."

He passed Arthur to her, then turned and disappeared from sight. In the few minutes he was gone, Millicent glanced at their surroundings. "It looks to be a fair-sized town, Isabelle. Either it's new or they all keep up their places. Did you notice the mercantile?"

Isabelle sank down beside her. "The towns all look alike. How can we be sure this is the right place?"

Light from another gas lamp illuminated a portion of the railway sign. "The sign says it's Gooding, and the rail porter called out the stop. We're in the right place."

Isabelle's head dropped. "It doesn't much matter where we are."

"You'll think differently when we get to the store. The living quarters are upstairs."

That was all Daniel had said. Though Millicent hoped he'd give more details, he'd spoken of the ground level in vague terms. Since he'd bought it from a cousin, maybe he hadn't bothered to ascertain the particulars. He trusted his relatives.

Boxes and crates appeared from one of the train's rear cars. Daniel gestured, and more followed. She'd been so preoccupied with her sister in New York, Millicent hadn't noticed just how much her husband had shipped to America.

He strode back. "That's it."

"You brought enough to stock the store." Compressing her lips, Millicent wished she hadn't blurted that out. "I apologize."

"Those are the goods for our home. The store is already well stocked, but I'll want to put my own stamp on things."

A lanky man walked up. "Dan!" He slapped him on the shoulder. "Took you long enough to show up!"

"Orville. As I telegrammed, there were extenuating circumstances."

The stranger flashed a smile at Millicent and Isabelle. "Well, well." He smoothed back his sparse hair and rocked from toes to heels and back. "You sly old goat! You mentioned a nanny, but I expected only one, and an old nag at best."

"Millicent is my wife. Millicent, this is my cousin Orville Clark." Daniel's tone carried icy reserve.

"Wife?!"

"Mr. Clark." Millicent gave him a polite nod.

"And the other lady is my sister-in-law, Mrs. Quinsby." Daniel moved between his cousin and Isabelle. "If you'll give me the key, I'll settle my family in."

"Sure. Let me get those bags." Orville hefted two.

Daniel took Arthur from her arms and murmured, "Arthur's too heavy for you to carry about."

Mindless of the hour and the fact that Arthur was asleep, Orville Clark prattled all the way across the street. Cramming the key into the lock, he shot her a sheepish look. "I've been runnin' back and forth, trying to keep this place and the feedstore going—it's two blocks over," he said, pointing. "It's tough, operating two businesses. If Dan wasn't my cousin, I wouldn't have waited all this time. Plenty of men wanted to buy my mercantile."

A bell jangled as the door opened. Arthur startled and screamed. "Shh." Daniel gently jostled him. "Shh."

"Guess your boy's gonna have to get used to that." Orville swept his arm in a grandiose arc. "After you."

"Sir, if you don't mind, could you please light a candle or lamp?" Due to the dirty windows, the light from the gas lamps on the street barely filtered into the building. Millicent couldn't see much from her post just outside the door, but what little she saw made her eager to grab a broom. She didn't—

mostly because she knew that as badly as the place needed a good cleaning, she'd not be able to withstand the temptation of whacking Orville with whichever end of the broom would reach.

"Okay, sure. Dan, I can take your boy if you wanna carry your wife over the threshold."

Millicent stood her ground and stared at Daniel. "Save your back for worthwhile pursuits, Daniel. Mr. Clark, is there a cot upstairs for the baby?"

"Better'n that. There's a sturdy oak cradle."

"A cradle," she said to Daniel, "won't do. Arthur's too old. He'll climb out. Especially since we've not yet looked about and cleared dangers, we simply cannot place him in a cradle."

"We don't have any cribs. Cribs is what we call 'em here. Since you're in Texas, you'll want to give things the right handle. Anyway, I just tell people to order 'em from a catalogue." Orville went inside and lit a lantern.

Millicent saw that the muscles on both sides of Daniel's jaw kept twitching. "I can keep Arthur beside me in the bed," she whispered as they followed Daniel's cousin into the store.

"I hadn't reckoned on you havin' a missus. Sorta planned on the nanny and shortstack sharin' one room, and I'd just bunk in the other room with you till Mrs. Vaughn moved outta the rooms above the feedstore. She's got herself a passel of kids. Five, actually, and the littlest one's just now crawling. I didn't have the heart to bump her out till I paid her all the cash money for the feedstore, what with her bein' a widow and all."

Isabelle let out a low, keening sound. The lantern illuminated her pallor and tears.

"Aw, don't go gettin' all upset. A little dustin' and scrub-bin' and—"

"Millicent, you and Isabelle remain here. I'll have my cousin show me the second level." Daniel took Orville's arm and propelled him toward the stairs.

"Daniel, don't you want me to hold Arthur?"

"No," the men said in unison. Orville tacked on, "We'll stick him in the cradle."

Daniel had started up the stairs, so she couldn't tell if he'd reacted at all to his cousin's assertion.

Her sister looked ready to collapse. "Isabelle, there's a chair. Have a seat for a few minutes." Millicent dumped down the bag she'd carried. "A sip of cool water will do you some good. Let me find the water bucket." She squinted at the jumbled shelves. Chewing her lower lip, she walked up and down the two small aisles and around the perimeter. No matter where she turned, messes surrounded her. A water bucket wasn't anywhere to be found. She made her way back to her sister.

Footsteps rang out on the stairs. "It's the practical solution." Daniel's voice sounded firm.

Whatever he's decided, I'm going to support him. My husband deserves my loyalty.

"I can bunk down on the sofa in the parlor. Mrs. Quicksly—"

"Quinsby," Daniel half growled.

"Yeah. Well, she and the baby can use that one room while you and your bride have the master bedroom."

Millicent jerked back in reaction, accidentally knocking over a display of Dr. Sheffield's dentifrice in a tube.

"Millicent, is everything okay?"

"Yes." *Sorry, Lord. I didn't mean to lie. It's just that I want everything to be okay. It won't be—not if I'm supposed to share Mr. Clark's bedchamber.*

Oblivious to the tumult his words caused, Orville blathered on, "The sofa's hardly ever been used, so the stuffing is good. I'll sleep like a baby."

Afraid the men would see the blush that set her face afire, Millicent bent to pick up some of the toothpaste. She wound up sneezing from the dust.

"Bless you," Isabelle murmured without any inflection or even a quick glance at her.

"That settles it. Millicent, I can't have you risk becoming ill. You, Isabelle, and my son will spend a few nights at the boardinghouse until we . . . tend to matters."

Relief poured through her. "The boardinghouse."

"Spendin' money needlessly. There's enough room here."

"The decision is mine." Daniel's tone brooked no argument. "Millicent, gather what you'll need for the night. Orville, I'll trust you to see that our goods are brought over from the train station while I get my family settled over at the boardinghouse."

The valises they'd used on the boat contained the essentials. A quick count reassured Millicent she'd have enough nappies for Arthur. Swiping up the baggage, she declared, "Ready. What about you, Isabelle?"

Isabelle gave her a lost look. "What am I to do?"

"You're going to the boardinghouse with Millicent and Arthur," Daniel said, keeping his tone mild.

I'm going to have to thank him for how gentle he is with her. There's probably not another man on the face of the earth who would

*have done what he has for us. I'll do everything I can to make sure
he doesn't regret it.*

"Millicent—" Daniel adjusted his son over his shoulder—
"I'm going to reach up and lift the bell so it doesn't sound.
When I tell you to, open the door."

"I will." Just as she and Frank strived to relieve Isabelle of
her worries, she and Daniel would work together to rear his
son, shelter Isabelle, and run his store. *A man can only do so
much. With all of those burdens, the last thing he needs is to worry
about me. I'm going to labor alongside him, pitch in, and take care
of myself.* Resolved to be as independent as possible, she curled
her fingers around the doorknob. "I'm ready."

As they walked down the boardwalk, Daniel murmured,
"It wasn't very gentlemanly of me to have you open the door;
but had I asked Orville, he would have made more noise than
the bloody bell."

Try as she might, Millicent couldn't help herself. With a
valise in each hand, she couldn't even cover her mouth as she
giggled.

For the first time in two days, Daniel smiled. "I ought to
apologize for my appalling language."

"That man wouldn't hush." Isabelle's comment made Millicent
miss a step. As Daniel steadied her, Isabelle continued.
"If you hadn't lifted the bell out of the way, I would have fed
it to that rude oaf."

It took a second for those monotone words to register. Millicent
and Daniel exchanged a shocked look, and she started
to giggle again. "Oh, Isabelle! He was horrid, wasn't he?"

The door to the boardinghouse was locked. That realization
scared Millicent into rapping smartly on the door. *I have*

to stay here. Otherwise, I'll be expected to share a room with . . . She swallowed hard and knocked louder and faster.

"Just a moment, please." A few minutes later, the door opened. A woman in a beautiful mauve dress stood back so they could enter. She'd lit a few lamps. The parlor and dining area both gleamed dully in the light, and the scent of lemon and beeswax told that she took pride in her business. "I'm Mrs. Orion."

Daniel entered last. "Mrs. Orion, I'm Daniel Clark, new owner of the mercantile. Until I tend to matters there, my family will need lodging. Do you have a room available, and have you a crib?"

"I have two rooms. If you'll give me a few moments, I'll see to the crib."

He noticed how Isabelle clung to Millicent. "What do you deem better—for you each to have your own room, or would you prefer to be together?"

"Together. Please."

"If you'll show us to the room, Mrs. Orion, I'll set my son down on the bed and assist you with the crib." They did as he suggested. When Daniel transferred Arthur to the crib and Millicent leaned over to cover him with his blanket, Daniel bent closer. "I've confided in Mrs. Orion about Frank's recent death. She's also widowed."

"Thank you." Gratitude washed over Millicent again. Daniel anticipated problems and nipped them in the bud. Things were going to work out.

Scant minutes later, Isabelle wearily laid her head on the pillow. Millicent pulled back the covers and started to climb in. Isabelle shot upright. "This can't be. It can't."

"Shhh." Wrapping her arms around her sister, Millicent started to lie down.

"I shouldn't be here."

"Yes you should." Millicent tugged the covers upward.

Isabelle threw them back down. "A w-w-wife should be with h-her h-h-husband."

"Oh, honey." Millicent fought tears of her own. "Frank's gone."

"I know." She looked devastated, and her tone sounded utterly forlorn. "But Daniel Clark's your husband. It's been a few days on the train, but this is supposed to be your w-w-wedding n—"

"Shhh." Millicent succeeded in covering her sister and holding her in a tight hug. Whispering in her ear she coaxed, "Sleep."

"But . . ."

"It's not that way, Isabelle. It's merely a marriage of convenience. He's shown us inestimable Christian charity." Weary as she was, Millicent lay in the bed and plotted how she could possibly repay Daniel Clark's kindness.

———

ThumpThumpThumpThumpThump Boom! Daniel bolted out of bed and tore open the door. A cloud of dust filled the air. "What is going on here?"

"Mr. Eberhardt asked the same thing," Millicent muttered.

"Millicent, where are you, and what does—" he caught himself just before saying *a dead man*— "Eberhardt have to do with this?"

"I'm at the foot of the stairs, stuck. And he's not here. He just thundered that same question at me in the very same tone the last time I saw him."

Upon hearing she was stuck, Daniel headed down the stairs. "Are you hurt?"

"No."

Dust motes still swirled heavily in the air. Squinting, he spied his bride. Both hands on her skirt, she yanked. He couldn't yet tell what kept her trapped, but if he left her to her own devices, she'd probably suffocate in the dust her movements stirred up. "Wait a minute, woman."

"I'm sorry." She used her wrist to push back an errant lock of hair. A smudge of dust slashed across one cheek, and her nose had a speck of something on it, too. "I didn't mean to awaken you."

"With the racket you made, you probably woke the dead."

Millicent's eyes widened and her lower lip trembled.

Why did I say that? I'm an idiot. "My apologies. I—"

She shook her head and straightened her shoulders. Quickly, she swiped her hand along the stair rail and held it out for him to see. Dust coated it liberally. "Impossible." Her voice shook, but she forged ahead. "No ashes. Just dust."

Her bravery stunned him. She had every reason to dissolve in a puddle of tears, yet she'd gathered her composure. He could do no less. Taking her cue, Daniel made it down the last few steps. He grimaced at the mess before him. "The place is inside out."

Gratitude glimmered in her eyes, letting him know he'd reacted the right way. A tiny smile tugged at the corners of her mouth. "I'd have said it's outside in. Fear not. You and I shall win this war."

He inspected the ungainly crate pinning her hem against the wall. He pushed against it and tugged her free. "I don't recall directing you to join the battle."

"Not yet, but since you prefer schedules and the like, I figured you'd probably be making plans." How could she, in one blithe sentence, dismiss any possibility that he'd disallow her to work at such tasks? Yet she did. Leaning forward, Millicent used the corner of her apron to wipe off an obscure label on the very crate that had held her captive. "Hmm. A boy's velocipede. From New York."

She brushed past him and pattered up the stairs. Her voice floated back to him. "This place needs to be scrubbed from top to bottom and organized at once. Until I do, you cannot possibly conduct business."

Daniel chased up the stairs after her. He stood in the doorway to the second bedroom and groaned. "It looks worse in the light of day."

Standing in a small aisle of space alongside a wrought-iron bed, Millicent surveyed the room. Boxes, brown paper–wrapped parcels, and an array of strange items jumbled around the perimeter of the chamber.

Anger coursed through him. "This is no place for a lady."

"But a wife's place is beside her husband, being his helpmeet." Millicent turned and *tsk*ed over a pair of grit-covered gloves. "Having run a successful business, you'll organize us. Things will come to order in no time at all."

"Go back to Arthur and Isabelle." Daniel raked his fingers through his hair. He'd promised her a thriving business, a nice home, a safe shelter—and yet she stood in the midst of a sty and in all earnestness planned to help clean it. "You don't belong here."

"From the way he pushed it all to one side and set the cradle by the bed, your cousin did make an attempt to prepare for your arrival." She chewed on her lower lip, turning red. "I forgot he planned to spend the night here."

"He slept elsewhere." Once he'd returned from settling the women and his son at the boardinghouse, Daniel met up with Orville and two other men who carried his trunks and such to the back storeroom. The last crate had no more than hit the floor before Orville invited them all to wet their whistles at the saloon. He'd been offended that Daniel hadn't gone. Changing the subject, Daniel frowned. "Why aren't you with Arthur and your sister?"

"Isabelle is going to mind Arthur for a few days. I'll help you here, and he'll keep her busy."

Daniel chose his words carefully. "Ordinarily, your sister would be more than equal to the task. Right now . . ."

Tears glossed Millicent's remarkable eyes. "Arthur noticed Isabelle was crying. He crawled up on her lap and kissed her. Children are sensitive—he knows something's wrong, and he's staying close to her. Mrs. Orion promised me she'd keep an eye on them both."

Slowly reaching over, Daniel brushed away the tears that escaped down Millicent's cheeks. "You're grieving, too. Go back and give yourself some time. I'll take care of this."

"I want to do this, to help you. The sooner we straighten everything up and get it done, the better. When we settle into a home and routine, Isabelle won't worry as much."

"Millicent . . ."

She whirled away. "I'll continue to clear some of the stuff while you find your shoes."

Daniel attempted to quell his irritation at being told what to do and resolved to devise a plan to keep Millicent out of this mess. He tied on his shoes and stepped into the hallway, immediately grabbing Millicent. "What are you doing?!"

Fourteen

Holding up a large piece of pasteboard, Millicent explained, "This goes beneath the boxes. It'll allow me to slide objects down the stairs more easily."

"The way it did with the velocipede?"

She hitched her shoulder. "It wasn't quite large enough for the velocipede. Halfway down the stairs, that crate slid off and—"

"Nearly killed you." Daniel robbed her of the pasteboard, set it aside, and hefted the box she'd planned to send downstairs. "Don't do anything more. We need to take a few minutes to assess the situation."

"I've made a list. It's on the counter."

He stared at her. "When did you make a list?"

"When I got here this morning. About an hour ago."

"I didn't hear the bell."

"Oh, I came through the back door." She wrinkled her nose. "The storeroom is a disaster. I'd hoped we could move items and stock into it while scrubbing down the shelves.

Instead, maybe we can pile goods on the cutting table and counter." She stood on tiptoe. "Is that a birdcage in the corner?"

"Don't try to find out." After realizing he'd barked the order, Daniel softened his voice. "First, let's go get some breakfast."

Millicent smiled. "Mrs. Orion is bringing over food in about thirty minutes. She was out of coffee, so she walked over with me. I hope you don't mind that I bartered a tin of coffee for our meal."

"Not at all." He looked pointedly at the pasteboard. "I'm taking things downstairs, starting with this box. Don't let me see you using that again."

As he gazed around by the light of day, Daniel realized the store looked . . . contemptible. He'd scrupulously sought to pay a fair price for a successful business, yet it would be a mercy if lightning struck the place and burnt it to cinders. He set down the box and walked up and down the few aisles and past the bins. Certain shelves overflowed while others lay barren. Whatever merchandise was on hand had been damaged by the grit coating every surface in the place.

"It's not as bad as I thought last night." Millicent came down the stairs with strange things poking out of her apron pockets and a mangled parasol under her arm.

"If you thought it was worse than this, it's a wonder you slept at all." In truth, Daniel hadn't slept all that well, either. He'd been exhausted, but twice he'd awakened and prowled around. He'd told himself the first time it was because he was concerned about Arthur and the women. The second time, he knew that was only part of it; promising them a better future, he'd brought them to disaster.

Unaware of his thoughts, Millicent nodded toward the list she'd put on the counter. "I figured I'd attack the upstairs first. Though the store is our priority, it would be foolish to clean it, then work up here. All the dust we dislodge will sift down and soil the displays."

"The store is not my priority. A man puts God and his family first."

"Oh, I do apologize." Instead of demurely dipping her head, she looked him in the eye. "I misspoke. You've already proven your priorities by selling off your business so you could be with Arthur. I merely meant that earning a livelihood was essential."

He stood akimbo. "Making sure my family is safe is foremost in my mind. That being the case—"

"We're of one accord." She whirled up the stairs.

"Stop right there." Daniel stared at her back in astonishment. She'd interrupted him, turned away, and defied him!

"Yes?" She turned, looking as innocent as could be.

A rapping on the window made him turn around. A woman smiled and waved to him, then motioned toward the door.

Daniel shook his head.

Millicent hurried down the stairs. "You called me back because you heard someone knocking!" She rushed over and opened the door, causing the bell to jangle. "Good morning."

"Hello. I'm Hope Stauffer and this here"—the woman beamed down at the spectacled little girl at her side—"is Emmy-Lou."

"I'm Millicent F— I'm Millicent, and this is my h-husband, Daniel Clark."

Daniel pretended not to notice how his bride almost gave her maiden name and stuttered about who he was. "Mrs. Stauffer, it's a pleasure to meet you and your daughter, but the mercantile is closed until further notice."

"Closed?" She gestured toward a buckboard. "But I have eggs, butter, and milk. Didn't Mr. Clark—I mean the other Mr. Clark—tell you about our arrangement?"

Millicent turned to him. "Did your cousin mention anything?"

"No." *There's plenty Orville didn't mention.*

Mrs. Stauffer shrugged. "Prob'ly slipped his mind, what with his firing too many irons."

Firing too many irons? Is that a Texas saying?

"Anyways, all the women do their marketin' on Thursdays. You're gonna be needin' my eggs and such. In the past, we always brung them in on Wednesday, but Mr. Clark's been doin' Monday, Wednesday, Friday, and Saturday at the feedstore. Tuesdays and Thursdays here. All the womenfolk in Gooding are gonna show up today, expectin' to buy up what they need for the next week."

The little girl pulled on her mother's skirt. "Mama, where's the little boy?"

"Mr. Clark said you got a nice little feller what could play with Emmy-Lou. While they swap howdies, what say I bring in the eggs?" She turned slightly, and her green skirt swished to the side, revealing a strange wooden tree from which half a dozen wire egg baskets hung.

"Mrs. Stauffer, my son is at the boardinghouse, and the mercantile is closed until further notice."

Millicent leaned forward and half whispered, "We mean you no slight. I'm sure your eggs are wonderful, but—" She let out a nervous laugh. "Not that they're your eggs. Your chickens' eggs. Nevertheless, circumstances—"

"Hold it right there." Mrs. Stauffer held up one hand. "I'm a plainspoken woman. Mr. Clark kept a good store. Tidy. Well, tidy, considerin' he's a man. Anyhow, once the sickness swept through town, he sorta let things slide. Folks still come for what they need. We dust it off, load it up, and tote it home. This bein' the onliest store for miles around, we're counting on you."

Having spoken her mind, the woman lifted her egg contraption and plowed ahead. Out of self-preservation, Millicent backed up. Hope Stauffer stopped cold. "Merciful heavens above! Did Orville leave the door open durin' that dust storm?"

"As you can see for yourself," Daniel began, "the state of the store is such that—"

"Ever'body needs to pitch in and help." Mrs. Stauffer set down the eggs and began to roll up her sleeves. "Emmy-Lou, you go on over to Parson Bradle's and tell his missus to gather up the ladies. Tell her I said the camel's wallowin' under the ditch."

"Mrs. Stauffer . . ." Daniel started in. He didn't want his own wife in the midst of this disaster, let alone more women!

She smiled at Millicent. "Seein' as we're neighbors, call me Hope. Go on with you, Emmy-Lou. That's a very important job I just gave you." A heartbeat later, she whispered, "Mr. Clark, I'd take it kindly if you'd peek outta the window yonder and tell me if she's makin' it over to the house that has the purdy roses. That's the parsonage. Emmy-Lou can't see none too good. Them eyeglasses help a bit, and we're tryin' to let her do things on her own. Millie, you're gonna meet the most nicest women in the world. Open hearts and willin' hands. That's the way it is in Gooding."

A child's welfare counted for more than someone seeing the sad state of the store. Daniel watched. "Mrs. Stauffer, your little girl just made it up to the door, and a woman opened it."

"That was mighty nice of you to keep an eye on little Emmy-Lou. Most ever'body in town does. If she bumps into something here and breaks it, Jakob will make good on it. Long as I'm jabbering, I'll tell you straight up that I can't read nor write. I'll have to rely on all y'all."

"We'll be happy to help you, Hope." Millicent hastily excused herself, plucked a handkerchief from her apron, and sneezed.

"God bless you." Daniel immediately followed that with, "This place isn't healthy."

"No, it isn't." Millicent immediately tacked on, "We can't possibly bring Arthur or Isabelle here until we fix it up."

"Plenty of help's on the way. Won't be long before this shop's shining like a brass penny." Hope halted beneath a sign and let out a full-throated laugh. "And the first thing they're bound to do is rescue me from this here sign. Mr. Clark, I don't aim to tell you how to run your place, but—"

Blood boiled as Daniel realized that their new neighbor was caught. He carefully pulled a fishhook dangling from the *Superior Bait and Tackle* sign from Hope's hat. "My deepest apologies, Mrs. Stauffer."

"Ain't nuthin' better than a bunch of country women to whip a place into shape."

A second fishhook jabbed his knuckle as he worked to free Mrs. Stauffer. "I fear for my own wife's safety here. I cannot permit you ladies in." As he freed the farmer's wife, he yanked down the sign. "This is ample proof why. Dangers abound."

Millicent came up beside him, dusting off a hat. "Here, Hope. I insist on you having this since that sign snagged the flowers on yours. Daniel, you needn't be worried. I've looked about, and the only dangers I've seen are the dangling signs and the dirt."

Daniel set the sign on the counter with great precision. The muscle in his jaw twitched. A married couple didn't air any disagreement—however great or small—before others. Millicent owed him the courtesy of expressing her opinion in private—if at all. *But she grew up in a lackluster boarding school, not in a decent one or in a family. She'll no doubt have to learn these things.*

Oblivious to his reaction, Millicent smiled at Hope. "If you'd like, you may have the hooks off that sign. They seemed to have an affinity for you."

"I'll take the hooks, but not the hat." Hope reached up and fingered the silk flowers along the brim of her hat. "Jakob—my husband—he thinks this thing's ugly as sin. In a few days, it'll be my birthday. I'm not 'posed to know, but he got me a new hat." She squeezed Millicent's hand. "Y'all just say something nice 'bout it right in front of Jakob, and that'll gladden my heart like nothing else in the world."

"We'll be sure to do that, won't we, Daniel?"

"Absolutely." Daniel took his wife's arm. "Millicent, I need a word with you."

The bell jangled. Millicent looked from Daniel to the front of the store and gasped. She felt him go rigid as five women flowed on in. Emmy-Lou walked alongside the first, announcing, "I got 'em, Mama!" A spate of introductions ensued.

Mrs. Orion came in last with a covered basket. Even above the almost overpowering smell of dust, delicious aromas wafted from it. "Mr. Clark, there's no way a man can accomplish a day's work without a decent breakfast and a cup of coffee."

"We can talk later, Daniel." It felt funny to call him by his first name. Then again, it felt strange to call him her husband, too. "Even with your great strength, you'll need all the sustenance available to manage the goods upstairs since you won't allow me to help." Millicent turned to Hope. "My husband is adamant that women cannot handle anything up there, and I must admit he's right. It's all ungainly or impossibly heavy. He rescued me from an enormous crate this morning. I'll have to tell you all about it once we set to work."

Millicent felt a rush of pleasure. She'd managed to concoct a solution whereby her husband still kept his pride and stood his ground, yet she'd be able to show him she wasn't a helpless, shrinking violet. Today she would prove her worth and let Daniel know that though they'd lost Frank, she could and would fill in and be able to fulfill many of the responsibilities Daniel had initially designated as his.

"Oh good," one of the women said as she spied Millicent's list on the counter. "Here's a list of things to be done." She started reading off the tasks and soon everyone plunged into action.

Daniel paced through the store, ripped down every sign and banner, moved heavy articles out of the way, and looked craggy enough to masquerade as a cliff. Millicent handed him his coffee. Jutting his chin toward the southwestern corner, he declared, "That's where we'll set up Isabelle."

"She can use the parlor upstairs to sew," Millicent whispered. "Things have changed. Without Frank, a dress shop isn't reasonable."

Daniel pivoted. "Ladies." The women fell silent at once. "My sister-in-law, Isabelle, is over at the boardinghouse today. She's an accomplished seamstress, and we'll be setting up a small dress shop for her over in that corner."

Millicent's nose tingled with suppressed tears—grief for Isabelle, and gratitude for Daniel's incredible generosity. "My sister's husband met with a terrible death a few days ago."

The women all murmured condolences.

"My wife suggested Isabelle might simply stay upstairs and sew in the parlor. My plan is far bolder: to bring Isabelle through this tragedy by helping her realize the dream she and Frank had of having a shop."

Hope Stauffer rubbed her hands together. "Never made sense to me, the notion of a woman havin' to hide away for a whole year when her man died. Goin' to Sunday meetin' once a week and being stuck in the house the rest of the time only makes her more lonelier. Nothin' better for an aching heart than to be surrounded by folks what care. Talk comes cheap. Deeds last. You folks tell us what you want where."

A chorus of agreement echoed in the air.

A deep groan followed it. A large man stood in the open doorway, dismay twisting his features. "Don't tell me I forgot to tell my wife about a missionary aid meeting or sewing bee or something."

While the ladies laughed, the pastor's wife said, "You needn't worry, Big Tim. Nothing was planned. We've gathered to lend a hand. The new owners have arrived."

Daniel walked over and extended his hand. "Daniel Clark."

"Tim Creighton." The man shook hands, then scanned the store. He didn't bother to hide his grimace. "You've got your work cut out for you. I can spare a couple of hours if you need a strong back."

Over the next few hours, more women arrived. Some came expecting to help; others arrived from the outlying area to do their Thursday marketing. Every last one of them pitched in—whether it was for half an hour or the morning.

Millicent lost track of the things Daniel and Big Tim hauled out of the upstairs. By the time they were done up there, the women had emptied the store shelves. All four of the brooms in stock were put to use. She had no idea exactly how many dustpans full of grit disappeared out the front and back doors.

As the day progressed, she tacked up sheets of paper and a pencil to a long string. It wasn't possible to keep track of everything, but when it became clear they were overstocked with an item, she'd write it on one sheet. Neighbors started listing things they'd like to have the store carry on another. Small piles of goods people wanted to purchase formed out on the boardwalk.

"Excuse me. Might I please speak to you, Daniel?"

Daniel stepped to the side.

Going up on her tiptoes, Millicent whispered, "These people have been kind to work on our behalf. I think a discount would be nice. What would you say about fifteen percent?"

His dark eyes held hers.

Doubts assailed her. "If you don't wish to . . ."

"As hard as they've all worked, more was well earned." He turned and raised his voice. "If I could have a moment, please."

The chatter and work ceased almost at once. Feet shuffled as women moved from behind displays so they could see him.

It's his voice. Strong and deep and sure. It commands attention.

"When Mrs. Stauffer told us we'd meet the nicest women in the world here, ones with open hearts and willing hands, it wasn't an empty boast." His large hand settled on Millicent's shoulder. No man had ever been so familiar with her. Was the warmth she felt just the physical imprint of her husband's contact? Unaware of the tide of confusion he caused, he continued to address the women. "My wife and I are thankful to each and every one of you for all of your assistance. We've determined to deduct thirty-three percent off anything you choose to purchase today as a token of our gratitude."

"Oh my," someone gasped.

The pastor's wife cleared her throat. "That's very generous."

"It's fair." Daniel paused, so Millicent nodded to add her agreement. He smiled his approval at her. "As your new neighbors, we deeply appreciate this warmhearted welcome. Then, too, any ethical business would assess items that had been weather-damaged and sell them for at least a twenty percent reduction. Your considerable help makes the figure we've chosen quite reasonable. As long as the door is open to the mercantile, I want you to feel certain you'll always receive fair trade."

"Then I'm going to go ahead and buy that ready-mixed paint for our barn," Lena Patterson declared.

"Was that any *one* thing, or off everything?" someone else asked.

"One-third off everything you buy and carry out of the store today." Daniel slid his arm around Millicent's shoulders. "One other thing: As a token of budding friendship, my wife wants each of you to choose a packet of Mr. Burpee's flower seeds. Isn't that right, Millicent?"

"Indeed, it is." She slipped away and hurried off. She didn't have time to stand around. Daniel might be cutting deals, but she wanted their marriage to be the very best one he'd ever made.

———

Late afternoon sun slanted into the store, golden now instead of chokingly gray with dust. Millicent scanned the emporium with satisfaction.

Daniel stood a few feet away. "It doesn't look anything like it did this morning."

"Thank God!" Millicent slapped her hand over her mouth. "I didn't mean that to sound blasphemous. Truly, the Lord sent us help. We needed it."

"We've cleared out quite a bit."

"With that generous discount, everyone was more than eager to take advantage of the sale. The shelves are as bare as Mother Hubbard's cupboards." She tried to use a perky voice and paste on a smile, but the truth left her livid. That afternoon, she'd dropped the store ledger. Though she hadn't meant to pry, the page it opened to bore the last entries—and they were six weeks old. The ugly truth was, Orville hadn't merely been busy with trying to run both businesses; he'd taken the money Daniel had paid in good faith for a well-run and decently supplied enterprise and continued to take money for the stock he sold—without replacing the stock or honorably leaving that money in the till.

Daniel bent over backward to be good to my sister; the least I can do is ignore the nasty truth about his cousin. Daniel hasn't said anything, and I'm not going to, either. I'll pretend I don't know he's been cheated. I wouldn't be surprised if Orville intentionally left the store open so the damage would hide his perfidy.

Surveying the stacks of crates and piles of merchandise pressed against one wall, Millicent pushed back a strand of hair. Her back ached. Even with the worst of the filth cleaned away, reopening the store would require long hours and hard work. *There's no time like the present. . . .* "Daniel, am I correct in presuming you'll want to place the shelves for the bolt goods over by Isabelle's corner? I'll—"

"Wash up."

"Yes, of course. We couldn't possibly put anything on those shelves until they're scrubbed." She leaned over and picked up a pail of sudsy water.

"No, Millicent. You wash up." He robbed her of the pail and pressed a cake of Ivory soap into her hands. "It's teatime. Go be with Arthur and Isabelle."

Certainly, Isabelle needed her. *But a woman's place is with her husband. I vowed to be his helpmeet. It doesn't matter that the marriage is one of convenience; if anything, that makes it even more imperative that I put him before all others. He's done so much for us and asked nothing in return. The least I can do is be true to the promise I made him.*

Slipping the soap into her apron pocket, Millicent tried to give him a smile. "In America, they don't have tea and a late supper; they just have an early supper. I'll go get Isabelle. While you play with Arthur, she and I can measure the windows for curtains. You wrote curtains on your list."

"That will wait." He sounded peeved.

"I set aside a couple of bolts of fabric that took the brunt of the dust storm. We'll not be able to sell the yardage, but it's suitable for curtains, counterpanes, and such. I'll fetch them so you can decide which you like best."

"Choose what you like—later." Daniel gave her a piercing look.

Millicent fought to stay composed as he studied her. Normally, she'd not feel in the least bit self-conscious if a gentleman paid her passing attention . . . but this was different. He was her husband. And she couldn't begin to guess what he thought.

"Millicent, we need to have a private discussion."

Fifteen

Private." Millicent wasn't sure that strangled sound had come out of her. Heat rushed to her cheeks, and suddenly she hoped dust completely covered her face.

Daniel nodded. "Privacy isn't something we've yet enjoyed."

Oh, dear merciful heavens. She swallowed hard.

He tugged her hand, and she followed woodenly. "Please have a seat." He led her to an oak press-backed chair he'd dusted off only moments before.

"Thank you." She melted onto the seat, her hands knotted in her lap. *I'm not a coward. I refuse to be.* She lifted her chin and looked at him.

"There are a few topics we need to cover. The first is rather delicate."

Delicate. Her lips formed the word, but no sound came out.

Daniel noticed her acknowledgment and continued on. "Sensibilities being what they are, some rules are best left intact for all involved. Other customs are not necessarily for the greater good." His deep brown eyes regarded her steadily. "Don't you agree?"

"I'm not sure." She fortified herself with a deep breath. Until she knew for certain precisely what he wanted, she didn't have the ability to answer him. "Could you be more specific?"

Clasping his hands behind his back, he walked away from her, then turned slowly. "Isabelle and Frank were very devoted to one another."

Sorrow slashed through her.

"Their affection for one another was unmistakable."

Not trusting her tongue, Millicent nodded.

Daniel approached her. He took her hands in his. "Sometimes, we make sacrifices out of love. I know what I'm about to ask of you is, as I said, delicate. Nonetheless, it is the best course of action. I noticed you set aside crepe for mourning. Veils made of it are unhealthful for the eyes and the lungs. Isabelle oughtn't wear them."

Relief bubbled through her. He was worried about Isabelle's health. "I'll speak with her. I'm sure she'll still want a veil, though. At least when she goes out to church. The list of fabrics and sewing notions we provided for you has black netting on it. That would work."

"Fine. Fine." He walked away yet again.

Oh no. There's something more? Well, the other request was quite minor.

"Often, sisters are the same size. If I'm not mistaken, you and Isabelle are similar."

"We are."

"Though Frank was your brother-in-law, I know you'll agree that Isabelle's loss is the greater. That being the case, she should be the one to wear mourning clothes."

"We both shall."

Daniel shook his head and came back toward her again. This time, he dragged over a box and sat on it. They were knee-to-knee. Millicent subtly shifted to break the contact—though completely innocent, it was by far the most familiar and intimate contact she'd ever had with a man.

"I propose you trade clothes with her: She takes all of your black bodices and skirts. In return, she'll let you wear her white and colored garments."

Eyes wide with shock, Millicent stared at him. "You cannot expect me to lark about in merry attire!"

Daniel leaned forward and clasped her hands. "We can and will acknowledge her loss. But I don't want to cling to the visual reminders of her loss. You and Arthur will be the instruments God uses within our home to help Isabelle recover."

She paused to think about what he'd said. Looking down, she saw how his hands curled about hers, lending them shelter and warmth. "I don't mean to offend you. But Isabelle's feelings need to be our foremost concern. For her to think I don't mourn Frank—that would crush us both."

"I concede that point. Ask her. Will you give me your word that you'll do so?"

Millicent stammered, "Since you've asked, I will. There's still another consideration. I represent this family and both businesses. We cannot afford for me to offend the community by ignoring or slighting customs."

"Tim Creighton remarked that he was glad you weren't shrouded in black. According to protocol, his wife ought to be

in second mourning for her father. He won't let her wear dreary
colors . . . and she's the former Lady Sydney Hathwell."

Millicent's lips parted in surprise.

"Hope Stauffer told me her sister-in-law is a recent widow.
When Hope saw you set aside the crepe, she yanked me into
the storeroom and told me her husband flatly refused to allow
his sister to wear anything black other than her shoes."

"I promise to speak with Isabelle." Millicent let out a sigh
of relief. "It seems our talk went well, Daniel. I wasn't at all
sure what to expect. Frank and Isabelle were always of one
accord, yet their neighbors indulged in appalling shout fests.
Knowing that you and I can talk and compromise is quite
reassuring."

"*Compromise*—" Daniel sat ramrod straight and folded his
arms across his chest—"is the other thing we're going to discuss." The tone he used for the word made it clear how he felt
about the concept. "I'm a man who believes in excellence—
doing my best, giving my best, and expecting others with
whom I associate to do the same. We're to work as unto the
Lord, and anything less is wrong."

Gawking at him in astonishment, Millicent said, "You mistake me! I don't mean to compromise standards by any means.
I simply meant that you are an orderly man and operate by
schedules and agendas, whereas I am accustomed to adjusting
to the vagaries of weather, children's sniffles, and serendipity.
No doubt, we will have to acquaint ourselves with what this
means to our household."

"Indeed. As you remarked, there are conventions which
reflect on the family and business. Having grown up removed
from a family setting, then minding children in a home where
the parents were absent, your exposure may be . . . lacking.

In the future, if you wish to express an opinion contrary to a stand I've taken, do so in private."

Was this the same man who just moments before had so kindly held her hands? Completely unprepared for his condemnation, Millicent sat perfectly still and stared at him. The best she could manage was a single stiff nod. Then came a crushing sense of humiliation. She'd worked her very hardest all day to prove her value to him; the only thing she'd done was given him cause to regret marrying her.

The bell above the door sounded, and Daniel rose, took one look at the man entering the store, and knew he needed to get rid of his wife at once. "That's all, Millicent. Go join Isabelle and Arthur. I'll be there shortly for supper."

She inclined her head in a genteel acknowledgment of his order and stood. Her moves looked rather stiff, but after all she'd done today, that didn't seem unexpected. Unless it wasn't just her muscles but her tender emotions that were smarting. *I don't know my own wife well enough to guess if that's the case.*

Once Millicent left the store, Daniel met the man in the middle aisle of the store. "Daniel Clark."

"Clive Keys. Only everyone calls me Clicky." They shook hands. "Local telegraph operator. I have two for you." Clicky handed over two crisp sheets of paper. "Want me to wait in case you'd like to send a reply?"

"Yes." Daniel looked at the first and scowled. *Girls well. Give Fairweather best. Alastair.* The abysmal lack of information in response to his query might be attributed to the butler's discretion. Providing the information that he and Millicent were now wed would likely ease the starch in the old retainer's collar.

Children well. Ignorant of death. Cease all contact. Fawnhill Academy.

Daniel grabbed the paper at once. He stared at Clicky. "I'm not one to confide in others, but in this case, I'll do so and rely on your discretion in order to protect my wife and sister-in-law. Two little girls whom they love have been orphaned. Until I can assure them the girls are safe and happy, I don't want Millicent or Isabelle to know anything."

"I'll keep all telegrams regarding that aside for you alone."

"Much obliged." Daniel immediately composed a couple of telegrams. The first went to Nellows, a man he'd used on rare occasions when he required sensitive information to be obtained quickly and discreetly. The complete lack of cooperation and information from both sources clearly spelled out a need for someone else to assist in gathering facts. This wasn't something that could wait.

He quickly jotted down the pertinent facts about his marriage to Millicent so Alastair could confirm the news for himself. Adding that he wished to spare his bride undue stress, he hoped to discuss the girls' welfare and future with their guardian before Millicent learned of the tragedy and to please provide identity and contact information of same.

To Fawnhill, Daniel wrote very decisively, *Foreboding rises. Eberhardt girls' welfare is ultimate concern. Wife, Millicent nee Fairweather, was nanny—wishes to maintain loving contact. Personal guarantee will not divulge tragedy. Will wire funds to permit supervised cable exchanges. Require identity of guardian.*

Clicky's eyes bulged when Daniel handed him four twenty-dollar bills. "Wire fifty of that to Fawnhill Academy and keep the other thirty to fund the other telegrams that'll follow. I appreciate your discretion."

Being late for supper would be rude, so Daniel dashed down the street. He barely made it there in time to seat Isabelle. Millicent didn't await his assistance. She took care of herself, but Mrs. Orion was carrying hot heavy platters out from the kitchen, so it might have just been thoughtfulness on her part.

The boarders were a talkative bunch that night, which suited Daniel just fine. Hungry and trying to anticipate what needed to be done next about the store, the Eberhardt girls, and his marriage, he didn't want to be bothered with trying to be social. After the meal ended, Daniel slid in the chair Millicent had vacated, then took his son from Millicent. "Mrs. Orion, I appreciate your kindness to my family."

The owner of the boardinghouse started stacking the dessert dishes. "If my daughter hadn't needed me so badly after my husband passed on, I would have withered up and blown away. Heidi gave me a reason to live."

The way Arthur cuddled against his shoulder sent a rush of warmth through Daniel. "Having my son has been a joy."

Arthur twisted around and thumped Daniel's chest. "Mine dadda."

Mrs. Orion smiled at Arthur's declaration, but her smile melted just as quickly as it started. "It's such a pity that Isabelle doesn't have a little one." The silverware tinkled as she gathered it up. "Your entrusting her with Arthur—that's the best thing you could have ever done."

"He's a handful. If he's too much for her . . ."

"He kept her busy while he was awake, but I made sure she napped when he did." Mrs. Orion lifted the dishes and walked off.

Arthur dove back into Millicent's arms. She cuddled him and seemed eager to wander off toward the window. Ever since their discussion in the store, Millicent hadn't spoken a dozen words. Was she in a pique? Chagrined? He owed it to her, though, to set matters straight at the outset. A man's charge was to be head of his home. Perhaps it was best that she lived here for a few days yet—for the sake of her tender heart and pride. With time, she'd settle in.

Arthur rubbed his eyes and yawned loudly.

Millicent kissed his forehead. "It's bedtime for a tired little boy."

Daniel strode over. "I'll carry my son upstairs."

Millicent looked around to make sure they were alone. "There's no need."

"I said I'd do it, and I will," he snapped. "I lost one wife and child because she fell down the stairs. I'm not losing another."

Millicent gasped, then clamped her lips into a tight line. With exaggerated care, she passed Arthur to him.

Daniel stared intently at Millicent. *It was the wrong way and time for me to tell her, but at least she knows. She ought to understand now.*

Her gaze went to how he cupped his son to his chest. Without a word, she slipped past him and up the stairs.

"Dadda?" Arthur sounded as tearful as he looked.

"Shhh. Daddy has you." Millicent deserved a few minutes to regain her composure. Daniel went out to the porch and eased down into a wicker rocking chair. The fibers crackled for a moment as they accepted his weight, then the planks beneath the runners let out a faint creak as he rocked. Arthur crammed his thumb into his mouth, then dragged it right back out. "Buddy."

"Buddy's upstairs. He's . . ." *What would Millicent say?* "Buddy's getting ready for sleepy-bye."

Satisfied with that answer, Arthur shoved his thumb back into his mouth and nestled in.

Night descended and the lamplighter walked down the street, singing as he fought back the darkness with the spark he carried from one light post to the next. With the creak of the rocker as a lullaby, Daniel anticipated Arthur would doze off.

Rubbing his eyes, Arthur whined, "Bankie. Buddy."

The ritual Millicent had created now robbed him of his ability to soothe his son to sleep. Daniel rose. By now, she would have realized the wisdom of his edict. He went inside and carried Arthur upstairs. Millicent had left the door open. Surely, that indicated she'd seen past his gruff words and understood.

The sisters stood over by the window, Isabelle wrapped in Millicent's embrace. Feeling like an intruder, Daniel considered quietly gathering Buddy, the blanket, and a few nappies. He could keep his son for the night.

Millicent caught sight of him. She tilted her head toward the crib.

As he crossed the floor, he wished with every step that the mercantile had been ready so there wouldn't be this quandary. Arthur pushed away from Daniel's chest and tumbled into the crib. "Seepy-bye."

"Yes, son. Sleepy-bye." Daniel leaned down, drew up the blanket, and kissed him. Afterward he glanced over at the women. Neither looked back, so he took that as his cue. He left, shutting the door behind him.

Purposeful strides carried him down the street to his mercantile. The way his thoughts churned, he couldn't possibly sleep. *Just as well. I'm going to get things done so I can have my family with me as soon as possible.*

The small store adjoining the mercantile lay vacant, but Daniel saw a shadow move inside. He stopped and peered over the *Eldo's Fine Photography* lettering on the window. The door opened, and Orville stuck out his head. "Whaddya want?"

"Is this place available?"

"I'm renting it until the widow Vaughn leaves." Greed lit Orville's eyes. "Wanna split the rent? You could use the downstairs for storage."

Several blistering replies came to mind. "The only thing we'll ever share is our last name." Daniel strode on to his store.

The bell jangled as Daniel let himself inside. The scent of ammonia no longer lingered in the air, but the gas lamps on the street now shone through the clean windows and illuminated his path to the counter.

Again Daniel felt his anger flare . . . at Orville for leaving the store in such wretched condition, but most of all at himself. His fears had caused him to snap at his bride, when all she'd done was want to care for his son. *He's her son, too.*

But even now, Daniel knew he couldn't apologize; it would be a lie because he wasn't sorry in the least for drawing the line he had. He had to do everything within his power to minimize any risk to his wife and child. Millicent would come to accept the fact, even if she didn't understand it.

Restlessness sent him pacing through the store. The base of the stairs was where he'd first seen Millicent that morning. She'd been pinned there—could have killed herself with that stunt. Women's skirts were wont to tangle and get in the way, and the way ladies cinched themselves in led to light-headedness. Those were already a dangerous combination, but adding in the heavy box Millicent had been moving—that was enough to make Daniel go gray. He'd exercised notable restraint in his reaction then, but the memory confirmed everything he knew: Stairs were treacherous. He'd make Millicent and Isabelle promise they wouldn't carry anything up or down the stairs . . . not even Arthur. Especially not Arthur.

When Millicent's skirts were pinned to the wall, it was the last time she'd been still all day long. Whirlwind. He'd called her one in that last discussion with Frank. At the time, he hadn't known just how true the word was. All about him lay proof of her energy and labor.

Crates with boxes of food and soap, large boxes filled with jars, barrels with countless items piled high upon them . . . Not a single item remained where it had been yesterday. Empty, dust-free shelves formed an alley down the center of the store. Fabric formed two stacks: one that was ruined by the dust and the other that God, in His grace, had shielded from ruination because a Turkish carpet hanging on display had blown against the bolts.

Row upon row of toiletries and patent medicine bottles lined up along a bench like soldiers at attention—Millicent had laughingly called it the "March of Promises" and agreed with him that they needed to sort through them and decide which needed to be discarded.

She'd located the store's ledger earlier in the day, had set it out for him to peruse. If she'd taken a peek inside, she hadn't let on.

Lists hung from the wall—an idea she'd concocted. Their customers happily scribed all manner of items they'd appreciate having available. There, in Millicent's handwriting, was Hope Stauffer's name with only one request: pecans.

Alongside the requests, Millicent had tacked her things-to-do list. Each time she'd crossed off something, jubilation lit her features. It didn't matter how small the accomplishment, she'd celebrated it with a powerful pencil stroke. Twice, when he'd been nearby, she'd handed the pencil to him and insisted upon his doing the honors.

He took his own list from his pocket and tacked it up. Already three pages long, it still didn't begin to cover all that needed to be done. *From the looks of this place, we could work a solid year and still not be open for business.*

His hand froze over the tack. *We.* He was thinking in terms of their working alongside one another—rather than setting her aside or having her stay upstairs with his son. Somehow, even while he'd been irritated at how she'd behaved, he'd come to think of her as his helpmeet. He accepted for certain that she'd still be there in a year, and they'd work together—yet given how strained the last part of the day had gone, those assumptions were significant.

That morning, when he'd said he wanted a word with her, Daniel had known exactly what that word was: submit. By the time he spoke with her at the end of the day, he'd been glad of the delay. He'd had the opportunity to soften his approach and realize she needed to be counseled and tutored. How could she have known what was proper when she had never actually seen a family in action? As her husband, it fell to him to teach her these things. Telling her to submit would have been wrong. Harsh. What he would do, though, was make lists and schedules to give her guidance.

The stairs drew his attention. To top off their sensitive conversation here in the store, the harshest words he'd ever spoken had come out when he'd forbidden her to carry Arthur upstairs tonight. If ever a marriage had gotten off to a rocky start, it was theirs. *Maybe come morning, she'll understand why I said what I did. Millicent isn't the type to hold a grudge. She's going to have to change, because I'm unyielding on this. She'll come around.*

Yet even as he told himself so, unease trickled down his spine.

———

Millicent lifted her hem and stomped up the steps. Part of her wanted the noise to awaken Daniel so she wouldn't have to endure the embarrassment of rapping on the door of his bedchamber. The other part of her hoped he'd take the hint that she was thoroughly miffed.

"I lost one wife and child because she fell down the stairs. I'm not losing another." Daniel's words echoed in her mind, taunting her. He didn't trust her with his son. He thought she'd kill his little boy on the stairs. That hurt. Furthermore, it was ridiculous. In fine temper, she made it up the last step, turned, and gulped. The door to the bedchamber hung wide open.

Either Daniel Clark was deaf or he slept like a brick. On more than one occasion he'd heard mutterings she'd hoped he hadn't; so she knew his ears worked just fine. That left the other alternative: Daniel Clark was one of those people who needed a hurricane to blow him out of bed. Come to think of it, she'd had to beat on his door forever that morning she told him Arthur was sick.

Shouting wasn't ladylike, and Millicent refused to resort to such behavior. Instead, she gave the doorjamb to the master bedchamber a solid kick.

Pain exploded, but she choked back a yelp.

Daniel bolted upright in bed.

Well, at least the pain's worth it. I woke him up.

"What are you doing here?"

To keep her from rubbing her toes, she shoved her hands into the pockets of her apron. "I was going to ask you the same question."

"What time is it?" He fumbled on the bedside table for his pocket watch.

It wasn't until then that it occurred to Millicent his chest was bare. Heat zoomed from her bodice to her brow, and she spun away. Her aching toes protested, but she continued to punish them by balancing on that foot until she regained her equilibrium. Only she wasn't sure she ever would. She'd never seen a shirtless man.

"Seven forty-five!" A solid thump made it clear he'd leapt out of bed.

"Yes." Why did she sound breathless? He was the surprised one. *Well, I'm surprised, too. But I'm not going to let that stop me from showing him how ludicrous he's being.* "We're waiting breakfast on you."

"You didn't need to do that."

"Yes we did. You said you're uncompromising, so Arthur is stranded upstairs until you arrive to carry him down."

"That's not going to change."

She stared at the stairs. Rustling of cloth let her know Daniel was getting decent. Her gaze traveled to the other bedchamber. Shame scalded her. She'd awakened her husband, scolding him like a harridan. He'd made one request of her—one. That edict didn't demand labor on her part—it meant he had to do more himself. *I'm being a fool. He's done so much for Isabelle and me.*

His hands rested on her shoulders, and she jumped at the contact. Wheeling back around, Millicent stammered, "I'm sorry. I'm . . . You . . ."

"You're not yourself right now."

She nodded. Of all the things he could say, that was probably the most true. Before she could let her irritation or pride extinguish her good sense, she blurted out, "You want only the best for your son."

"I do."

Dark stubble covered the lower half of his face. Yesterday, had it been there? Everything blurred together and she couldn't remember.

His hands remained on her shoulders, his thumbs slowly rubbing her collarbones. "Which is why I want you for Arthur. You're the best."

"You're impossible." She let out a mirthless laugh. "In one breath you say I'm what Arthur needs, and in the next you tell me not to take care of him."

"By having me carry him up and down the stairs, you *are* taking care of him and yourself."

"Your shirt is buttoned crooked." She groaned. "I'm going back to the boardinghouse to tell Isabelle and Arthur that you'll be there shortly." Fearing she'd blurt out something more she'd regret, she headed down the stairs. *He can't even button up his shirt correctly, but he thinks he can take care of two women and a baby. Lord, you're going to have to help us all.*

"Millicent?"

She continued down the stairs, pretending not to hear him. *So help me, if he comments about my wearing a white blouse, I'll forget every rule of comportment I ever knew. I'd rather have him consider me a shrew than let him know Isabelle insisted it's a bad omen for the marriage if the bride wears black.*

"Millicent?"

She stopped one step from the bottom but didn't want to turn around. *I refuse to be a coward.* Forcing a smile, she looked over her shoulder. After all, it was a decent compromise—even if he didn't like compromises, she could still make them in her heart. "Yes?"

"Arthur isn't just my son now. He's your son, too."

Sixteen

S uch a good boy." Phineas Stahl scratched Nicodemus on his withers, then gave the bay gelding a solid slap. The workhorse walked from the trough toward the field. Phineas had already cleared the two milch cows, Hope's mule, and the mare from the stubble-covered field. Today, they'd hitch a plow to the beasts and plow under the stubble to enrich the soil for the next crop.

Looking at his boss, Phineas grinned. "Jakob, the liniment worked. Nicodemus walks without a hint of limp."

"Might not be the liniment. I threatened to bring out Doc Wicky."

Walking along with Jakob toward the field, Phineas snorted. "I've heard he's taken up treating animals, but I sure wouldn't summon him."

"Nor would I. He's not fit to treat man nor beast. Town council is looking for a replacement."

"Speaking of replacements, your wife sounds impressed with the new storekeeper and his wife."

Chuckles spilled out of Jakob—a miracle, given the deep grief Jakob had endured until Hope breezed into his life and turned it upside down. "Given the state Orville left the mercantile in, any woman who didn't dissolve into tears or indulge in hysterics deserves some credit. That being said, Hope is wont to overestimate the goodness in others. After supper last night, my sister said Hope could make a mute leper sound like an ideal house guest."

Stopping dead in his tracks, Phineas rasped, "Annie said that?"

A smile stretching across his tanned face, Jakob halted. "Ja. There are times when a glimmer of the old Annie shines through."

The old Annie—the young girl Phineas had adored at school as they were growing up. Lively, helpful, and compassionate. He'd had nothing to offer her—no land, no money— so when her father married her off, Phineas moved south to Texas and became Jakob's farmhand. For years, Annie endured untold abuse at her husband's hand until Jakob unexpectedly went home and discovered the truth. He'd brought her here, and they'd protected her.

Now Konrad was dead, and Annie was beginning to emerge from the terror that once claimed her. Taking off his hat and swiping his brow, Phineas grinned back at Jakob. "Your sister—staying here let her know she was safe physically, but in her heart and mind, she was still held captive. Now the fetters that held her lie broken at her feet. For her to say such a thing—it shows she has finally begun to heal."

Jakob stared off at the horizon. His expression remained as bland as could be. "Ja. This is true."

Now. Now was the time. "I want her for my wife." There, he'd said it.

Jakob turned and arched a brow. "And Johnny?"

The thought of Annie's newborn son brought a rush of delight. "Johnny is the son of my heart, and well you know it. I'm the only person who's made a bigger fool of himself over that baby than you have. I want to adopt Johnny and give him my name."

Anguish darkened Jakob's eyes. "Even with that pledge to take Johnny on as your own son, she won't marry yet. Her fears will be too great. You yourself just said she has just begun to heal. It will take time—a long time."

Along with the love he felt for Annie, an ache lodged in Phineas's heart. "I'll prove to her what a special woman she is, that I cherish her and will always be tender. With God's blessing and the Holy Spirit's help, Annie will come to trust me."

Jakob gave him a sideways glance. The corner of his mouth pulled as it did whenever he was about to say something wry. "So you want God's blessing and the Holy Spirit's help, but you don't ask my permission to court my sister?"

"I don't need it." Phineas kicked a small stone and sent it sailing. "Remember the time we were swimming at the water hole and she—"

"Ja." Jakob didn't like to be reminded of that embarrassing incident.

"On that day, you told me I could have her." Laughing like a simpleton, Phineas couldn't thank the Lord enough that the time had finally come for him to realize his dreams. "You gave Annie to me, and you are a man of your word. All these years, she's been worth waiting for. I haven't changed my mind. It's good to know she'll finally be mine."

"Thank you for watching Arthur." Daniel started steering Millicent out of the boardinghouse. "I have every confidence he'll have a happy day with his aunty while we inventory stock today."

Still trying to accept the fact that she'd become Arthur's mother, Millicent hadn't taken that next mental step. "Did you understand what he just said, Isabelle? Arthur is your nephew!"

Isabelle blinked. "He is, isn't he?" For the first time since Frank died, she smiled.

The whole way down the boardwalk, Millicent kept thanking Daniel. "You have no idea how important that was to Isabelle. She and Frank have been married awhile, and well . . ." Heat filled her cheeks. "Isabelle loves children. She adores Arthur, you know."

"I wouldn't leave him with her otherwise." Daniel let go of Millicent's elbow and opened the mercantile door.

Maybe now that he's turned loose of me, I can think clearly. That hope fled just as soon as they got inside and Daniel started rolling up his sleeves, revealing strong wrists and muscular forearms. Millicent wheeled away. In a decade or two, she might not feel quite so abashed by his actions. It took a moment for her to realize the nail holes and cracks in the walls had disappeared. "Oh, my gracious! When did you do all of the plastering?" *He stayed up late last night. That's why he was asleep this morning.*

"It's a matter of using time wisely and adhering to a schedule. As it's Friday, we must telegraph our orders today so stock will begin arriving next Wednesday." Neatly drawn diagrams lay on the counter. Daniel touched each. "Stockroom, store, and Isabelle's shop. I've plotted where to place the goods for maximum efficiency." He plucked a list from the wall. "Requests first. By supplying the items the clientele wants, the store will begin on a good footing. First impressions last."

"In all the confusion, it's possible some of the things requested are actually in stock."

Daniel's features darkened. "There's no use wasting time on such a doubtful errand. The first request: Hope Stauffer wants pecans."

"I want to do something special for her. She offered friendship and help without a thought of anything in return. Could we give her a bag of pecans as our very first order since she has such a heart of gold?"

"Gold." The paper in his hand crackled protest as his fingers tightened into a fist. "I ran across a receipt for jewelry, but there's none to be found other than the silver already in the case. Supposedly there are four gold rings, a brooch, two pendants, and a bracelet."

"That's a lot." *Expensive jewelry.* She cleared her throat. "With Mr. Clark spending the bulk of his time at the feedstore, perhaps he felt it prudent to tuck such valuable items someplace special for safekeeping." Millicent didn't believe it, but Orville was Daniel's kin. She wanted to give him every chance to prove himself to be of good character. In the meantime, she decided to revert back to discussing Hope. "Yesterday, Hope said something about—"

"The camel wallowing under the ditch." Daniel nodded. "I was still trying to figure out what she meant when she said Orville was probably 'firing too many irons.' "

"Yes!"

"Tim Creighton told me Hope is famous for mangling clichés. Her husband adores how she does it, so no one corrects her."

Millicent gave a small sigh and smiled. "I like it here."

Daniel scanned the store and grimaced. "This isn't what it was purported to be."

"We're a good team and have wonderful neighbors, Daniel. I'm not about to let a nasty dust storm ruin my opinion." *I know the dust storm wasn't the cause of the problem. Was that a kindness, or was that a lie? Lord, you're going to have to guide and forgive me. I don't have any idea how to be a wife.*

Tearing paper from his tablet, Daniel felt a spurt of satisfaction. "We'd best send off some of these orders. As the day progresses there'll be more, but since I'm a little ahead of schedule, it's prudent to get shipments on the way."

Humming as she had been all morning, Millicent rounded the corner. "I finished inventorying the ready-to-wear clothing, so we can send in the order for garments, as well!"

"You were to do canned goods."

She nodded. "I will. They're right here on the list you gave me."

Never had he imagined he'd have to explain something this basic. Daniel tamped down his irritation. "Millicent, I list tasks in order of importance. The things I expect to be done first are at the top of the list. I need you to count every jar of food on that shelf over there at once."

"What about—"

"That's all, Millicent. There's nothing more to be said."

Her smile melted, leaving her features stiff. "I see. Now that I've been instructed, I'll try not to disappoint you in the future."

He nodded acknowledgment, and she disappeared back around the aisle. Seconds later, the scrape and clink of jars sounded in the otherwise deafeningly silent store. No doubt, Millicent was embarrassed. She couldn't conduct herself in a willy-nilly fashion in the business world. Teaching her that lesson early on, and in private, was the wisest and kindest course of action. She might not see that now—but in the days ahead, she'd look back and understand.

Daniel decided they would see to another task once Millicent completed her inventory. Though the telegraph office was a mere stone's throw away, it would make for a pleasant stroll. They could go together and get some fresh air. That might help cool her temper a bit, too.

Or so he thought. As they walked down the boardwalk, Daniel realized once again his bride wasn't at all like his first wife. Millicent was neither biddable nor predictable. He could say something about the necessity of adherence to schedule, but she'd worked with remarkable speed to tally the number of cans of every conceivable fruit and vegetable. Surely that meant she'd taken his lesson to heart. "I discovered last evening why there aren't any men's shoes in the store. See Matteo's place just to the left? He specializes in custom leatherwork—boots for men and boys, saddles, and the like."

Millicent gave him a sideways glance.

"His carrying saddles and boots is to our advantage. Those items take up significant space."

She gave him a tiny nod as he opened the door to the telegraph office. "Good day, Clicky!"

Alarmed, Daniel asked, "Have you met?"

"Your son introduced us." Clicky grinned. "How may I help you?"

"Sending out orders to stock the store." Daniel handed over the papers.

Scanning the first slip, Clicky pulled the pencil from behind his ear. "I need blue jeans something awful. Stauffer, Toomel, a couple of cowboys on the Forsaken ranch, and me all wear the same size. Do you mind if I add on another two pair to this order just for myself?"

"Please do." Millicent broke into a smile. "It was kind of you to inform us that the store needs to stock more in that size. In addition to the two pair for yourself, please add on another pair. We're happy to take requests, Clicky. Is there anything else you'd like?"

"Just the jeans, thanks."

She's turned chatty again—proof that she indulged in a childish snit. I can't conduct business if I have to mollycoddle her. The one extra pair of jeans would suffice, but Daniel decided to make a point. "Make that three additional pair, Clicky."

"Good, good." Clicky was already looking at the next sheet of paper. His head shot up. "Dan, you have shovels and rakes and such on here."

"From the fine gardens I've seen, I'll need to supply gardening implements."

Clicky grimaced. "Since Orville took over the feedstore, he's started selling shovels, hoes, rakes, and spades there. We all figured he'd arranged that with you; but he didn't, did he?"

More betrayal. Daniel jutted his chin toward the orders. "Send off the orders as they're written with the exception of those items. I'll be back later with the next batch and tell you what I've determined."

————

Millicent arranged the spices alphabetically. They made more sense that way—or did they? What was the difference between black pepper and cayenne pepper? Peering around the corner, she established that Daniel was busy taking stock of the rifles, guns, and ammunition. Good. Well, maybe not good. After how he'd discovered Orville had double-crossed him again, Daniel had ample cause to be livid. *Lord, don't let him do anything rash.* The best thing she could do was keep her husband busy. She'd been upset earlier, but all that faded in light of what they'd learned. Her husband needed her support. If he ran out of things to do on his list, she'd started thinking of things she could add.

Back to the spices. Peppers. A little twist, and the top of one tin came open. Brick red?! Cayenne pepper was brick red and it smelled . . . she took a whiff and her eyes started to water. Texans could enjoy that vile spice—she'd gladly do with ordinary black pepper. Unless it wasn't the same as what they'd had back in England. Millicent opened that tin, as well. One sniff and she started sneezing.

"God bless you."

"Thank—*chooo!*—you." Closing the tin, she started to laugh at herself. She should have expected to— A brace of three more sneezes tore from her.

"Bless you. Here." Daniel appeared holding a dipper of water and a handkerchief. "You've worked too hard and are taking ill."

"Stacking spices wouldn't overtax a toddler." She accepted the water, took a sip, and held the dipper up for him to have the rest. "I am sick at heart, though. You turned the other cheek when Orville cheated you regarding the store. We've not spoken of it, and I'll not say anything of it again—but the truth was plain. There's nothing more shameful than for a man to betray his own family. Learning that he's trying to steal part of the business that he sold to you—it's enough to crack a heart of stone."

Daniel's brows furrowed. He took the handkerchief and pressed it to her nose. "It's over and done with. There's no use in becoming so distraught. Come sit down." Millicent tried to take the handkerchief, but he nudged her hand away. "You've worked yourself straight into a nosebleed."

Nosebleed? *The cayenne!* Nervous giggles spilled out of her. "It's nothing, I assure you." She grabbed the hanky, dabbed away the evidence, and presented her face again. "See? Now back to the important matter. You're a man of integrity; your cousin is nothing but a scoundrel. It must have been terrible, learning the truth. But as the Bible says, the truth will set you free. Sooner or later others will see him for what he is. In the meantime, I'm steadfast on your side."

"Is that so?"

"Of course it is! What kind of wife do you take me for?" She held up a hand. "Don't answer that." *Not after the way I behaved earlier.* She ticked off others on her fingers. "You have me, Isabelle, Mrs. Orion, and Clicky, but most of all, you have God. So don't be disheartened."

"Stop fretting, wife. From his conduct, I'd surmise Orville isn't walking with the Lord. He's a man to be pitied. So how are you doing with the spices?"

She flashed him a smile. "They took my breath away."

Daniel forced a chuckle as he walked off.

After she finished the spices, Millicent consulted her list and let out a sigh of relief. Soaps, laundry soap, toiletries—she knew about those. Walking toward that area in the store, Orville's betrayal still weighed heavy on her heart. "Daniel? Are you going to just let Orville sell the rakes, hoes, and shovels?"

"That's exactly what I'm going to let him do."

Millicent wheeled around. "Orville can't stop you from selling them, either, can he?"

"No."

"So if yours are better quality and cost less . . ."

Daniel motioned toward the sparse supply presently in the store. "Those are nothing more than passable." Tapping his pencil on a small leaflet, he stated, "I'm ordering the best."

Millicent looked at the soap, then at her husband. "Daniel, counting bars of Pears and Ivory will have to wait. I have a wonderful idea!"

———

The rocker's rhythm faltered, then stopped as Phineas rounded the corner and climbed the back steps to the veranda of the Stauffer farmhouse. Hectic color filled Annie's cheeks, and she didn't meet his eyes. Johnny's lusty grunts and gulps from beneath the shawl explained why. In the six weeks since she'd had him, Annie had nursed her son up in her bed-chamber whenever Phineas was around. Catching her unaware embarrassed her. Sweeping off his straw hat, Phineas let out a low whistle. "It's hotter today than I expected. Far hotter."

"I'm sorry."

"You've nothing to be sorry about, Annie." He walked up the steps. "You didn't make it hot." She apologized for the least little thing—even though it wasn't her fault. Her husband had torn down her spirit to a distressing degree, but Phineas didn't want to rob her of the privacy she'd sought when Jakob rescued her. Until recently, Phineas had had to act as if he knew nothing about how she'd been mistreated. Finally he felt free to give her the assurances he'd had to withhold. "Days like this make me grateful for a light breeze, the shade of the porch, and a tall glass of that sweet tea you and Hope always keep on hand."

"I'll get you—"

"No, I'll get my own glass. Would you care for a glass, too?"

Her eyes went huge. "It is not done. The woman serves the man."

Smoothing her shawl over her shoulder, Phineas gave her a tender smile. "You are serving a man, Annie—your sweet little man-child. I'd be a selfish wretch if I demanded a mother set aside her hungry babe to get me something I could easily fetch for myself."

"You should not have to—"

"Ah, but Annie, I want to." He longed to touch her. "I have no family, yet you have all welcomed me into your home and at your table. The very least I can do is make allowances for you to mother your son." Running his fingers along the smooth oak arms of the chair, he grinned. "It is fitting—you suckling your son here. The night you gave birth to him, I sat in this very chair, praying to the heavenly Father to grant you His mercy and compassion. To have you here with Johnny now is God's way to remind me He answered my prayer. Ja, He did—above and beyond all I could ever ask or think, because Johnny is the finest baby I've ever known."

Annie drew in a sharp breath. "You cared for many babies before the orphan train brought you . . ."

"Ja, so I know. Almost two years I took care of babies. Our Johnny is beyond compare. Surely God has done a great work." Johnny shifted beneath the shawl and snuffled. "Now I'm getting some tea. Would you like a glass, too?"

Her lips formed the word *please* but no sound came out.

"I'll be right back." The screen door slammed behind him, and he started toward the icebox.

Hope grabbed his hand, squeezed, and whispered, "Jakob told me you were wantin' to court. I'm happy as a lamb over it."

Footsteps sounded, so she raised her voice. "Hey there, Phineas. Can I get you something?"

"I'm grabbing some sweet tea for Annie and myself. Would you care for a glass?" He set another glass on the counter for her.

Emmy-Lou came in with a kitten under each arm. "Mama, Daddy said I could keep one kitty. He forgot about Aunt Annie's baby. It isn't fair if I get a kitty and Johnny doesn't. He can have the boy kitty, and I can have the girl."

Sitting on the floor, Hope pulled her daughter onto her lap. "We need to be sure animals go to good homes. Johnny's just a baby. He could pull a kitten's tail or poke out its eye without meaning to."

"I wouldn't let him, Mama."

"We'd all be careful, but that's not the only thing. You talk of fairness. You just had your birthday. Don't you think Johnny

225

should have to wait until his fifth birthday to have his very own kitten? That would be fair. Isn't that right, Phineas?"

The rest of the litter was spoken for. Only one kitten didn't yet have a home. Hope was being a good wife and backing up her husband's decision. The least he could do was agree. He set down the pitcher. "That's a fact."

The screen door opened and Annie came in. She stared at the kittens. "They are brother and sister. The sister doesn't want to go away. She feels safe with her brother. Happy."

"It's not the sister, Aunt Annie. I'll keep her. It's the brother that has to go away."

Phineas strode over and picked up both kittens, which had started to frolic on Hope's green skirts. "They were born in the barn, and I check on them first thing each morning and last thing before I go to bed at night. So helpless at first, and now look at them." He chuckled as the all-white female climbed across his shirt and poked her nose between the buttons. The male kept trying to bite his fingers. "Sometimes a brother and sister are meant to stay together. You know, I think everyone else in Gooding was offered a kitten. I wasn't. But I'm going to take one."

"You are?!" Annie, Hope, and Emmy-Lou exclaimed in unison.

"Of course I am." He handed the female back to Emmy-Lou, then picked up a glass of sweet tea and pressed it into Annie's hand. He glanced at the kitten in his hand, then at the child in her arms. "In my heart, there's lots of room to love a baby boy."

———

Fawnhill Academy regrets to report Eberhardt children no longer in attendance. Daniel crumpled the latest telegram in disgust.

The previous evening, Clicky had delivered a new telegram from the butler. Daniel hadn't had the heart to show it to Millicent, even though it was intended for her. *Felicitations upon marriage. Personal assurances girls fine. Alastair.*

The subterfuge and maneuvers obscured his ability to ensure the children's welfare. In the world of business, strategies were part of the game; but Daniel had no tolerance for ruses now. The butler had pointedly omitted sending the guardian's identity. Nellows hadn't reported in, so questions abounded. Had the guardian taken the girls? If so, where? Millicent would be desolate if she lost touch with Audrey and Fiona.

———

Just after eight the next morning, Clicky sauntered into the store. "I'm hankering for some lemon drops."

Millicent stopped arranging kerosene lanterns and went to the candy jars. "As busy as we've kept you, it's the least we can do."

Clicky slipped a telegram to Daniel while her back was turned, then went over and distracted her with an idle conversation for a few minutes.

Daniel turned and read Nellows' message. *Girls removed from Fawnhill. Whereabouts unknown. Several irregularities in murder case. Proceeding with all speed and caution.*

It would be far too dangerous to keep the telegram in the store or even in his pocket. Daniel scribbled a reply. As Clicky left, Daniel handed him both pages. "I'm glad you stopped by.

We came to the startling realization that there isn't a single Bible in stock."

"I'll take care of things right away."

"I'm depending on you."

———

"There!" Millicent stepped back from the decorative bunting on the counter, scurried toward a shelf, and swiveled a few jars so the labels lined up just so. Next, she disappeared around the corner and reappeared with a spool of scarlet ribbon. It fluttered behind her like a banner. "We need to put a ribbon on Hope's bag of pecans. Oh! And I just had an idea."

"An idea?" Daniel removed the shears from the cutting table and handed them to her. He didn't trust her not to go running off with them. "Like the one where we painted the gardening tools bright colors and branded them with the store insignia you designed so neighbors can borrow them for free?"

Snip. "They weren't of a quality you wanted to sell. It was a nice solution, and we've met several of our neighbors in the past few days as a result."

He grabbed the scissors again. He'd methodically accomplished all but the last two things on his list for the day and set aside the rifles he planned to display next. Instead of giving his wife a list for today, he'd given her free rein—and she'd run wild.

"The velocipede. What if we put it out front and feature it as a grand opening prize?"

"You mean the velocipede that smashed you to the wall?"

She finished tying the bow with a flourish. "I wasn't smashed. Just . . . inconvenienced."

"The same velocipede that landed on your toes the next day? Don't think I haven't noticed you're favoring your right foot."

She blushed brightly. "You cannot blame that on the velocipede. The schoolyard is full of boys. Surely one would be proud to have such a fine toy."

"You think we'll garner goodwill from our patrons if we foist that contraption on one of them?"

"It'll be a noontime grand drawing. Only those who are interested will participate." A puckish smile crossed her face. "Since you're holding the scissors, why don't you cut some entry slips?"

"You do it. I'll go pry that monster from the crate."

Daniel went back to the storeroom and picked up the crowbar. All day long, he'd opened crates and barrels; but if he turned his back, Millicent tried to open another. Her curiosity was endearing; her will to work, amazing. She'd put together imaginative displays, tied ribbons around posts, nailed a yardstick to Isabelle's cutting table, and helped him fill the shelves. Working with her was an exercise in exasperation and delight. She couldn't follow a schedule to save her soul, but she managed to get a lot done and have fun accomplishing it.

She'd worked harder than ten men this week, bringing order to disaster. Early morning until suppertime, she worked side-by-side with him. They went to the boardinghouse for meals. During that time, Millicent had changed. She was still herself, but subdued. He made a habit of taking his son for a stroll after supper so she and Isabelle could have time alone. Several times, he'd suggested that she stay with Isabelle and

Arthur, but Millicent had steadfastly refused. According to her, she and Isabelle both needed to keep busy.

He'd done the same thing after losing Henrietta—thrown himself into work as if the physical and mental exhaustion would somehow blunt the grief. In a way, maybe it had. The details and demands of selling a business, immigrating, and taking over another business forced him to focus on something rather than dwell on the emptiness and guilt. More than anything, though, was how Millicent had brought him back when she'd showed him how to be a real father. Hope for a good future had dawned when he knew he'd become the kind of earthly father God would have him be.

He longed for Millicent to have a sense of peace for the girls she'd mothered for years. *I'd give up every last thing I own to know the girls are safe and have Millie be mine.*

His thoughts were disrupted by heavy footsteps. Daniel set down the crowbar and turned.

"Orville."

Seventeen

Orville lounged against the back door of the mercantile. "Heard you were busy, so I stayed outta the way."

"Your absence hasn't gone unnoticed."

Orville shrugged. "Fancy talk like that's not gonna do you any favors here."

"Then I'll be blunt: You—"

"Howdy there, Mrs. Clark." A sly smile slid across Orville's face. "Us being cousins, I reckon I'll just call you Millie and you'll call me Orville."

Millicent's hands plunged into the pockets of her apron, a sure sign she had feelings roiling under the surface. "We looked for you at church Sunday."

His grin broadened. "So you missed me?"

Daniel wasn't given to violence, but pitching his cousin out the door seemed like a fine notion.

"Since you're a stranger, I cannot honestly say so. Your personal belongings are in that burlap bag in the corner."

She pivoted and beamed at Daniel. "Daniel, I've cut up three dozen slips. Do you think that will be sufficient?"

Fighting to control his anger, Daniel pulled the velocipede from the packing straw and spun the oversized front wheel. The whirring sound filled the storeroom. "Better make four dozen slips for the drawing."

Orville reared back. "You can't give that bicycle away in a drawing! Do you know what it's worth?"

"He's right, you know." Millicent moistened her lips. "It's valuable. It'll cause problems."

"Now you're talking sense." Orville smirked. "Tell him."

Millicent wandered over. She never wandered unless Arthur and she were going for a stroll. For once, Daniel didn't care that his wife wasn't sticking to his schedule or list—she was up to something. Running her hand along the handlebars, Millicent sighed. "Such a grand prize is bound to cause problems. It's a *boy's* toy. We didn't think about anything for a— Wait! I know!"

"What do you have in mind, dear?" Eager to see what plan she'd concocted, he leaned forward.

"Remember how the ledger shows Orville bought some lovely jewelry? It's nowhere to be found and hasn't been sold. That can only mean Orville is safeguarding it until we take care of clearing the dust. Well," she said, flashing a bright smile, "the dust has cleared."

"Orville, please retrieve the following items." Daniel listed off the exact number and type of jewelry, removing any opportunity for his cousin to withhold anything. "My wife will select whichever piece she thinks is best."

"Oh, thank you, Daniel. And thank you, too, Orville." Millicent looked at Orville expectantly.

"My wife is waiting." Daniel leveled him with a stare.

"They're uh . . . upstairs. I'll have to get them."

Daniel wasn't about to let his cousin wander about unattended. Two minutes later, the small cloth pouch freed from the secret compartment in the false-backed dresser drawer, the men descended the stairs. Tension crackled between them.

Millicent had wheeled the bicycle out by the counter and fussed over creating a bow for it. "Orville, I do hope you'll come celebrate our grand opening."

He muttered something under his breath, grabbed the burlap bag, and stomped out.

Millicent rested her hands on her hips and made a disgruntled sound.

"Due to your clever thinking, we have the jewelry." Daniel set it on the counter. Surely, that would please her.

She ignored the gold entirely. "Even after all he's done, you've forgiven him, so I've tried to like him, Daniel. Truly I have. He's your family, and it's the least I can do."

"Don't bother. I've determined I don't like him at all."

Millicent heaved a sigh. "I don't blame you one bit. He walked straight through here and didn't say a word about the handsome job you did painting the store."

———

"I'm not feeling particularly well." Isabelle clenched a handkerchief. "Perhaps I should just stay here with Arthur."

Daniel glanced at his pocket watch. Quite a group had gathered after breakfast in the living room of the boardinghouse.

Sydney Creighton, Big Tim's wife, stopped playing her game of peek-a-boo with Arthur. "It's your grand opening, too, Isabelle! You have to be there! Besides, I only have a few more months to gain experience with babies." She blushed. "I have to learn to care for them by myself."

"I'm so excited to show you what Daniel did for your shop." Millicent took her sister's hand. "The fabric and notions arrived yesterday just as he promised."

"Your sister did most of it." Daniel took his wife's other hand. "Isabelle, you must be present to discuss your services. We'd best leave now. There are details which require attention before the store opens."

"I wish it weren't a school day," Heidi Orion pouted. "I want to go, too."

Millicent wriggled loose, and Daniel bristled. *I just said we need to leave.*

Down eye-to-eye with the little girl, Millicent gushed, "Your mother tells me Saturdays are very busy, too. What if you have a lemonade stand out in front of the store on Saturday?"

Heidi squealed. "Really? May I?"

Millicent rose and turned to Mrs. Orion. "Since it will bring in more business—especially from the noontime train—Daniel and I insist upon supplying the lemons and sugar, don't we, Daniel?"

His curt nod seemed to thrill Mrs. Orion almost as much as her daughter. Millicent then took more time to embrace Heidi, Mrs. Orion, and Mrs. Creighton. His throat ached not to roar. "We must be off now, ladies."

Of all the days to dawdle, this was the worst. Shadows moved faster than the women. It exercised every last shred of his patience to get his wife and sister-in-law down the street and into the store. Once there, Isabelle bit her lip and traced her fingers along the sewing machine, then stood by the dress form. Her shoulders began to shake. "If only Frank were here."

Millicent embraced her. "He is, in all of the little details for the shop that you dreamed of together."

Realization dawned. *Millicent knew. She knew her sister was struggling because Frank wasn't there and they'd planned for this moment together. She'd lagged to give Isabelle time.* "Well said. Pastor Bradle will come to say a blessing outside before we open, but I'm going to say a prayer of dedication now." He tucked an arm around his wife and braced Isabelle's arm, then bowed his head. "Gracious heavenly Father, we give you thanks for your providence and strength. As we open today and every day hereafter, let us not only serve the material needs of our neighbors, but help us to minister to their hearts and souls, as well. We ask your guidance and direction as we now dedicate this store and Isabelle's shop. In Jesus' precious name, amen."

"Amen." Millicent gave her sister a squeeze, turned, and gave Daniel an impulsive hug. Suddenly realizing what she'd done, she blushed and pulled away. "My list. You'd better give me a list. Otherwise, I'll wind up doing . . ." Her mouth snapped shut.

Returning her embrace felt so natural—but he'd caught himself in time. "Your list is on the counter."

"Never thought I'd be thankful for that list, but I am," Millicent muttered under her breath as she scurried away.

Isabelle bit her lip and ducked her head.

Daniel didn't share her sense of mirth. Undoubtedly once Millicent read the list, gratitude wouldn't be among the sentiments she felt for it. He pushed a bolt of fabric in a half inch to buy a few seconds before addressing his sister-in-law.

"Isabelle, women notice how mindful a dressmaker is of the latest fashions. You've said you could promote the trend of gored skirts in Texas." She nodded, so he stated, "I'm hiring you to sew one for Millie."

"You don't need to hire me! She's my sister."

He'd written *AGREE WITH ME* at the top of Millicent's list in bold letters. Had she read it? If so, would she comply?

"Isabelle, you ought to be working on something so customers can see how talented you are." Millicent gave him a we'll-talk-about-this-later look. "I do need a black skirt."

Isabelle recoiled. "Absolutely not. It's bad fortune and bad faith for a bride to wear black. Celadon to match your eyes." She started looking through the bolts of cloth. "But you're not hiring me."

"Then you're not sewing me a new skirt."

Daniel declared, "Isabelle will choose the color and accept the commission."

"Fine." Millicent grabbed his hand and pulled him away. "Daniel, the list said to hang the bracelet for the drawing over the counter, but I'd rather hang it in the window. It's sure to garner more attention there. I'll need your help, though."

They went to the window, and she immediately turned loose of his hand. "It wasn't my intent to disagree with you, but this is a more noticeable place to display the bracelet." Pulling the bracelet from the pocket of her apron by a length of red ribbon, she stared at it and sighed. "I'm still trying to adjust to living by your schedules and lists. I know you prioritize and put what's important first, but I'll never manage if you expect me to agree with everything you say all day."

"Do your best." A realist, he'd known she wouldn't agree with everything. "If there's a problem, we'll discuss it in private."

Tension drained from her shoulders. "Very well. Then I'll see to the buttonhooks as you— Oh! Daniel! We're going to need a sign to tell about the drawings." In a flurry of skirts, she was gone.

She'd tried to adhere to his list, yet off she flew when this notion overtook her. *I never had to trouble myself with these issues when I was married before.* Just as quickly, his mind shot back, *Henrietta didn't have the fire, intellect, and spirit Millicent does.* They did need a sign. Though he usually kept track of details, that one had slipped past him. What would it hurt if he tended to a few more last-minute chores so she could see to that task? After all, she was covering for his lack of foresight and planning. For the first time, the term *helpmeet* started to make sense to him.

At eight o'clock sharp Pastor Bradle stood out front and said a prayer. Afterward, he turned to Daniel. "So the drawings are for boys and girls. Are you limiting the age of entrants?"

Leaning on her cane, an old woman declared, "I'm a girl, no matter how many wrinkles I have!"

The pastor chuckled. "Daniel, this is Mrs. Whitsley. Her grandfather founded Gooding. She's got more vim and vigor than most girls do at twelve. Before you answer her, I'm going on inside to be out of the range of her cane!"

Daniel looked to his wife and escorted her into the shop. "What say you, Millicent?"

"I say everyone who desires may have an entry slip. Put your name into whichever drawing you wish."

The telegraph operator entered the store, and Millicent inhaled sharply. "I don't know what I did with your breeches!" She turned toward Daniel. "Daniel, I can't recall what I did with this gentleman's breeches. I don't even remember what I did with yours. I—" Her voice died out and she went crimson as customers started to laugh.

"The jeans we special ordered are in the stockroom."

"Thank you. I'll fetch them at once." Millicent straightened her shoulders and passed by him, muttering, "I'm not saying another word all day."

Old Mrs. Whitsley stuffed her name in the bowl for the drawing and tapped him on the chest with her cane. "You got yourself a handful, don't you?"

"Yes, ma'am." He smiled. "I do."

"That's the good kind of trouble. You've got the other kind a-comin'." Mrs. Whitsley tilted her head toward a woman storming toward him. "You'd best tell Widow O'Toole that you don't have spirits. Otherwise, she'll climb up on the counter and start haranguing your customers about the evils of alcohol."

"I don't sell distilled beverages."

"Mr. Clark!" The woman hadn't even made it five feet past the door before she bellowed his name. She stormed up and thrust a bottle at him. "What is the meaning of this?"

He glanced down. "Ma'am, this product is for halitosis. I take the welfare of my patrons seriously and provide for dental health with Sheffield toothpaste, as well."

"He's got Mum deodorant on the shelf." Mrs. Whitsley's eyes narrowed as she glowered at Mrs. O'Toole. "Maybe you ought to get some of that for the stink you're raisin'. Cowboys can go buy a lot more beer for the money than a bottle of mouthwash. They do it, too, so stop your hollering here because the men who're drinkin' are at the saloon, not in the mercantile."

Mr. and Mrs. Smith came in with a woman everyone called Grandma. All three of them lined up to put a slip in the bowl for the boy's bicycle. "I've got nine children," Mr. Smith explained. "They'd ride the wheels off that thing!"

Grandma stuffed her bit of paper into the bowl. "You folks have done a jim-dandy job on the store. Good quality work shirts for the men."

As they wandered off, Millicent whispered, "Daniel. A word with you, please." Daniel looked down at her. She'd remembered to speak with him confidentially. Excellent. Millicent went up on tiptoe, and as he started to lean down, he caught himself staring at her lips and planning to kiss her. He jolted upright. *What am I thinking? Not here. Not now. Not at all. Not ever. Not unless everything changes.*

"With nine children, it's no wonder his shirt is worn and faded. We have those shirts your cousin stocked."

It took a moment for her statement to sink in. Daniel winced. Orville's stock of ready-made clothing left him disgusted. "I'm going to burn them with the trash."

"The fabric in them is decent; the workmanship was the problem. Do you mind if I offer them to the Smiths?"

"Not at all. Do what you feel God leads you to do."

She breezed away, and Daniel took a long, steadying breath. Temptation hadn't ever looked or smelled so sweet. *Lord, grant me strength, or give me freedom to make her mine.*

The bell jangled all morning. Millicent buzzed around, mentioning selling points of various products and helping locate items.

A young couple with a tiny baby came in with Hope Stauffer. Following on her heels was a big man holding Emmy-Lou. Hope looked around. "Yoo-hoo! Millie, where are you?"

Millicent nearly flew around the corner. "Hope!"

"I brung my kin. Millie and Dan'l, this is my husband, Jakob. This here's my sis, Annie, and her boy, Johnny. Phineas here's the most bestest farmhand in the world, and you already know Emmy-Lou."

"It's such a pleasure to meet you." Millicent reached for the baby. "May I?"

"Ja." Annie passed Johnny over to her.

Millicent glows when she's around children. Women long for babies, and because I married in haste instead of waiting for God's blessing, I may have robbed her of that dream.

"Arthur is a year and a half, Annie." Millicent snuggled the baby. "Our sons will grow up together."

Jakob looked past Daniel. "Do you mind putting a song on the Gramophone? We'd just be enjoying it—it's not something I could buy."

"Music would be pleasant. We have several records."

Daniel joined Jakob and Phineas at the Gramophone. Phineas said in a low tone, "I wish to give Annie a courting gift. What do you recommend?"

"Jewelry is always a fine choice. The sentimental value grows more dear over the years." He glanced at the clock. "You know, we're having a drawing in five minutes. There's a bicycle as one prize, and a gold bracelet for the other. You could put your name in and hope for the bracelet before spending your money."

A minute before noon, Tim and Sydney Creighton brought Arthur over. Folks thronged to see him, and he grew scared. "Anny! Dadda!"

"Have you already met him, Annie?" Pastor Bradle asked.

"I was Arthur's nanny before I became his mama." Millicent handed Johnny back to Annie and claimed Arthur. He clung to her.

"It's time for the drawings, isn't it?" someone over by the shoes called out.

"Indeed. We'll draw for the boy's bicycle first." Daniel scanned the room. "Emmy-Lou, why don't we have you pull out the name?"

She drew a slip of paper, and Daniel silently read the name. Puzzled, he showed it to Millicent.

"This name must have accidentally been put in the wrong bowl."

"Who is it?" Mr. Smith craned his neck to see.

Millicent handed the slip back to Daniel who said, "Mrs. O'Toole."

"Well, glory be!" Mrs. O'Toole let out a whoop. "How do you like that?"

"What," Lena Patterson asked, "are you going to do with a boy's bicycle?"

"Why, I'm going to ride it, of course. They said we could put our slip in whichever bowl we wanted, and that's just what I did. I won fair and square!"

"Silly old woman," Mrs. Whitsley huffed. "Give it to someone who will enjoy it."

"I'm going to enjoy it. Nobody's going to tell me different."

"Nobody's going to tell her anything at all," someone grumbled.

Millicent announced in a slightly too-loud voice, "And now the drawing for a golden bracelet. Our Arthur will draw the name." Millicent took Buddy from Arthur's hand. "While he's doing that, Phineas, you're by the window. Could you please untie the bracelet and bring it here?"

Daniel took the little slip from his son's hand. "The winner of the bracelet is Mrs. Whitsley."

"Aha!" Mrs. O'Toole smirked. "The shoe's on the other foot now. Why don't you give it to someone who will enjoy it?"

"Any woman would enjoy it," Annie said.

Mrs. Whitsley got a twinkle in her eye. "Since a woman got the boy's gift, I'll give the girl's gift to a man. Phineas, the bracelet is yours to do with as you'd like."

Eyes huge, he asked, "Are you sure?"

"Just as sure as I am ornery!"

Everyone laughed.

Phineas shouldered his way across the store. "What I'd like most is to offer this bracelet to the lady I wish to court." He got down on one knee. "Annie, I would be honored if you would accept this."

Daniel watched as Millicent's eyes went misty and her smile was tremulous. *Never once did I do anything in the least bit romantic for her.* A woman deserved little gestures and tender words that made her feel cherished. Theirs wasn't a marriage in the physical sense, but it still could be in the emotional sense. He thought of how Millicent treasured the silver bracelet those little girls gave her—he could have taken that cue and realized tokens of affection spoke to her heart. Like a savvy businessman, he'd told Phineas jewelry made a wonderful courting gift.

The results of the gift and his declaration were unmistakable. Joy lit Annie's face.

Patrons filled his store and the cash box couldn't hold much more—but the signs of success meant nothing now. Not when the realization rocked him: *I did it again. I got so involved in business that I didn't put my wife's needs first.*

———

"What a wonderful day!" Millicent sat across the dinner table from Tim and Sydney Creighton. They had been so supportive of Daniel and Millie as they'd prepared for their grand opening, and Millie was grateful when she had heard Mrs. Orion invite them to join the group for dinner.

"Isabelle, you sold several yards of fabric today. Did you take any orders?"

"Mrs. Whitsley chose some lawn. I'll be making her a few things." Isabelle didn't specify what, but since lawn was such fine cotton, no one used it for anything but small clothes. She pushed her meat around on the plate. "Mr. Toomel asked if I could alter a suit for him. He'll bring it in next week so I can determine whether it will be worth his while to invest in the work."

"A good suit is always worth it." Daniel barely grazed Millicent's hand. "Might I have the butter?"

"Of course." She passed it to him. "I didn't meet Mr. Toomel, did I?"

"He's a farmer." Mercy Orion lowered her tone. "He ducked out of the store when the Richardsons came in. Their eldest daughter, Linette, is wearing her heart on her sleeve for him."

"For him and any other bachelor for miles around." Tim and Sydney's housekeeper, Velma, chuckled. "I oughtn't laugh, and I don't mean to be cruel. Linette's a nice gal. Problem is, she's not got a single nibble, and the two sisters just behind her both have weddings planned."

"It doesn't help that her parents cut off her hair when she had the fever." Sydney sighed.

Tim grinned at his wife. "I fell for you when your hair was short."

Velma laughed so hard, she snorted. "You hacked it off. If I didn't know better, I'd think you did it on purpose to keep other men away."

Sydney's lips twitched. "Millicent and Daniel, you may as well learn my shameful secret now. I masqueraded as a boy when I came to Texas. Tim thought I was a boy when he took a knife to my hair."

"If you thought she was a boy, you need glasses." Daniel finished buttering his bread. "I have several pairs of spectacles and an eye chart."

"Talking about medical things . . ." Velma waggled her knife at them. "This isn't gossip—it's dire warning. Doc Wicky here in town's a quack."

Tim nodded. "Town is bound by contract to keep him another ten weeks. Anyone needing help either hops the train or sends for Velma."

"The Lord blessed Velma with the ability to tend to the sick." Sydney turned rosy. "When my time comes, more loving hands couldn't catch our baby."

"I've seen examples of the babies Velma delivers. Yours is certain to be a very beautiful one." Millicent felt Daniel's light touch on her arm. Taking his cue, she handed him the honey. He liked butter and jam on scones, but butter and honey on rolls.

"Thank you, dear."

Dear. Daniel had taken to calling her that. His voice dropped ever so slightly when he said it, too—as if there were true affection behind the sobriquet. It left her feeling oddly pleased. Millicent managed to tell him he was welcome, then asked what Arthur looked like when he was born.

"Arthur was bald and wrinkled when he was born. Come to think of it, all he needed was a monocle to resemble the physician who delivered him."

Isabelle started to giggle. "A monocle. Baby." Suddenly her giggles dissolved into tears. Huge sobs soon wracked her.

Daniel scooted Isabelle's chair from the table and lifted her as Mrs. Orion took Arthur from Millicent. Millicent raced up to the room they shared and swept back the bedcovers just before Daniel eased Isabelle down. Velma hustled in and divested Isabelle of one of her half boots.

Rolling to her side, Isabelle pulled the other pillow to her chest. She hugged it as shudders wracked her. Broken words spilled from her lips, but the gist of it wrenched Millicent's heart. Isabelle wouldn't ever have babies with Frank.

"Is there something we can give her?" Daniel asked Velma.

"Time." Isabelle's second half boot thumped onto the floor. "I don't hold with numbing grief with powders or laudanum. All it does is delay the pain. Time and tenderness are what she needs."

Daniel reached over and curled his big hand around Millicent's. A sense of warmth and comfort wrapped about her as he drew her closer. Resting his other hand on Isabelle's shoulder, he bowed his head. "Lord, we lift our sister Isabelle up to you. You know the grief that has her in its grip. Though we thank you that she and Frank will be reunited for eternity, we know you understand mourning. Just as Jesus Christ wept at Lazarus's death, Isabelle's heart cries out now. Grant her rest and restoration, we pray. Amen."

Tears streamed down Millicent's cheeks. Unabashedly wiping them away, she tried to speak, but the words didn't come out. She hoped Daniel could read her lips as she mouthed *Thank you.*

Daniel took his leave, and it took seemingly ages to peel Isabelle out of the layers of clothes. Velma gave the strings on the corset an impatient yank. "Idiotic contraptions. At least she's not wearing a bustle and those stingy narrow hoops a rooster couldn't hop through."

Isabelle's crying changed from body-shaking sobs to choppy tears of exhaustion. Once she was in her pale pink flannel gown, she hugged the pillow once again.

Velma pulled out the last of Isabelle's hairpins. "Time and tenderness . . . and tears. Remember that." She left the room, and after drawing up the covers Millicent followed.

Daniel waited in the hallway. "Go ahead and retire now, too. You've been taking care of everything and everybody but yourself."

"Right up until the end, it was a wonderful day, wasn't it?" She didn't want this to spoil the fresh start he was making. "Your store—"

"Isn't worth anything at all if my family's not well. Go on to bed, Millie."

Mrs. Orion cleared her throat. "I don't mean to intrude, but I do have that empty room. If you'd like it for the night, you'd both be close by if you're needed."

Millicent stiffened and felt tension sing through Daniel. They'd agreed to a marriage of convenience, but that was a very private arrangement. No one ought ever know . . .

"Thank you for that kind offer, but my wife is where she belongs, Mrs. Orion." His fingers lightly trailed down Millicent's cheek. "Sweet dreams, dear." With that, he left.

As she lay in bed, Millicent couldn't sleep. Her thoughts drifted to Tim Creighton, who positively doted on Sydney. Hope and Jakob Stauffer couldn't take their eyes off one another. Unashamed of showing the world his feelings, Phineas had declared his intentions for Annie. Isabelle and Frank had adored each other. But witnessing Isabelle's ravaging grief proved that deep love exacted a great price. Was it worth the cost in the end?

Did it matter?

She hadn't married because she and Daniel were madly in love. They had married because he was honorable and generous, considering the needs of Christian sisters and his son instead of what he planned for himself. A woman couldn't—shouldn't—ask for more than that.

I made my bed. Now I have to lie in it.

———

I've got to be able to put this bed together, Millicent told herself the next morning. *At this rate, Arthur will be grown and married before I get this cot assembled.* The screwdriver slid from her control and jabbed her hand. "Ouch!"

"Millicent?" Daniel called from down in the store.

She pressed the heel of her left hand to her mouth—both to stop the sting and to remain quiet. She'd sneaked in and didn't have much more time before she had to get back to Arthur. Mrs. Orion had offered to watch him for an hour or two.

This escapade made her rethink fashionable clothing. Only three minutes into being there, Millicent had come to the dismaying realization that she wasn't dressed for the job at hand. Velma was right about the stingy hoops. Millicent's metal wire rings were far too narrow and impossibly uncomfortable to leave on as she knelt on the floor. Practicality being what it was, she'd undone the latch and let them fall into a stack of twenty-five rings only eighteen inches in diameter.

"Are you up there?" Daniel persisted.

Don't come up here, don't come up here, don't come up here, she inwardly begged.

"Dear?" Daniel appeared in the doorway.

Oh dear.

Shaking his head, he picked his way across the floor, pulled her hand away from her mouth, and frowned at the reddened wheal forming on her palm. "Are you kissing it better?"

She scanned the pasteboard, thin wooden braces, and clumps of packing straw that littered the floor all about the room. Relief flooded her. One of the lengths of pasteboard covered her hoops. "All is well."

His fingers slid beside the mark on her hand. "No it's not. You hurt yourself. Why didn't you wait and let me do this?"

Her palm tingled. Millicent snatched her hand away. "I'm doing just fine. Mrs. Orion's minding Arthur whilst he naps." Injecting confidence into her voice, she said, "I'll be done with this and back before he awakens."

Brows scrunched, Daniel moved his attention to her workmanship. Getting down on his knees, he looked at her over the rail. "I'll fix it."

Millicent stared through the white-painted iron slats. "I'll figure it out. You have work to do." *My bustle hides that my hoops are missing. I have to get him out of here before he realizes—*

"I'm right where I belong."

She clutched the screwdriver. "Piffle. You have customers."

He swiped the screwdriver, and his voice dropped to a conspiratorial hush. "I'm hiding out up here. Isabelle is showing unmentionables to Mrs. Richardson and her daughters."

"I was hiding, too." *Far more than you'd guess.* "I wanted to surprise you by having this done."

"There's not a man alive who wouldn't be surprised to find his wife in the center of an upside-down baby cot." Applying the screwdriver, he twirled a few screws free.

"You can do so many things—plaster, paint, hammer, drill—I thought businessmen used their minds instead of their hands."

"Jesus worked with His hands before He assumed the ministry God had for Him. I aspire to be like Him in all ways." He undid one more screw, then tugged gently. The side of the cot let loose. "Come on over here beside me."

Gathering up her petticoats, skirt, and apron while walking on her knees left little opportunity for grace. Millicent moistened her lips. "Close your eyes."

"Why?"

He knows. He hasn't said anything, but he knows. She huffed.

Daniel wrapped his hands about her waist. "The world won't stop turning if I see the hem of a petticoat."

A nervous laugh bubbled out of her. "Then why aren't you downstairs helping the Richardsons?"

"Their petticoats haven't been hemmed yet." His fingers tightened, and he lifted her in an arc. Her skirts swirled about them both as he set her down close to his side. He didn't let go. "And you're my wife."

Her breath caught. *I'm not that kind of wife.* Flustered, she blurted out, "I'm Arthur's mother, too—and not a very good one. I can't even make his bed."

"You weren't supposed to. It wasn't on your list."

"You'll grow accustomed to my doing more than is on my list." She smiled. "Now, how do we fix this so it's usable? Or will we need to return it? I could repack it, if necessary."

Daniel looked around and cocked a brow. "Re-forming the box and trying to shove the pieces back inside would be akin to putting an octopus into a teacup."

"I might manage it if it were a teapot."

"You have more important things to do. You cannot veer off schedule, Millicent. I rely on your accomplishing what I place on your list." He realigned the wide ladder-like crib side to the piece.

Millicent supported the piece, and Daniel shot her a funny look. *If he thinks I'm going to leave this task half done and run off to do something else, he can guess again. It's nice to know he relies on me; but we're in a mercantile, not the merchant marine!* "I may as well hold this so you can do whatever else you must." She leaned closer to watch. "So I had the screw in the wrong location. Pray tell, then what are those other holes for? And why don't they match up with the ends?"

"The base of the cot rests on braces attached to these holes."
He attached them with ease. "You connected the rail segment
too low. Made the cot tipsy." A few rotations of his wrist, and
the last brace was screwed in securely.

"Don't tell Widow O'Toole. If she catches the slightest hint
of something being tipsy, she's liable to pitch a fit. From all
accounts, she's quite a woman."

"No, Millicent. She's a character; you're quite a woman."
He stood and extended his hand to help her rise.

She accepted his assistance. "Thank you." Fluffing out her
skirts, she said, "Mr. Smith will come by tonight or tomorrow.
Evan is supposed to let you know when."

"Who is Evan, and why is Smith coming by?"

"Evan is Mr. Smith's . . . well, he's not his son. Mr. Smith was
married before. Grandma is his former mother-in-law. Evan is
her grandson, so I suppose that makes him Evan's uncle. Only
he calls all of the children his. Isn't that wonderful?"

"Yes, that's most kind of him."

Millicent gave him a startled look. "I wasn't thinking it was
nice of Mr. Smith. I was thinking how blessed he is to have
more children to love and call his. Remember the verse in the
Bible about 'happy is the man that hath his quiver full'? Well,
Mr. Smith is that man."

Daniel nodded his understanding. "So why is this happy
man coming by?"

"He's taking the Turkish carpet."

"The carpet?" Her husband's jaw dropped.

"Oh! I didn't give it to them. I traded."

"Millicent." His tone held censure.

"I can explain!"

Eighteen

"They won't keep the carpeting, Daniel. Let me explain. It seems Texans like to barter. Have you noticed that? Well, they do."

Daniel's strong fingers clenched around the iron slats. "So you're letting them borrow the carpet."

"No. Mr. Smith and Daisy wouldn't accept the work shirts, even though I pointed out that the stitching will fall apart. Daisy said she can clip them apart and resew them, so we worked out a deal: Mr. Smith will come get the rug and put it over their clothesline. It'll keep their children busy, beating the dirt from it. When he brings back the rug, he'll take the shirts."

"Did it occur to you to include me in this discussion?"

"I did. At the grand opening, when I asked you about the shirts, you told me to do as the Lord led me," Millicent reminded him. Being a wife was hard work. Every time she said or did something, she had to worry about whether her husband would approve. "It's a fair trade, don't you think? If anything, the carpet is a very expensive item. I think it's a lopsided deal in our favor, but I wasn't sure how to even it out."

"You like the carpet?" Her husband's shoulders rippled as he turned the crib upright.

"It's one of the loveliest things I've seen in a long while. It's hard to believe Orville could choose something that tasteful, and then get some of this other junk."

"Like that idiotic birdcage." Daniel nodded toward the corner.

"What is wrong with the birdcage? It would be quite fetching with a little canary in it."

"Do you want me to answer your question, Millie?"

Something in his eyes made her hesitate. Curiosity got the better of her. "Of course I want to know."

"Nothing should be crammed into a wire cage. Not a little bird, and certainly not a beautiful woman." He lifted a large metal frame that bore a wafflelike wire grid. *Clunk.* It slid inside the crib with a satisfying sound. "There. Nice and sturdy."

Her voice croaked as she stared at the cot. "That's a wire cage."

"In a manner of speaking, but it's temporary, and for safety." He bent and started to gather up the packing.

"I'll do that!" Desperation shot through her. She grabbed the other side of a piece of the pasteboard covering her hoops. For just a moment, they engaged in a silent tug-of-war.

"I'll carry it out and burn it."

Her eyes widened. "You can't!"

"Millicent, I won't have you carrying this trash down the stairs."

"Then do it later!"

"Why?"

"Because . . . it's bad manners to carry trash out of the store when you have customers. Yes. That's why." She nodded to emphasize her point.

He turned loose of the pasteboard. *Ching!* The wire hoops it landed upon sang.

Millicent promptly let go of her end and stepped on the board to silence the sound.

Daniel stared pointedly at her hem. "I'll have my son in a cot. I'll even consider a bird in that cage. That's two out of three wire cages. Two out of three is the best deal you'll get out of me."

"Then take out the birdcage!"

"No."

"You're not making a fair deal." *I only have that one gored skirt of Isabelle's. Everything else is cut for tight hoops and a bustle. I don't have time to make other clothes!*

He shrugged. "I'll sweeten it a little so you feel the deal is fair. On Sundays and special occasions, if you want to be caged, I won't complain." Daniel didn't wait for a response. He headed down the stairs.

Millicent thought for a moment, then a slow smile formed. Her husband didn't know it yet, but she was going to make every day a special occasion.

Daniel headed downstairs and to the sanity and order of his list. On a separate sheet, he also kept a schedule listing when the train was due to arrive, what time patrons said they'd return to pick up orders, when he'd send telegrams, etc.

"Dear," he said when Millicent came down the stairs, "I've added another thing on the calendar. Come take a look."

She came over, her petticoats rustling and the faintest hint of a floral perfume swirling about her. Longing rose up within him to slip his arm about her and shelter her beside himself. Two becoming one wasn't only an act of passion in bed—it was also a closeness of spirit and a sense of completion when being together. Daniel struggled with how he'd draw the line at what was acceptable in God's eyes. Since he'd not felt he'd been given a release from the Lord yet, he'd denied himself anything at all.

Eyes alight with curiosity, Millicent asked, "Yes?"

"I've drawn in a timeline of how long it would take for your letter to reach England, then arrive at the girls' school, and for a reply to cross the Atlantic and come clear over to Texas."

Millicent followed the expanse of time and moistened her lips. She looked up at him and gave him a wobbly smile. "I've had a horrid feeling for so long—this terrible foreboding. I can't explain it. I'm probably being silly. It's just that I've never been separated from the girls. Seeing the way you have this all marked out so logically makes me feel I oughtn't let my fears take hold. I should be trusting the Lord to keep His ever-loving hand over Audrey and Fee. Thank you, Daniel."

As she walked away, shame scalded him. *I'm no better than that butler who's sending platitudes and giving no information. Lord, I promised Frank I wouldn't unnecessarily burden Millie or Isabelle about the girls. Please keep them safe, and let me get the assurances soon.*

As the day progressed, he checked chores off his list, but none of those accomplishments meant anything.

Isabelle continued to spend time with Mrs. Richardson and her daughters, their quiet murmurs and muffled titters making it clear she continued to show them small clothes. Mrs. Orion had told Millicent that Mrs. Richardson would be buying her daughters' trousseaus, so Millicent had ordered a plethora of sheer, lacy goods. Daniel had opened that box and itched to select some for his wife. Slamming it shut, he hated how temptation lurked in the most unexpected places. *Thank God Isabelle is here today to sell those goods to the women!*

"Here we are!" Placing half a dozen discreetly wrapped small packages on the counter, each with three or four prices penciled on it along with either Kathryn or Marcella's name, Mrs. Richardson simpered, "Everything is going perfectly."

"Is it?" *If only it were. Not in my walk with God, not in my marriage, not with those little girls . . .*

"We found every last thing on our list."

Daniel forced a smile. "We strive to carry everything you need."

Isabelle came up to the counter with eight pair of stockings and two pairs of slippers. "Your organization helped tremendously." She set all of those goods on the counter, too. "You'll notice Daniel has a list right there. He's quite the proponent of lists and schedules."

One of the daughters smiled. "I never thought they were important until now. With our trying to plan a double wedding, it's the only way to keep track of everything, isn't it, Marcella?"

"Yes. Oh, Mama! Wouldn't it be the talk of Texas if Daddy bought that Gramophone and we played music from it for the wedding and reception?"

"No doubt, your mother puts important things like that on her list." Daniel tallied up the goods. "Women speak with their husbands about such matters. It makes for a solid, happy marriage. This comes to three dollars, two cents, Mrs. Richardson. Would you like me to put that on your account?"

"Yes, please. Girls, take this on out to the buckboard." The girls gleefully scooped up their booty and left. Mrs. Richardson turned back around. "We already discussed the Gramophone and want to purchase it. Isabelle, can you copy a wedding dress? Both girls want to wear my gown, and if you could do that . . ."

"I'd have to see it."

"I reckoned you'd say that. Sydney will bring it over. What with the land deal and all, it's a wonder I can keep my head on straight."

"Land deal?" Daniel gave her a puzzled look.

Mrs. Richardson covered her mouth and colored. "I wasn't supposed to say anything." She looked around, then like a child who couldn't bear to keep a secret, she blurted out, "Leopold Volkner—Marcella's intended—had a farm next to Jakob and Annie's old homestead. Their land is far more fertile. Jakob came to us and proposed a trade: He would give us the land and house for Marcella as a wedding gift if we'd deed him the acreage we've left fallow for the past two years that adjoins his property. With Annie having a son, he must want him to have land for a farm of his own someday—but I think he wants to surprise her, so please don't tell anyone."

"I won't tell a soul," Isabelle promised.

"It's hard to keep secrets from a wife," Daniel said.

Mrs. Richardson giggled like a girl. "Of course you can tell Millie. I'd never expect a man to hide anything from his wife!" With that she was off, leaving Daniel feeling worse than before—if that were possible.

A moment later, Millicent descended the stairs—completely encased in that cage once again. "A quick word, dear." Daniel crossed off number seventeen on his list. "All the paint is lined up out on the back porch. Selecting the colors for our rooms must be done. Would you care to have a hand in the choice?"

"I'd love to! Let me go fetch Arthur first." She drew close and murmured, "Isabelle's not eating well. If I bring Arthur over, we could have them share some of those new Fig Newtons and milk."

Arthur babbled merrily as he ate his cookies, then tagged along with Millicent out to the porch. Daniel thought choosing paint colors would be a straightforward, five-minute task; an hour later, she delightedly called him and Isabelle outside. Arthur wore no less than nine shades of paint on his chubby arms, and Millicent had a speck on her cheek. A variety of old discarded cans dotted the entire porch, all now containing a mere dab of paint that she'd mixed. Topknot sliding one way and apron slipping the other, Millicent held up a gallon of green paint. "Daniel, what do you think of this?"

It's an absurd mess. He opened his mouth to tell her so, but the pleasure in her eyes stopped him. "Nice."

Beaming, she set it down and tapped a gallon beside it. "I thought eggshell would complement moss. Then, with the leftover yellow paint, I thought I might repaint Arthur's toy box. It got horribly scratched up on the way here."

Daniel surveyed the porch more thoroughly. Why women gave colors all those strange names was beyond him. She'd concocted at least two dozen shades—but he far preferred the one she'd settled upon.

Isabelle looked at them, too. "These will dry up. If we save them, I can reconstitute them with a drop of turpentine. I could paint birds and trees on the toy box if you'd like."

After she'd fallen apart just last evening, Daniel recognized she was signaling she'd regained her equilibrium. "Capital idea. Our home will look grand indeed, ladies." Securing lids back on the paint, he said, "It'll be ready for you to move in tomorrow, as planned."

"There we go!" Millicent's enthusiasm astonished him. Wheeling around, Daniel realized she was talking to Arthur. She'd soaked the corner of a rag with turpentine and cleaned the paint from his little arms. "Daniel, could you please carry Arthur upstairs now?"

"You're supposed to be getting ready to move. It's on your list."

Millicent reached up and secured her hair as she bobbed her head. "Indeed."

"Then why would you go upstairs?"

"Because the kitchen cupboards must be scrubbed out, the walls washed, and the wood polished. Then the mirrors and gas lamps . . ." Millicent rattled off a list, and her sister chimed in on other details.

Left to their own devices, they would scrub the place until the building was whittled down to a toothpick. Daniel knew how to limit them. "I budgeted only this afternoon for move preparation. The schedule won't allow any more time."

"Daniel," Millicent said, trying to hide her exasperation, "could I have a word with you?"

"Dear, say whatever you please, but I'm not changing my mind. My son's been away from me far too long. Arthur will be under my roof tomorrow."

Millicent sucked in a loud breath and grabbed her sister's hand. The two of them disappeared up the stairs.

It being Friday, the store wasn't busy. Daniel took his son, went up, and moved things for the women. He also pulled furniture away from the walls in the nursery. While there, he laid a pair of chairs sideways across the head of the stairs to block them off so Arthur couldn't fall down them. When the bell downstairs jangled, Daniel clambered over the arrangement.

Two strapping blond men stared at him from the bottom of the stairs. "Do you need help moving the furniture?"

"No. My son's a busy tyke and likely to tumble if we don't block off the stairs. I need to devise a gate."

One man elbowed the other. "Karl, you take the measurements. I will draw the plan."

"My brother has no manners. I am Karl, he is Piet. We are the Van der Vort brothers—the blacksmiths. This gate—it is important. A child's safety comes before all else. We will do it for you now, ja?"

"Daniel Clark. And yes, you're hired."

The men lumbered up the stairs. Once at the top, Karl went down on his knees to greet Arthur. Piet winced. "I did not think about the women being here. We are not suitable." He cast a disparaging look at his sooty leather apron.

Millicent ceased scrubbing the kitchen cupboard and came over.

"This is my wife. Millicent, these are the blacksmiths—Piet and Karl van der Vort."

"Ma'am," they said in unison.

"It's lovely to make your acquaintance. My apron is every bit as soiled, so let's look upon one another as industrious, shall we?" She didn't wait for a reply. "Isabelle, come meet our neighbors."

Isabelle wilted into a chair and shook her head.

"Is she ailing?" Piet wondered.

The anguish in Millicent's eyes tore at Daniel. He murmured, "She lost her husband very recently."

"So she moves to a new country and loses her man? It is too much." Piet shook his head.

Millicent's eyes glistened with tears. "My husband's been most kind to Isabelle. In fact, as soon as he paints the nursery, we'll move over from the boardinghouse. Settling in will help."

Karl rose from the floor with Arthur on his shoulder. "Ja, and so we will help." A few seconds later, Daniel discovered he wasn't referring only to manufacturing the gate. The Van der Vort brothers volunteered to paint.

"Isabelle, Arthur's bound to get into the paint. Could you take him back to the boardinghouse with you—maybe do some hand sewing there?" Millicent tugged Daniel toward her sister. She whispered, "Daniel, hurry and carry Arthur downstairs. Isabelle, run back and ask Mercy if she can cook enough to allow us to have the Van der Vort brothers as supper guests."

Jealousy speared through him. The way to a man's heart was through his stomach, and he didn't want any other man getting any warm or affectionate feelings for Millicent just because she thought to feed him. *She's mine.*

Just before supper, he still fought those feelings as he began to walk her back toward the boardinghouse. Millicent wouldn't intentionally betray their marriage vows; but her friendly ways and breezy nature could lead a man to think she held special feelings for him. *What am I to do about this, Lord? She's as maddening as any woman can be, yet tender to a fault. Unpredictable as the wind, but just as refreshing.*

"Daniel, I've been thinking about your concerns regarding the stairs. Knowing about the gate relieves my mind. I cannot fathom how much deeper your worries have been. Reflecting upon that makes me realize how inconsiderate I was to challenge your decision regarding the stairs. I might forget, but I'll not ever intentionally go against your rule and carry Arthur up or down the stairs."

Relief streamed through him. "Good." He nodded and started to escort her across the street.

They'd made it about halfway when someone shouted, "Beware!"

Nineteen

The world swirled around. Daniel had swept her up, taking two strides before something streaked by. *He's so strong and fast.*

Dark, serious eyes looked down at Millicent. "Are you all right?"

"Nothing happened, thanks to you." Immediately after saying so, she reconsidered. *I'm fluttery inside like a silly schoolgirl.* Patting Daniel on the shoulder, she whispered, "You must put me down now." He obliged as if he couldn't wait to turn loose of her. Both relieved and a tad disappointed, Millicent babbled, "I cannot for the life of me fathom what that was, though. Did you—"

"Beware!"

He grabbed her close once again. Pressed against one another, they stared at the spectacle. "Daniel," she groaned to his shirtfront, "is that . . ."

"Mrs. O'Toole. On the velocipede."

"In bloomers!" Horrified she'd spoken that shameful realization aloud, Millicent let out a squeal and whirled away in time to see cowboys scatter like buckshot as Widow O'Toole plowed through their midst.

"Dan!" Orville shouted as he stomped over. "I told you it was a mistake." He shook his finger. "That old battle-ax is trying to ride that bicycle!"

"I don't know any old battle-axes." Daniel threaded Millicent's hand through his arm.

"Widow O'Toole," Orville almost spat. "You gave her that velocipede."

Pushing aside her embarrassment over having mentioned unmentionables, Millicent smiled up at her husband. "I'm so glad she's enjoying herself. Don't you think it admirable for an individual to try to learn something new?"

"Indeed." Daniel patted her hand. "Excuse us, Orville. It's our family's suppertime, and we've invited guests to join us tonight."

———

He'd figured it out. After a lot of soul searching, Daniel had come up with a solution. Though they weren't fully wed, he owed Millicent as complete a marriage as possible. That meant kind words, courtly praise, and the gestures that made a woman feel cared for. He'd do all of those for her. Surely, with her seeing he'd set up separate bedchambers, she wouldn't feel he'd suddenly changed his mind or was trying to seduce her. Honor had never come at such a steep price. God had not released him to reveal his true emotions to Millicent, so Daniel prayed for the strength to conduct himself with the chivalrous love of medieval knights.

He made a list of things he could do, and the next morning he showed up at the boardinghouse for breakfast with a bouquet of wild flowers. "Good morning, dear." He held out the bouquet to Millicent.

"Oh, how lovely!" She looked utterly surprised. "Thank you, Daniel."

Prepared to compliment her outfit, he gazed downward and frowned upon noticing the hoops beneath her skirt. "Millicent, we have a deal about—"

"But this is a special occasion! Now that the store is open and Arthur's cot has arrived, I can move into our home above the store!"

He couldn't help smiling. As odd as their marriage might be, she found some measure of happiness in it. "I concede, that makes it a special day."

Once they got to the mercantile, Millicent arranged the flowers and carried them across the store. *She's showing her sister. Isabelle will be happy Millicent's receiving the little attentions a husband ought to pay his wife.* Isabelle managed a weak smile, but Daniel lost his smile entirely when Millicent set the vase down on the corner of Isabelle's sewing machine and left it there.

Humming, Millicent referred to the schedule and chore list and went to tidy up the dishes, then on to the stockings and socks. When she went around the corner and rearranged the shoe polish display, he asked, "Dear, why are you fussing with those chores?"

Looking completely baffled, she said, "You put them on the list."

Laughter rumbled out of him. "The list was the things we most need to unpack."

Giggles spilled out of her, but they stopped abruptly when the store bell jangled. Orville sauntered in. "When you packed my stuff, you didn't stick in my favorite decoy."

Irritated, Daniel snapped, "We're not open yet."

"That's mine!" Orville swiped the decoy from up by the rifle display and set it on the counter, serving Daniel an outraged scowl.

Arthur spied the decoy and lunged for it. "Guggy!"

"He said *ducky*!" Millicent hurried over. "What a clever boy you are, Arthur."

Beaming at her, Arthur boasted, "Mine."

"Oh no. That's *my* lucky mallard." Orville reached for it.

"Mine!" Arthur wound his arms about the decoy.

Millicent gave Orville an apologetic smile. "Arthur soon will grow weary of it."

Lena Patterson opened the door a crack. "Hello! I know you're not open yet, but I'm in the middle of a recipe and I'm out of eggs!"

"We can't have that!" Millicent reached for an egg basket. "One dozen, or two?"

Daniel watched his cousin saunter over and pick up a box of Glycerole. While reading its instructions on how to oil and dress shoes, his right brow hiked upward. He set it down and pulled the Jacquot and Company blacking from beside it and positioned it in front. Next, he rearranged the measuring cups and spoons Millicent had just displayed.

Daniel clipped out, "I'll bring the decoy to you at the feedstore, Orville. You don't need to wait around here."

"I'll have to shop here, so I may as well become familiar with where you moved things. You'll sell more stockings if you have 'em by the shoes, like I did."

"Nonsense," Lena whispered to Millicent. "Men's work shirts were on the other side of . . . *them*. I can't count the times I went without because a man was buying a shirt." She paid for the eggs and left.

Moving on, Orville opened the thread cabinet. "Clark Thread Company. The name was good for doing a little advertising for the store, but I didn't like the stuff. See here? They call it 'Mile End' for a reason. Takes forever for women to use up a spool. Can't make a profit on that."

Daniel didn't bother to respond. His cousin had outstayed his welcome.

"You sure shipped in a lot of yardage." Orville surveyed Isabelle's shop. "That was a big mistake, you know. Those cotton sacks the staples and feed come in provide for folks' needs. Fancy wares and stylish clothes don't belong out here."

Isabelle looked crushed.

"That's enough." Daniel glared at his cousin. "Go tend to your own business. I'll tend to mine."

Orville shrugged. "Fine by me." He headed straight for Arthur, and Daniel moved to thwart his approach. Orville folded his arms across his chest. "Spoilt rotten. That's what your son is."

Daniel didn't even draw a breath before Millicent swooped in. "You'll apologize at once for speaking about our son in such manner."

"Ba man!" Arthur clung to the duck like a limpet. "Mine!"

"Spare the rod and spoil the child. That's what the Bible says." Orville tried to get the duck again.

Daniel's hand shot out and clamped around his cousin's wrist. "Don't."

"Little hellion," Orville muttered.

Millicent pressed close to Daniel, but her arms curved around Arthur in a show of maternal protection. "You're picking on a helpless little child and calling him names? Shame on you, Orville Clark."

Arthur made a face at Orville. "Ba man!"

"Orville, you'll not speak ill of my family, nor will you come here and sow discord." Daniel shot daggers at him. "Get out."

The glass in the door rattled as Orville jerked it shut. A second later, he shouted, "No! Get out of my way. I—"

Millicent and Daniel both headed for the door. He stormed outside; she stayed in the open doorway. Daniel barked, "Orville, you will not raise your voice at a child." As he spoke, Daniel reached over and tucked Heidi Orion behind himself. He felt Millicent tug her to safety. Taking another step forward, he repeated himself.

"She's not yours. It's none of your business," Orville replied.

Daniel stared at him coldly. "Children are everyone's business."

Sobbing, Heidi said, "All I did was ask if he wanted lemonade."

By now, people had congregated to see what was happening. Old Mrs. Whitsley let out a crack of laughter. "Heidi, honey, Orville Clark is so sour, he doesn't need any lemonade!"

Folks got a good chuckle out of that. One of the farmers named Toomel, who'd come to have Isabelle fit his suit to him, pulled a coin from his pocket. "Lemonade sounds mighty good to me."

Daniel grabbed Orville's collar and yanked him close. "I've turned a blind eye when it was just me. No more—not when you're picking on women and children. This is it. You stop, or I'll stop you." He gave his cousin a mighty shake, turned him loose, and Orville slouched away.

Daniel turned the OPEN sign into the window and watched as his neighbors flocked to buy lemonade. Millicent breezed past him after staying outside all of two minutes. Once inside, she gave Arthur a cookie and set him on the floor.

"How did you do all of that?" Daniel asked, gesturing outside. "In two minutes, you changed Heidi Orion's hysterics to hilarity, greeted half of the town by name, arranged cookies on a platter, and kept Arthur from taking any of them."

Millicent laughed. "Daniel, I had the easy part. You're the one who dealt with Orville. He was perfectly dreadful, and you handled him magnificently. Anyway, we're not going to let him ruin today."

"Very well." Never again would he allow Orville to act as he had. The only good thing about the entire episode was that Millicent had responded with all of the protective instinct of a riled she-bear. She loved with unswerving loyalty. If ever a woman ought to have a dozen children about her, surely it was she.

Ping! Something ricocheted off his shoulder. Daniel looked around. *Ping! Ping!* He traced the source of the hairpins and strode to the storeroom. Clicky's eyes were round and bright. "You're not going to believe it!" He shoved a telegram at Daniel.

Daniel made sure Millicent wasn't around, then opened it. The message made him suck in a deep breath. He handed back the paper. "Reply immediately. Yes."

Clicky dashed back out.

"Daniel?" Millicent's footsteps drew near.

"Dadda?"

He paced out of the storeroom, clapped his hands together, and rubbed them briskly. "Let's go upstairs and start getting you settled in."

Millicent gave him a playful smile. "In a while. After I finish my chores down here."

Isabelle walked by with another package of Fig Newtons. "Go on, Millie. I'll remain down here to wait on customers."

Placing his hand at the curve of Millicent's back, Daniel guided her toward the stairs. His pulse kicked into a gallop. Rose. She smelled lightly of rose. He didn't know a lot about flowers, but everyone knew roses were the flower of love. *I'm on dangerous ground. Instead of thinking of her as my wife, I'll think of her as Arthur's mother.* "Arthur, we're taking Mama upstairs."

"Anny." Arthur scowled at him. He babbled a few things that made no sense.

Millicent paused on the stairs. "Arthur doesn't understand who I am."

"We'll fix that right away." They made it to the top of the stairs. "Son, this is your mama now."

Arthur held the decoy and gave him a quizzical look.

Millicent tapped Daniel on the chest. "Daddy."

"Dadda!"

Tapping Arthur on the chest, she said, "Arthur."

He wiggled happily. "Bee boy!"

"Yes, Arthur's a big boy."

Daniel wanted to coax the name from his son. He cupped Millicent's shoulder. "Mama."

Emphatically shaking his head, Arthur said, "Anny."

"Daddy changed her name. She's Mama now."

"Like when Arthur was a baby, but now he's our big boy. I was Nanny, but I'm Mama now."

Arthur thought about it for a moment. He clung to Orville's duck. "Mine."

Daniel laughed. "You have to share Mama with Daddy. We all belong together. This is going to be our new house. We have a cot ready for you."

"No, no seepy-bye."

Millicent smiled. "No, it's not nap time yet. Daniel, I'm so relieved that you're having that gate put in."

"It'll be in later today. The parlor will be good-sized once we clear out the steamer trunks and chests. I climbed back and got a look behind the screen. That back portion is unfinished. I plan to plaster it and create more rooms."

A fetching blush tinted her cheeks. "I suppose that would be wise."

Does she hope things will change? That we'll have a true marriage and children together? He cast a look at the nursery Millicent, Isabelle, and Arthur shared. *Even if we don't have children of our own, we'll need a room soon.*

The bell downstairs jangled. "I'll leave you to settle in up here." Daniel stood motionless a moment and fought the urge to give her a hug—maybe even a quick peck. Times like this, when they'd just tried to teach Arthur to call her Mama, everything felt so sweet and cozy—so right. Being a family didn't require having children together. Even so, Daniel couldn't fool himself. He was becoming acutely aware of just how attractive and appealing Millicent could be. Any liberty she might invite or allow would be a huge temptation.

———

Isabelle finished hemming draperies at the same time the Van der Vort brothers arrived. They carried the bundles of fabric upstairs as a favor since Daniel had a handful of customers.

Millicent gazed at the gate they'd made. "Oh, that is so beautiful. You must have made the supports for the awning out front, too. This matches."

"Ja, we did." Piet looked proud that she'd noticed.

"Piet—" Karl sounded upset—"the curtains, she's hanging them on broom handles."

Piet scratched his arm. "There are rods that would work back at the smithy. If you give me about two hours, I can add finials to the ends to make them look handsome."

Millicent thought of all the expenses the store had incurred. It would take weeks—even months—to recover financially. "It's a nice suggestion, but we'll do this for now."

The burly brothers exchanged a sheepish look. "You could trade us. Two bachelors don't cook so good."

Neither do I, Millicent thought ruefully.

"Supper tonight and next Saturday," Piet said. "That would be fair for curtain rods, don't you think?"

Millicent remembered something the pastor's wife had said. *Lord, are you opening a way for us to minister to these men?* "Supper on Saturdays for the whole month if you promise to attend church on Sundays. We're new here, and I know Daniel would be glad to have friends surrounding him in the sanctuary."

The brothers conversed in another language—Millicent didn't understand all they said, but their Dutch still had a lot in common with German. Piet wasn't happy with the idea; Karl wanted to accept the deal.

"I tell you men what: You don't know what kind of bargain that is. Let's make it so you come to supper tonight. After you've had a taste of what we can do, then we can forge a deal that will be fair for everyone involved."

"Ja," Karl agreed. "This is fair." They finished installing the gate and left.

Millicent stared at the stove. *Goodness, what have I done? I've invited guests for supper, and I don't know how to cook!* The very advice she and Frank always gave to Isabelle now filtered through her mind: *"Stop worrying about later when you have things to do today."*

But I have to feed the men today. Not just the Van der Vort brothers, but my husband. I should have told him I can't cook before we got married.

Millicent figured she couldn't begin to cook unless she cleaned the stove and fired it up. Lifting one of the burners, she saw that clinkers and ashen bits of charcoal abounded. Millicent groaned.

"Anny owie?"

She sank down and pulled Arthur to her. "Mama's fine. I'm going to take icky stuff out of the stove. Later on, we'll put yummy things in to cook and eat. Find your horsey and giddyup while Mama works here."

With single-minded zeal, Millicent cleaned the inside of the stove, then polished the outside. A scuttle of coal allowed her to fire it up, but she had no notion what to cook—or how.

Piet brought over the curtain rods and installed them. He sniffed. "I don't smell anything. What are we going to eat tonight for supper?"

"You'll just have to wait and see! For now, I need to tuck Arthur in for a nap."

Isabelle came upstairs and laid a garment on the back of the couch in the parlor. "It's all hand sewing right now, so I thought to come up. I heard you tell Daniel we'll have company at supper." Isabelle leaned close and whispered, "We'd better talk about what to fix."

"I thought ham and scalloped potatoes." No one could botch ham, and scalloped potatoes were one of the few dishes she made well.

"Okay. Want me to make something for dessert?"

"Would you like to, or are you too busy with your sewing?"

"I'd love to cook. You can set the table. It would be nice if you brought up the flowers from downstairs."

Setting plates and silverware on the plain pine tabletop seemed gauche, but Millicent didn't find any table linen. She dashed downstairs, took a length of white material, and used her sister's sewing machine to hem the edges. Remembering a few remnants she'd seen in the storeroom, she grabbed them, cut, and hemmed them into serviettes.

"I went ahead and put your potatoes in the oven. When they come out, I have a pie ready to go in."

"Bless you!" Millicent gave her sister a hug.

Daniel came upstairs an hour later. He grinned at the table. "Very nice. Homey."

"There are the flowers you picked," Millicent said.

"So I see." He seemed quite pleased. After shoving the empty trunks behind the screen, he surveyed their place. "It feels like home."

Millicent's heart soared. She was fulfilling her part of their bargain—she'd been minding his son and making his home. Dinner was even turning out well.

The Van der Vorts arrived and bowed their heads respectfully as Daniel asked a blessing. In a matter of minutes, it became clear that they could eat far more than she'd planned. Millicent hopped up, sliced more ham, and fried it.

"The food—it is *goed*." Piet nodded.

"Thank you. The ham is one Daniel started carrying in the store called Our Trade-Mark. Daniel, that company also makes bacon. Perhaps we should try it."

"Definitely."

Ten minutes later, inhaling the last bite of pie, Karl decided aloud, "The deal—it is fair. Four Saturdays, four Sundays." His brother nodded agreement.

After dishes, Daniel invited Millicent to take a stroll. Once out of the store, he asked, "To what deal did Karl refer?"

"Oh! Please forgive me, Daniel. I should have spoken with you first. From now on, I will."

"I'd appreciate that."

"Well, at least I'll try to remember. If I forget, you'll have to forgive me. I haven't been married before, so I'm no good at this yet. Anyway, you saw the wondrous curtain rods the blacksmiths made for us. I traded them, but we get the better deal by far. We'll cook four Saturday suppers for them, and here's the best part: They'll come to church the day after."

Daniel cocked a brow. "The way to a man's heart is through his stomach. I've never heard that's also the route to his soul."

Then you and I are never going to be close. The way I cook, it's liable to send you away if it doesn't kill you first.

Twenty

Daniel lay in bed and sniffed. Something was burning. He bolted up and out of his room, then skidded to a halt.

"Oh, bother." Millicent stood by the stove, fishing a lump of something from a smoking pan. Waving a potholder back and forth to disperse the acrid fumes, she had no idea he'd seen what she was doing. When she didn't remove the pan from the fire, it became apparent she didn't know what she was doing, either.

"Good morning, dear." He took the pan and scooted it off the fire. What appeared to be a tangle of fried worms hung from the fork she held aloft. An underlying scent rescued him. "Bacon!"

"It was going to be bacon." She sounded woeful.

"I like my bacon crisp. You remembered my telling that to Mr. Tibbs aboard the ship, didn't you?"

The church bell began to peal. Millicent stared at the stove. "That's probably the fire alarm."

"Millie!" Isabelle dashed out of the nursery. Daniel noticed she skidded to a halt at the same place he had. She caught sight of him and fell silent.

He winked at her. "We've started breakfast. Millie's got the bacon nice and crisp."

"Burned to a crisp." The rashers broke into dozens of little shards as she dropped the glob onto a nearby plate.

Isabelle gathered her robe about herself and approached. "We ought to scramble eggs and sprinkle the bacon and some cheese on top. How does that sound to you, Daniel?"

"Delicious."

Arthur started singing his wake-up song. Isabelle quickly urged, "Millie, you go see to the little one. Daniel, would you be so kind as to hand me a mixing bowl?" As soon as her sister was out of earshot, Isabelle whispered, "Daniel, you ought to know my sister can't cook."

He looked her straight in the eyes. "I'd never have guessed."

Something between a gasp and a strangled giggle came from her.

Daniel gave her a big grin, and Isabelle's eyes widened. "Let's salvage her pride, shall we?"

Isabelle nodded in agreement, a small smile lighting her features.

———

True to their word, the Van der Vort brothers attended church. While Piet stood thin-lipped as the congregation sang, Karl hummed along. Jakob Stauffer did the Bible reading from Psalm 119. " 'Trouble and anguish have taken hold on me: yet thy commandments are my delights. The righteousness of thy testimonies is everlasting: give me understanding, and I shall live.' "

Arthur let out a loud yawn, then curled up on the pew and rested his head in Millicent's lap. She tucked Buddy into his arms and turned her attention to the minister.

Pastor Bradle spoke about walking with God and trusting Him even during the storms of life. Daniel sensed Millicent's sadness, felt how she tried to be strong. He slid one hand over hers and the other over Isabelle's. *Jesus, you said those who mourn are blessed because they shall be comforted. Grant comfort here now, I pray.*

Isabelle soaked her handkerchief. Daniel silently passed her his, and soon it became a sodden mess. Piet sat on her other side. He slipped his handkerchief to her, and his so-called whisper probably carried to most of the congregation. "I would take you out of here if you want. You do not have to stay if it brings you so much grief."

The pastor stopped.

Piet stood. "I mean no disrespect. The widow—her heart is broken." His own voice thickened. "God . . . He takes someone, and even the kindest words cannot fill the emptiness."

He extended his hand to Isabelle.

Millicent gasped as her sister accepted his help and rose.

Isabelle didn't turn loose of Piet's hand. "You've lost some-one, too."

He nodded. "Ja."

Karl didn't budge from the pew. "Our baby brother, Lars, drowned."

No one in the congregation said a word. They all sat in absolute silence. Here and there, people bowed their heads and their lips moved in silent prayer.

Piet turned to the pastor. "He was two. He did nothing wrong, but God took him."

The pastor's words came out slowly, thoughtfully. "If anyone knows what it is like to lose a child, it is God."

"Jesus lived. He grew to His manhood." Piet shook his head. "He chose to die. It is not the same. I don't understand."

"Neither did the psalmist." The pastor reread, " 'The righteousness of thy testimonies is everlasting: give me understanding, and I shall live.' David knew God would redeem us in the end, but he didn't know how or why. He confessed his confusion. Even in his confusion, David didn't turn away from God; he turned toward Him. Christianity doesn't mean we understand everything; we don't. When we don't understand, we have faith that God is all-wise and all-knowing."

Piet shook his head. "In my heart, I cannot find peace with this. God did not need to take my brother to heaven."

"Heaven wouldn't be heaven without babies." Isabelle's head tilted up toward Piet's. "My biggest regret is that I didn't give Frank a child. He loved children so very much. I know Frank's with Jesus. Your brother is with Jesus, too. Now—" her voice quavered—"I can picture my Frank holding your baby Lars. Church is the place I want to be most." She sank back down onto the pew. "I look at the cross, and it reminds me that the pain I feel isn't forever."

Daniel rose. "Piet, you told Isabelle she didn't have to stay here if it caused her pain. You offered to accompany her out. She'd like to stay, but I'm making the same offer to you. If being here is too hard for you, I'll walk out alongside you."

Piet shook his head. "You stay. There are times a man must walk alone." He looked at the pastor. "I am sorry for the interruption."

"I'm sorry for your pain, but I'm not sorry for anything you've said or done." Pastor Bradle waited in silence as Piet left the sanctuary. "Let's close in a time of prayer, seeking to deepen our own faith and asking the Lord how He would use us to make a difference."

Karl lifted Arthur and carried him back to the mercantile after the service. "It feels good, holding a little boy. Mrs. Quinsby, if this is how your husband feels in heaven, holding my little Lars, then they both must be very happy."

Isabelle nodded.

It seemed wrong to take Arthur away at the moment, so they had Karl carry him upstairs to his crib. Afterward, Daniel took the blacksmith aside. "Karl, it wasn't right for us to include attending church in that bargain. Please let Piet know that neither he nor you ever needs to go to the house of the Lord unless you want to."

"I'll tell him." Karl paused a moment. "For me, I'm glad I went. It's been a long time, but it felt good in my heart to be there."

"I'd be honored to have you join my family there any time you'd like."

———

"A picnic?" Millicent turned from the cupboard. "Today?"

"Sure." Daniel sat on a dining chair and tied his shoes. He'd changed from his Sunday best into a pair of Levis. *They look good on him. Rugged.*

"It's a nice day. From what Tim said, it'll start getting cooler soon, so we may as well enjoy the weather while we can. We'll raid the store for some crackers and cheese. Sunday's a day of rest. Why bother cooking when we can have a nice meal without the fuss?"

After this morning's debacle, I'm sure he'd like to excuse me from kitchen duty.

"I'd like to go visit Mercy." Isabelle resituated her mourning veil. "You go on and have a good time."

"Isabelle, if you want to spend the afternoon with a friend, that's fine." Daniel gave her hand a light squeeze. "But you're always welcome to be with us."

Wistfully tracing Arthur's curls, Isabelle asked, "Would you mind . . . well, Heidi Orion adores Arthur. I'd like to take him with me."

Millicent held her breath until Daniel said, "Arthur, Aunt Isabelle is going to take you bye-bye."

"Bye-bye!"

Isabelle grabbed Buddy. "Daniel, if you'd carry Arthur down the stairs, I could hurry on over to the boardinghouse and help Mercy serve dinner."

A few minutes later, Daniel looked up at Millicent as she descended the stairs. He watched every step she took, so Millicent made a point of holding the banister to allay some of his worry. As she reached the bottom step, he cleared his throat. "That dress—isn't it fancy for a picnic?"

Millicent looked down at the dress. Isabelle had spent countless hours applying brown twill and gold soutache braid in an intricate pattern around the gored skirt and the hems of the sleeves. The brown and gold mingled in a simpler complementary design along the neck and bodice front. Spreading the skirts, she said, "It's two, almost three years old, so it's seen a lot of wear and washing. Besides," she said, flashing him a self-conscious smile, "since it used to be my sister's, the skirts are gored and don't require a . . . cage."

"So I see." He slid his finger beneath his collar and eased it. "I've a basket by the door with a blanket, some oranges, and crackers in it. Go get some cheese while I take care of dessert."

"Dessert?" Millicent smiled at him. "Isn't having a picnic enough of a treat?"

"It's not a picnic without salt water taffy." They gathered those last few items, then Daniel pulled something from behind the nearest shelf. "Voilà! A Chinese kite. I loved these when I was a kid."

She looked at his shining brown eyes and lopsided smile. "At the moment, you could easily pass for a little boy."

"Each day, looking over at the schoolhouse and watching all the children scramble and play, I think it won't be long before Arthur gets to dip little girls' plaits in the inkwell."

"If he ever tries such a vile stunt, I'll . . ." Millicent caught herself and shrugged. "Actually, I have no idea what I'd do. After four years with Audrey and Fiona, I'm well versed in little girls, but I'm woefully ignorant on boys."

"Is that so?" He let out a playful laugh.

"Until now, I planned to rely upon you. After that laugh, I'm not so sure!"

They wandered down the boardwalk and through a field at the edge of town. Daniel checked the direction of the wind. "There's a nice patch of shady grass. I'll spread the blanket there."

Millicent helped him with the blanket. "Would you like to eat first or set the kite to flight?"

"I'm hungry, but if I get orange all over my fingers, the kite string will be a mess."

She sat down and carefully spread her skirts in such a way to allow him plenty of space. "We could have the crackers and cheese first."

Daniel dropped down on the blanket, careful not to crowd her. They had a wonderful lunch, talking about Arthur as well as their favorite childhood toys and books. Daniel popped the last cracker into his mouth. "Let's see about the kite."

Watching Daniel get the kite aloft was engrossing. For the width of his shoulders and the length of his jean-clad legs, he moved with lithe grace. She'd never studied a man's motions before. His shoulders rippled as he paid out the string and the wind took hold of the kite. The vermilion and black kite suddenly wheeled about and crashed. He coiled up the string and carried it back to the blanket.

"It didn't break, did it?"

"No, but it needs a little more weight—the tail's too light. Would you mind if I took the ribbon from your hat?"

"Not at all." As she removed her hat, hairpins shifted. Millicent made a few quick moves with questionable results.

He started pulling the ribbon from her hat. When she didn't move, Daniel gave her an excessively patient look. "Millie, you and I are the only ones out here. I daresay no one will see you with your hair down, so go ahead and fix it."

No sooner had she removed the remaining pins and let her hair uncoil than Daniel looked up at her. "Your hair—it's beautiful. I didn't realize it was that long."

Embarrassed, she blurted out, "You had to know. I made an utter cake of myself that night I thought the ship was sinking."

He handed her his pocket comb. "I thought you quite brave. You put Arthur in the only life preserver on hand." Cocking his head around so she could see his smile, he added, "The only reason I even noticed your hair that night was because you told me you learned to tie knots when you tried to braid your hair. I marveled no one shaved you bald if you knotted your hair as thoroughly as you strapped my son into the vest."

She started coiling her hair and let out a nervous laugh. "The first time we met, I wouldn't have imagined you'd have such a sense of humor."

"The first time I saw you, I couldn't imagine you were nanny material. Miss Jenkin was twice your age and stout as a barrel. She also smelled of camphor. When Mr. Tibbs went to fetch a replacement, I expected a pudgy, older woman."

"Am I to deduce you thought I smelled of camphor?"

Daniel set aside the hat and held the ribbon with as much pride as a fisherman who'd caught an enormous trout. "Alas, no. Why else do you think I instructed Mr. Tibbs to find other candidates?"

"It boggles the mind to consider that on a vessel the size of the *Opportunity*, you didn't locate a woman who met your criteria."

Tying the ribbon to the kite tail, he mused, "Camphor seemed quite sensible. It had to overlay the smell of Arthur's nappies, yet none of the candidates I interviewed exuded that particular aroma." He tugged on a knot. "There. Now let's see how it does."

When he stood, she blurted out, "You look like a knight with his shield."

Fingering the ribbon, he grinned. "Knights wore a favor from their fair lady when they entered tournaments. I'll be jousting with the wind, but I suppose that's better than Don Quixote tilting at windmills."

Again, he strode off and worked to get the kite aloft. Millicent studied his every move as she tried to figure out how she'd come to regard Daniel as a friend. She'd never had a male friend. Nonetheless, she felt quite certain other men wouldn't be as interesting to converse with. Daniel's strength was undeniable, yet he tempered it with a gentleness that surprised her over and over again.

What do I have to give in return? He's gone far beyond what any other man would do—Isabelle and I would have been stranded without him. Yet all I offer in return is to mind Arthur, clean his home, and do his laundry. I can't even cook his meals. The memory of burning the bacon made her wince. *I'll have Isabelle teach me. I've never had much exposure to a kitchen. Surely it's a matter of applying myself.*

"What do you think?"

She spotted the kite and clapped. "You've won the joust, Sir Daniel!"

"Nay, fair lady. Instead of fighting an enemy, I turned the wind into my ally." He sat down beside her and gave the string a light tug, then played out a little more length. "Why don't you hold it?"

"But you sent it aloft."

"We'll take turns. Besides, those oranges are looking very inviting." His hands overshadowed hers. "Here. You've got it now. It's a little like riding. Keep a firm but gentle hand."

His nearness muddled her mind. Millicent pulled away. "Isabelle and I can both drive a buggy. She worries about it the whole while, so she prefers for me to take the reins."

"I could have predicted that." His tone seemed a little wry, but Millicent kept her eyes trained on the kite. A moment later, the sweet fragrance of an orange filled the air. "Here." Daniel held a segment to her lips.

"Mmm. Thank you." She bit into it, and the juice squirted all over.

"Mine now." He popped the other half of the section into his own mouth, then pulled out his handkerchief. "Turn here."

"I'm as messy as Arthur, aren't I?"

"And every bit as cute." His smile was true, but it died rapidly. "Millicent, it's probably an act of God's mercy that Isabelle went to the boardinghouse this afternoon. It will permit me to discuss something with you."

His tone sent a whisper of unease up her spine. "Whatever is wrong?"

"First, I want to give you Alastair's personal assurance that Audrey and Fiona are fine."

"Oh. Good!" Relief flooded her. Then just as quickly, Millicent's eyes narrowed. "Wait . . . Alastair?"

"Allow me to start at the beginning. I admit, what I say will cause you distress. Please hear me all the way through, though."

Millicent bit her lip and nodded slowly. Still holding onto the kite string, she listened as he told her of the Wanted poster on Ellis Island and the initial telegrams, and her mouth went dry. Daniel mentioned that the academy wasn't cooperative, then that the girls hadn't been told about their father's passing. Tears filled her eyes, and she started to shake.

Daniel slid his hand atop hers. "I gave my word of honor to Frank that I wouldn't speak of this to you or Isabelle until we could give assurances that the girls were safe and happy."

Unable to keep silent any longer, she blurted out, "But you've lied to me. All along, you've known the truth and perpetrated a falsehood."

"I gave my word of honor to Frank—the last promise he asked of me before he passed on. He knew it would distress Isabelle and you too greatly and wished to shield you. Granting a dying wish is—"

"Important, I grant you. But is it any more sacred than a wedding vow?"

"No, Millicent, it's not. In keeping that pledge to Frank, I've been secretive and even deceitful with you. I behaved that way because I wished to spare you further grief when you were already suffering from the loss of your brother-in-law. Even now, I feel Isabelle oughtn't know anything. I received word late yesterday that Alastair is willing to serve as an emissary to transmit letters and telegrams between you and the girls. As soon as I knew the girls were safe and you could communicate with them, I've come to you. Had I said anything before now, it wouldn't have served any purpose other than to have heightened your anguish. At this time, Millicent, the girls still don't know about their father, and Alastair feels they ought not be told yet. Since he is able to see them, we need to trust his judgment."

"He can see them?"

"Yes, he's seen them."

Those words gave her a small measure of comfort. Alastair loved Audrey and Fee. He'd keep a close eye on them. He wouldn't let terrible things befall them. It was still a tragic situation and so much needed to be done, but at least now she could trade notes with her girls and remind them of her love.

"I'll continue to investigate the matter further."

She rubbed her forehead, then gazed at him. "I can't believe it."

Daniel gave her an irritated look. "I did what I had to do, Millicent. I was honor-bound."

"No, Daniel. I can't believe that you've put up with me. I've been sitting here finding fault with you when you did your best to act with compassion and principles. I hope you'll forgive me for reacting too swiftly and harshly." Tears filled her eyes. "It's hard to imagine you did all that for me and two little girls you've never met."

"Things that are important to you matter to me, as well."

"Thank you."

"You've taken on Arthur as your own. How could I not care for the little girls you love?"

His tone carried such conviction, Millicent felt sure God had blessed her with the best husband in the world.

"Hey!" A couple of children dashed up. "We saw your kite!"

"Isn't it beautiful?" Millicent saw the longing in their eyes. She glanced at Daniel.

"Millicent, dear, do you think the children would like to have a turn?"

She turned the kite over to him, and he knelt alongside the younger boy. She'd once heard a man was never taller than when he stooped to help a child. *It seems I've married a giant.*

Sadness threaded through her. *I shouldn't be this way. I made a deal. Isabelle would be counting her blessings if she were in my place.* Still, a strange longing persisted.

———

"Daniel? Daniel?"

"Huh?" He rolled over and squinted at the door. "Is that you, Millicent? Something wrong?"

She stuck her head in his bedchamber and whispered, "I didn't want my sister to hear, but I have telegrams for the girls. I should have asked. Are eight words apiece too expensive?"

"Eight?" He sat up.

She averted her gaze and whispered, "I'll shorten them."

"I don't care if they're one hundred eight words apiece."

Appearing shocked, she turned back to see if he was teasing. He cocked an eyebrow and virulent color washed over her, and she dashed away. When he emerged for breakfast, she handed him three slips of paper and an I-dare-you smile. He glanced down to see that she'd written telegrams to both girls and a third to Alastair. Just to show his wife that for all her sass, she'd met her match, he looked down at her skirts and back up at her face. "It's Monday."

"But it's a special Monday. This is the beginning of the first whole week your mercantile is open!"

He walked off to hide his grin. She'd told him yesterday that he looked like a boy with his kite, but this was going to be a game with her. Millicent's girlish streak counted as a good sign; she wouldn't play like this if she wasn't starting to feel at ease around him. No doubt, she would concoct a reason—however flimsy—to declare each day to be special so she could keep on wearing that silly wire hoop cage and bustle. But she was right—this was the first full week the mercantile would be open, and that was exciting. Then, too, as long as he played the game, she'd wear the hoops. Heaven only knew how badly he needed her to. When she'd come downstairs yesterday with that gored skirt softly flowing down and accentuating her womanly shape, he'd wanted to fill his eyes forever; he found he needed to close his eyes and beg for strength. He'd have Isabelle work on other people's orders first—saying that she needed to take care of their commissions long before his. After all, she and Millie both agreed they had sufficient to wear. He'd also keep this silly game going with his wife, so she'd continue to concoct reasons each day was special.

Phineas Stahl came into the store. He bought a ready-made pair of trousers and shirt for himself, then stood by the case and vacillated between hairpins and combs for Annie. Sheepishly, he looked up from the case. "I'll take both. My Annie—she deserves all I can give her."

"She seems to be a fine woman."

"Ja. I have loved her for many years and longed for her to be mine. I had to wait for God's timing."

Daniel teased, "I didn't realize yours was a case of unrequited love."

Phineas hitched his shoulder. "You could call it that. A few times I had plans, but in my soul I knew they were not right. It was not to be—not then."

"I apologize. I shouldn't have made light—"

"I take no offense." Phineas looked at him with a directness that carried a wealth of feeling. "It is a testimony. God has worked His miracles for my Annie and me and done away with the barrier that kept us apart. You helped start us anew, too, with that bracelet in your drawing."

Chuckling, Daniel said, "Millicent deserves the credit for that."

After Phineas left, Daniel bowed his head. God had answered Phineas's prayers—but it had taken years. That knowledge alternately reassured and depressed Daniel. There was hope, but could he hang on long enough?

Folks trickled in and out of the mercantile as the morning progressed. He'd come down immediately after breakfast to open the store, but Isabelle stayed upstairs to help clean up. When she came down, Daniel ambled past her and murmured, "I appreciate your working alongside your sister and teaching her. We're blessed to have you."

Just before lunch, Isabelle dashed up and down the stairs to fetch a collar she'd crocheted. Not long thereafter, the yeasty scent of fresh-baked bread drifted down. At lunch, Millicent brought sandwiches to them. How anyone could botch a sandwich was a mystery, but Millicent had managed. The bread and ham looked like a drunkard had sliced them. After the first bite, Daniel set the sandwich aside for a moment and took care of a customer. Millicent pattered back upstairs. Once the customer left, Daniel stalked over to the sewing machine and took Isabelle's sandwich. "Courage is one thing; foolishness is another." He took them through the storeroom and tossed them out to where any of the stray dogs or cats would snap them up.

Millicent came down to help as Arthur took his nap. When Daniel's stomach rumbled loudly, Isabelle looked up from her sewing machine. "There's going to be apple pie soon."

"The pie!" Millicent ran for the stairs.

"What's this about apple pie?" Tim Creighton came in through the back with a bucket in his hand. "Might be that

I have something worth trading for." Tim lifted the bucket. "What do you say, Dan?"

"I say you haven't tried my wife's cooking." As soon as he said it, Daniel realized he'd been indiscreet. "I've got quite the bride."

Tim chuckled. "You had me going for a second there. When Sydney started cooking at the ranch, Velma kept bicarbonate of soda on hand for us. Thanks to Velma's help and the Richardson girls' lessons, my wife can more than hold her own in the kitchen now."

So if I swallow enough bicarbonate of soda and am patient, then maybe there's hope . . .

Tim set the bucket on the counter. "I need to order a half dozen traps. Coyotes are heavy this year—took down a cow and her calf last night. No use in good meat going to waste."

"You set the price and I'll sell it—or did you want to barter that for the traps?"

"Nah. We all help one another out around here." The aroma of fresh pie flooded the store, and Tim's nostrils flared.

Daniel called, "Millie? Dear?"

"Yes, Daniel?"

"Tim brought by a bucket of fresh meat. That pie's got both of us . . ."

"Hankering." Tim grinned.

The bell rang and Mr. Smith came in. "The rug's done. I'm pretty sure my kids beat the last bit of dust out of it." He stopped and inhaled. "I must be going crazy, because I could swear I smell baked apples."

Millicent's laughter flowed down the stairs. "Daniel, Arthur's climbing up on a chair to get to the pie. If you men want a piece, you'd better hurry."

Gesturing toward the stairs, Daniel said, "Gentlemen. Isabelle, the bell will sound if we get a customer. Come join us."

As they started to eat, Daniel watched Millicent blush as the men paid her compliments on her baking. He mused, "You spent time in boarding schools, so this isn't an old family recipe, is it?"

"Isabelle—"

Isabelle chimed in, "Shared the recipe."

Tim turned to Smith. "What brought you to town?"

"I'm delivering a carpet. After being up all night last night, I'm surprised to see you here."

"Likewise." Tim shoveled the last bite into his mouth. "I came to order traps."

"Traps?" Millicent gave Arthur a bite.

Eyes bright, Arthur bobbed enthusiastically. "Nummy, nummy nummy!"

"We're all in agreement on that." Daniel reached over and casually fed Millicent a bite. "Coyotes set upon the Creightons' livestock."

"Oh no!"

Tim heaved a sigh. "It happens every year. It's not often, though, that they take down both a cow and her calf. The last two years, the coyotes have grown far bolder. I've not used traps before now, but this was by the house."

As soon as they finished eating, Daniel rose. "Millie, can you keep Arthur in the nursery for a few minutes?"

"I'm going to put him down for another nap. He just babbled and played when he was supposed to be napping earlier this afternoon."

"Fine. We're going to bring up the carpet now."

"You're going to bring it up? Here?"

He nodded.

She pressed her fingers to her mouth. "I'm sorry. Could I please have a moment with you?"

He nodded tersely and led her to his bedchamber.

Twenty-One

The minute Daniel closed the door, Millicent whirled to face him. "Daniel, that carpet's expensive!" She paced away and back. Still in a whisper, she said, "You know our finances; I don't. But after having to restock the entire store, I understand we have to be careful."

Daniel watched her, noting she couldn't stay in one place. She went over to the window and back, then changed direction and measured the distance to the armoire a few times. The whole while, she fretted in a hushed voice.

Suddenly she wheeled around and came back once again. "The carpet isn't ruined at all, if that's what you're worried about. I'm sure the Smith kids beat every bit of grit straight out of it. As tightly woven and knotted as that carpet was, the grit didn't stand a chance of getting past the surface. If you're concerned that a customer would be offended that it's had that negligible mishap, then you could discount it a little. Yes, you could." She brightened up. "Even up to thirty-three percent like you did the other goods. You'd still recoup a fair price. It would sell in an instant. I'm sure of it."

"Are you?"

She gave him an exasperated look. "Of course I am! The colors and pattern are exceptional. Any woman would be proud to have such a fine piece in her home. And the quality will make it last forever. You're a man—"

"Glad you noticed."

She huffed and continued. "You know it would be a sound investment for a family man to purchase that carpet for his home. He'd not have to replace it over and over again as he would a cheaper piece. I know most of our neighbors are living on a very tight budget, but there are others who could easily afford a quality Turkish carpet. Once you display it, it'll sell and someone else will see it lying in a parlor and ask you to order one for them, too."

The countless knots she'd tied in the life preserver now made sense. When Millicent was rattled, she couldn't help herself. She had to move around and talk. Only this time, instead of praying, "O Lord, O Lord, O Lord," repeatedly, she was talking to Daniel. Just like that prayer, she kept repeating herself. Daniel snagged her as she passed by.

"Millicent, calm down."

Worry darkened the green-gray of her eyes. "I am calm. I'm thinking quite clearly. You have to agree that I've made several very important points. Once you give it a moment's consideration, you'll realize that those points hold merit."

"Let me sum them up." He was sure she didn't realize she was clasping his hands like lifelines. "The carpet is a work of art. It's expensive and of laudable quality. A man might consider it as an investment; a woman would appreciate the warmth and beauty it would lend her home."

She nodded and waited expectantly. When he didn't continue, she leaned a little closer and said in the barest whisper, "You forgot about the money—the finances and that you could sell a few more once it's known you can procure such an elegant piece."

"The money doesn't concern me, Millicent."

She tipped her head back and let out a long-suffering sigh. "Daniel, I know you believe God will supply our needs according to His riches, and He's been more than faithful. But we have to be good stewards. I don't want to say things like that to you. Bossy women who try to direct their husbands in spiritual matters aren't heeding biblical principles. I won't say anything more. Please, though, will you give it consideration?"

He nodded, and she almost wilted in relief.

A few seconds of complete silence stretched between them. Daniel rubbed his thumb back and forth over the pulse at her wrist. "Millicent, I've thought about it. I've decided what I must do."

"You have a big heart, Daniel. I want you to know I appreciated the gesture."

"Dear, I sold a very lucrative business to come here."

She smiled. "Of course you did. And this mercantile is already promising to become a business you'll be proud to pass down to Arthur someday."

His wife didn't have the slightest notion of how wealthy they were. Keeping hold of one of her hands and pressing the fingers of his other hand to her lips, he continued to look into her eyes. "Dear, we have funds that more than cover all of the expenses, and I'll always endeavor to be a good and faithful servant to our Lord and Savior."

"Dan?" Smith's voice came through the door.

"I'll be right out."

Color flamed Millicent's cheeks. "I've kept you here when he needs to go. I'll hurry on down and get the shirts for him. Daniel? Did you pick up on how Tim had the Smith women over to help butcher all night long? He did that so he could give them meat in payment of the services. With a big family like that, Mr. Smith undoubtedly needed the food. Do you mind if I give him some of the material that got a little dusty? I'm sure they'd put it to good use."

"Yes, that would be nice. We'll even tell him it's in thanks for helping with a little project I have underway." He opened the door. The carpet now stretched across the parlor with the settee and wingback chair positioned precisely where they'd been.

Isabelle exited the other bedchamber. "I put Arthur down for his nap."

"Thank you." Millicent followed her sister's gaze and let out a gasp. Grabbing his hand, she started to fret again. "Daniel, they didn't understand. Don't worry. I'll—"

"They did understand." He smiled at her. "You did say it was a special day, Millie. In the years to come, we'll look at that rug and know it began our first full week with the mercantile. Now come on downstairs."

Millie held the banister and Daniel's arm, as well, to descend the stairs. She took a deep breath.

Daniel stopped and reached to brace her waist with his other hand. "Are you all right?"

He's scared of me fainting or falling. She straightened to her full height. "I'm perfectly fine, Daniel Clark; but I've come to the conclusion that you are a rascal. I'm going to have to be on my guard around you, aren't I?"

A slow grin tugged at his mouth.

"Don't you give me that rakish look. It's going to have me worrying that you're plotting and planning something more."

His smile grew. "I am."

"Two can play at that game, you know." She pulled her arm free and scurried down the last few steps. His chuckle followed her.

Just before Smith left with the work shirts and fabric, he remembered needing a few nails. Millicent spied Orville's decoy and pushed it into Daniel's arms. "Daniel, I'll help Mr. Smith with the nails. You promised your cousin that you'd take over his favorite hunting decoy."

"Thanks for reminding me, dear. I'll take care of that in a moment." Without so much as drawing another breath, he gently returned it. "You know how important this is to Orville. Will you please hold it for me in the meantime? Smith, why don't you tell me about the hunting hereabouts while we get those nails."

Millicent didn't look down. She watched and started plotting as her husband went to the nail bin. Yes, two could play, and he was a worthy adversary. Without missing a beat, he'd not just sidestepped the duck—he'd gotten the upper hand. But not for long. *This is war.*

During the following lull, Daniel solemnly took the duck. "I am a man of my word."

"Yes, you are." Millicent felt a twinge of guilt. "It's one of your many fine qualities."

"Thank you." He left the store. How did he manage to hold the decoy with such dignity? Millicent watched through the window as he strode down the street with the mallard balanced in his hands as if he were one of the three kings, delivering a priceless gift. Indeed, he was as noble as a king. He'd agreed to one arrangement when Frank was alive; he had every reason and right to have simply taken his son and left her and Isabelle to go back to England. *But he didn't.*

The bell chimed. "Annie! How may I help you?"

"I need some thread." Annie fumbled in her apron pocket. "Brown. Black, too."

"We're having a sale. If you buy three spools, you get a fourth for free."

Annie chewed on her lower lip. "White, then. And . . . blue. Dark blue." She followed Millicent over to the Clark Mile End Thread case. Once there, Annie changed her mind about the colors of thread several times. Finally, she whispered, "Oh, you must forgive me. My mind's not right these days. I know he respects me, but holding hands—it just does not say as much as I feel. I just wish Phineas would kiss me."

"I know how you feel! It's so frustrating, isn't it?" Millicent blurted out the words, then pressed her fingers to her lips. Her face went hot. *How could I have divulged something so revealing— even betraying?* Patting Annie's arm, she stammered, "It's hard for us. Women aren't allowed to express their innermost feelings. We carry our affections within our hearts, yet we cannot so much as hint at them. Ladies are taught that men must always take the first step, so we live in hope and fear."

"Yes!" Annie grabbed her hand. "That is exactly how I feel!"

"When the time is right, things have a way of working out. I promise you, the love in Phineas's eyes is strong."

"I do see the love in his eyes," Annie admitted.

"Will there be anything else?" Millicent headed toward the counter.

"No, thank you. That is all."

"Let me get a lemon drop for Emmy-Lou." Millicent opened the jar. When she turned back, Annie looked pale. "Is anything wrong?"

Annie gave her an odd look and slipped two cents onto the counter.

Millicent stepped close and murmured, "I'll hold what you said in confidence, Annie."

She flickered a smile, tucked the thread and lemon drop into her apron pocket, and left.

As she left, Millicent turned and closed her eyes against the sting of tears. No matter how deeply she felt for Daniel, was she going to spend the rest of her life alone and untouched?

Isabelle called her over. "Could you please help me measure this sleeve? Mr. Toomel's shoulders are wide, so I need to let out a little more on the jacket."

Millicent shook off her dark feelings and went to assist her.

"I'm so glad to see you and Daniel having fun. The playfulness you shared just a while ago was precious." Isabelle's smile was bittersweet. "A wife should cast a little levity into her husband's days."

Millicent looked at the tears in her sister's eyes and heard the courage behind her words. "I don't want to offend you, Isabelle."

"No, no. You won't do that in the least. I wish I would have been more playful with Frank. I worried and fretted so much, but he cheered me with the lighthearted little things he did. I've worried that my state would dampen the spirits of your home, and I won't have it. Frank wouldn't want it."

Millicent took the tape measure from her sister and enveloped her in an embrace. "He knew how contented you were. Your marriage was full and rich. Don't ever doubt that you were a good wife. Frank often boasted that he had the best wife God ever created."

"Millie?" Isabelle pulled away very slowly. "I don't want to interfere in your marriage, but you need to reconsider something. Don't you think you ought to be sleeping in the other room?"

Drawing in a noisy breath, Millicent shook her head. "It's not like that."

"A husband deserves the . . . comfort only his wife can give. Babies, too, if God blesses them."

That longing she'd felt came back again. "No, it's complicated, Isabelle. Daniel told me Arthur is more than enough for him. Just before we took our vows, we agreed this would be an in-name-only arrangement. He even said we'd not discuss the matter again. He's been so very honorable and good to us. How can you suggest I go back on my word? I won't."

"Maybe you misunderstood him. Maybe he's changed his mind."

Could he have? Millicent quelled the hope that sprouted in her heart. "Nonsense."

"He's acting like a man who's courting."

"It's all for the sake of appearances. Isabelle, he feels it's his fault that his wife died. She fell down the stairs when she was with child. You see how he is already about the stairs—I understand why he's so careful. A man can't admit he's terrified of something, but deep in my heart, I know Daniel is afraid the nightmare will repeat itself. He's making sure it won't happen again."

"You're fond of him."

"Yes." Millicent wished she hadn't answered quite so quickly and emphatically. "But you're fond of him, too. He'll be back any moment. Let's concentrate on the sleeve here." When her big sister gave her a we'll-talk-about-this-more look, Millicent flashed her a cheeky grin. "I'll take your advice to heart, though. Being playful is a grand idea. In that vein, I think we should give him a housewarming gift."

"Have you asked him what he'd like?"

"Of course not! Then it wouldn't be a surprise."

Shaking her head, Isabelle warned, "Daniel isn't the kind of man who likes surprises."

"It's our duty to teach him. How will Arthur ever learn to graciously accept presents if his father doesn't provide an example? I'm going over to see Clicky. He'll help me place an order and arrange for delivery."

"You'd be wiser to concentrate on preparing the roast Tim Creighton brought in that pail."

"Let's go put it in the oven right now."

An hour later, Millicent was well on the way to instituting her next grand plan. She'd be everything Daniel needed in a wife. The fact that Isabelle wasn't offended by their lightheartedness put her at ease. If anything, Daniel would be her partner as Frank had been her sister's. They'd have fun and cheer up Isabelle all at the same time.

"Daniel?" she called down the stairs. "I wanted to take Arthur for a stroll. It's such a nice day. Do you think if I hold the banister with one hand and hold his hand with the other, maybe he could bump down the stairs on his little bottom? We'd be very careful."

"It's no bother for me to fetch him."

"Not at this very moment, it's not. But with Thursdays and Saturdays being the busiest days, I thought we could teach him how now. That way, when you're serving the customers, we'll have a safe alternative."

Halfway down the stairs, Arthur gleefully shouted, "Dadda! Me bump bump!"

"Yes, you are. There's Daddy's brave, big boy."

"Bee boy!"

Daniel reached up, wrapped his big hands around his son, and pulled him off the stairs. When Arthur began to object, Daniel lifted him high and jostled him. "The big boy is high! Look, son. You're up high!"

"Wheeee!"

As he set Arthur down, Millicent murmured to him, "I'm more proud of you than of Arthur. He was learning something new; you were banishing ghosts."

"Don't think my memories are that easily erased, Millicent. Some things, a man never forgets. He just learns to control them the best he can and live with them."

His words pounded in her mind as her boots measured the length of the boardwalk. Arthur held her hand and ambled alongside her, babbling happily. Suddenly, all of Daniel's schedules and lists made sense. If he could write everything down, he could control it—only she'd been blind to how important those lists really were to him. She hadn't looked past what they were and seen why they were so necessary. Daniel used them as a tool so he could be a good head of their home—and he succeeded at it. All these days, she'd tried to bring spontaneity into Daniel's life when what he needed most was what he'd asked of her from the very start—someone to mind his son and adhere to his schedules. Isabelle had been right—Daniel wouldn't appreciate the gift she'd arranged for, and it couldn't be returned. Millicent tried to convince herself that he might actually surprise her and appreciate it a little, but from here on out, she wouldn't make that mistake again. *Lord, help me be a good wife and mother. I need your guidance. Grant me wisdom so I can be the woman Daniel needs me to be.*

"Your box is overflowing." The postmaster stamped the back of Arthur's hand with an ink stamp, then handed her an appreciable stack of mail.

Millicent riffled through the envelopes, hoping in vain for a letter from Audrey and Fiona. Disappointment flooded her. Without a photograph, the bracelet was her only tangible link to the girls. Mr. Eberhardt's promise to the girls that she'd never take it off wasn't exactly accurate, but Millicent never allowed it out of her sight.

Arthur tugged on her skirt. "Up peasssss. Amma, up."

Her heart skipped several beats. Millicent dropped the mail and knelt beside him.

"Uh-oh! Boom!" Arthur squatted down and started picking up the envelopes.

Mr. Tyson came around the counter to help. He frowned at Millicent's tears. "Is something wrong?"

Heart overflowing, she shook her head. "He called me mama."

Twenty-Two

"D adda!" Arthur shouted as he ran past the shelves and toward the counter. "Dadda! Preee!"

Daniel hefted him. "Yes, Mama's pretty."

"No. Mine! Pree!" He stuck out his hand to show off the ink stamp.

Daniel whistled. "Now, that's something."

Thrilled with the attention, Arthur wiggled. "Down! Iz-belle!"

"Yes, Aunt Isabelle would like to see that. Here you are." Daniel set him down, then straightened up. He looked at Millicent and waggled his brows. "I still say Mama's pretty." As she drew closer, he saw traces of tears. He rasped, "You've been crying."

The sweetest smile he'd ever seen sketched across her face. "Arthur called me 'Amma.' "

"Then I'll forgive him for not calling you pretty just this once."

Trilling laughter, Millicent handed him the mail. "I don't know your system. Your organization is beyond me." She coiled up some loose string for tying packages. "Arthur is a very bright boy. Clever." She sharpened two pencils.

Daniel opened the letters, sorted out the bills—

"So I'm sure you'll agree with me that it's essential." She brandished the feather duster and attacked the rifles.

Pitying the rifles, Daniel walked over and took the duster from her. "What's essential?" Had he missed hearing something while glancing at the mail?

Gusting a sigh, she looked for something more to do. Daniel kept taking whatever she picked up away from her. "You're a businessman, Daniel. Think of it as an investment. A clever boy like Arthur needs books to wind up his imagination and stimulate his thinking. Books for him now will mean brilliance later. We simply must do this for him. After all, the town has no library."

This is all about books! "I have a crate full of books upstairs from the nursery back home, Millie. I'll locate it for you."

"You're a scamp, Daniel Clark. If your son—"

"*Our* son."

"If *our* son grows up to be half the man you are . . ."

"It will be because his mama loves him."

"Of course I love him!" She straightened her apron. "If I stand here much longer and try to reason with you, the roast will burn."

An amused expression crossed his features. "If you *stand* here?"

"I can take a hint. I really do need to get back upstairs. Will you please carry Arthur up?"

"Yes. Millicent?"

She watched him stoop to pick up Arthur. "It's very difficult to carry on a conversation with you. Did you know that, Daniel? It would be ever so much easier if you'd just stay still."

He forgot what he was going to say. Once she and Arthur were upstairs, Daniel looked at the trail of merchandise in odd locations that marked Millicent's crazy path through the store. Putting them away, one of Millicent's ideas took root. Books could be a solid investment. Especially cookbooks.

———

Isabelle shadowed Daniel's steps. "Millie's worried about her girls, Daniel. I told her it's too soon for a letter to reach here from England, but you ought to know that she can't help fretting. She has a big heart, so it's not that she loves Arthur any less."

"I know. We've sent a telegram. We're bound to have news soon." He said as much as he dared.

"That's terribly expensive."

Daniel finally faced her. "Millicent said the same thing. Allaying my wife's troubled heart is worth whatever the cost."

"She's growing very fond of you," Isabelle whispered.

"Isabelle?" Millicent's voice drifted down the stairs, sounding uncertain.

"Excuse me." Isabelle went up the stairs.

Daniel wondered if Millicent had overheard her sister and was trying to silence her. They were confidantes. Had Isabelle been trying to tell him something but he'd not comprehended her meaning? Her grief kept her so subdued, he found it impossible to understand anything about her at all. Other women were so much alike—they attended those finishing schools and all resorted to the same little phrases, tactics, and ploys. They were trained that young ladies behaved thus and so. Only his Millicent—she was a rule unto herself. At times, Daniel found that refreshing and delightful, but sometimes, like now, he wished it wasn't so. He'd like to be able to tell if she was genuinely happy or just humoring him.

Phineas Stahl came in. He looked about the store, then asked in a low tone, "Is anyone else here?"

"No. Is there a matter you need to discuss? Would you like to open a line of credit?"

Phineas shook his head. Grim-faced, he stared at Daniel. "My Annie was here to buy thread." When Daniel nodded, Phineas continued, "She came to me. She saw it—the list you made for your wife."

"Yes?" Daniel had no idea where the conversation was headed.

Flexing his hands at his sides, Phineas leaned forward. "Annie's a widow now, but her husband treated her bad. Very bad. Each day, he wrote a list for her, too. My Annie was here today and saw the list you made for your wife and came to me, weeping. She is worried for your wife."

Daniel let out a hearty laugh. Shaking his head, he grinned. "Millicent could no more follow that list than she could sprout wings and fly. They're suggestions. She knows the first few things are the tasks I consider the most important. Our very first days of marriage, I was foolish enough to expect her to follow the list, but I soon learned different. I once told her I didn't believe in compromise, but that's exactly what we've done—she tries to do the first three or four things, and I try to ignore anything else that doesn't get done. The rest of the time, she has free rein over things upstairs in our home, and I do as I please in the store."

Phineas grinned. "The things we do for the women we love, ja?"

Daniel extended his hand. "Any man who is willing to put a woman's safety ahead of his own comfort is the kind of man I'm proud to call my friend."

He finished the work day, turned over the CLOSED sign, and locked the door. Once upstairs, he declared, "Something smells great!"

"Dinner will be ready soon. We're having the roast Tim Creighton brought." Millicent stopped stirring for a moment and popped Arthur into the high chair they'd gotten in with their last order. She kissed his crown, then went back to the stove. A sound of dismay escaped her lips.

"Millie, will you please put the potatoes on the table?" Isabelle shoved the bowl at her and took over at the stove. She started stirring the gravy furiously.

Biting her lip, Millicent placed a bowl of mashed potatoes on the table next to the roast.

"Goo food!"

That seemed debatable. Nonetheless, Daniel bowed his head and asked a blessing. The roast was dry and the gravy plopped out in lumps. Mixing them with the mashed potatoes made the meal edible. Millicent looked ready to cry, so Daniel served himself seconds. Smiling with each bite he took, he gradually revised his order. He would send for two different cookbooks. No, three.

After supper, Daniel played with Arthur as the women did the dishes. Millicent refilled the sink and tested the water. "Arthur, bath time."

"Baff! Baff!" Arthur bounced with glee. "Bows?"

"Bows?" Daniel gave Millicent a puzzled look.

"Bubbles. We sometimes dip my bracelet in the soapy water and blow bubbles through it."

Daniel unbuttoned Arthur's gown. "No wonder he's excited. It sounds like a lot of fun."

Standing around and watching Arthur splash was a delight. When Millicent dipped her bracelet into the water and held it up, Arthur's "blows" turned out to be squeals of joy. Millicent ducked down beside him and timed her puffs to coincide with his efforts so he could think he'd created the bubbles.

Sleeves rolled up to his elbows, Daniel swiped the bracelet. "Son, let's make one together."

Nothing happened. They tried it four times, and Arthur grew impatient. He grasped the bracelet and thrust it toward Millicent. "Amma do peassss."

She made it look so easy. Arthur giggled as he poked his fingers through the bubbles and popped them. "One more, Arthur, then it's bedtime." Millicent blew that bubble, then Daniel lifted his son from the water. Looking over his shoulder, Millicent frowned.

Daniel turned. Isabelle had fallen asleep in the wingback chair. "Her grief drains her," he murmured. "When she minded Arthur over at the boardinghouse, Mrs. Orion made sure Isabelle napped."

"I tried to get her to nap today. She wouldn't."

"Mark my words: She'll nap from now on. I'll blackmail her."

Millicent gave him an outraged look. "My sister's never done anything—"

"Ah, but you see—" he slipped her bracelet back onto her slender wrist—"I'll tell her if she naps each day for a week, I'll send a telegram to Alastair and ask for a photograph of the girls for you."

———

Daniel spread his hand wide and rubbed his temples in disbelief. Just when he'd thought they were doing better . . . this. He pitched his voice to keep from waking Arthur and Isabelle. "Millicent!"

She rushed down the stairs and skidded to a very unladylike halt. "Yes?"

"Just what," he asked, pointing at the monstrosity in the corner of the store, "is that?"

Suddenly intensely interested in a tiny spot on her apron, she announced, "Our gift to you."

"Whose gift?"

"Your gift."

He glowered at the hideous birdcage that he'd wanted to throw out since the first day they'd taken possession of the store. Millicent had polished the stupid thing until it glittered. Ornate, overblown swirly things dipped and looped around the cage. Cleaned up, it looked worse than it had when it was covered in dust. Daniel closed his eyes and gritted his teeth to keep from saying something that would hurt her tender feelings. "Just whom am I supposed to . . . thank . . . for . . ." His voice ground to a halt as something yellow flitted behind the foliage and silk flowers. "Don't tell me there are birds in that thing."

"Of course I wouldn't tell you that."

Relief eased through his neck and shoulders. He should have known Millicent had better sense than to—

"It's rude to tell someone about their gift. They're supposed to discover it on their own."

"Millicent, get your list."

She pulled it from her pocket.

"Did you, or did you not, recently say that you would adhere to your schedule and our agreement?" As soon as he asked, he saw the hurt look on her face. He thought for a moment. She'd accomplished the main tasks he'd asked of her for the day.

"You're the one who said it was acceptable." Her voice remained steady.

"I did?" *She's been under too much strain. . . .*

Millicent didn't just nod, she looked quite certain of herself. Still holding the list in her hands, she recited, " 'I'll have my son in a cot. I'll even consider a bird in that cage. That's two out of three wire cages. I'll sweeten it a little so you feel the deal is fair. On Sundays and special occasions, if you want to be caged, I won't complain.' "

He stared at her in disbelief. He'd said those exact words.

"When I went to order the lovebirds, they seemed like such a wonderful present. Clicky didn't have to help me order them at all. He knew Mrs. Vaughn needed to sell hers since she's moving. Everything seemed to work out so perfectly. Who wouldn't want their home to be filled with beauty and music? But then, things . . . made me realize how very different you and I are."

"Things."

Slowly putting her list back into her apron, she said, "I see the birds, and you can't see past the cage. When I look at it through your eyes, a cage is a sorrowful gift indeed."

"If you want the birds that bad, keep them."

"What I wanted was to make you and our home happy. I should have known better than to think something could do that. Only God can."

———

The distinctive sound of retching woke Daniel. He'd suffered a case of indigestion late into the night. It made sense that Millicent and Isabelle were miserable. He pulled on his robe and went to the kitchen. Adding some bicarbonate of soda to a glass of water, he mentally steeled himself. Being anywhere near someone who was violently ill made his own stomach lurch.

The nursery door opened. Millicent appeared, her nightgown peeping from beneath the hem of her dress. A sickly shade of green, she held the covered chamber pot.

He tugged it from her. "Go back to bed. I've got this."

"But—"

The stench from the chamber pot made him shove the glass into her hands. "Bicarbonate."

After emptying the mess, Daniel stood on the back porch of the store and drew in a few deep breaths of fresh morning air. *Poor Millicent.*

He went upstairs to find his wife at the stove. "Dear, go back to bed."

She shook her head. "No, no. Tea and toast . . ."

"I'll bring them to you. How is Isabelle?"

"Shaky."

He nodded and curled his hands around Millicent's waist. For a moment, his mind went blank. He'd touched her in a similar manner before, but this time her small waist gave slightly to his touch. She hadn't laced on her stays yet.

"Truly, Daniel—"

"Go." He turned loose of her when all he wanted was to pull her closer and— *She's ill. I'm being a selfish beast.* "Go."

Millicent gave him a strained look. A second later, the nursery door clicked shut.

When he took the tray with cups of tea and some toast to the door, he poked his head inside and ordered, "Give me Arthur. I'll take him to the diner for breakfast so you don't smell anything cooking."

Gratitude made the gray striations in her eyes shimmer. "Shall I fetch the doctor?"

"There's no need. Truly, there isn't."

Keeping Arthur out of trouble while he shaved might pose a problem, so Daniel carried the high chair into his bedchamber. Soon, his son giggled as he got a good view of Daddy's funny faces. "So you're entertained, are you?" Daniel used the brush and daubed a few spots onto his son's jaw.

Arthur stared at himself in the mirror and squealed with glee.

Breakfast at the diner tasted fair. With all of the traveling he'd done, Daniel thought he'd developed a cast-iron stomach . . . until last night. He finished feeding Arthur and lingered over a cup of coffee. He wouldn't open the store for another half hour, and if he kept his noisy little boy out of the place, maybe Millicent and Isabelle could catch a little more sleep.

The school bell rang twice. The second call for families who didn't own a clock. The system seemed quite effective: a single ring for a half hour, two when school would start in fifteen minutes, and three times when the school day had begun.

When Daniel heard three rings, he rose. Everything at the store was spic and span. All he needed to do was show up and open the door. Mopping up Arthur, he chuckled. "You make funny faces like Daddy does when he shaves."

Carrying his son down the boardwalk, Daniel heard someone call his name. He turned. "Reverend Bradle."

"Daniel. I wanted to speak with you about what happened at church last Sunday."

Daniel nodded curtly.

"I want to thank you for what you did. We've been inviting the Van der Vorts to church for years. No one's wanted to pry as to why they refused. I've been praying for the Lord to send someone who could reach them. Sunday, Piet told us why. Instead of condemning him for his outburst, you offered to walk beside him."

"It wasn't a slight to your preaching."

"I didn't take it as such."

The men spoke a little longer. Finally, Reverend Bradle said, "Piet's grief isn't fresh like your sister-in-law's, but it is every bit as raw. Karl shook my hand after church and plans to return; let's agree to minister to both of the Van der Vorts in whatever ways the Lord directs."

"Let's."

"Good. Good then. I'm off to visit the Vaughn widow. Now that you've arrived and your check for the mercantile cleared the bank, Orville paid her off for the feedstore. She made arrangements to leave at the end of the week. My wife wants to have a departure dinner on Thursday night. We hope you can attend."

"Pastor, something's not right. I wired Orville full payment for the mercantile from England seven full weeks ago. He should have been able to pay off Mrs. Vaughn back then. Frankly, his dealings with me have been less than scrupulous, but I've chosen to forgive. If Orville was willing to be dishonest with a male family member, I have grave concern—especially upon hearing that he's been dishonest about the transfer of funds—that he might take advantage of a grieving widow. It's imperative we look into this at once. I trust you know the person or persons who'd handle the situation. If any cost is incurred in determining this, I'll fund it. The matter must be seen to immediately."

"Indeed. I happen to know the bank president is gone at the moment. I'll have to summon the board of trustees."

Daniel headed back to the store. The day started out bad and had gotten progressively worse. A bellyache, a sick wife, and a swindling relative. *Lord, you promise not to give more than we can take. I think I've hit my limit.* Opening the door caused the bell to clang. Daniel was surprised to see Tim and Sydney Creighton's housekeeper trundling down the stairs.

Millicent followed her. "Thank you for coming, Velma. It was so very kind of you to drop everything."

"Glad to help." Velma patted Arthur's back as she passed by and left.

Daniel tilted Millicent's face up to his. She was a little pale. "Are you all right?"

"I'm fine." Tears filled her eyes.

Arthur grabbed for her. "Mmm-ah! Amma aw bear."

Millicent kissed his baby cheek and cuddled him close. "Daniel, did you think I was sick?"

"Yes."

"I'm perfectly fit." Color filled her cheeks. "Isabelle's . . . still queasy, but it's nothing to worry over."

Suddenly, Isabelle's tiredness took on a completely different significance. "Is she . . . ?"

Millicent smiled and nodded.

Daniel heard a faint rustle. The hem of Isabelle's black skirts appeared at the head of the stairs, and his blood ran cold. "Isabelle," he rumbled, "don't you move. You're not going up or down those stairs unless I'm with you."

Twenty-Three

I was so happy for Isabelle, I didn't even think about Daniel's feelings. What kind of wife am I? He lost his pregnant wife because of stairs, and now he's going to be faced with that horrible memory every single day for the next eight months.

Daniel escorted Isabelle down and beckoned Millicent. "We need to pray."

"Yes, we certainly do."

They joined together. "Heavenly Father, we come to you and give thanks for this very special blessing. Grant Isabelle health and safety, we pray. Amen."

He was putting up a good front, but Millicent knew the truth. He'd prayed for Isabelle's safety. Well, she was going to be praying for that, too—in addition to begging the Lord to give Daniel peace of mind.

"You aren't upset?" Isabelle half whispered.

Daniel smiled at her. "We've known you longed to have a child. God heard your desires. If it's a son, will you name him Frank?"

Pressing her hand to her heart, Isabelle made a funny little sound that was a mix between a sob and a laugh. "That would be so sweet."

He turned to Millicent. "I see you're all dressed. I presume this news is your reason to declare today is special?"

Millicent nodded. She wasn't fooled for a moment. Daniel completely sidestepped Isabelle's question. To his credit, he didn't lie; but the truth still wrenched Millicent's heart. Daniel didn't want a pregnant woman under his roof. The irony of it all was too much. In trying to protect Arthur and Isabelle, he ended up sacrificing his peace of mind.

"Isabelle, will you take note of this?" Daniel let out a chortle. "Your sister is so surprised and excited, she's speechless! It's going to be quite a year for her. Arthur just started calling her mama, and your little one will soon call her auntie."

Isabelle let out another of her little sob-laughs and threw her arms around Millicent.

Returning the embrace, Millicent looked over her sister's shoulder. In that moment, Daniel's smile slid away and the muscle in his jaw twitched. He turned and strode off—almost as if he wanted to leave, keep walking, and never look back. He'd become a prisoner of his past in his own home.

———

"Daniel?" Slipping into the storeroom, Millicent whispered, "Could I have a word with you?"

"This isn't a good time."

"It's probably the safest time. Isabelle just left to go tell Mercy Orion her news, and there's no one in the store."

He didn't bother to turn around. "Then why are you whispering, and where is my son?"

Stunned, Millicent stood stock-still. "*Our* son went with my sister."

Her husband pivoted toward her.

"As for whispering, I don't know why I am." Her voice was low, but it built in volume. "I was worried about your feelings. Fool that I am, I actually thought you might have some and appreciate a friend!" She whirled around and raced out of the storeroom.

The bell over the door jangled just as Daniel came out and called her name. She hastened up the stairs as the gentleman asked, "Is this the store that gave away the bracelet?"

Widow O'Toole clomped in. "And the one that gave away the bicycle. I won it."

Biting her lip, Millicent kept from crying. She didn't know what she was doing at all. According to Daniel, she hadn't done anything right since the day he put the ring on her finger. Emotions roiling, she decided to tackle the area of the upstairs that was blocked off. Daniel said there were books for Arthur, and she was tired of waiting. Goodness knew what other useful things she'd find there. He'd shipped half of England here, and there were still assorted oddities left over from Orville. She soon lost track of time; if only she could lose some of her memories as easily.

"Dear?"

Millicent heard Daniel, but she refused to answer to that sobriquet. It was a lie. A painful one, too. She'd been foolish enough to actually cherish how he'd called her that.

"Millicent?" His footsteps crossed the parlor floor and halted by a steamer trunk. "What are you doing?"

"Getting the books for Arthur and organizing."

He stepped over a few crates and around another obstacle. "I had getting the books on my list for today."

Swinging her arm in a wide arc, Millicent invited, "By all means, take care of your task, then. I've not yet been able to locate them."

Scanning the space, he shook his head. "I don't recall seeing half of this stuff. It's a good thing they labeled everything so we can tell what's inside." He prowled around and found the box of books for Arthur. "I'll put this in the parlor."

She nodded. He was acting as if nothing were amiss. Nothing happened, nothing changed. *Almighty Father, how am I to conduct myself? As your daughter? As a lady? As a . . . am I a wife? I'm so confused.*

"Hello up there!" Heavy footsteps sounded on the steps. "The replies came. I brought them straight over."

Daniel sprinted to the stairs. A moment later, he sat beside her on the settee. Millicent wasn't sure if she wanted him that close, but it was a small price to pay since he held the telegrams.

Her hands shook as he handed her the first paper. It seemed strange to see Clicky's large, masculine script to represent Audrey's careful penmanship. *Dear Nanny Fairweather, I love you. I miss you. I am fine. At school they said I was too smart so they made me learn with the bigger girls. I liked your lessons better. Please come see me. You can be my teacher again. That would make me and Fiona happy. Love, Audrey.*

She closed her eyes and pressed the telegram to her bosom. Dear Audrey. So grown up, so responsible and cautious.

Daniel gently tucked a wisp of hair behind her ear. "She sounds well."

Millicent steeled herself with a deep breath and read Fiona's. *My nanny, you are my dear nanny. I miss you. Alastair can bring me your letter, so he can bring you to me, too. Come right now. I am sad because you are gone. The school was mean. They were bad to me. They took Flora away. The end. Love, Fee.*

"No!" Millicent hung her head.

"Who's Flora?"

"Her doll. I made it for her for. . . ." Her voice died out. Daniel had cut himself off from her, yet he expected her to bare her heart to him? She shook her head. "Thank you for arranging the telegrams, Daniel. I'm more grateful than I can say."

"Make another doll, Millicent. We'll send it to Fee."

She nodded.

Daniel cleared his throat. "Did you want to share these with your sister?"

Millicent thought for a moment. She couldn't spoil Isabelle's precious day with the shadow of this worry. "No." Carefully folding the papers, she slipped them deep into her apron pocket. "It would be best for Isabelle not to know." Always before, she'd been able to share her joys and burdens with someone—her sister, Frank, the cook or housekeeper at the Eberhardts', and more recently, even Daniel. *I can't share this with anyone but God.*

———

Daniel awoke to the sound of the door creaking open and bolted out of bed as if his life depended on it. In fact, it might. Millicent's cooking could very well kill someone. He threw on his robe and raced out to the kitchen.

Counting under her breath, Millicent was dumping spoons full of ground coffee into the pot. She counted six twice. Eleven, too. She stopped at twelve.

It won't be too bad. As she hastily shoveled in four more, grumpiness overtook him. "Making coffee isn't on your list; it's on mine."

Yelping in surprise, Millicent almost spilled the pot. To Daniel's disappointment, she didn't. "I was up first. I told you I'd do things that weren't on my list."

"Not coffee. It's on my list; I will brew it each morning."

Eyes a stormy gray, she snapped, "Do you ever do anything that isn't on your list?"

"I married you!" He couldn't believe what he'd said. Raking his hand through his hair, Daniel said, "I'm sorry."

Millicent set the coffeepot on the stove with exacting care and turned to face him. Hands deep in her apron pockets, she half whispered, "So it's come to this."

"I'm sorry I spoke without thinking. I didn't mean I'm sorry I married you."

Millicent lifted a hand. "Don't. Don't try to explain, Daniel." Her shoulders went back and her chin rose a notch. If it weren't for the ache radiating from her eyes, she might have fooled him by hiding behind her regal façade—but she didn't. "We agreed at the outset this marriage was for Arthur and Isabelle's sake. They are both doing as well as can be expected, so I have no reason to complain."

"They are doing well, but you've done far more than you should, Millicent."

"I, too, apologize. I vowed to obey—so I'll let you make coffee, and I'll try to follow your lists. Now that that's settled, can we please forget this conversation ever took place?"

"No." Daniel folded his arms across his chest. If he didn't, he'd grab her and hold her tight. "I vowed to love you. If we're—"

She gasped and turned scarlet. "But there are different kinds of love. Christian brotherly love is not to be dismissed."

Is it all our marriage will ever hold? The thought grieved Daniel deeply.

Tears welled up in Millicent's eyes, yet she kept her chin high. "If your regrets run that deep, it's possible to get an annulment."

"No." He stared at her, willing for her to see how deeply he felt. "I could never let you go."

She tore her gaze from him, the hurt and confusion in her eyes letting him know she hadn't detected the merest fraction of his devotion. "Please, Daniel. We've done well." Millicent wiped away the tears streaming down her now pale cheeks. "Can't we please forget about this? Pretend it never happened?"

Seeing her suffer like this tore at him. *Lord God, I acted rashly—let me bear the consequences. Please, shield her. She was confused and grieving and I convinced her to marry me. I told her it was the right thing—I confess, Father. But I can't go back and undo it. Now I've spoken harshly and the wounds of those words will leave scars on her tender heart, as well.*

Dressed in his robe, he didn't even have a handkerchief to offer her. Slowly, he reached out and cupped her face in his hands. She wouldn't look him in the eyes—a fact that sickened him. Brushing away her tears with his thumbs, he agreed in a muted voice, "Nothing would make me happier than to know you'd forgotten it all."

Arthur started singing in the other room. Millicent eased past him and fled from the room.

Daniel dumped out the coffee and started a fresh pot. He set some water to boil in case Isabelle needed tea to settle her stomach. Millicent murmured her appreciation and took tea and toast in to her sister. She helped Arthur with his breakfast and refilled Daniel's coffee cup before he realized it was getting low. As she returned to the table, Daniel's head jerked up. "You're wearing a new skirt."

She nodded.

He hated it. She hadn't wanted a gored skirt; he'd ordered her to agree to having one. She'd indulged in her game of making each day special and wearing her outdated bustle and narrow hoop cage. She'd even had it on just fifteen minutes ago. Only now she'd shed it. He'd been a fool and made a vibrant, loving lady think conforming to a list was more important than the joy of being the woman God made her.

"I found something yesterday." Her voice sounded a little forced, but she'd asked him to pretend that everything was exactly as it had been. She was trying to act that way, too. "I assume it's one of your cousin's odd marvels." She pulled a strange wooden gadget from behind a trunk.

Daniel walked over and examined it. "The McGaffey Whirlwind. Precisely what does it do?"

"I believe it's one of those sweeping machine devices." Millicent lugged it to the parlor carpet. Setting it down, she allowed the large upright wheelbarrow-handlelike stick to rest against her breastbone. "From what I gather, the belt that goes to the bottom and loops around these bicycle pedals up here is supposed to cause suction. I tried it, and it's woefully awkward."

"How are you supposed to get it to go across the carpet if your hands are busy cranking the pedals?" Daniel studied it. "I fail to see how this wooden thing is airtight. It would have to be, to create suction." He pulled it from her, gave it a quick try, and shoved it to the side. "I don't want you touching any more of my cousin's follies."

"The velocipede was lovely."

"I recall awakening to it smashing you to the stairwell. I'll take this one down lest the temptation overcomes you. There's to be a farewell for Mrs. Vaughn and her children tomorrow. I thought to ask you to put together a box for their train ride. I'm sure you'll create a collection that will feed and occupy the children."

"I'd be happy to."

"Millicent?" he said, longing to bridge the gap between them. "I thought it would be fun if you made dolls to send to Audrey and Fiona. Maybe sew dresses they could wear that match like the little girls did at church on Sunday."

"Very well." She smiled. It was a tentative one, and short, but any glimmer of hope counted.

————

While Isabelle and Arthur napped at midmorning, Millicent started gathering a variety of things on the counter. It would be a two-day train ride for Mrs. Vaughn—but with five children and the youngest still a little babe in arms, the trip would be difficult. A tablet of paper and a pair of pencils, the sock "balls" she'd made for Arthur on the ship, and two picture books would help keep them occupied. She folded two handkerchiefs into shapes as she had so often for Audrey and Fiona.

"What is this?" Daniel picked up one and gave it a perplexed look.

Millicent picked up the corners of a matching one and gently swished it from side to side. "Babies in a cradle."

His eyes darkened as he ceased looking at her hands and focused on her face. "You love children."

It wasn't a question—it was a statement of fact. She nodded and swallowed a lump in her throat. "About my sister . . ."

He set down the folded handkerchief. "I can't help worrying, Millicent. Don't tell me not to."

She bit her lip and nodded.

"I enjoy children. It'll be good for Arthur to have others around."

Millicent looked up at him. "It'll be nice, won't it?"

He looked at her steadily. "Yes, dear, it will. I've determined that with the store doing so well and our family growing, it makes sense to expand into the space next door. I've bought it from Mrs. Whitsley, and I plan to have the wall between the upstairs opened."

"There's plenty of room for the baby with Arthur and Isabelle and me. It's quite cozy, being together. We like it."

"Shhh, Millie. I'm not meaning to indicate that Isabelle and her baby are a hardship or unwelcome; on the contrary, I'm saying I wish for them to feel comfortable to remain with us all through the coming years."

Millicent studied his features, wanting to believe him, needing to believe him.

He met her gaze and slowly reached up to twirl a tendril of her hair about his finger, then slip it behind her ear. "Remember what Velma said that night Isabelle fell apart? She said three different things were needed to overcome sorrow: time and tenderness and tears. I fear for all the tenderness you've given me, I've given you tears in return—but give me time, Millie. I'll do my best to make it up to you."

In that moment, Millicent dared to hope that maybe things would work out. Something in her expression must have given away her thoughts because Daniel winked. "Keep praying, dear."

"I do pray, Daniel."

"I know. As do I." He cleared his throat and picked up the babies in the cradle. Swinging them back and forth, he mused, "With two little ones, it only makes sense to have a proper nursery. Did the girls still sleep in the nursery, or were they old enough that they'd moved into a bedchamber?"

"By the time they were five, I had them in a bedchamber, but we used the nursery as a schoolroom and for crafts and any number of projects. Why?"

"I'm curious. All of the little girls who come in here have a favorite color."

Oddly, the memories didn't hurt. "Audrey loves lavender, and Fee likes pink. It made decorating their room simple. Alastair's wife, Cook, the cook for the estate—I never did know her true name—she was quite an artist. She painted a chain of wild flowers around the girls' room." Millicent shook her head. "If we do create a nursery, the buttery yellow would be cheerful. Since you'll undoubtedly want to check in on Arthur whenever the mood strikes, we'll arrange for a curtain or screen by Isabelle's bed."

Daniel waved his hand dismissively. "It'll be far more practical to arrange for her room to have a door open directly to the nursery."

The bell sounded, and they turned around. Orville blasted, "You ordered traps for Creighton. Traps are a feedstore item.

I didn't expect my own flesh and blood to knife me in the back like that."

Daniel didn't back down. "While cleaning the mercantile, I found a variety of traps, Orville. Don't get on your high horse and make accusations when the truth is that you're trying to carve out another segment of the business you sold me."

Millicent bit her tongue to keep from cheering and scurried about the store gathering a pair of tin cups, candy, cheese, crackers, jerked beef, apples, and cans of Borden's milk for the Vaughns' basket.

"More important, Orville, you told me you were renting the store next door."

"I am."

"From whom?"

"What business is that of yours?"

An undercurrent captured Millicent's attention. She turned and watched as Daniel locked eyes with his cousin. "The elderly widow, Mrs. Whitsley, was the owner of record of the property. I decided I'd like to expand the mercantile, so I went to ask about purchasing the place, and she offered to allow me to buy it today. You lied. You cheated that old widow out of rent."

"That old bat won't miss it."

"I warned you to cease taking advantage of others—particularly women and children, or I'd stop you." Millicent spun about to keep busy. If she stopped, she knew she'd yield to the temptation to speak her mind, contrasting what the Bible said about the righteous man and about the ungodly man. One of each stood in the store before her, and she thanked the Lord He'd allowed her to wed the right one.

Orville's tone suddenly altered. "Don't tell me you're going to have another drawing! That's a genuine Whirlwind."

"My wife"—Daniel's voice carried a wealth of amusement—"is the only whirlwind I want or need."

Millicent clapped her hand over her mouth to hold back her laughter. Daniel was right—she'd been in a flurry the whole time they'd been talking. The real reason she wanted to laugh, which was far more important—Daniel's sense of humor had returned.

"A pure gold bracelet and a sixty-dollar bicycle weren't enough?"

Her knees went weak. Pure gold? Sixty dollars?

"Evidently not," Daniel said in an utterly bored tone.

"That was always the problem with you. You always had too much money." Orville left with a bang of the door.

Millicent slumped on the counter. Beneath it was the Lovell bicycle brochure. She'd never ridden a cycle. Never looked at them and figured they probably cost about the same as a baby's pram or a deluxe child's wagon with the adjustable parasol. Those ran between five and eight dollars. She had to know the truth. Opening the cover, she bit back a cry. The least expensive child's bicycle was twenty-nine dollars, and a Lovell Diamond safety bicycle cost eighty-nine dollars! Sound roared in her ears.

"Dear?"

Weakly, she pushed at the brochure. "I didn't know they cost so much. Why didn't you tell me?"

He tucked it back into the stack. "You're not fretting over that, are you?"

"Of course I am!"

"When I woke up to find that velocipede pinning you to the wall, it almost ended up being kindling. At least with the drawing, it made someone happy. And Phineas knelt in this very spot and declared his love for Annie with that bracelet."

"He did, didn't he?"

"Yes. So don't entertain any worries. I hold no regrets whatsoever." He picked up a bottle from the counter. "Dear, Mrs. Vaughn's hair isn't half as luxurious as yours, but I don't believe she needs Baxter's Curative for Baldness."

Millicent knew he'd closed the topic. The sudden hope she felt about their marriage led her to be a little sassy. "Daniel, it's not for Mrs. Vaughn; it's for her baby."

A low chuckle rumbled out of Daniel, and Millicent flashed him a smile. "I'll put most of this back. Honestly, Daniel, I had to stay busy. If I didn't, I would have wanted to chase Orville out of the store. Unmitigated gall—that's what he has. Accusing you of trying to cheat him! There's not a more honest or generous man to be found."

"Thank you." The bell clanged. "Look, dear. It's Mrs. Orion and Miss Richardson. May we help you ladies?"

Linette set a basket on the counter, then reached up to tug her hat down lower over her mannishly short hair. "We're hoping we can help each other."

Mrs. Orion set down a tray of baked goods. "Have you noticed Gooding doesn't have a bakery?"

"Seeing what you have there makes that a crime," Daniel said. "Don't you think, Millicent?"

Feeling completely inadequate for burning bacon and ruining coffee, she nodded.

"I could use a little help at the boardinghouse, but not enough to hire someone—that is, unless I start baking. Linette brings her little sisters to school each morning, so she could stay in town for a while each day."

Linette blurted out, "If we bake stuff, will you sell it?"

"With all of the bachelors around and the train stopping in, baked goods should sell quite well." Mrs. Orion fished a slip of paper from her apron pocket. "I've surveyed newspapers. Bread goes for thirteen cents a loaf. We could provide it to you for eleven cents."

Daniel placed the paper facedown on the counter. Millicent grabbed the pencil and handed it to him. He was about to exercise his generosity again. "You've identified a keen need, but our arrangements should be such that it's financially worthwhile."

Linette's shoulders drooped.

"Your prices are based on paying full price for the staples." Daniel scribbled down some figures. "It's only fair for you to purchase them at wholesale cost if you're selling the finished product here. It's wrong for me to profit twice from your labor. Here are the prices upon which you need to calculate your costs. I must insist, though, that any arrangements we make remain completely confidential. In the business world, that is an absolute."

Mercy turned to Linette. "I won't breathe a word. Will you?"

Linette shook her head.

They all paused while a stranger came in to buy a book and a box of crackers. Once he left, Daniel said, "Your business proposal couldn't have come at a more auspicious time. Millicent was just preparing a basket for the Vaughns to take on their trip. A loaf of bread—"

"And the cookies," Millicent added. "See how God provides?"

After the women left, Daniel said, "You're right. God provides. I worried that the aroma of cooking might be difficult for Isabelle."

Arthur's wake-up song drifted down to them. Millicent looked at the heavily laden counter. "I'll be back to take care of this in a minute." As she went upstairs, she tried to devise something simple she wouldn't ruin for lunch. *It's a pity man does not live by bread alone. That would have solved everything.*

————

Almost an hour later, a man entered. Daniel greeted him. "May I assist you?"

"I heard you had a good selection of jewelry."

"The jewelry case is here. Are you interested in a brooch, or perhaps earbobs?"

Daniel showed him the stock, and the stranger pulled a face. "It's not exactly what I had in mind. The one locket there is passable, but not quite right. Have you anything more, perhaps a ring?"

"I've shown you all we have in stock. We had a grand opening drawing and gave away a gold bracelet. Since then, I've sold four other bracelets and a few other pieces of fine jewelry. I'll be getting more in—probably tomorrow. If you have anything particular in mind, I'd be happy to special order it."

"I'll be sure to check back in. Thank you."

The gentleman left, and three more customers came through. Daniel tended them all, then went to check on Millicent. "That bracelet we gave away at the grand opening has brought us all sorts of business." He handed her a catalogue. "I was thinking perhaps we ought to stock a wider variety— maybe carry a few more wedding rings and a few lockets and stickpins. Could you take a look and let me know if you see anything pretty?"

"Of course. Daniel? Widow O'Toole needs some birdseed. Could you stop by the feedstore and buy some for her?"

He studied her carefully. "I still wonder if I should have kept those birds for you."

Millicent shuddered. "Goodness no! I had no notion just what a mess a bird and birdcage could be!"

He let out a booming laugh and drew her into his arms.

The bell over the door jangled. Jakob, Hope, Phineas, and Annie entered.

Suddenly self-conscious, Millicent disentangled herself. She patted her hair and scampered over toward Annie. "You look lovely! Is that a new dress?"

"It's my Sunday best, but Hope made me a new collar."

Phineas tugged Annie toward one of the cases. "We've come for two reasons. I want to buy Annie a wedding band."

"Oh, felicitations!" Millicent embraced Annie.

Annie hugged her back. "It is to be a quiet wedding at the parsonage. Just us. But Johnny and Arthur will grow up together. You and Isabelle and I are friends now, and Phineas and Daniel are, too. We'd be proud to have you come, if you don't mind closing the store for a few minutes."

"We'd be honored to come." Daniel took Phineas over toward the jewelry case. Millicent grabbed Annie. A spritz of lemon verbena, a tiny spray of silk flowers pinned into her hair, and a new white Bible to carry had her set.

As they stood in the parsonage, listening to the vows, Daniel encased Millicent's hand in his. When she looked up at him, he wondered if the longing in his eyes would be evident. For the first time since their own wedding day, though, he felt like there was actually hope for them.

———

The kerosene lamps cast an eerie glow around the feedstore. Eight men sat there—seven of them silent out of disgust. Orville hadn't stopped fast-talking since they'd all gathered.

Patience lost, Daniel rose and stalked toward him. "Shut your mouth."

"It's easy for you to swagger around. You're rich! Some of us have to work for a living."

Daniel roared, "You consider bilking a widowed mother of five out of a third of her funds 'working for a living'?"

"She can read and cipher just as good as I can." Orville folded his arms across his chest. "Nothing's wrong with a man doing a business deal that sways in his favor."

"Sheriff," Jakob Stauffer demanded, "do something. We cannot stand for this."

"He hasn't done anything I can charge him with in a court of law."

Tim Creighton and Karl Van der Vort both looked ready to tear Orville limb from limb.

Knowing full well what the answer would be, Daniel leaned back and allowed Orville one last moment to gloat. He then wondered, "Why can't he be charged, Sheriff?"

"The bank didn't have Mrs. Vaughn sign the loan papers on the business or transfer the funds. Mr. Blevens planned to see to the matter before closing the bank, but a family emergency came up, and he hopped aboard the train. Until those papers are signed, the feedstore legally still belongs to Mrs. Vaughn."

Orville shot to his feet. "This place is mine!"

Daniel asked one of the bank trustees, "So the down payment Orville planned to pay Mrs. Vaughn was never taken from his own account?"

"Nope. Every last cent is still there. None of it changed hands, and Mrs. Vaughn didn't complete the papers since Mr. Blevens wasn't there to advise her on signatures."

The sheriff stroked his beard. "So let me get this straight. You're saying that Orville tried to pull a fast one on the widow Vaughn and it didn't work."

"Yep. That's it exactly." Mr. Richardson served Orville a dark look. "I've got me six daughters. Any man who'd cheat a woman out of money just because he thought it was easy pickings is lower than the stuff I scrape off my boots. The trustees have met and voted you're not a reliable risk, so we won't be loaning you the money for the remainder of the mortgage on the business. You'll have to move on down the road."

"I'll get a mortgage loan from another bank."

"That's not necessary." Daniel straightened.

Greed lit Orville's eyes. "That's right! You're my cousin! You can give me the money! You tell them!"

Daniel shook his head. "You mistake my meaning. Before this meeting tonight, the feedstore was purchased in full. Blevens isn't in town, but his presence wasn't required. Mrs. Vaughn owned the business free and clear; the buyer paid cash."

"This ain't right." Sweat ran down Orville's temples.

Piet snorted. "So you will tell us all what is right? You, who would cheat a widow woman?"

"I was making smart business decisions."

One of the tellers spat a wad of tobacco into a spittoon. "Like you did when you took top dollar from your cousin for the mercantile, then ran it into the ground before he got here?"

Murmurs swelled, and Orville shouted, "It was smart business." Then he shook his finger at the teller. "And it was none of your affair." He turned back to Daniel. "I bought stuff for the feedstore here with my own money—those hoes and rakes, and I put up those shelves and bricks, too!"

"It's unwise to invest in a holding until it's legally yours."

"Guess you ain't so good at that smart business stuff after all, huh, Orville?" someone jeered.

Eyes narrowed, Orville spat at Daniel, "You did this to me, didn't you?"

"No, you did it to yourself."

"I'll take my boy home for his bath." Millicent tried to take Arthur from her sister.

Isabelle wouldn't turn loose of him. "You can't carry him upstairs when you get him home."

Millicent laughed. "It's a good thing you're having a baby of your own. You're getting possessive!"

Mercy Orion crooked her finger at Heidi. "Go get a towel and soap. We'll give Arthur a bath in the kitchen!"

"Baff!" Arthur clapped his hands, then looked stricken. "Bow, Amma?"

Millicent thought of the telegram she'd received promising a picture of her girls. She wriggled the bangle from her wrist. "Yes, poppet. Aunt Isabelle will help you have pretty bubbles." Millicent embraced Mercy Orion. "I'll send Daniel over to pick them up when he gets home. If I dash home now, I can do several little chores so I can spare Daniel from having to write them down on my list."

The gas lamps lit the street with their warm glow, and Millicent looked at the town with contentment. Things were turning out well. Isabelle had the wonder of her baby to help soften her grief, and Arthur was a constant source of joy and pleasure. She and Daniel, after a painful patch, were doing well.

Deep in her heart, she wished their marriage was . . . different. More.

I'm wrong to feel this way. I knew what I was agreeing to. This afternoon, I felt there was hope, and now I've decided I can't expect anything. Lord, what am I to do? Her steps lagged. The doors to the church lay wide open, and someone was inside, practicing the piano for their Sunday special. The lyrics to the hymn came to mind as Millicent stopped and listened.

> If earthly parents hear
> Their children when they cry,
> If they, with love sincere,
> Their children's wants supply,
> Much more wilt Thou Thy love display,
> And answer when Thy children pray.

Pray. She'd prayed for everyone but herself. She'd prayed about everything except the aching loneliness she felt. She hadn't even been able to speak to her own sister about it. Isabelle had told her a man needed the comfort his wife could afford him—but never had she even alluded to a wife wanting to be embraced, cherished, to sense the sweetness of knowing someone's eyes searched for and met yours. The fairy-tale stories she recalled Mama reading to her had never dimmed—and somewhere deep inside, she'd never outgrown those childish fantasies.

God, you're my heavenly Father. I've felt so silly, so I've not prayed over this. I'd be so sad if Arthur wouldn't come tell me something because he feared I'd think he was silly—yet I've been too proud to be honest with myself and with you. Lord, I love my husband. I want him to love me back, so I'm laying my heart before you now and putting my trust in you.

She stumbled up to the store and let herself in. Tears blurred her vision, and she soaked the corner of her apron.

A man stepped from the shadows by the counter. "I came for the bracelet."

Twenty-Four

Terror streaked through Millicent. Then just as quickly, a sense of calm poured over her. Isabelle and Arthur were safe. "I'll have to ask you to give me a moment. I have something in my eye."

The man stuck out his hand. "Just give it to me."

"I'll set aside the entire shipment so you'll have a selection from which to choose."

He kept coming toward her. He stuck out his left hand. "Don't play with me."

"I don't understand."

Click. A wicked-looking knife swung open. "I'm sure this will refresh your memory. Now give me the bracelet." He kept coming toward her.

Millicent shuffled backward. "Oh, Lord," she prayed.

"He gave it to you before he died. He had to. It wasn't anywhere else."

He must mean the bracelet Mr. Eberhardt gave me. But why would anyone want that? "Before he died? Mr. Eberhardt—"

"We took care of him." He brandished the knife. "Give me the bangle, else I'll do the same to you."

Millicent reached for her left wrist, but her right fingers found nothing there. *It's with Isabelle and Arthur.* "O Lord, O Lord, O Lord, O Lord."

"Shut up and give it to me."

"I don't have it." She lifted her arm so he could see her wrist. "See? I don't have it."

"You have to. I searched all over the store. It's not here."

Pressing her hand to her bosom, Millicent sagged against the wall.

A lurid chuckle hovered in the dim store. "So it's upstairs, huh?"

Millicent prayed his greed would make him leave her. In a faint voice, she trembled, "False back. Top dresser drawer."

He wasn't taking such a chance. Dragging her upstairs, he growled, "You'd better not be lying. You can't get past me. If this is a trick . . ." The knife slashed through the air in a potent threat.

———

The whole business with Orville left him disgusted, but Daniel was glad to have it over. Mrs. Vaughn wouldn't have to worry about finances any longer. Daniel would have to hire someone to run the feedstore, but that oughtn't be too difficult. More than anything, he wanted to get home to his wife and son.

Halfway down the street, something made him look at the store. His heart stopped, but his feet stumbled forward as he saw his wife crawling out of the upstairs window. "Millicent!"

Startled, she looked out at him and teetered.

He couldn't take his eyes off of her as he ran down the street toward the store. "God, please—"

She fell. Onto the awning.

It split.

Daniel caught her shoulders. One of her boots was stuck in the ironwork. As he reached up to free it, she babbled, "Man. Knife!"

Until that moment, Daniel hadn't appreciated that most Texans wore a gun. The men who'd been at the meeting swarmed about them.

"How many men?" Daniel demanded.

"One. I think." Millicent tried to keep him from plowing into the store. "He has a knife!"

"What about a gun?" Piet demanded.

"I-I don't know."

"Hey!" someone yelled from behind the store. "Gotta man down back here. Landed on his knife when he jumped out the window. Don't look too good."

Millicent kept straightening out her skirts and slapping Daniel's hands away. "I'm fine." She then patted him. "Did I hurt you? Daniel, you can't touch me like that. It's not decent."

"You have half the awning hanging off of you. The town could have a revival meeting under all this canvas, and there'd still be room for a circus."

"Revival meetings and a circus are fine, but we're never having a grand opening drawing again!" She burst into tears.

Daniel lifted her up and carried her back inside. "Why's that, Millie?"

"Because I don't like jewelry anymore!"

Daniel was determined not to let go of her. He sent Parson Bradle over to the boardinghouse to arrange for Isabelle and Arthur to spend the night. Before the assailant was hauled over to the jail, the men argued about whether to have Dr. Wicky render aid to the criminal. Wanting simply to care for Millicent, he snapped, "Get him out of here and give him medical care."

Jakob Stauffer rubbed the back of his neck. "Dan, that is the problem. The doctor—he's so bad, it might be better not to use him."

Daniel left them to decide and carry the man away. Three volunteered to stay and keep watch over the store in case the man hadn't been acting alone.

After dispensing with Millicent's apron and shoes, Daniel made sure no real harm had befallen her, then tucked her into his own bed. She wasn't in any state to object. She couldn't get over her shivers, so he bundled her in the quilts and pulled her onto his lap, where she nestled into his keeping until she finally fell into an exhausted sleep.

Parson Bradle tapped on the door. "How is she?" he whispered.

"Terrorized." Daniel bit out the word in wrath.

"But she's not harmed—else she wouldn't lean into you so trustingly." The pastor looked at him. "Your calm assurance will give her peace, just as God's serenity gives us a resting place in the storms of life."

Tenderly fingering her tresses, Daniel asked, "Have you ever wanted anything with all your heart and had God tell you no?"

"I suppose it depends on what you mean by 'all your heart.' Folks toss that phrase around pretty cheap. Matthew seven, verse eleven says, 'If ye then, being evil, know how to give good gifts unto your children, how much more shall your Father which is in heaven give good things to them that ask him?' God is our Father, and He sets desires within us. When God gives us gifts, it pleases Him for us to accept them. It would be a travesty to turn away from a gift He offers because we feel we are making a spiritual sacrifice out of a mistaken sense of loyalty.

"The four of you under this roof have all been battered by life. God brought you together and has special plans for you. Daniel, He counted you worthy of the charge, and He'll give you strength and wisdom as long as you put your trust in Him. We'll all be praying for you."

Long after the pastor left, Daniel held his wife and smiled into the dark. All this time, he'd been making it so difficult when the truth was plain to see. He'd even seen part of the picture—he'd recognized how Millicent helped him past his grief and showed him how to be a good father. He'd been attracted to her from the start. God stopped the ship in the middle of the ocean and gave Arthur chicken pox . . . and still, Daniel didn't see the truth. He wanted to wake Millicent up and kiss her silly—but that would have to wait. For now, he rested and savored the peace he felt with the Lord and with his bride.

———

"Millie? Millie, honey, wake up."

Millicent snuggled into the warmth of her pillow, but it moved. She tried to pull it back, but it was—"Daniel!"

"We have to go. Come on."

"But it's dark out. Where are we going?"

"I can't say. Here. You need your shoes."

Thoroughly disgruntled, Millicent put on her shoes. Daniel laughed, and she saw nothing funny about the fact that she'd gotten her boots on the wrong feet. "It's your fault. Couldn't you wait to take me someplace at a decent hour?"

"I'll make it worth your while." He kissed her nose and shoved something over her hand.

"My bracelet!"

"Here's her shawl." Someone tossed it over her shoulders and tugged her to her feet. "You must go now."

Daniel decided she was too slow, so he swept her up and carried her across the road to the railroad tracks, sat down on something, and it started to move. Millicent gasped and clutched him. "I have you, dear. All is well."

Everything didn't seem exactly well, but being in Daniel's arms felt nice. It took a moment for her to realize the little platform on which he sat was somehow connected to a railroad handcart manned by the Van der Vort brothers. "I don't recall what I cooked for supper, but I'm never eating it again," Millicent muttered. "I've never had a wilder dream."

Daniel tucked her face into the hollow of his neck and murmured, "God willing, this is going to be a night for dreams."

When she opened her eyes again, they were in the next town. Daniel set her on her feet and walked her to the sheriff's office. The sheriff stood by his desk, and several papers fanned across it. From the way he glanced at his pocket watch, he'd rather be home in bed. Another man stood next to him. He extended his hand to Daniel. "Clark? Jones."

"Jones." They shook hands. Daniel wrapped an arm about her waist but didn't present her.

Mr. Jones overlooked that omission. "Mrs. Clark, the matters we will be discussing are highly sensitive. Before we go any further, I must have your vow of confidentiality."

When he'd merely said names, she hadn't known his nationality; with his speaking more, Millicent identified Mr. Jones as being English. "Daniel, you know about this." She caught herself. "Of course you do. That's why you brought me here. Mr. Jones, I trust my husband implicitly, therefore I agree."

Jones nodded. "Mr. Eberhardt served Her Majesty, which was why he absented himself from the children. The last day he saw them, Mr. Eberhardt had reason to suspect confidentiality had been breached. Considering the dangers associated with his profession, Mr. Eberhardt had provided for his daughters' future and named a guardian if anything befell him. By sending the girls away, he'd ensure their safety. After Eberhardt's untimely death and until matters could be legally settled, the butler used some letters of business authority and wrested control of the girls."

Jones paused a mere second. "He also provided for our country's security. A code we've sought for some time finally came into Eberhardt's keeping. Your bracelet, Mrs. Clark, contains that code."

"I'm sure that's quite important, but please tell me about the girls. There was no family. Mr. Eberhardt relied heavily upon Alastair. I would expect he'd—"

Smith shook his head. "He designated you, Mrs. Fairweather-Clark."

Already reeling, Millicent let out a strangled gasp.

"As you are married, Mr. Clark had to consent to the responsibility—"

"Privilege," Daniel corrected. He wrapped his arms around her. "I instructed him to bring our daughters to us at once."

"Daughters." She could scarcely form the word. First, he'd taken on her and Isabelle. Then, Isabelle's baby. He'd always been exceedingly kind about Audrey and Fiona, but exercising compassion in no way compared to taking on the lifetime commitment of rearing two children. Her husband could have quietly refused, and she would have never known; yet he'd wanted them right away. And he'd called them . . . *ours.* "Oh, Daniel, thank you."

He held her tight. "Where are they, Jones?"

Jones's chin lifted ever so slightly. "They'll arrive tomorrow. Circumstances require retrieval of the artifact you possess. As lives have been lost over it, leaving the girls in the care of others was the safest choice."

"Dear, we need to sign the adoption papers, and Mr. Jones needs the bracelet."

She couldn't take off the bracelet fast enough. "Why did we come here to conduct this business?"

Jones checked the bracelet carefully and seemed more than satisfied with it. The sheriff behind him finally spoke. "Security measures, ma'am. For you and the girls. Meeting away from your hometown seemed wisest."

The handcar ride back to Gooding went fairly fast. The brisk night air had Millicent huddling in her shawl, and she kept tying knots in it. Daniel looked down at her and cuddled her close. She pushed away, but then started shivering and decided cuddling was acceptable after all. Hadn't she just prayed about this very thing?

"Millie? Is something wrong?"

Panic overtook her, and she blurted out the first thing she could think of. "My boots are still on the wrong feet."

"Tying the fringe of your shawl won't remedy that."

"You should have scheduled more time for me to put on my boots." She snuggled a little closer. "I won't be cross, though. After all, you brought over my girls."

"From now on, they're *our* girls." He sounded as proud as could be.

Stars twinkled down on them, and he held her tight as the countryside whizzed past. He'd said it was a night of dreams coming true, and he'd been right. *The only thing that would make it perfect would be if he'd kiss me.*

Daniel's head dipped down. Millicent's heart skipped a beat and her breath caught. His lips brushed beside her ear, making her tingle all over. "If you're concerned about being ready for the girls, fret no more. Piet and Karl plan to paint a room and put up a pair of white wicker beds. Hope and Annie promise to sew curtains. I can't remember if the flowers on the material are sweet peas or snapdragons, but they're pink and lavender."

Gathered tight in his embrace, Millicent gazed up at him. Tears of joy filled her eyes. He'd bothered to do the little things that would make Audrey and Fee feel at home.

Arms tightening a little more, Daniel lifted her slightly. Before Millicent knew what he was about, he'd oh-so-gently pressed his lips to hers, then brushed his lips to her cheek and whispered, "We need to talk later."

They came to an abrupt halt. "So," Karl said, slapping Daniel on the back. "Was she surprised with her wedding gifts?"

Millicent let out a nervous little laugh. "You've not known me long, Karl, but have you ever known me to be quiet? The whole way home, I've been speechless!"

The Van der Vort brothers roared over that. They all went back to the mercantile, and the men scoured every nook and cranny of the store to be sure no one was there. Finally, everyone else left, the doors were locked, and she was alone with her husband.

After taking a big gulp of air, Millicent shuffled back a step. A clump of knots at the front of her shawl swayed forward, then banged and struck her in the midriff with surprising force. She put her hands there, beneath that clump, and started worrying the hopeless tangle of fringe. "Did you remember to get birdseed for Widow O'Toole?"

"I was busy. She can have all she wants tomorrow."

Millie caught a glimpse of herself in the reflection of the window and about shrieked. She'd been thinking starry-eyed, romantic thoughts, yet she looked like a guttersnipe! "I . . . You . . . Your list. You need to write it on your list. It's important. It should go on the schedule, Daniel." She threw her head back and moaned. "Look what you've done to me! You've made me think about lists."

Slow and steady, he stalked toward her. "You might think about them, but you never stick to them. You're in no danger of becoming organized, Millicent." He paused. "And I wouldn't have you any other way."

Hope mingled with uncertainty. Millicent looked at him.

"I love you, Millie." He hadn't just said the word. Emotion resonated in his deep tone, shone in his eyes, and caused him to trail his fingers down her cheek. "Since the moment you tied a knot into that pillowcase and yanked out Buddy's ears, I've been captivated. We've had a rough start, but God's pouring His blessings out on us."

She backed away from him as her fingers scrabbled with the tangled fringe. "Daniel, please don't say anything more. Not right now."

He yielded no ground. "Why not?"

"I'm not going to ruin such a special moment in my life by telling my husband I love him when I look like a gust of wind blew me in."

The most handsome smile in the world lit his face. "Too late. You just did." His arm wrapped around her waist while the other hand cupped her head. "I'm glad you love me." His head lowered, his lips met hers, and she went weak in the knees. When they parted, she was breathless.

"Admitting you love me wasn't all that bad after all, now was it?"

"Oh, Daniel." She sighed. "I may as well admit that I've longed to say I love you for half of eternity."

He rested his forehead against hers. A sweet sense of intimacy surrounded them. All of the passion she'd longed for now glowed in his eyes. "Millicent . . ."

She started to giggle.

He pulled away. "Precisely what is so funny?"

She tried to wiggle out of her shawl.

He laughed in disbelief. "What are you doing?"

"I don't want to hear my very first declaration of love when I've knotted myself into a shawl!"

Daniel's smile took on a decidedly rakish tilt. "You'll recall from the life jacket incident, Millicent, my love, that I'm adept at doing away with knots."

Epilogue

Four days later

"Daddy, don't stop!"

Daniel reeled in the kite string. "It's lunchtime, Fee. We'll fly it again later."

Wrapping her arms around his knee, Fiona hugged him. "Okay."

Millicent had spread a huge blanket in the field for a Sunday afternoon picnic. It would be their family's first, and the family had grown tremendously. Daniel hadn't told Millicent the other part of the surprise: The girls hadn't traveled alone. Daniel invited Alastair and his wife, Cook, to immigrate with them. They'd accepted with alacrity. Alastair and he were masters of schedules and order. Thanks to Cook, burned food was but a fond memory and bicarbonate of soda no longer qualified as a nightly dessert.

Plopping down on the blanket, Daniel mentioned to Millicent, "This morning, Phineas asked me how to go about arranging an adoption."

She turned so quickly, he wound up with a half dozen dev-iled eggs in his lap. "Annie's boy?" Hurriedly cleaning up the mess, Millicent enthused, "That would be so wonderful!"

"You made it possible by suggesting the bracelet for the grand opening drawing. We men struggle to find a way to win a woman's heart."

Fiona crawled over and sprawled between them. "Are you talking about fairy tales?"

Millicent caressed Fiona's pigtails. "A real-life fairy tale."

"I fried enough chicken to bury Napoleon's army," Cook said as she passed out the plates. "You can tell your stories later."

Arthur stuck his plate on his head like a hat, folded his hands, and prayed, "Foo goo!"

"He's your son, but I don't know why you let him act like a Chinaman," Cook muttered.

After lunch, Fee tugged on Daniel's sleeve. "You promised."

"I did." He reached for the kite.

"No, not that. The fairy tale."

Millicent smiled at him. "Their very favorite thing."

"Mine, too." He winged out his arms, and the girls settled on either side of him. "This is a true story. A wonderful, Jesus-made-it-happen love story."

Audrey sighed with bliss and Fee wiggled. Millicent watched him, her brow puckered a little with curiosity. He smiled back.

"Once upon a time, there was a fair maiden. She was the most beautiful girl in the land, and this is the story of her whirlwind romance. . . ."

Acknowledgments

Special thanks to Barry Moreno, the librarian at Ellis Island. I've been to Ellis Island three times. After speaking to Barry, I long to go back and see it all again at least twenty more times. When I exhausted all other avenues of finding an answer to something, Barry proved to be an unfailingly kind and professional resource. His encyclopedic knowledge of the island is fascinating, and he has my deepest gratitude. Our nation is very fortunate to have someone of his caliber and dedication serving as he does. Thank you, Barry!